REVAMP

BECK SHERMAN

ISBN: 978-0-9857327-0-7

PROLOGUE

FOR THREE DAYS, IT WAS DARK.

News reporters scrambled. This was the biggest story to come along in weeks.

They called it a blackout.

The last one was in New York City in 2003, but this one was different, special, because the grids in six major cities across the country had been fried, kaput, see-you-next-Sunday. Everyone with some jurisdiction blamed each other, and when there was no one left to blame, terrorism rode in on its gallant steed.

It was the media's fault. They were so busy stuffing fanatical Muslims with a penchant for Allah and decapitations down the American citizen's throat, that they never saw it coming. I guess I shouldn't be too hard on them.

They were partially right.

It was *terror* after all, but a whole new kind. And when the lights came back on, things had changed.

The dark had brought us visitors.

CHAPTER ONE

WHEN I WOKE, I WAS FALLING.

Something smashed and a guess had my new bedside lamp biting the dust.

It took ages to find the right one.

A truck roared by outside, and the wind followed, rustling trees and leaving eager branches scratching at my window. I was back in my bed, but apparently I had never left. A hand rested on my shoulder.

"You alright, mate?"

Sullivan Smith: tall, musical, a way around the natural order of things. I sighed, not appreciating that my nightmares had staged a return, or that the guy I had been dating for over three months was still calling me "mate." It was a British thing but no less annoying for that fact. There was no one he didn't call mate, and this served as a constant reminder of the casualness of our relationship. I let my body slump into the mattress. Sullivan leaned over me to check the time and the status of my lamp. He laid a kiss on my lips.

"I didn't know you were such an active sleeper," he said, rubbing his eyes. "Next time I'll bring body armor. We'll make it a game of sorts." Sullivan flashed me a devilish grin. His skin was pale blue in the darkness of my room. The headlights of a passing car climbed the wall and streaked his face. Even with just a couple hours of drunken slumber, he was still beautiful.

"Well?"

"What?"

"A bit of role-playing to get the blood going?"

"If it's games you want, I've got a deck of cards that I'd be more than happy to bring out. Anytime."

Sullivan laughed. "You know I'm never playing cards with you again. Last poker night you left me a pauper with just a pair of knickers to my name."

Some people had dads. I had a useless talent that my dad had given to me before he left. I honed it.

"Yeah, well, when my mom was teaching me how to read, my dad was teaching me how to tell who's got the flush and who's got the pair of twos. Story goes he won our last name off some poor guy in Vegas with one helluva bluff." I stretched my limbs over the side of the bed. I hated talking about my dad, but sometimes it just happened, like a cough or a sneeze.

"Emma Spade," he said, as if trying my name on for size.

"Don't wear it out."

I separated myself from the blankets and made the cold dash to the bathroom. My skin prickled, and my breath escaped as tiny ghosts. I had a radiator in the room but suspected it wasn't working to its full potential, despite the landlord's protests. Usually I kept the door open to let the heat in from the hallway but not when Sullivan was over. Information was a drug to my roommate.

"Hey, Em…what was your dream about?" Sullivan asked, leaning his naked chest over the side of my bed to pick up the broken pieces of lamp.

"I don't remember." I flicked on the bathroom light and closed the door tightly behind me. There was no need to share that stuff with Sullivan. Not yet, anyway.

I waited with my butt against the door and scribbled a note on my brain: *Change bulb to 40-watt.* I rubbed my eyes, encouraging them to adjust. My stomach tensed. Screwdrivers, aspirin, and butterflies—together at last.

The television turned on in the bedroom. *Great.* Another sleepless night. I pried myself off the door and tiptoed my bare feet across the cold tiles. I snuck up on the mirror, because post-finals, post-party, post-booze, post-sex, that was the only way to do it.

"Nice look," I whispered at my reflection.

Finals week had been a killer. I sleepwalked through the last two the previous afternoon, and what followed was a night of good ole college binging. Besides the onset of spring break, there was a lot to celebrate. Sullivan's band scored a gig downtown, my roommate got a crush on the lead singer (giving me a partner in crime), and I was off to Los Angeles to scope out graduate schools. Minus my nightmares, things were peachy.

My stomach gurgled. I bent over the sink and turned on the cold tap. *A splash will do the trick.* I flailed for a towel as water dribbled down my face and neck, soaking the front of my pajama top. I dried and flung the towel back over the rack. My mom's hazel eyes returned my gaze in the mirror. A wet auburn curl stuck to my cheek. I huffed. *Unruly hair be gone!* I opened the medicine cabinet, grabbed the melatonin bottle, unscrewed it, tipped it over my right hand, watched a dozen or so pills spill out onto the floor, had the quick idea of squatting down to pick them up, silently scolded myself for having such a silly idea at such a ridiculous hour, popped one, screwed the cap back on, closed the cabinet, and had a final look in the mirror.

"It's nothing eighty billion years of sleep can't fix," I whispered.

4

I opened the bathroom door. Bright light confiscated dark from my bedroom. Sullivan was lying on his stomach, watching television with his feet kicked in the air. His black hair slanted to the side in a gel-meets-hair-hair-meets-pillow state. He squinted.

"*Ah*, turn it off. My eyes are melting."

"Because a blind drummer would be a bad thing," I said, nodding. "With all the ogling of groupies to be done."

I turned the light off. The bedroom was now bathed in flashing blues and reds from the television. A salesman named Big Al wanted us to buy a car, "*Now, now, now!*"

Sullivan jumped off the bed, moving faster than I thought he could in his current condition. He threw me into a dip. Our noses touched. He spoke, his breath all whiskey and cigarettes.

"As far as I'm concerned, you're the only groupie worth my ogle."

His lips smiled, and the smile brushed my cheek. My heart pirouetted.

"I am *not* your groupie," I said, stuffing the lovely feelings back from whence they came.

"Okay, you're not." Sullivan let me up and took his place back on my bed. "But you are the most frustrating woman on the face of the earth. Maybe good frustrating. Jury's still out." He chuckled. "Done primping for me? Can we go to bed now?"

My eyes zoomed in on a pillow.

"Seriously…no more horseplay. I'm knackered and there's a bug going around. We need our sleep." He gave me a "come on" look, and I made the executive decision to whip the pillow at him anyway.

~

I awoke for the second time that morning. This time, the bed was empty. Just me, myself and I. Dull sunlight nudged me through the cracks in the blinds. It spewed lazy patterns across the carpet and onto my packed suitcase. My nose was Antarctica. I reached an arm over to the other side of the bed and slid it into the indent which not long ago, but no longer, held Sullivan. In his place was a note. I rolled onto my stomach, entangling myself in the bed's layers. The note read:

Meeting guys for practice
Have fun in L.A.
XX Sul

Nice and casual. Exactly what I pretended to want and exactly the opposite of what I wanted. When will men learn? I put the note back where I found it, as if having a bit of Sullivan—even a torn corner from one of my notebooks with his writing on it—was better than no Sullivan at all. My phone buzzed.

"What up, bitch?"

It was my roommate Josie calling from the room next door. Her voice made me wince.

"How many packs did you smoke last night?"

"Enough to make Jesus weep. How's Stint's sexy drummer?"

"Not here. He had practice."

"Oh, the sacrifices we groupies make," she said. I heard her inhale and then enjoy a long exhale. Josie was to smoking what Mother Theresa was to charity. "It's worth it, you know."

"I am no groupie."

"Keep telling yourself that, babe," she said. "So, did you do the dance of joy when you handed in your psychotic paper this morning?"

Oh no.

The clock said 11:45 which meant my psych paper was due across campus in fifteen minutes. Some things never changed.

"I gotta go," I said, flinging the phone onto the bed.

At noon, the doors of most campus buildings were locked, papers were shoved into briefcases, and professors got off to wherever professors got off to for spring break. I threw back the covers and bolted over to my chair-not-for-sitting across the room. I tore away rejected garments from the night before and found my paper at the bottom, safe. It hadn't been consumed by a black hole as I suspected. The title stared up at me:

PSY 401: THE CRIMINAL MINDS OF COPYCAT KILLERS

The print curved into a mocking smile.

"You sweat your soul for me," it said, "and now you're going to go racing across campus, and the doors will be lockedy, lock, locked!"

If they were, I was truly toast.

I took the paper off the chair, slipped it into a notebook to keep it from bending, and put both in my backpack. I stripped down and surveyed my clothes in a colorful orgy on the floor. I disentangled my favorite pair of jeans and slid them on. I couldn't find a bra but triple layered. A baseball hat completed the ensemble. I grabbed my backpack and headed for the door, stepping over discarded items from my night with Sullivan: a crumpled pair of jeans that reeked of stale smoke, my license with a wine-stained twenty wrapped around it, an unfamiliar sock.

The floor creaked going past Josie's room. I waved and mouthed goodbye to her closed door. A picture of Kate Moss stared back at me anemically.

I knew my roommate had gone back to sleep after calling. The concept of daytime was foreign to Josie. If it were possible for her to drag herself from bed before noon, she would protest her ability. Most likely she'd hire someone to protest it for her. Her parents taught her that money could buy anything. Josie's father was a cardiac surgeon and nurse hopper, her mother a world traveler and hired-help hopper. She had written a book called *Mothering in Minutes* which said that the best nurturing could be done in intervals of ten minutes or less. Also, *Say It with Cash: An Unspoken Language To Save Time and Emotion.* I love you (*$100*), I hate you (*$100*), I'm going away for a while (*$100*), I'll be leaving with the gardener (*$100*).

School was a formality. Come graduation, Josie would walk despite rarely having been to class because her dad's name was on half the campus buildings. But under the circumstances, she was level-headed enough. We met at a fraternity party sophomore year and got an apartment off campus senior year. Having nothing in common seemed to work for us.

~

The first step outside was painful. The cold was not my friend. It took advantage and seeped through any skin not triple-protected. It laughed and had fun making icicles of my bones. I shaped my mouth into an O and exhaled. I looked up at the sky and cringed. *Overenthusiastic with the gray much?* I thought, to no one in particular.

The walkway was covered with ice. I took big but careful steps. Down the street, dirty snowdrifts and swanky SUVs competed for space. Not a backpacked soul, as far as the eye could see. I made my way toward the crosswalk. The traffic light was red, but the hand began to flash, so I broke into a sprint. I jumped a yellow snow blower somebody had decided to store in the middle of the sidewalk and barely missed an uncomfortable moment with a tree.

I arrived at the crosswalk just as the hand went solid. When I was halfway across the street, the rumbling began. But it must have started sooner than that and I was too preoccupied to notice. On my right, a truck's shiny grill was fast approaching. I leapt forward into a pile of snow as four eighteen-wheelers drove by, horns blaring. I stood, dusted my knees, and watched as the trucks separated at the next intersection, the first one pulling into the driveway of a red house, the other three bombing toward south campus. I waited a minute for the driver of the parked truck to get out, and when no one did, I left, time being what it was.

~

On the quad, snowflakes kamikazed ahead of me. The wind changed direction and slung shot its best fighters into my face.

The campus was dead, and I wondered where everyone had gotten off to. I felt like the last person on earth, and as life didn't play fair, I was stranded in sub-zero temperatures and not on a warm desert island. *Soon, Emma, soon.* Highs were reaching the eighties in Los Angeles. I was warmer just thinking about it.

I climbed the stairs of Huntington Hall and winced as my right knee started to throb. A thin streak of blood and two smaller spots above it had seeped through my jeans, resembling a smiley face.

I stood outside the entrance and made a silent wish before trying the doors. They opened and heat greeted me in the lobby with a big hug. I took off my gloves and wiggled my fingers.

"Welcome back, guys."

The psychology department's main office was on the fourth floor. I opted for the stairs and was huffing by the time I arrived. It was all the extra layers, I told myself confidently. The office doors were wide open and the lights on inside. I walked up to the front desk, placed my backpack on the counter and removed the notebook that held my term paper. I put the notebook flat and took my paper from between its pages.

Behind the counter, three desks sat unoccupied. The office usually had a nice view of Marshall Street, but today the shades were closed. A half-eaten sandwich was on the desk by the windows. Egg salad. Syracuse's mascot, Otto, smirked at me from beneath things and behind things and on top of things. I jumped when a phone rang on the desk nearest to me, then held a hand over my heart and laughed uncomfortably.

"Whew," I said, in case anyone was paying attention.

The phone stopped ringing after two rings. *Wrong number. Check the phonebook next time, buddy.* I noticed a smaller room off the one I was in.

"Hello in there? Can I get some help?"

No answer.

I picked up a stray paperclip and pinched it between my fingers. I looked at the clock on the wall and my watch for a second opinion. Noon. *I could leave it*, I thought. On one of the desks perhaps, but not the main counter. Someone would make off with it. They'd get a boring read, but people did the oddest things sometimes just to screw with other people's lives. I knew leaving it next to the food was a surefire way to get it noticed fast and dropped in the right hands.

I released the paper clip and drummed my fingers on the countertop. *Sigh.*

I couldn't leave it. I perspired coffee for three months and the project had managed to set off my nightmares again—nightmares I had kept at bay for years.

I retrieved my scattered possessions and headed toward staff offices. The hallway was dimly lit by circular lamps. They cast a yellow glow and reminded me of chain Italian restaurants. I passed four shut doors. Through their opaque, rippled glass, dark outlines of objects that helped people learn and teach. Professor Winthrop, or Winnie, as he was called by most of his students, had the last office on the right. Although rumors reputed him as a drunk, he was good enough at what he did to get the corner room with the view.

His door was closed, but a light was on inside. I knocked. No noise came from within.

I grabbed the door handle. It didn't move. I pressed my forehead against the glass and cupped my hands to the sides of my face. *Gray fuzz.* I got the idea to slip my paper under the door, dropped everything, and got down on my knees. There wasn't much space between the carpet and the bottom of the door, if any. It was possible the carpet would have some give, but enough for 50 pages?

This could end badly, I thought, stuffing my paper into the slit. It went halfway, before stopping. I tried coaxing it with a side-to-side motion but no luck. I pulled and heard the sound of ripping.

"No…no, *please*."

Click.

The door's lock turned over.

11

I stood, leaving my paper behind. The door didn't open, but on the other side a throat cleared.

"Come in."

I opened the door slowly, and my mind squealed as the cover ripped and half of the paper tore away from the other half. I retrieved the carnage and entered Winnie's office.

The room was dark and smelled of labored knowledge. The shades were closed, and a small brass lamp provided the only light. In the corners, blackness bunched. Winnie sat behind an oak desk big enough to swallow him whole. His hand scratched a pen feverishly across an open notebook.

"Professor?"

The pen in hand continued its cycle. Back and forth. Winnie's gray hair bobbed. It flared into points on both sides of his head and went missing down the middle in a reflective runway.

"I have my term paper," I said. "It's a bit late. I had an accident. Nothing serious but enough to make me…late." I laughed. My palms sweated and tingled. I feared my hands might fail me and I'd end up having to deliver my paper to him in my mouth, like a dog.

"So, uh...here it is," I said, searching for free space on his desk. I found some between an "I (heart) NY" coffee mug and a framed black and white photograph of a young couple sitting at a café table. They looked perfect. There was no way it was real. There was no way those people were any relation to Professor Winnie. I put my wrecked paper down, thinking maybe I should have inquired about a stapler and a fresh sheet to patch it, and turned to go.

"Ms. Spade?"

He was out from behind his desk, and I hadn't even heard him get up. *Did he have time to get up?* Seeing his face for the first time since my arrival made me gasp. His skin was pale and stretched over protruding cheekbones. Dark circles hung like sick crescent moons under his eyes. Hair halfway between stubble and beard poked through his chin. A bacon-strip Band-Aid stuck to his neck.

"Are you alright, professor?"

"Did they come?"

"Did who come?"

"*Them*," he said. "Death."

I shook my head. "I don't know what you mean."

"Let them in when they do."

Old Winnie was putting me on. Either that, or my professor had hit rock bottom and I was there to bear witness. Bring my nose close to his mouth and I was sure to smell the remnants of some lethal concoction. I might even get light-headed.

"You're bleeding."

I looked down. The smiley face was gone, a red carnation in its place.

"You know...I should go take care of this." I couldn't get to the door fast enough, but when I got there, I stopped. My backpack was where I had left it, unzipped and gaping in the hallway. "Maybe you could call someone, professor? A relative...or a friend?"

Against my better judgment, I looked back. Winnie smiled and waved his fingers at me. Saliva bubbled out from the corners of his mouth.

"Bye," I said, snatching my bag off the floor.

I ran past the front desk, where no one had returned to accept a late paper or finish a sandwich, down four flights of stairs, and out the

13

main entrance, back into the blustery cold.

It was the last time I saw Professor Winnie alive.

CHAPTER TWO

THE GRAY CHOKED THE SUN.

It wasn't nice at all.

I got back to my apartment in record time. There was no sign of the trucks, or anyone for that matter. I felt alone in an off-white world.

The place was quiet. I shed two layers, including my stained jeans, and threw the items onto a chair next to the dining table. I went into the kitchen, filled the kettle with water, placed it on the bottom left burner, and turned the stovetop on.

The kitchen and lounge were adjacent, separated only by a wall which ran half the length of both rooms. A window in the wall above the sink allowed the chef to watch her guests starve to death while she pretended she hadn't just burned the main course and was not now frantically preparing a box of shells and cheese. At least, that was what I'd heard it was for.

I opened the cabinet next to the stove and flipped through an assortment of tea bags, registering my mood. I was definitely tense, which called for Chamomile. I took out the yellow envelope and plucked a mug from the drying rack. My knee still throbbed. I leaned over it to get a closer look. Three small cuts. They had stopped bleeding. I prodded to feel for glass or splinters that might have gotten stuck in the wound. It didn't seem so. *What tea would help me not die from blood poisoning?* I replaced the Chamomile with a sigh and flipped through the bags some more.

"Green it is."

The kettle screamed. I prepared my tea and shuffled to the lounge. I sat on the sofa and put a blanket over my bare legs. The sofa was long, and I could stretch my body out and still not touch the end. I loved that. Rescued from a thrift store in the city, it was blue-velvet, sweet vintage and the only piece of furniture I had insisted on. Josie's parents wanted to import a lambskin leather sofa from Italy, handmade by naked virgins, but I put my foot down. "Character over cost," I had said, or something like that.

I took a sip of tea and fingered one of many cigarette burns on the armrest. Josie was a chain-smoking fool. On more than one occasion, she had passed out with a lit cigarette between her rouged lips. On more than one occasion, our lives had been saved by my simple sofa that refused to go down in a blaze of glory.

There was a soft pack of Marlboro Lights on the coffee table. It looked beaten—too many hours in the back pocket of tight, designer jeans. On the front, two Ku Klux Klan men still carried the banner. Had they not tired of all that? I picked up the pack and flicked the bottom. Four cigarettes shot out half the way. I poked three back in and put one in my mouth.

All I could taste was cancer. Rotting, holey, messy cancer.

A doctor at the campus clinic had ambushed me with the infamous black-lung photo when I checked in with a run-of-the-mill cold my freshman year. I couldn't remember his name, but to me, he'd always be "Dr. No."

I quit straight away with mixed feelings of love and hatred for Dr. No. It was all Erin's fault, and I was okay with blaming someone else for my former addiction. Erin was my best friend in high school. We were at Rick Cheller's end-of-the-year bash, because his parents were on vacation and trusted their pot-dealing son with their entire life's possessions. She surprised me with a cigarette the way Dr. No had surprised me several years later with the photo. She told me she would no longer be my friend if I didn't smoke it. Peer pressure at its finest. So I smoked it, Erin stayed my best friend and gave my high school sweetheart a blowjob beneath the bleachers two years later, and I got stuck with no boyfriend, no best friend, and a habit that made Swiss cheese of your lungs.

I removed the cigarette from my mouth and replaced it in the pack. I took a sip of tea and grimaced. Why did things that were good for you always taste so bad? I put the mug on the table and retrieved my *Marvin the Martian* phone from the bookcase. The receiver was part of his hat and I'd never seen another like it. I stretched the cord as far as it would go, to stay comfortable on the sofa, and dialed my mom's number. I had promised to call her before leaving for California, and I didn't think I could let another minute pass without sharing my day thus far with someone.

First that parade of trucks nearly running me down, and then the strange encounter with Professor Winnie? Sure, teach had always been a bit eccentric. He'd wear flamboyant hats to class and show *The Little Mermaid* twice a semester because, he would claim, the movie's link to forensic psychology was astounding. Of course, no one else ever saw the connection and Winnie always refused to elaborate. But there was no mistaking his brilliance. He had been published numerous times in all the most distinguished journals, and there was a two-year waiting list for his class. Most students signed up for Winnie's class to reap the benefits of his mind, but there were those few who sought entertainment and knew the professor could deliver.

I usually enjoyed both aspects equally, but I had never seen him the way he was that afternoon and didn't find it entertaining in the least.

The phone rang at the other end. My mom's voicemail answered after three rings: "Hello, this is Sophia Spade. I can't get to the phone right now so make sure to leave a message or I won't know to call you back!" *Beep.*

"Hey, mom. It's me. Uh…I'm leaving for L.A. in about two hours or so. I'm flying American Airlines, Flight 145. It leaves just after six. Not sure when we arrive—I think it's about a five-hour flight. Anyways, I'll try you again from the airport. Love you. Oh and be careful because I hear there's a flu going around and I know you have your thing coming up. K…bye."

That thing was the real estate exam. My mom had spent her whole life waiting tables at Joe's Café. Not the one in Brookline but the one in Framingham off of Route 9. She quit high school before graduating to marry my father, and after he left, she went back to what she knew, which was being a waitress. My mom's boss Joe was a decent guy, and the friendship they formed got her the good shifts. A year ago, she took the GED and passed. She confided that that piece of paper made her feel like the world was her oyster—something she hadn't felt in a very long time. When an old friend suggested she try real estate, claiming that selling houses was good, easy money, my mom jumped at the chance. After 13 years in a backbreaking, unappreciated job, pushing new homes sounded just like heaven.

I replaced the phone and sat back down to contemplate my next move. I was packed, basically. Calling the cab company to confirm my pick-up was a must. I contemplated contacting someone on campus to let them know about Professor Winnie. Whose responsibility would it be? The dean's? Would he even still be around? My objective wasn't to get the professor in any trouble. I wanted to avoid that. I liked the guy.

My roommate's door opened down the hall.

"What up, girl," Josie called out.

"It's alive," I said. "I was starting to worry." I wasn't really. Afternoon was early for her.

Josie appeared under the hall archway. Above her hung an assortment of post and greeting cards from around the world. Most were from her mother, with special hellos from the gardener Juan.

Josie wore an oversized Yankees tee and plaid flannel pajama pants. She was about six inches shorter than me at 5'4" and very well-endowed, which was the first thing most people noticed about her. The second was her Long Island accent.

She squinted through smoke and hazy sunlight. A cigarette hung from her mouth, as one always did. She walked to the couch and collapsed, as if her trip there had been a trial. She exhaled, and it was worthy of an erupting volcano.

"How did the paper-handing-in-thing go?" she asked.

"It went. Winnie was acting weird."

Although Josie was a Philo (one who studies philosophy) and, when drunk, could wax poetic about the sound of one hand clapping, Professor Winnie's antics had given him a reputation that crossed majors and even degrees.

"Winnie is always acting weird," she said.

"No, but he looked ill. Whatever—I got it in. Hey, do you know the people who live in the red house with the white shutters?"

"Just past the intersection?" I nodded. "The twins," Josie said,

19

pausing to take a drag. "Abigail and Anita. Their father's like some big shot somewhere. An ambassador, I think. They are queen snobs. Why?" She exhaled. I always wondered where the smoke would go to when she talked. It never seemed to come out of her mouth until she was ready to let it out.

"There was this eighteen-wheeler that nearly ran me over today," I said. "It pulled into their driveway."

Josie shrugged, and I could see her measuring the importance level of my story. I imagined it was a measurement between one and ten, ten being of the utmost importance, and generally having something to do with my roommate, and one being of no importance, i.e., not involving Josie in any way.

This story was in the lower numbers. I read it on her face. She nodded once, made little eye contact, and changed the subject almost immediately. Indirectly, it had something to do with Josie, us being roommates. But because I survived and was not maimed in any way, her present was not interrupted and her future not altered. I wasn't mad. It was just her way.

"You won't believe what happened to *me* last night," she said, fanning her face with her hands to establish drama. She stabbed her cigarette into the ashtray and went for another. Once lit, she started.

"After you and Sul left," Josie said, "Adam asked if I was up for an after-hours down by the old factories on Geddes. It's one of the ones that's always moving around—you know, with a different venue every week? Sounded kind of cool."

I nodded confirmation. She continued: "Adam's fucking hot, Em, and he can belt, he really can," she said. "And I was on some stuff. Uppers, downers. All of it, really. Long story short, I was off my head, and maybe I shouldn't have gone...but I did, okay? I did, and I think something bad might've happened."

THEN:
JOSIE

Josie was pleased.

She gave Adam a long look, drinking him in. *Fuck, he's gorgeous.* A cross between Joaquin Phoenix and Matt Dillon in his younger days.

The ecstasy pill had taken effect, and the world looked bright, shimmery, and clear. Some people Josie talked to never got horny on the stuff, but she felt the urge between her legs every time.

They were in Adam's car on the way to a shifting club called Die Mortem. It was your typical techno-trance-drug-induced-flailing-til-the-wee-hours-of-the-morning type club. Josie preferred rap to techno, techno to trance, and trance to rock, in that order, but where Adam was concerned, she was willing to make a whole lot of exception.

Josie flipped the visor mirror down. Her pupils were huge. They reminded her of doll eyes. She giggled and ran her hand through her hair and down her neck.

"How you feeling, baby?"

"Like everything's beautiful," Josie said, smiling dazedly.

"I think you're beautiful."

Josie looked at him. *He's an angel. Perfect in every way.* She felt the urge and leaned over to massage Adam's cock through his jeans. It was already hard, and this made Josie feel good. Special.

Adam moaned.

She undid his pants and tugged the waist down. Then Josie reached through the front opening of his boxers and pulled out his cock. Taking a hand off the wheel, Adam slid his seat back, enough to make some good space to work with, and motioned her over. She climbed carefully over the gearshift and straddled him. She teased the tip of his cock, before moving her panties to the side and slipping him inside her. Adam swerved to the left, then righted the car and slowed to 50 miles per hour. He half laughed, half moaned.

Josie rode him nice and easy at first, with one hand on the roof of the car, and then faster until they both came. His cock was big and it filled her up, so when she orgasmed, her insides had something good to grip. *Damn that was amazing.* It was second only to the best sex she ever had with Juan the gardener.

"I love you so much," she said.

"I love you too, babe."

Both were lying. They had met five hours ago. The drugs were talking and sometimes they talk so sweet. Josie kissed his forehead and lifted herself off Adam's cock. She slid back into the passenger seat and adjusted her skirt and panties.

"Where are we?" she asked.

"Fuck if I know," he said, turning his head to check out a passing street sign. "*Ha*, I got you, you bitch." Adam pointed at the sign. "Should be the next street."

He took the next right and then another onto Ontario. He steered the car down a side road and pulled up behind a Cadillac, which might have been baby blue to begin with but was now too rusty to be sure. Adam put the car in park and got out. Josie waited for a second for Adam to come around and open her door, before realizing he was already standing on the opposite sidewalk waiting for her.

She opened her own door.

Josie got out and looked both ways. There were lots of cars parked, but, like the Caddy, they had all seen better days. The only streetlight to grace that shabby part of town was out, of its own accord or someone else's. Big buildings stood erect behind barbwire-topped fences, like dark, watching soldiers. Josie was still rolling, but the wad of hundreds in her handbag flashed warnings in her head.

"Is it safe?" she asked, stuffing her new Gucci deeper into her armpit.

Exaggeratedly, Adam put his arms out to each side and looked both ways.

"Of course it's safe. There's no one here!"

That was exactly what worried her, but the drug reassured, and the world began to look heavenly again, with all its bad, scary bits forgotten.

The after-hours club was in a warehouse down an industrial drive. The building's entrance was a little green door. "For the leprechauns," Josie had said. The door was in the back of the building, camouflaged by overflowing trash bins. It was well-hidden, and that they had even found it was a miracle. Plus, the directions had been bogus, given to Adam by a guy whose girlfriend he had fucked the week before. They were put on the right path by another angel in a red sparkly dress.

~

The place was packed. At least 300 people and most of them were dancing. The *avant* song was old Chemical Brothers. That was what Josie called the song that started her night, *avant* meaning *before* in French. It was a stupid thing her and her girlfriends started in high school. You could be looking sexy in the freshest Dior with some tasty eye candy on your arm, but none of it mattered if your *avant* song sucked. You might as well just turn around and leave, because the night was on a downhill slope.

Josie's night had started a while ago, but this was her first major entrance anywhere with Adam, so she thought the rule could still apply. She wasn't religious, but she looked up at the ceiling and offered a silent prayer, just in case. *Thank you for not playing P. Diddy. Amen.*

They walked down a narrow, metal staircase. They were like fire escape stairs, except on the inside, and Josie's heels kept getting stuck, leaving Adam to pull them out. It was all very romantic in Josie's mind.

Once on solid ground, Adam went to get drinks at the bar. Josie didn't like the idea of being left alone. Being alone on ecstasy made her feel vulnerable and at the mercy of whoever came along. But she nodded and smiled up at Adam, and before she could count to one, he had disappeared into the crowd. Josie tried to dance, but she got dizzy and took a seat near where Adam left her so there would be no confusion when he came back with the drinks.

The inside of the building was huge, and it was all open space. Wooden crates of various sizes and with red words and symbols on them were stacked up against the walls. Some of the words were in English (THIS END UP and FRAGILE), but most were in another language, German it looked like. One of Josie's nannies had been from Germany. She was a stout woman with mud-colored hair, a thick neck, and cankles. Josie had been young at the time, but she went to the library and did her research. She started greeting the nanny each day with a hearty *Seig Heil!* and it wasn't long before she quit.

Besides the boxes, the place had been gutted. There were lots of doors leading off to other rooms. Possibly, everything had been pushed into them. One door was marked OFFICE. Josie grunted, imagining colorless people in a windowless room banging out numbers about boxes and collecting faxes about boxes. *How boring*, she thought, sitting on her chair waiting for Adam's return. She felt grateful she'd never have to have a job like that.

Josie closed her eyes and swayed to the music and the voices of the people around her. The DJ was playing something she recognized, a slower song except it had been sped up and put to a dance beat. She hated when they did that. She hummed the slow version of the song and tried in vain to think of the band's name. A man spoke nearby. His voice was strong and commanding. Josie knew he was speaking German, not because of her old nanny, but because she had traveled a lot with her family as a teenager. "Forced Family Travel" she had called it, and despite valiant efforts, she became partially fluent in three languages along the way. One was German.

"Die Zeit ist gekommen," the voice said.

Something has come, Josie thought. *The people or the day or...time...the time has come.* She looked to her right. A short man with brown hair, in his mid-fifties, possibly sixties, was talking to a peroxide blonde with thin features. He was dressed in a black collared shirt and tan slacks. She couldn't quite make out his face and strained from her seated position before giving up.

Must be the club coordinator or something, she thought, and then recalled the name of the club and nodded. Die Mortem. Right, German. Her eyes were drawn to him again. *He has money.* Josie was attracted to men with money, or rather, men who had more money than her family did. Adam had no money, but if he stuck with the music and quit the drugs, she was willing to bet he'd be making a nice stash of green some day. Of course, Josie would be long gone by then.

The man turned and she saw his face and like the song playing it was familiar but different. *Flatten and darken his hair,* she thought. *Grease it, apply a bit of color to his face, and add some facial hair, like a...moustache?* At this, Josie began to laugh uncontrollably. People stared. She couldn't breathe. This fit was caused partly by the drugs in her system and partly by the name that goose-stepped into her head:

Adolf Hitler

Josie laughed so hard that it took her a few minutes to notice Adam's hand on her shoulder.

"Hey, you okay?"

He held one drink in his hand and the other he had put on the floor by her chair. Both were pink in pint-sized, plastic cups. Josie pointed at the man, and the fits would not desist.

"Hit...hit...*HITLER!*" she managed, between bouts of laughter.

Adam looked, but the man had moved into the crowd and was already gone.

"There's no one there, baby," he said. "Hey, sorry I took so long but the line was to China. Looks like you don't need me for entertainment though, huh?"

Josie got control of herself and breathed. She tugged the cigarette pack from her jeans' pocket and worked one into her mouth. She offered one to Adam, but he declined. He leaned over to pick up her drink and hand it to her. She lit her cigarette, took a drag and a tiny sip from the cup.

"There was a man...a man there," she said, pointing again to where she had seen the man. "He looked exactly like Hitler. He even spoke *German*."

Adam nodded, clearly expecting more of a story, and when none came, he spoke: "Shit, that must be a bitch on his sex life. That man was *not* pretty. Plus you have the whole genocide thing." Adam snickered to himself and looked at where Josie had pointed. "Poor guy."

Josie laughed and hit him playfully on the arm. He took her hand to help her up. She gulped her drink until it was half-empty or half-full. It tasted like castor oil.

"Let's fucking dance," Adam said.

~

The floor was jumping. They moved into the center of the crowd and let the music control them until sweat dripped from every orifice. It was at this time, when the X was starting to wear off, that Josie noticed them. The ones with the vacant eyes and outdated clothing. The ones with the pale faces and not a drop of sweat glistening on their bodies.

They've been dancing longer than we have, Josie thought.

The nape of her neck tingled. She grabbed Adam's hand and pulled him off the floor, through the crowd, and toward the exit. Adam stopped, forcing her to stop too.

"Hey, hey...wait," Adam said. "What's going on? Where are we going?"

"We need to leave *now*," Josie said, taking back her hand and renewing her pace to the exit. Adam chased after her.

"No, wait...Josie, wait." He got a hold of her waist and drew her to him. "What's wrong, baby? You were fine two minutes ago."

"Did you see them?" she asked. "The people wearing those weird clothes and they had the white faces?" She whispered: "Something's wrong with them."

"Oh, baby, baby, baby," Adam said, laughing. "It's a Goth thing, and the rest is just the drugs talking. You've been coasting all night. Let's just go back to the bar—"

"*No!* I'm leaving now," she said, with an unfamiliar urgency. "You stay if you want."

Josie turned to go. Adam didn't try to stop her again. She thought she heard him mutter something about her sanity, but she didn't care. She climbed the stairs and pulled her own heels out. When she got outside, she ran. When she thought she might collapse, she called a friend to come get her. Josie didn't think about Adam until she was safe in her friend's car and on the way home, and then only one thought occupied her mind: *Oh no, I left him there with those things.*

NOW:

Josie finished what must have been her fifth cigarette, stubbed it out in the ashtray (a.k.a. the tobacco graveyard), and lit another.

"You know your lungs are going to hoist themselves out of your body and run away," I said, smiling. I was always on her case about the smoking, but it was just because I cared.

"That can't be all you have to say?"

"I don't know, Josie," I said. "You were on a lot of drugs last night. You saw Adolf Hitler. Do you know how old he'd be if he was still alive?"

28

She looked at me expecting an answer. I attempted the calculations.

"He'd be dead," I said. "That's how old."

"Well, I only said I saw a guy who looked like him...that's all. I *know* I was fucked up." She nodded and took a drag. Her cheeks sucked in like a supermodel's. Tobacco crackled in its paper sheath. She exhaled a perfect ring before blowing out a long, thin line of smoke. "I know," she said, nodding again. "I know."

"You know?"

"I know. I was über fucked up," she said, smiling now. "What was I thinking? Never again...never ever ever."

"Until next time?" I said, making a scissors in front of her face. She handed the cigarette to me, and I took a puff, then gave it back. It tasted like I had just licked the bottom of my shoe.

"Of course, until next time," she said, shrugging. "We're young. Our minds might say no, but our bodies say *yes, yes, yes!*"

I laughed. "You're a dork."

I got myself up off the couch. It was time to finish packing.

"Hey, what happened to your knee?"

"Oh." I looked down. "Remember, the truck? I landed in a snow bank."

"You better see to that. I have no plans to wheel your ass around final semester senior year."

"Gee, thanks."

Josie winked at me. "You know I love you, bitch."

I was halfway down the hall when I thought of poor Winnie again.

"Hey, Josie?"

"Yep?"

"What really scared you about those people...the ones from the club?"

A long pause followed. I was about to repeat the question, when she answered.

"I'm not sure," she said. "They just gave me a bad feeling, you know?"

I think I did.

CHAPTER THREE

IT GROWLED, ITS MOUTH WIDE WITH DANGER.

I sat and bounced.

Stupid suitcase, I thought, knowing that it wasn't, and never was, the suitcase's fault.

I had already removed several items from the bag, but it still wouldn't close. Removal was meant to equal closure.

"I'm annoyed," I said aloud, as if that would change everything.

I opened the suitcase and decided on showing no mercy. I did it like Noah: two interview suits, two pairs of shoes (one for my interviews and one for leisure activities), two pairs of nylons, two bras, two bathing suits, two pairs of jeans, two dresses (one for evening and one for the beach), two tank tops, two tee shirts, two pairs of sunglasses, and two books (*The Zodiac Killer* by Robert Graysmith and *High Fidelity* by Nick Hornby). The things that I was okay with not doing it like Noah: underwear, suntan lotion, makeup and assorted bath and body products, iPod, cash, passport, and paperwork.

There was a pile of discarded items next to me now. I picked the pile up and transported it to a corner of the room, to be organized upon my return. I went back to my suitcase.

"Come on, you bastard."

The zipper zipped, and the suitcase closed with no body weight necessary. I imagined the chosen pairs of various articles getting frisky when the lights went out and producing offspring. By week's end, the bag would be impossible to close again. *Maybe that's what happens?*

31

It was as thrilling as my single sock vortex theory.

I was officially ready for California. I'd be there for a full week. It was more business than pleasure but more pleasing than standing in snowdrifts. I had three interviews lined up—one every two days, starting the day after arrival, which would give me enough time in between to rewire. My interviews were with the University of California, Los Angeles, the University of Southern California, and Pepperdine. I would attend one of these schools for my post-graduate studies, exit cum laude with a master's in clinical psychology, buy a house at the age of twenty-eight, have my own practice by thirty-one, marry at thirty-three, one child by thirty-four, retire by 50 somewhere in Europe. My life plan in a nutshell.

I was really a planner at heart but never spoke of my long-term goals with anyone. If you put it out there so it's floating around in the universe, someone or something will stop it from happening. That might sound crazy, but that doesn't mean it isn't true. John Lennon sang about making plans as if it was a hindrance to appreciating life, but I think maybe John had been a fellow planner at heart even though he didn't present himself in that way. Then, one day, he made the fatal mistake of speaking aloud a long-term goal.

BANG, BANG!

I picked up the note from Sullivan, read it again, crumpled it, and tossed it in the trash. A future with the writer of very short notes was unlikely. We had different goals, and I suspected he had what my mom liked to call "ants in the pants." It was the reason my mom gave me when my dad left. I was seven, and for two years, I thought an insect problem in my father's trousers had driven him away from us. The concept was preferable to him falling out of love with my mom and me and moving to the city of sin to live out his dream of becoming an Elvis impersonator. Sometimes you just want to go back to believing what you did when you were younger. Usually you can't.

I looked at the windowsill. A tiny, plastic Elvis struck an eternal pose. It was a gift from my father before he left with a signature shimmy and lip curl. I remembered watching him drive down the street in our swamp green wagon, and the wagon and my father becoming a small dot in the distance.

There was a knock at my door.

"Enter."

My roommate, still well-done from the night before, filled a quarter of the doorway. She held a cigarette in one hand, poised for penetration near the lips, and her cell phone in the other. The knuckles of the middle and index fingers of her smoking hand were mustard yellow. She was smiling—last night's fears melted away.

"So Adam just called," she said. "Apologized for last night. Wants to come over." Josie caressed the side of her face with her phone, as if it were a tiny Adam in her hand.

"That's good, right?" I asked.

"Very good. Says he's got a surprise for me. Oh boys...so easy to wrap." She held up her pinky finger and winked. "What time you out of here?"

I looked at my watch. It said three o'clock.

"In about a half-hour."

Josie walked over to me with outstretched arms.

"Have fun, bitch. As much as you can have without me."

We hugged. It was one of those uncomfortable hugging moments—the kind you can have after knowing someone for a couple hours or 20 years. I patted her on the back.

"Okay…say hi to Adam for me."

"Will do." She released me and gave a half wave. "Ciao, chica. Time for me to get beautiful." She turned and danced out of the room, lifting her hands in the air and singing, *"California…California."*

The limited-lyrics song continued down the hall and into the bathroom, behind the shut door and well after the water pipes groaned to life. I went to my window and raised the blinds halfway. It was still snowing. I put one cheek against the cold glass to try and get a look down the street, at the red house with the white shutters, but it was too far. I would go see the twins after the break. Ask them about the truck. There was no time now, which was the perfect excuse to put it off.

~

At a quarter past four, my cab was officially late.

I spent ten minutes searching for their card, which was originally in the menu drawer next to the fridge, and another ten searching for my phone, which I thought I had packed but found under the bed mingling with elastic bands and dust bunnies.

And I was irritated before the whole process began.

I phoned Timely Cabs, and a man with a heavy accent answered. He told me he was on his way and that three of his drivers and the operator hadn't shown up for work, which left just him to handle all the calls and rides for the evening. There weren't a lot of either, but there was the weather too. I nodded and pictured the driver nodding at the other end and a passenger in the backseat nodding in sync. There was always the weather excuse in Syracuse.

"Give me 15 minutes," he said. I heard a siren, and the line went dead.

34

"Sure," I said.

Thirty minutes later, a horn interrupted my pacing in the living room. I grabbed my bags and headed out the door.

~

The cabbie was polite but didn't have much to say. The taxi smelled oddly of bananas and baby powder, and I stayed occupied with my purse's contents to quell my queasiness. I was getting way too old for all-night binges.

My purse was big, and if I was a British nanny and inclined to put a floor lamp in it, I probably could have. I rifled and found one reason for the bag's shoulder-dislocating weight.

I pulled out the folder and opened it. The behemoth contained all of my handwritten notes from my psychology project, plus photocopied pages of various studies. My paper had been on the psyche of copycat killers, with a concentration on the media-dubbed "Heart Attack" murders.

In 1988, on the day I was born, a 22-year-old girl was murdered in the suburbs of Albany. Her heart was ripped from her body. The killer wrote on the wall in her blood: *Until we meet again.* The organ was never found, likely taken as a trophy. She was victim number six, of the same gender, similar age, and murdered in the same way as five others since the first incident in 1883.

Records from a murder investigation were recovered from the attic of a former deputy in Lexington, Massachusetts. The first girl had her heart ripped out while soaking in the bath. No charges were ever filed. Another girl in 1903 was walking home from a dance in New Orleans when she was dragged into an alleyway. No killer found. A Benjamin Lamb, 39, was convicted and put to death in 1943 for the murder of two girls, one that same year in Florida and the other in 1919 in South Carolina. It was a media feeding frenzy. They called him the Heart Attacker, among other things. Lamb gave a full confession and could describe both crime scenes in detail. In 1966, long after Lamb's execution, a student attending Suffolk Law in Boston was stolen off her fiancé's doorstep. A shoe salesman, James Bailey, was convicted. Papers noted the similarities to the Heart-Attack killings and called him "Lovelorn." He was later acquitted on account of the prosecution tampering with evidence. Bailey was dead by drug overdose when Maura Sims, the final victim, was kidnapped and murdered in 1988.

To confess, my birth day attracted me to the project initially. It's not every day you come across someone who was being taken out of the world when you were being put into it. Some preliminary snooping and the project took on a life of its own. I did the work, but information came easy. The papers hadn't even dug deep enough to find the first two girls and connect the earlier murders to the later ones. But I did. And I found out at least three of the victims were born the day of a murder. The papers didn't get that either. This discovery bothered me more than the gruesome photographs and the gory details. It meant I had something in common with the dead girls that wasn't as simple as age or gender. I was at the library that night, but from the chill coursing through my body, I might as well have been at the morgue.

The cab was pulling into Hancock International Airport, and I stuffed the folder back in my purse. My plane was scheduled to leave in 22 minutes. I decided to let the driver know I would be seeking compensation from Timely Cabs if I missed my flight. But when we arrived at Departures, I thanked him profusely and dropped an extra fiver in his hand.

Having family in the service industry made tipping compulsory. I hardly ever had the money, but I'd tip anyone who'd take it. My mom lived off of her tips, and every day, for too many years, she had to put up with crap from people who deserved to be zapped off the face of the earth. Those who served worked thankless jobs. Sure, the cabbie was late, but that wasn't his fault. His co-workers had bailed on him. There was always a back story. Most people were just too self-important to care.

When I arrived at my gate, the last passengers were boarding. A woman with short brown hair and wearing a blue skirt, white blouse, and red bow tie reached her hand out impatiently for my ticket. I put on my best sorry face.

"Doors are about to *close*," she said, as if she were speaking a new language and any word beginning with the letter "C" had to be spit venomously from the mouth.

She, too, has a back story, I thought. *Breathe.*

"I apologize," I said, handing her my ticket. "My cab was late."

"Sure," she said, offering me my stub and a fake smile. I withheld a gasp when I noticed she was missing three teeth, two at the top and one at the bottom. Her gums were blood red. She noticed me noticing and her smile deepened and blue eye shadow caked onto both lids avalanched bits of blue to her cheeks. "Enjoy your flight."

"Thanks, um…you…too."

The door shut behind me. It made a loud clunking noise that reverberated everywhere. When I got on the plane, I realized that those last passengers were the only passengers. I counted 15 as I dragged my stuffed carry-ons through first, business, and coach. A stewardess, much less Appalachian than the previous one, moved aside for me to pass and informed me that the flight wasn't full and I could change my seat after takeoff.

I looked at my ticket stub. "Twenty-one E," I said aloud.

I checked the corresponding numbers above the seats and found mine near the front. I deposited my bags on the seat and glanced around for babies with flight-ruining potential. No babies, but vomit was in the air. Three passengers near me were already gripping barf bags. I retrieved my carry-ons and made my way toward the back. Several others followed my lead, getting up from their seats, gathering their belongings, and relocating to the back of the plane. Screw the rules. No one paid for projectile vomit.

I found a new seat, three to be exact. It was an entire row just for me. I took the aisle and planned on managing my time between aisle and window. It was like managing time between Luxembourg and the Isle of Capri, except slightly less exotic.

Lethargy hit me. I closed my eyes.

When I reopened them, I noticed a man sitting in the middle aisle, two rows ahead. He had dirty blonde hair and was dressed in a charcoal gray suit. From the angle, he was about thirty, give or take a few years. His computer was on his lap, and he pecked at the keys, his fingers punching them before rising slowly and coming down again.

As I watched, he quit typing and raised a hand to his neck. His middle and index fingers lingered on two small cuts, at first caressing, but then scratching. The cuts began to bleed and his fingers stained red and blood spread in long thin lines down his neck and along the bend of his starched white collar.

He stretched his neck out, looking like a dog attacking a flea, and blood speckled the seat in front of him. Skin peeled and hung loose, certain to tear away with the next fingernail that dug in. The man hissed in pain, before his fingers, stained now to the knuckles, returned to the keypad. But he didn't continue typing. His hands floated a half-inch above the keys. The black of pupil filled the corner of his left eye, and before my mind could register what was happening, the strange man whipped his head around to focus all attention on me. I stared straight ahead, memorizing the fabric pattern of the seat in front of me.

Squares in squares in squares with little dots in the middle of the center square.

I heard a rustling, flinched, and then exhaled when the sound of fingers hitting keys resumed. I undid my seatbelt, gathered my things, which had already spread into pockets and beneath seats, fetched a bag from the compartment above me, and moved.

Five rows remained to choose from. After that, I'd be joining the flight attendants in the back. A man dressed in black leather, with shoulders the width of Texas, sat in the last row. The vest he wore had at least ten Harley Davidson patches on it, and a tee shirt underneath read "I ate your grandma today."

Perfect.

I squeezed by him and plopped myself in the window seat. Despite his appearance, I'd be willing to bet he was a big softy—a food pantry worker by day, just a man recapturing his youth by night.

I kicked my bag under the seat and sat there for a minute watching the men in orange load the luggage onto the plane, looking for mine and wondering what kind of apparel offspring I would find when I opened it in California. *Mama needs a new pair of shoes.*

I decided on a nap. A couple hours of sleep, then some light reading or a movie perhaps? If I missed the movie, no big loss. Airlines showing only one movie played the same drivel people refused to see on land. Just when you thought you could escape it by taking to the sky...*fat chance*. Playing a bad movie in a confined space like this was a crime against humanity. There needed to be laws. I'd write a letter.

I reached into my purse and felt around for the melatonin bottle. I pulled it out. The natural drug could knock me ten-kinds-of-sideways. Directions said one tablet, but sometimes I took one, sometimes a half of one, and sometimes two. It all depended on what level of unrest I was in and how much time I could allow for unconsciousness. I captured a pill and couldn't be bothered splitting it. I popped it, swallowed, and replaced the cap on the bottle and the bottle in my purse. I got out my iPod and plugged my ears with the buds. I had made a play list for the flight, and now I put it on.

The music relaxed me.

After setting my watch to L.A. time, I slept.

~

I'm on a carpet of pine needles. Across from me is Mack the Clown. My mom bought him at a yard sale for two dollars. I named him Mack, and it fits because he looks like a gangster. He's plastic and has black plastic hair. He has a black suit and tie. His mouth can move up and down if you want it to. His red lips are set in a frown, and his face is dirty because the kid who owned him before me didn't love him as much as I do.

Behind Mack are my mom's special books to help him sit up. They're the books I'm not supposed to touch. She keeps them up high, because she doesn't understand that I'm nine and I have my ways. There's a tea cup and saucer between Mack's legs.

40

"Drink your tea, Mack," I say.

I look up at the sky. Big fluffy clouds of different shapes and sizes float above our heads. "Do you see the giraffe, Mack?" I ask. "And look! That cloud's like a big daisy. And over above Katy's house—that one looks like a big lollipop. What about you, Mack? What do you see?"

A strong wind comes and knocks Mack down. He's in a perfect cloud-watching position now, just like me, and I'm proud of him and I smile and smile. He speaks, and I get a good fright because Mack's just a doll made of plastic and thread. His voice is scratchy like Mr. Allen's who lives down the street and sells old stuff out of his garage.

"Know what I see, little girl?" Mack says. "I see a fuckin' naked body without a head and the guy has a hard-on the size of a baseball bat. Oh, and over there I see a big, bad-ass dog chowin' down on someone's intestines. And oh boy, looky over there, I think I'm gonna piss myself. It's a bloody torso being filleted over a fire." I hear the sound of plastic cracking and Mack's lips split into a smile. "You're right. This *is* fun. Pass the fuckin' teapot."

Something rips. Mack's head is turning, even though it never could before, and he has teeth, and they're very, very sharp.

"I have a game we can play."

My heart's beating fast. I'm not sure what I'm feeling. I'm only nine, after all. It might be anger. Mack was ruining my tea party. I stand and walk over to the clown. His head follows me, though it never did before.

"Timeout for you, Mack!"

I bring my foot up over his head and down really hard. The doll's face cracks in half. He laughs, and it sounds bad. I lift up my foot and

41

lower it again and again. Blood and little bits of brain matter spatter my pretty white sneakers and my legs and my nice china teapot. I stop when he stops laughing. My foot is sore. Mack's head is in a billion pieces on the ground. I think of Humpty Dumpty. I like Humpty Dumpty.

"No one's putting you together again, Mack."

One of his little pointed teeth has landed in my teacup. I lean over to pick it up.

It gets dark, then.

Purple clouds reach across the blue sky like needy fingers. It starts to rain. A drop lands on my cheek. Another one follows, landing on my lower lip. I look up and open my mouth wide to taste the rain on my tongue. My friend Katy and I do this all the time. It's a competition to see who can catch the most raindrops. I lie, but I know she does too.

I catch four in my mouth and gag. It tastes different.

Like wet salt.

My eyes start to sting. I run for the cover of a nearby tree and wipe my eyes with my sleeve. *That's better.* But it's not—not really. There's blood on my sleeve. I look down as drops stain my shirt red.

"What's this?" I say.

A car window shatters.

There's a loud thumping on the roof next door. Something else is falling from the sky. Something heavier. It smacks me across the face and knocks me onto the wet, sticky grass.

I'm soaked now. My clothes are sticking to my skin and any movement makes a horrible noise that has me feeling ill. It's raining harder and I can't see. On the ground, I drag myself back to the tree and lean against it. I try to push my hair out of my face, but it's matted and sticky and not going anywhere.

I'm wearing a shirt with a pelican on it, and the bird's head is clean. I use it to wipe my face. I can see again, and I look closer at what has landed on the ground.

There are many red balls around me.

No, they're not balls at all, but irregular lumps. Some have pinker sections. I inch over to one and poke it with my finger. I recoil and scurry back against the tree. I know what they are, and *God* my nine-year-old brain won't allow itself to wrap around the idea. The world starts to blink out.

No.

I push myself up and run toward the street. I try to avoid them, but they're everywhere. I step on one and it squishes and almost sends me to the pavement. A block away, the front door of a brown house slams open.

"Help me, please!"

A little boy in yellow boots and a matching slicker runs out of the house and into the street. He puts his hands up in the air and laughs. He jumps in a puddle of blood accumulating by a drain, and the blood splashes onto and slides from off the bottom of his bright slicker.

A couple stands in the doorway of the brown house. The man has his arm around the woman. They are both smiling. The man walks briskly down the steps to the front yard. He's whistling. He grabs two of the lumps from off the grass. He hops back up the steps and hands one to the woman and brings the other one to his own mouth. He bites down and gives an expression of sheer joy, like he has just bitten into the biggest, juiciest red apple and not what it actually is.

Not a warm, bloody heart.

The man is about to take another bite. His upper lip curls back, and his teeth stick out, sharp and stretched like daggers. He notices me and gives a friendly wave before returning to his snack. When it is all gone, he rubs his stomach.

Doors open, one after the other, like dominoes down the street. These monsters pour from their houses, laughing, talking, and throwing Frisbees like it was just another beautiful day in the neighborhood. Blood is everywhere. It flows along the pavement inches thick and tickles the back of my ankles. It slops down foreheads, over noses, into mouths, and through clothing.

Heavy sobs climb my chest. I collapse onto the ground, and a dark shadow gets on top of me and puts its hand over my heart.

"I believe this is mine."

My chest feels gripped, squeezed, and tugged. The flesh between my small breasts is being eaten away.

I cry out in pain.

~

I opened my eyes and sat up, digging my hands past multiple cotton layers to touch the skin beneath them.

I exhaled to no end.

I closed my eyes again and wiped away the cold sweat sprouting just below my hairline. It was then that I realized things not being right.

Maybe having my eyes shut gave me some sort of sixth sense? That's how the self-professed psychics do it. They close their eyes to really open them. But no, I think I was aware of my predicament when I awoke and my mind was only okay dealing with one scare at a time.

Second crazy dream of the day. Breathe. Done. Then…

You are alone on this plane.

I opened my eyes, and it was true. The 80-year-old woman reading a book titled *Hard Harry*. Gone. The man that looked like he was about to upchuck everything he'd eaten since age three. Gone. Creepy scratching guy. Gone. My biker bodyguard who had occupied one and a half seats next to me. Gone. I held my breath to better listen and waited for a sound, a peep, laughter... anything?

Nothing.

I shoved the shade open and looked out the window.

It was nighttime, and we had landed. *I can't believe no one woke me.* That was what I got for sitting next to a man with an identity crisis. Those things came hand in hand with intimacy issues. Even a tap on the shoulder would have been too much for him to bear. I checked my watch and struck it with a fingernail even though the second hand was moving along at a normal pace.

"It can't be one o'clock," I said, tapping the face again.

I looked out the window. Darkness clung to the runway. Below, a cart spilled luggage. Three suitcases leaned against the vehicle. Nearby, immense planes with empty windows seemed anxious for people to fill them and fly them.

I released my seatbelt, dropped my iPod into my bag, flung both purse and duffel over my shoulder, and bolted toward the front of the plane. I glanced at the empty seats. People had left stuff—a book here, a makeup case there—but that was what people did, right? *They forget things. It's only natural.*

I panicked thinking the plane's door might be locked and I would be trapped, but it was wide open, and my feet hit the carpeted tunnel like they were on fire. I took to the staircase two steps at a time.

Beneath me, reproachful gonging. I saw the doorway to the main terminal up ahead and laughed. I was acting like Josie and I couldn't blame drugs or booze. At least I was semi-qualified to be my own shrink.

Emma Spade, you're crazy, I thought.

"That will be fifteen hundred dollars. Cash or credit, please," I said aloud, breathlessly.

They forgot me, plain and simple. I was sure it happened every day. Maybe there had been a fire drill? That would explain the absence of people. *Do airports have fire drills?* I wondered. Did they line up by height? Did someone call attendance when an agreed-upon location was reached? It was possible they were calling my name at that very moment. *Five hours after the scheduled arrival?* Yes. We'd all have a good laugh.

LAX by reputation was one of the busiest airports in the world, and I would walk through the gate and there would be people everywhere. Congestion would be an understatement. Passengers would be like so many ants scurrying and weaving to and fro with their oversized loads. I would be willing all the people away and longing for my next iota of peace. I gripped my bags and opened the door and...

...nothing was as it should have been.

CHAPTER FOUR

THERE WERE HUNDREDS OF THEM.

In various shapes, sizes, and patterns. Some were intact, others spilled their innards out onto the polished airport floor.

It was a battlefield without bodies. I stood not able to move, staring out at the abandoned bags and struggling to hold open the gate door, which had hit the wall and flung back at me. It was the heaviest door in existence.

My arms began to weaken, and my legs followed suit. I gasped for breath. At any second, the airport walls would start closing in on me. They would collapse and I would be flattened and pushed into the ground and a hundred years from now they would find my flat body and exhibit it in a natural history museum as the *Flattened Airport Woman*. I forced myself to relax and felt better.

I walked out there.

I couldn't even go a couple of feet without having to avoid one of them. Sometimes I looked down, sometimes I didn't. I did when I passed a bag with its contents coming out. I couldn't help myself. Why did people slow down driving past traffic accidents? Besides, the abandoned bags, especially the open ones, could've held clues as to the fate of their owners. Why had these ones been opened and others not? Maybe something important had been taken from them before…?

It had to be a terrorist threat. They grew on trees since 9/11.

A phone rang relentlessly at the Delta counter, interrupting my thoughts and fiddling with my last fraying nerve. *The only sign of life in this huge place is a fucking phone ringing.*

But wait. There was life at the other end of that line.

I jumped over several suitcases and ran toward the vacant counter. I wasn't sure what I was going to say to this person when I answered. The truth, I decided. My fingers touched the edge of the counter just as the ringing stopped. I slammed a fist down and regretted it as pain surged up my arm to my elbow. I shrugged my bags off and slid my butt to the floor.

Quiet was sometimes the loudest noise in the world.

I had felt alone before. Everyone does at some point in their lives; the feeling is not easily evaded. People enter your life and exit without a sound. You come to the conclusion that the only person who will always be with you is you and here's to hoping you don't get sick of yourself. This aching awareness throbbed inside me as I eyed the hundreds of suitcases erect like so many gravestones—reminders of those who had traveled before, but, for one reason or another, traveled no longer.

My brain heaved and hoed, clinked and clanked, calculated and reasoned, spitting out possibilities at numbing speeds. *It must be a bomb scare.* Possibly. Could the airport have been evacuated? *Yes.* Would they have made people leave their luggage inside? *Maybe.* Wouldn't there be cops, FBI, bomb squad, and anyone else dressed for importance swarming about? *Yes.* Could they be at the other side of the airport? *Yes.* It was a big building. Was I in any danger? *Possibly.* Should I leave? *No time like the present.*

I reached over the counter and picked up the phone that had been ringing. An irate busy signal beat through my eardrum. I threw the receiver down, not bothering to put it back in its cradle. I started to run.

Fast. I carefully fed my hand to my purse, so that nothing would spill out, and found my cell. I flipped it open.

Fuck it. No signal.

I passed gates, stores, and restaurants. The trail of bags did not end, but thinned. I slowed outside a souvenir store where an abandoned *Curious George* doll was lying on its back. The monkey wore a red baseball cap and a red tee shirt with its name in yellow. It had dirty, matted fur and black cloth eyes. Its right arm was hanging on by a couple of threads, and stuffing bled from the monkey's shoulder. The toy had been loved for many years. I knew the likelihood was slim that a child had dropped the doll without looking back and causing a fuss. I was also pretty sure that the good guys wouldn't force a kid to abandon its favorite stuffed animal.

Maybe the airport had been taken over by terrorists and they had no plans to bomb it. They held the passengers and workers hostage and were planning on picking them off one by one until their demands were met. What kind of outfit could kidnap an entire airport? It had to be a big one.

I needed to be careful and stick to the shadows—easier said than done in a brightly illuminated airport with not a bulb out of service. I spotted payphones against the far wall. If they were working, I could call home and see if there was anything on the news. LAX was an international airport—something bad happening there was being reported on.

At the phones, I found my phone card, the one I had purchased on the previous spring break, and dialed the necessary digits followed by my mom's cell number. There was a click and then a ring.

"Come on, mom...pick up," I said. The fourth ring began and then half the fifth. I slammed the phone down when voicemail answered.

"Damn it!"

My palms were sweating. I dialed Sullivan's number. He answered on the first ring.

"Sullivan," I said, feeling such relief to hear his voice that my knees nearly buckled.

"Hey, mate," he said. "I thought you were Adam. Lazy bugger didn't show up for practice. Owes me $60 for studio time. You in L.A.?"

Jumbled up words spilled from my mouth, as if my vocal cords had become possessed. I paused for a breath and realized I couldn't even understand what I had just said, so how could he? I pressed my forehead hard against the top of the phone, as if that would allow me to smoosh through and find a place to hide.

"So you got off the plane and the airport's been evacuated and you're calling from a payphone in the airport?"

I loved him.

"Exactly," I said. "I mean…I'm in the airport but when I say I have not seen anyone at all, I'm being serious. There are just bags everywhere. If this place had been evacuated, there would still be people around…outside…the authorities…someone. I have a *really* bad feeling about this. It's like everyone's vanished."

There was silence at the other end. I half-expected the *da, da, dummmm* from an invisible orchestra pit.

"If you're wondering, Em," Sullivan said, "I'm gesturing the international sign for *you've gone completely fucking mad*. It's like I'm dating Josie and her issues, and I thought I left that honor with Adam." Sullivan had a usually quiet dislike for Josie. His collected British coolness clashed with her in-your-face New York City abrasiveness. "Believe me when I say this, Em. You have nothing to worry about. I mean, what do they do in L.A.? They make movies. They close down streets and airports and completely disrupt people's lives for the sake of brilliant filmmaking. I don't know...the crew's out to lunch or something." He laughed. "A few minutes earlier and you would have interrupted the most riveting scene. It's when the sexy but headstrong stewardess realizes that the world has been taken over by little green men who are vicious with anal probes."

I laughed. "I hate you," I said. My eyes hurt. I closed them and massaged the lids with my fingertips. My eyeballs bobbed. "Are you sure nothing's going on? There hasn't been anything on the news?"

"Haven't even seen a telly today—been running around like crazy. We've got that massive gig coming up, and uh...well, I just wanted to say that I want you there...in the front row. I mean, it means so—"

Sullivan continued speaking, but his voice faded in and out of my head like a faraway signal through a shortwave radio. Some words came loud and clear. They were words I had been longing to hear but words which were now like so much nothing against the dreadful tugging in my bones.

Hard, distant footsteps echoed. Either a giant was approaching or several people walked as one in synchronized, practiced steps. And just like that, they were not very distant anymore, and I knew it was their purpose that made them so damn fast. When I was little, my uncle and I watched old black and white war movies together. Uncle Benny, my mother's brother, wore funny wigs which he'd pull off and spin around his head until I was laughing so much I'd almost pee my pants. At 42, he died of liver cancer. Uncle Benny. The synchronized footsteps in

51

those old movies always meant either death or salvation.

A voice made me jump. It was Sullivan in my ear. "You there, mate?"

"Someone's coming. I have to go."

"Did you hear what I said?"

"We'll talk later." I hung up with all my things left unsaid. *We will talk later*, I thought. Sometimes convincing yourself is the hardest part.

~

Four—no, five. Five men came around the corner.

They were in a V formation, like geese, and all in black. They were too far away yet to make out faces, but the uniforms I could see. Each wore a cap, a fitted shirt with a red and white band around the left bicep, cargo pants, and army boots. Dressed as they were, they could have been any division of military or law enforcement. They took wide strides in sync, and before I knew it, they were standing in front of me, like time and space had turned a blind eye. I raised both hands slowly.

"I'm Emma Spade. I'm an American citizen." I wasn't sure about confessing that last part since being American was a liability nowadays. I guess I figured they would find out sooner or later.

On approach, I observed them all to be men, and men that didn't fit the terrorist profile. They had square, thick builds. I had to look up to see their faces, which at my height was rare. The rims of their hats fell to just above the eyes, so I couldn't tell if their hair color was different, as none was showing. With the exception of the man in front, they looked like cookie cutter images of each other.

The front man, who I dubbed "Burns," had neatly trimmed gray sideburns which poked out from under his hat. I could see his eyes, and they were clear blue. My roommate would've called them "easy" eyes,

52

meaning they were easy to fall into—a comment which was usually followed by certain things falling into her. He appeared older than the others. He was a few inches shorter than his men, yet still taller than me.

No one spoke. Burns offered a quick smile that lacked pleasantry. He turned, and I could see his armband in detail. It had two red stripes on the top and bottom and a thick white one going through the middle with the letters U V F on it.

After a minute, Burns addressed two of his men in an unfamiliar language, and the men sprinted off in the direction they came. He turned back to me with another quick smile.

"Ms. Spade, is it?" I nodded. "Were you traveling with anyone today?"

"No."

"Good. Please come with us," he said. "We need to ask you some questions... in private."

I glanced around. "It's kind of private here, isn't it? Who are you? Am I in any trouble?"

"That depends on what you think of as trouble, Ms. Spade." He smiled, and this one lasted longer than the others and had wickedness behind it. He gestured me forward.

I had two options: run or go with them. They weren't armed from what I could see, which I found strange. If I ran, that would get them pissed. They'd chase after me, catch me, and snap me in half over their thick bodies. But if I went with them and cooperated, I had a chance of finding out what all of this was about.

My heart beat double time in my chest. The two men positioned themselves on either side of me, with Burns in front. My chance of escape, if I decided on that course of action, had just narrowed considerably.

I complied, and we hadn't traveled far before stopping at a door with a red RESTRICTED AREA sign on it. They ushered me through, and we entered a hallway with beige walls and framed photographs of old planes and the pilots who loved them. There was no more abandoned luggage, which I was happy about. The rubber soles of my sneakers let out tiny squeaks, sounding weak next to the solid *clomp clomp* of the men's boots.

Before the hallway branched right, we stopped outside another door with an eye-level, glass and wire-meshed window. It was double paned, and the inside glass was fogged as if someone had breathed on it not long ago. Burns opened the door. Inside the room, a skinny man who looked like a caricature of himself sat at a long, cafeteria-style table. The table was one of three pieces of furniture in the entire room, with two folding metal chairs completing the set.

The man's black hair was slick and parted to one side. He had pale skin and a long nose that curved to a tight knob over paper-thin lips. He wore a white lab coat, a dark shirt, and gray trousers. The tips of his stretched fingers met over a pad of paper in front of him. The man smiled when he saw me, and his lips turned a paler pink, while his cheeks dimpled. Burns made introductions.

"This is Mr. Myers. Mr. Myers, Emma Spade. Mr. Myers will be asking you a few questions. Answer them as best you can. You'll be assuring the safety of yourself and others in the long run."

With that, Burns was gone. I turned to Mr. Myers. I wasn't sure which man I preferred, but my preferences at that moment had nothing to do with anything.

"Sit down," Mr. Myers said.

Sure his manners sucked, but in theory, the sooner I cooperated, the sooner I'd be out of there. I had no real reason not to believe that. I sat across from him and took in my new surroundings.

Four walls. The wall behind me was bare. The other three had a poster tacked to each. An advertisement for the Red Cross was on my right. The poster was white with the standard Red Cross symbol in the middle. Underneath, it read: DO YOUR PART. GIVE BLOOD. In front of me, a drug deal was taking place. A white boy in his teens had his hand out to receive a bag of pills from an older Hispanic man wearing a red bandana. The boy looked forlorn. At the bottom of the poster, it read: LIFE IS A TERRIBLE THING TO WASTE. PLEASE JOIN THE PARTNERSHIP FOR A DRUG-FREE AMERICA. A door on my left had a poster attached to it showing a pregnant woman surrounded by flowers. She was smiling and looking down at a little boy with an ear to her enormous belly. In the sky above them, yellow letters in a crayon font spelled out: THE JOY OF MOTHERHOOD!

"Wonderful, aren't they?" Mr. Myers said.

His voice startled me, and it might have been this that pleased him for immediately his lips broadened into another smile. Myers gazed at the posters like they were Picassos. His eyes were unusually large for his face, making me wonder if he was good at noticing details.

"Yeah, I guess," I said. "A bit strange for an airport, though."

Myers nodded. "Well, the characters that this room generally holds don't have the highest moral code. Airport authority hoped that these posters would give them a push in the right direction. You know, turn criminals into weeping saints." He laughed breathily but stopped when he realized no laughter was being returned. "Let's get on with the business at hand, yes?" His brows arched.

"Do I need a lawyer, Mr. Myers?" I asked.

"No, you will not need legal representation," he said. "This is query only. Besides, do you really want to get a dirty lawyer in here? Because they are all *dirty*." The way he said dirty made me feel like I needed a bath. "They'll suck you dry, Ms. Spade. They'll. Suck. You. Dry."

Myers' lower lip began to tremble, but he turned his head to the side, and when he turned it back the tremble was gone.

"These questions that I'm about to ask you are for your own well being. In fact—" Myers hit the table resolutely with the flat of his hand. The table jumped. "—I'm going to take a chance on you, Ms. Spade, and let you know what's going on because...well, because I like you."

Never trust anyone who says that they like you within the first few minutes of meeting you.

"You've heard about that nasty flu going around?" I nodded. "In truth, it's bio-terrorism. They're targeting wealthy Americans in positions of power. But the virus spreads easily from person to person through the air. A sneeze or a cough. A vaccine does exist, and the government's getting it out, but they want to make sure they're sending it through the appropriate channels. That's where I come in. We don't want to cause any unnecessary widespread panic, so the vaccine will be sent discreetly through smaller channels. We're pulling people aside and questioning them to make sure that the vaccine reaches all corners of the country and everyone receives the same treatment." Myers pulled his hands apart in a there-you-have-it gesture and brought them back together with a clap. "So let's begin, yes?"

"Don't you have the census for this type of thing?"

"The census isn't accurate. Everyone knows that."

"Could I be infected already? What about all those people? Are they in quarantine?"

"All what people?"

"The owners of the bags."

Myers sighed. "Most of those people are being questioned right now. Just. Like. You. Now, if you have any other questions, Ms. Spade, do make it quick."

He was lying. I knew it. He knew it. Even Johnny "Strung Out" and Martha "Bun in the Oven" knew it and they were just fictional characters in public service campaigns. I clutched my purse beneath the table, pressing my fingers into its fabric.

"What does U V F stand for?" I asked.

Something crept behind Myers' eyes. Shadows appeared on his face where there weren't any before. He leaned forward until his chest touched the table and jerked his head to call me closer. I leaned in and felt his warm breath in my ear.

"If I told you that, Emma Spade, your tongue might end up splayed and garnished on a rusty platter." He hissed a laugh, and before I could pull away, tiny drops of Myers' saliva catapulted into the depths on my inner lobe. I straightened and covered my mouth with my hand to reinforce my locked lips. Myers shook his head.

"I'm only joking with you, Ms. Spade. Removing your tongue from your mouth in a forceful manner would be illegal, and I work for the government. We frown on such activities. Now. Let. Us. Start. State your full name with middle initial."

I cleared the fright from my throat. I was going to get through this one way or another.

"Emma Spade…I don't have a middle name." It was the truth. My parents couldn't agree on one, so they decided just two names would be enough.

"Oh, you poor dear." He picked up the pencil and pad and scribbled something.

"Age?"

"Twenty-one." He looked pleased and scribbled.

"Full current address with zip code?"

"Eight hundred Sigmund Street in Syracuse. That's 13229."

Could he possibly know the area, I thought. *Oh God, his nephew went there and he'll grab the back of my head with his hands and pull my face closer to his and say you and I both know that there is no Sigmund Street in Syracuse and then he'll put his cold frog lips on mine, catch my tongue in his teeth, and...calm down, Emma...please calm down.*

"Occupation?"

"Student."

"Unemployed." Skribble, scribble, scribble.

"Major?"

"Psychology."

"Not. Very. Useful."

For the next hour, give or take, Myers asked me for details on the lives of my family, friends, enemies, boyfriends, neighbors, roommates, classmates, professors, and more. The list was endless, the questions basic, but the real reason fueling them was unknown and therefore disturbing. I had decided from the get-go that there was only one thing to do until I knew what was going on and that was lie through my teeth.

I lied a lifetime's worth, and I won't lie, it wasn't easy. Making up names, addresses, phone numbers, occupations, and relations on the spot and with such uninspiring surroundings was a talent one acquired through years of practice. I had to throw in some truths, mostly about myself, to ease the pressure.

"Well, Ms. Spade. Our interview has come to an end. I want to thank you for taking the time to help your government. You've performed a great service for your country…and so on and so forth, blah, blah, blah, bullshit, *BULLSHIT!*"

Myers' face contorted, reminding me of a doll I used to own with a big knob on top of its head which you could turn to reveal one of four faces. Someone had turned Myers' knob to the crazy face while the sane one slid behind follicles of greased-up hair.

"Nobody likes a big fat liar 'round here," he said. "You know what happens to liars? They end up drooling in a gutter, their skin choked by a dress five sizes too small, praying to their god that all of those dark figures will just pass them by. But they won't. Oh no, they won't. They're going to feed."

I shot up from my chair, sending it into the wall behind me. I turned and lunged for the door handle.

Locked.

"Mr. Myers," I said, holding my hands in front of me. "I have no idea what's going on here, but I told you the truth. I wouldn't lie to my government. I'm a very patriotic person."

The room plan was in my head. It didn't offer much: one table, two chairs, two doors (one locked), three posters, and one mental institution escapee. If I were *MacGyver*, I could've made a tank and busted the hell out of there.

"Please, call me Harold. We'll need to be on a first-name basis..." Myers reached under the table "...for what I'm about to do to you."

Myers had a gun in his hands now. He pointed it at me.

"No! Don't!"

The gun went off. Something pierced my neck. A dart. I pulled it out and opened my hand to let it fall onto the floor.

"What did you do?"

Myers replaced the gun under the table and reached into his pockets. He pulled out a pair of Latex gloves and put each one on with a loud *snap! snap!* He started for me.

"You will lose the use of your legs. Only temporarily. You see, less struggling in that area increases the efficiency of the exam."

My calves tingled. Myers was in front of me, his bony fist smacking my cheek. I fell and he stepped over me, lowering his rubber-gloved hands toward my face. They grabbed a bundle of my hair and pulled. My skull felt like it was on fire, and white explosions blurred my vision. He dragged me to door number two, and the glowing pregnant poster lady stared down at me.

Yes, I was fucked but you're fucking in for it. You're fucking in for it.

We entered another room. Blood was on the floor, and it soaked through the back of my shirt. A foldout examination table with stirrups and straps loomed over me. The blood was coming from the table—from in between the stirrups—and each drop made a patting sound when it hit the floor. A naked bulb attached to a naked cord hung from the ceiling.

Myers released his grip on my hair, and my head smacked the floor with a horrible sound. I was about to become a vegetable and now I was a nauseous soon-to-be vegetable and that blood *pat patting* on the floor was the constant reminder of what would happen to me if I didn't get out of there fast—a life reduced to the incessant dripping of bodily fluid.

I heard a clanging sound, metal on metal, and looked up. Myers had his back to me. He faced a small cart. He began to sway, moving his stick hips back and forth. He hummed and his voice wouldn't have been all that bad if he wasn't about to kill me.

"*Hmm, hmmm. Hmm, hmm, hm, hmmm. Hmm, hmm, hm, hmmm. Hmm, hmm, hm, hmmm hmmm.* Like Frank? He was my hero. Sorry about the mess. The last girl couldn't take the pain. She was the fifth one to die from my prying hands. I tell *them* it's not my fault. I tell *them* it's just been a while since I practiced. In my day, medicine was new. I have determination, and that can only lead me down the path to perfection."

Myers had stopped dancing. He was getting angry. Battling some fucked-up cause with a "them" I never wanted to meet.

"But not to worry. I think you're going to be my first success story. I have a very good feeling about you." He turned to face me with a speculum in his hand. It was bloody like everything else in that damn room. My jaw hurt and my head was swimming and I wasn't sure if it was from my fall or whatever drug Myers had shot into me but I spoke and when I did I made it sound like how Myers spoke—slow, enunciated words, all emphasis and period.

"Have. You. Ever. Heard. Of. Hygiene. Harold?"

Myers came at me and fuck it was fast. He crouched down to grab my hair, and I yanked my head away, at the same time sending a fist between his legs. I grabbed what I hoped were his balls and squeezed hard.

Myers wailed and fell to his knees.

His face fell forward, and I took advantage of the downward movement, grabbing the sides of his head with both hands and digging my outstretched thumbs into his eyes.

The left one popped first, then the right.

A mixture of blood and cloudy fluid oozed down my thumbs and splattered onto my forehead. I rolled right just as Myers collapsed onto the floor, his mouth wide with shock and what was left of his eyes retreating from their sockets and down his cheeks in liquid form.

I reached for a leg of the cart and shook it, knocking the cart over and sending assorted scalpels landing dangerously close to my limbs. I grabbed the meanest knife and positioned it midair, ready to strike.

Myers lay catatonic on the floor next to me, his face in a puddle of goo. I laughed and it sounded foreign to me in that nasty, smelly, sticky room. The psycho was down for the count, and I would be away from that nightmare very soon.

~

I'm not sure what I was doing when I saw it, or how much time, if any, had passed. The window was over six feet off the floor and its view obscured by a curtain. In my wrecked head, it was a magic window, appearing when I most needed my hope restored. In reality, it was plain as far as windows went. And what was on the other side was anyone's guess. A wall? Another room? Heaven? Hell? I would knock it in, find an exit, claim my cloud, and hell? Well, wasn't I already there?

The window looked small, but I would squeeze. I didn't know how

I'd get up there with my legs failing me, but I had to try. The cart I had tipped over was on wheels, which gave me an idea. I checked the bottom of the death table. It, too, was mobile.

Nothing like torture on the go.

Still holding a knife in case Myers recovered, I shimmied closer to the examination table, using my arms more than my legs. I wasn't sure which, use or nonuse, could put off the losing-them part, but one thing was for sure—I was going to need my legs to get out that window.

I pulled the table toward me and positioned it parallel to the wall. I shoved hard, and it flew forward. Blood sprayed the floor, and the specks made designs on the tile which looked more like art than violence. The table rolled straight, hit the wall and stopped beneath my magic window.

I held my breath to listen for the sound of boots approaching.

Myers was still passed out, or dead. Either way, he wasn't coming after me—just how I liked it. I had a quick, unreasonable pang of guilt looking at his body, then pushed the feeling away for a later date. I put the knife handle in my mouth, bit down and crawled to the table. My legs felt like they were being stuck by a million hot pins. I stood carefully, swung each leg onto the surface of the table and assumed a position on my knees, with my calves tucked beneath my thighs.

The window was in front of my face now. My nose brushed the curtain. It was scratchy and smelled like broccoli. I opened it and saw a black wall beyond the glass, which, as my eyes adjusted, became an unlit parking garage. There were no soldiers that I could see—just ten or so shadow-wrapped cars.

The window was latched. I grabbed the lever, turned it down and pulled the window open. It moaned like it had been a while, then slid open like that while had been way too long. My legs were spasming now. The table vibrated along. I stood, chucked the knife through the window and climbed in after, headfirst.

~

It wasn't a long drop, but my legs were now like bags of sand and would make the fall that much harder.

With my waist lodged in the window, my hands were still a few feet off the pavement. I wiggled my hips in an attempt to ease my legs out of the window, but they dislodged suddenly and toppled over the rest of my body, causing it to flip. I landed on my neck and shoulders. My breath left me at once.

But it felt more like my soul leaving. I started to sob.

I wanted to go home. I was drugged, I was hungry, I was angry, I had just committed my first murder, and I was covered in other people's bodily fluids.

California was not at all what I expected.

I gave myself a few seconds and held my hands over my eyes. I moved them away, clearer in my mind but physically spent. My legs were not my own—at least it felt that way. As if someone had sawed off my stems and replaced them with another person's and didn't bother to attach them properly. They were scratched dead weight, and I wondered how long I'd have to drag them around.

My head felt like a bowling ball and not one of those candlepin balls either. The big serious ones with the holes. I squinted the darkness away and spotted the knife. It was more of a scalpel—small but oh so sharp. The closest car was a maroon Chevy with a sad dent in the front right wheel well. More cars were parked on the down ramp. An orange elevator with a giant four on it was at the bottom.

The only noise was my breathing, until my stomach clenched and what was in there came out. When I was done vomiting, I wiped my mouth, breathed and debated my next move.

Up or down?

Not having the use of my legs made going down a more viable option. I could roll to the elevator, get to ground level and get the hell out of there. That was in a better world. I doubted there was currently a garage-to-door service for people like me. I pictured a squat chauffeur waiting outside, looking bored and holding a sign reading: ANYONE DISABLED BY POISON DARTS AND SET UPON BY INSANE GYNOS.

I had to figure that if anyone was waiting at ground level, it would be the soldiers, and I had to assume that if they had the main terminal, they had the rest of the airport too. I thought of my mom's favorite toast on those rare occasions she'd have a drink. It was always in celebration of something, but her words remained the same. *To the confusion of our enemies*, she would say.

I'd go up.

Before I started to roll, I looked back at the window.

Myers was there.

His eyeless head was afloat in the magic window. He waved at me.

Do you like Frank?

He wasn't there really. My imagination was accosting me. I grabbed the knife and started my rolling descent to the elevator. I stayed close to the parked cars for shelter. If someone drove around the corner or got off the elevator, I could take cover.

I sat up when I arrived at the orange doors and smacked the button to call the elevator to the floor. It came for me right away.

I didn't hide when the doors dinged open and harsh light escaped the carriage to flood the depths of the garage, but I wanted to. When you're escaping, light can be the other enemy.

I dragged my body onto the elevator, my arms shaking from the strain. The carriage smelled like piss, but who was I to complain? I propped myself up beneath the panel of buttons and scoped out the floors. Anything higher than four would do. I'd go to six. I pressed the button and jumped in my sticky skin when the doors closed and the elevator started to move.

Down.

"But I didn't press *down*," I said aloud.

My eyes darted around the small enclosure. I glanced up. In the movies, there was always a loose panel at the top of the carriage, perfect for escaping by. Based in truth or not, I wasn't getting up there in my condition.

I saw no place to hide. I couldn't walk or run. I could only sit and wait.

My knife looked tiny in my hand. I started to doubt whether I could do damage with the thing. Size mattered.

Size always mattered.

I pictured an eyeless Myers waiting for me. His face was stained with dried blood, but the blood still flowed, and it flowed down his face and his neck and his white lab coat and his smart pants and made a deep, thick puddle at his feet. His hands, still gloved, worked the speculum—opening and closing it. Open and close, *clink*. Open and close, *clink*.

"No, he's dead," I said.

The elevator stopped its descent.

The doors opened.

I pressed up against the side of the elevator, panting and sweating, trying to make myself minimal. *Could this be when it happened? Is this when it all ends? I escape only to get caught again and taken back to that...that horrible room.* No, I couldn't go back there. I wouldn't. They would have to pry me from that carriage and good luck to them because it wasn't going to happen. After a few seconds, I dared a look out, and only an empty garage and darkness waited on the other side.

There was no button to close the doors, so I banged on the SIX button repeatedly with my fist. I wondered how much adrenalin a body and mind could take before going into meltdown. It felt like an eternity before the doors finally closed and the elevator hopped to an ascent.

The elevator arrived on the sixth floor, and the doors opened. It took some time to gather my courage, and I ended up having to throw myself between the doors as they closed. *Thanks for the ride, buddy,* I thought, once back on solid ground.

My body wanted to collapse, but the adrenalin coursing through it said *NO!* Abandoned cars speckled the floor, like the bags from the terminal. I made myself into a human rolling pin and caught the down ramp.

I rolled to a silver Honda with a red, white, and blue sticker on the bumper that said PROUD TO BE AMERICAN and found my home for the night.

CHAPTER FIVE

A SLIM JIM WRAPPER STUCK TO MY FACE.

It clung to the tip of my nose, flapping in my breath. I wondered how it had chosen its landing spot and decided anyplace was fine when you had no more purpose in life. I blew it away and sat up. There was a quick moment of blessed confusion until the reality of what happened the night before settled back deep in my gut.

"You've got to be kidding," I said. But nothing else could explain the condition of my body or why I was in the backseat of a strange car.

I looked at my legs and bent one at the knee and then the other. I wiggled my toes in my shoes until satisfied that I had my mobility back and that that garage and the airport and Myers would soon be just an unthinkable notch in my past. My legs were scratched and sore from being dragged around, but they'd get me from A to B and then whatever letter I had to get to from there.

The proud American whose backseat I had borrowed was also a clean American. Besides the wrapper, there was a pink polka-dotted umbrella and a Rubix Cube with its square, colorful stickers crooked.

In the front seat, I found a stick of Wrigley's and two quarters. I checked for a spare ignition key under the driver and passenger side floor mats, behind both visors, and in the glove compartment. In the movies, these places were gold mines and spare keys were waiting here for heroes to come along. In reality, not so much.

At that moment, I was running on instinct. My brain was telling me to get out fast and use any means necessary, but I wasn't sure stealing a car from the garage was the best idea. It was too quiet, and noise woke things up. The soldiers could be on me before I reached ground level. No, the best thing to do was to get out of the garage first and find transportation from there.

I felt an overwhelming sense of dread and had to swallow to force down the vomit inching up my throat. I liked my controlled environment: my little Honda, my dark backseat, and my Rubix Cube to settle the soul.

I wrapped a tight fist around the gum and change. It wasn't much, but when you have nothing, not much can be pretty good. I had left my bags in the interrogation room. I wasn't kicking myself for it—I had been busy—but I toyed with the idea of going back for them, before good sense slapped me across the face and left a mark.

It's time to go.

I popped the gum, pocketed the change, and opened the back door.

I was outside the garage in five minutes flat. My intense need to stay put was replaced by an intense need to release myself from anything keeping me in. The sun felt unfamiliar to me, and I squinted up at it as if it were a stranger offering candy.

I ducked behind a tree and searched the departure drop-off. There were the usual suspects, cars and bags, but no people. A giant crow with glossy feathers flew down from a telephone pole and hovered over me, flapping its wings. I thought it might land on my head, before it went high and dove into palm brush. I spotted a parked yellow taxi and ran to it in a crouched-down position.

Inside, the cab reeked of something gone bad. The door was unlocked so I let myself in, but I was so overwhelmed by the smell that

I had to kneel by the side of the car to regroup.

A ray of sunlight fell on a Dippin' Donuts bag on the passenger seat. I reached for it. There were two jelly donuts inside, one half-eaten and covered in green and white mold, the other sans mold but flattened with jelly sprouting from tears in the dough. My stomach growled. I gave the contents a longing look of food lost, before closing the bag and chucking it on the grass. I shut the door and settled behind the wheel.

I pictured the mutant donuts flinging themselves from the bag and onto the car window, smearing a path of jellied guts.

We will get you for throwing us away so callously, Emma!

I remembered my old social studies teacher telling the class that if we didn't study hard we'd end up working in a donut shop and pumping jelly into pastries for the rest of our lives. *Or they'd pump jelly into us*, I thought.

I got down low in the seat so as not to be seen and gathered my bearings. A plump set of keys dangled from the ignition. It was a lucky break and about damn time. To the right of the ignition was an L.A. Cabs identification card with a picture of miserable-looking-fuck number 3021. The man had cold eyes and a frowning mouth. The only feature with some semblance of happiness was the driver's moustache. It dipped downward from his nostrils, curved upward at his top lip, stretched outward to each cheek, and twisted inward forming two tight curls. The man had loved that moustache, if nothing else. I was inclined to say he had come across something to make him even more miserable, something to make him wish he was still driving his crummy, old cab. My heart sank for the miserable fuck who maybe never really knew how good he had it until things got very, very bad.

I turned to check the backseat with high hopes of finding a map, but no luck. It was my first visit to the city, and without my cell phone, navigating would be difficult. I needed to find a phone, people, and the police, not necessarily in that order. Each could lead me to the other.

I budged up so I could see over the dashboard and turned the key in the ignition. I pressed the gas lightly, and the car coughed and shot forward. It wasn't the quiet exit I had hoped for, but it was an exit nonetheless, and for that I was grateful. The radio burst on in static and nearly sent me onto the curb. I adjusted the tuner, and my hand shook like an addict's on the knob.

"Tell me something, baby," I said.

Indecipherable sounds and voices stretched across stations.

"Damn it." I turned the radio volume down and checked out a road sign above me: WEST CENTURY.

My foot fell heavy on the pedal once I cleared the airport, and I eyed the speedometer climbing past rational speed. The need to get somewhere drove me, but right there with it was the need to race by the fact that there was no one anywhere. Only crows and cars and even crows in cars. I spotted one on the steering wheel of a tire-less El Dorado.

The birds lined power lines, tree branches, and roofs. Two flew right up to my window and beat their wings hard and angry against the glass as if I had sent them an invitation and then not allowed them in. I laid on the horn and they flew off to rejoin their fellow feathered conspirators.

With every empty bus stop, every empty street corner, every empty car, my heart thumped my chest as if it didn't believe the visual messages being collected by my eyes and was telling me off for the deception. I slowed my breathing. I refused to die of a heart attack at my age. There was a reasonable explanation for all of it. I promised myself I'd laugh when I heard it—a nice, hearty laugh, the kind that hurts so good and makes your eyes water.

My right foot pressed heavier on the gas. The roads were empty, giving me the luxury of speed. My head flicked back and forth, my mind registering poles, trees, mannequins, elevated head rests, and anything else that had an iota of human resemblance as that thing that appeared to be gone.

Life.

I took a left onto La Brea and drove a few miles before realizing that the gas light was on, and a few more before the cab rolled to a stop in the middle of an intersection. I opened the door, moving quickly so as not to give myself an opportunity to assume the fetal position. I had yet to do a thorough search of the taxi, so I started under the seats, followed by the glove compartment and behind the visors. This time, I found a pack of cigarettes, a book of matches from a place called "The Rusty Screw," and some more spare change—seventy-eight cents, to be exact. I was morphing into a piggy bank.

I put the new change in my right front pocket, with the two quarters I had sequestered from the Honda. On the bright side, I would have money for a payphone, since my phone card was in my wallet, my wallet in my purse, and my purse back at the airport.

I got a cigarette from the pack, lit it, and stuffed the pack and matches in my back pocket. I took a drag. It still tasted like dirt, but I was hungry and the nicotine would suppress my appetite. I exhaled.

"La Brea and Venice," I said, reading the street signs out loud. "That doesn't help at all."

A snicker escaped my lips, recalling my plan to not even glance at a map in L.A. I was going to take cabs to and from interviews and wing the rest. I wanted the adventure and was averse to looking like a tourist.

"I could be dressed like Minnie Mouse," I mumbled.

I left the cab with all four doors open (because what did it matter) and shuffled to the sidewalk. My body was still sore. My head ached. My right cheek felt separate from my face. With each step, a quick spasm of pain sprung from my lower back to the spot I had fallen on between my shoulders and my neck.

Around me, bungalows and brightly colored apartment complexes were gathered like mushrooms. In front of me, a single-story pink house. A car sat in the driveway with a dream catcher hanging from the rearview.

A crow screeched far away, and a chorus of out-of-tune birdcalls followed. I hurried to the house. Once on the front step, I made a comb of my fingers and ran it through my hair. The screen door was unlocked. I held it open, knocked twice on the second door and waited. There was no answer. I knocked twice, again.

The birds had quieted. I knocked and put my ear to the door. I pulled away and hung my index finger over the doorbell. I paused before concluding that I had given the knocking thing a fair chance and was now allowed to pursue more disruptive means. With still no answer, I used the tentative knock-try-the-lock method. The door gave way, and I pushed it in enough to stick my head through.

"Hello," I said. "Anyone home? My car broke down...I need to use your phone."

I waited for an answer. None came. I stepped into the house and shut the door behind me. "Just come right in, young miss," I said in a whisper, putting on my best old lady voice. "By all means, use the phone and feel free to take a shower and clean yourself off. I've got some biscuits coming out of the oven, and they've got your name on them, they do. It's been so lonely since my Bobby passed."

I had succeeded in creeping myself out and hadn't even meant to. I wasn't going crazy, I was just keeping myself company. Plus, the voice made me feel better about the intrusion.

The front door opened into the living area. I went to the window and pulled a cord to raise the blinds and get some light in the room. A dust cloud landed on me, and I sneezed. The newly invited sunlight stretched across a rust-colored rug. Most of the space allotted to furniture was occupied by a fluorescent pink sofa that hurt my eyes and a matching loveseat with dented cushions. Meatloaf sat in a microwaveable container, on a plate, on a serving tray, on a stand in front of the love seat. Bites had been taken out of the TV dinner, hopefully before it had become shriveled and off-color.

What remained of a glass of milk rested on top of an old RCA television set, the kind in sixties sitcoms with the bubble glass screen. Whoever had been eating the meal, it seemed, had gotten up to turn on the television or change the channel and had been interrupted. I put the glass of milk on the tray. The liquid had soured, and white jelly bounced against the sides of the glass as I carried it.

I returned to the television and pushed the power button. Electronic snow pulsed across the screen. I turned the dial. It was stiff, and I had to put some weight into it. The channels clicked over with still no reception.

I glanced around the room and found a phone next to the sofa and behind a stack of *Reader's Digest* magazines. The top one featured an article titled "Ten Surefire Ways to Get Happy!" I was so frantic or ecstatic or frantic about the phone that I toppled the entire stack and took a china statue of a cat down with it. The bang made me jump. I replaced the thankfully unbroken statue on the table but left the magazines as they were for now.

The phone was an old rotary. My ear was damp with perspiration as I pressed the receiver against it. There was silence at the other end. I jostled the hang-up, with no joy. I checked the cord, tracking it a short distance from the phone to a jack in the wall behind the sofa. Everything was connected.

I smiled and shrugged because I was a person getting used to disappointment. My time in that city had a theme: expect the worst and then expect things a lot worse and that won't even begin to cover it.

I walked in a daze from the living area to the kitchen, which was just as oddly colored with yellow countertops and bright purple flooring. The counters were decked out with appliances for all occasions. I blankly wrote in dust on a pasta maker:

Em was here.

I opened the fridge. A small Tupperware container of salsa, a can of spray butter, a Saran-wrapped plate of bacon, and a liter of orange Crush sparsely filled the fridge.

"This just in," I said. "Unhealthy eating habits may cause color blindness."

I removed the salsa and the bacon. The bacon smelled bad. I put it in the sink. The salsa seemed okay. I found an unopened bag of tortilla chips in the cabinet next to the fridge and opened it. I removed a chip, dipped it in the salsa and ate it. The salsa was tasteless, but the chip had some spice to it and enough taste for both. I would have tossed the salsa, but I needed vegetables and the salsa was the only thing that came close in that kitchen.

I grabbed the chip bag and the container of salsa and went to check out the rest of the house. I would return later to have a look in the remaining cabinets. My stomach growled. *Easy tiger*.

~

The hallway was dimly lit. The ceiling light flickered behind its globe and seemed to be in its final throes.

Two rooms were off the hallway, both doors shut. A smell I didn't recognize was up my nostrils. It wasn't a bad smell—just a smell. The bathroom was beyond the first door, and it was shy compared to the house's other rooms, with white walls, a white shower, a white basin, and a yellow rubber ducky.

Next was the bedroom, with an emphasis on BED. The door banged against it, and I had to squeeze myself through the narrow opening. Full down pillows and clothes were piled on top of the oversize mattress. It was Mt. Vesuvius. I gripped the food under my left arm, unwilling to let it go, and picked through a few items of clothing. They were hideous, all sequins and flash.

Something moved above me.

It took a split second to realize the movement was just my reflection in a ceiling mirror. That was the longest split second of my life. I climbed up on the bed and reached out to my reflected face. I ran my fingers down my reflection's hair. It wasn't auburn anymore but dark brown. My curls were gone except for a few at the bottom. A thick strand of hair stuck to my face, glued there by dried blood and separated into smaller pieces that spread like veins across my swollen cheek. A bit of green matter clung to my eyebrow. I swatted at it and detached it onto my fingertips. I flicked my hand violently several times before the unidentifiable matter released and splatted onto the wall. I laughed.

"Gross," I said.

I looked back up at the mirror feeling like my sad spell had been broken by something truly disgusting. I was covered in blood and guts, but the situation was too *out there* not to have any humor in it.

The rest of me was in the same state of mess. My cheek was blue and the size of a baseball. My clothes were brown and crispy, like my hair, and cracks were starting to form in my repulsive armor. I looked down at my hands and knew that anyone who saw them would understand that something had died brutally by them. Blood had dried under my fingernails. It tattooed my palms like henna, from the tips of both thumbs to halfway down my forearms. I spit a chip out of my mouth and dropped the bag and container of salsa onto Mt. Vesuvius below. I jumped off the bed, tugging at my shirt.

There was a rustle in the closet.

I froze. "Who's there?" I asked. I pulled the shirt back over my body and waited. "I *said*, 'Who's there?'"

I thought of the knife and knew I didn't have it on me. I tried to remember whether I had brought it into the house or even recovered it from the Honda.

It might just be something settling, I thought.

Yes, that was it.

I walked to the closet with my arm out. My red right hand reached for the door's knob. I could open it really slow or really fast. If I did it slow, I would have time to close it again if I didn't like what I saw. Doing it quickly gave me the element of surprise. Slits were in the door. The thought that someone might be watching me through those slits unnerved me. I grabbed the knob and yanked the door open.

Something pushed by me. A blur of black.

I fell backward. My head hit the mattress, and I landed on the floor. There was a clicking behind me. I smelled that smell again, but this time it was stronger, more acrid. And then, a growl.

It was a dog.

The dog looked like a Doberman, except smaller and with longer hair. It moved its snout close to my face. It snarled and both sides of its mouth rose like a curtain being brought up for show time. Sharp, wet teeth were centimeters from my nose.

I tried to think of a good course of action, but everything ended with my face as dog food. Any move that I could make would take longer than what the dog had to do to finish the deal—open up and chomp down. I stayed still and prayed the canine would lose interest, knowing full well that his kind despised all intruders. The thieves and the girl scouts.

A thick growl started from somewhere deep beneath that fur. The noise climbed the dog's throat and spilled out around its enormous teeth before turning into a whine and going away completely. Then the canine moved its warm nose across my face, smelling every inch. It sneezed and unfurled a long pink tongue.

The dog licked my face for several seconds before whimpering and jumping up onto the bed. It climbed Mt. Vesuvius to get to the bag of chips, sparking an avalanche of clothes. The creature took the bag between its teeth and shook its head. Tortilla flew in every direction.

I stayed put until I was certain that the dog had no more interest in me, then I sat up and watched as the mutt inhaled the scattered contents of the bag.

"You're crazy," I said, from the floor. "Schizophrenic, even." The dog paused in its binge to look down at me. I pointed at the salsa container on the bed. "There's salsa, too." The dog smelled the container and exhaled suddenly through its nose.

"I know, it's pretty bad."

A better look told me that the mutt was a *he* and *he* was close to starvation. The animal's ribs jutted out in all the wrong places, and his pelvic area dipped unnaturally close to his back. I struggled off the floor and walked over to the bed. I reached out to touch the top of the dog's head. I scratched it, and the dog stopped eating and leaned into my hand, his jowls spreading into a satisfied grin. I got in there, working behind his ears and down his back. He groaned and shook his stub tail. It was hard to believe that this softy was just ready to bite my face off.

"Poor schizo dog," I said. "How about we find some real doggy food for you. There has to be something around here better than those chips."

He raised his head from his meal, his ears moving like satellites receiving important data. Pieces of chip stuck to his muzzle, and his tongue came out to clean up. He looked at me with wide brown eyes and glanced at the remaining chips on the bed. I walked to the door, and the dog filled his mouth with what he could and followed.

~

The light was changing outside. It slid through the cracks in the

79

blinds and bathed the living area in an orange glow that made the room almost beautiful. Having finished off the chips, the dog made a beeline for the meatloaf, jumping up on the loveseat and falling face first into the antiquated meal. Peas, which must have been hiding under the congealed gravy, escaped and rolled off the plate, off the tray, and onto the floor. As if it was his duty, the dog hunted down every last one.

I went into the kitchen, grabbed two bowls from a cabinet and filled one with water and the other with some dry dog food I found under the kitchen sink. I put the bowls on the floor, and my new companion came over to investigate. He looked up at me, gave a quiet groan that sounded so close to words but not any in particular, and dug in.

"You're welcome, Schizo." I thought the name would do for now.

I left Schizo eating and walked down the hallway, peeling off my clothes as I went. I opened the bathroom door and stood in the doorway naked, looking for the mirror so I could avoid it until after my shower. There was a nail protruding from the wall above the sink, but nothing hung from it.

"No mirror," I said. "My luck is changing."

I turned on the water and waited. I got in when the steam rose in thick plumes and I was satisfied that it was hot enough to wash away what that nasty day had left on my body. I stuck my head under and watched the water turn brown and vanish into the drain.

I tried to block out the bad thoughts, but they always have a way of getting in. Something was wrong at school before I left. That strange flu, Professor Winnie, and the trucks? I clutched a bar of soap retrieved from the sink and started to scrub. *I'll stay here tonight*, I thought, and felt my shoulders relax. Rest would get my head straight. Anything not done today could be done tomorrow.

I felt eyes on me—watching me. I threw the curtain open, with raised soap. Schizo ran from my line of fire, then poked his head around the corner to see if the situation had changed. I lowered the soap and he returned to his position in the doorway, sitting and staring.

"Schizo, go lie down somewhere. This isn't a peep show." He turned his back to me and settled in the doorway.

"Fine, have it your way. But there might be more peas in the lounge, *oh boy!*"

He was ignoring me now. The peas were gone, and he knew it. Maybe he just needed the company. I did too. I wondered how much time he had spent in that closet. *Too much*, I thought, by the look of it.

"I'll get you fixed up, boy," I said. "No worries."

My stomach clenched. I had abandoned the chips after getting a look at myself in the mirror. When I was clean, the kitchen was my destination. I'd do a more thorough search. Whoever lived there was gone for the time being, but they *were* living there at some point and they had to eat something besides chips, spray butter, and bacon.

Schizo whined outside the shower. I watched as he came into the bathroom, walked to the window, turned around and walked out of the bathroom and out of sight. A few seconds later, he reappeared and repeated his movements.

"Settle down, Furry," I said.

I turned off the water, took a towel from a shelf above the toilet and wrapped it around me. I returned to the bedroom, my feet leaving wet tracks on the floor. Schizo followed me after completing his pace down the other end of the hall. I sifted through the clothes on the bed. A chip fell from a shirt with a shiny gold heart on it. I held the morsel out for Schizo to take, but he just sat and stared up at me.

"Go on. It's for you. You can't be stuffed already?" He continued to stare, so I popped the chip in my own mouth. "Don't mind if I do."

I searched through the clothes, and what was left of Mt. Vesuvius fell. I tried to be respectful, folding anything I pulled out of the pile. Most items were too formal, and I couldn't think of an occasion in the near future that would call for a backless, sequined dress. Besides, the woman who lived there was almost a foot shorter than me.

I went to the closet Schizo had come out of. It smelled of piss. I sifted through clothes on hangers and took out a jean skirt that was meant to be long but when held against me fell to my knees. I also grabbed a hot pink, long-sleeved top that had *BITCHIN'* written across the chest in silver sequins. I would cover up this abomination with a zippered gray sweatshirt, which looked brand new and must have been left behind by a guest. My mucked-up sneakers would finish the ensemble since all the shoes in the closet were a size four.

I dropped my towel and put on the clothes. Once dressed, I made room on the bed and lay down to look in the ceiling mirror. *Well, you look like a freak but a noticeably cleaner freak.* I saw a small tin on the bedside table and reached to pick it up. Inside were some unused Trojans and a twenty. I wondered why cash and condoms were so often stored together and what it said about society's views toward the two. *Save it for class, Emma.*

Schizo whined again, forcing me from my thoughts. I pocketed the cash and got up to see if I could calm him down. I took a mental note to write down what I borrowed before I left so I could replace everything when my situation improved. I liked calling it that—a *situation*. A situation was never that bad. A situation was a problem that could be fixed without too much fuss. *Yes*, I thought. It was all just a situation.

I brightened but the room dimmed as the sun was ready to retire for the day. I stood and something snapped beneath my feet. I stepped away to find a broken cross on the floor.

The cross was in the shape of Jesus, but the job was messy, possibly done by a child. Jesus' facial features were slits stabbed into the wood, and his hands and feet were a few simple lines. The carving had been two pieces of wood bound together in the middle by string, but now it was three. I had just broken the savior at what I estimated to be his pelvic bone.

"This can't be good," I said to myself.

I picked up the broken cross and placed it on the bed. Schizo peered at me from around the corner of the bed, and before I could stop him, he had grabbed the top half of the carving and made a dash for the door.

"Schizo, get back here with Jesus!"

I ran into the living room. The dog was sitting by the front door with the cross still in his mouth. He stood when he saw me and wagged his tail so his butt wiggled back and forth.

"We are not playing fetch-the-Jesus," I said, getting my hand around the drool-lacquered wood.

Schizo growled. I let go. "Fine, have it your way. I'm just trying to save your soul."

The dog whined. He stood on his hind legs and scratched at the door. I noticed several deep claw marks in the wood and wasn't sure if the dog had just made them or if they had been there all along.

Schizo stopped scratching and returned to all fours. He moved in frantic little circles with his eyes on me the whole time. I wondered if he might have to go to the bathroom, but this wasn't a dog that abstained from urinating inside. In his defense, he had been locked up and didn't have much of a choice.

"Need to go to the bathroom?"

Schizo stopped circling. He gave a quiet moan before continuing his movement. I had a bad feeling and some people might believe it is ridiculous to base major decisions on what you think an animal is trying to tell you, and maybe they're right most of the time, but not this time. Schizo knew something, and even though I had just met the mutt (and he was prone to erratic behavior), I felt I should follow his lead.

"Alright," I said, holding my hand out to calm him. "Just give me a sec to get some things together, and then we'll go."

I ran to the bedroom. The only bag I could find had pandas on it. I don't know why I even gave it a second thought. I just needed it for spare clothes and food, and I didn't hate pandas though I heard they could be mean. Regardless, I spent an extra couple seconds searching the top shelf of the closet for another bag, before feeling okay with the pandas.

I thought about stuffing my old clothes in the bag but decided that the trash was the best place for them. Since I had already been through the clothes on the bed and in the closet and found nothing, I decided there was nothing in that room for my bag and I could move on.

Schizo met me in the hallway and stayed close as I moved on to the kitchen. I got the bottle of orange soda from the fridge, emptied it and filled it with tap water. It was heavy but necessary. I found a small jar of peanuts and an open box of granola bars in the cabinet. I threw the jar in my bag and upended the granola bar box. The contents included four chocolate chip granola bars and one dead fly.

I found a carving knife in the utensil drawer and picked it up, shifting it between both hands. This one was bigger than the last and made me feel safer. I stuffed the weapon and the dry dog food in my bag, and these items occupied the last remaining space. I found a leash under the sink and put it in my back pocket. Lastly, a note:

Girl in need. Used shower. Took necessities. Borrowed dog. WILL RETURN ALL.

I looked down at Schizo, who was looking up at me. "That's it," I said. "Let's blow this pop stand."

I flung my new bag over my shoulder. I had filled it to capacity, but it was medium-sized so not too heavy. I gave a quick look around and headed for the door. As I passed the television set, something caught my eye that I hadn't noticed before.

"What's that doing down there?" I stopped. So did Schizo.

It was a door about three feet tall and two feet wide. It was the same color as the wall, with a small silver knob.

"That's odd," I said aloud. "A teeny little door. I guess it's storage."

I moved the TV stand, which was on wheels, and crouched down for a better look. *There could be something I need in there*, I thought. I reached out and touched the knob and had to know what was in there. It was a need unlike any I had ever felt before, and for an instant, ripping the door off its hinges was just another way to open it.

I pulled, but the door didn't budge. I pulled harder. I sat down, positioning my feet on either side of the little door, and pulled more. It moved outward a bit. Loose plaster detached from the edges and landed on the floor between my legs. I felt a pain in my right foot. It was nothing at first—a barely there pain which hardly needed my attention while I was involved in something so important. But the pain increased tenfold until my eyes focused and I saw Schizo's jaw clamped around my foot. He had enough of my size ten in his mouth so that only the top part, where the laces tied into a bow, was visible.

I stopped pulling on the door and released my hands from the knob. The pain burned.

"Get off me!" I screamed. I kicked, but Schizo didn't detach. I moved away from the door, dragging the dog with me until we were both back in the middle of the room, and he let go.

"What is your problem?"

Schizo replaced my foot with the broken cross. It was the first time since he ran off with the thing that he had been without it. He sat between me and the front door, splitting stares between the two. I got up from the floor and expected the worst, but it wasn't so bad. The dog had showed mercy. I looked down at him and wondered whether it was safe to be traveling with such an unpredictable animal. He whined. *I can't just leave him here*, I thought. Who knew how much longer he'd be left alone, and there was only enough dog food for another day or so. I limped over to Schizo with a finger raised.

"Chew Jesus. *Jesus*. Not my foot, you hear me?"

We shared an unspoken agreement.

I picked up my bag, put the leash on Schizo, who strangely didn't object, and opened the front door. I didn't give a second thought to that odd little door. The need was gone.

It had been kindly forced out of me.

CHAPTER SIX

THE AIR WAS SUFFOCATING.

Before we left the pink house, my watch said four o'clock, but it felt like midday in Death Valley.

Wild orange clouds draped the sky as if the fires of hell had relocated. Buildings were fast becoming silhouettes. The only sign of life was the black squawking mass of birds above us. They were restless, but they were leaving us alone and that was good.

The leash was taut as Schizo pulled me along the sidewalk. I started to feel like he had a destination in mind. We passed lots of houses, but they were all dark inside and the idea of entering another house and finding nothing made my heart hurt. So dog led, and we pressed on.

The last bit of sunlight left, night fell, and the world I never knew existed made its grand entrance.

The noises and sights started from far away, then passed by us and continued down the block. A security alarm went off, a car door slammed, a horn honked, an engine roared to life, a heavy metal song blared, street lights illuminated, and a red door swung open. It was just like in my dream. I stopped from fright, stopping Schizo with me.

A woman in a black skirt-suit appeared in the doorway. Her hair was cut in a bob that bounced when she moved. I realized I was staring but couldn't do anything about it, and the woman stopped to stare, too, when she spotted us. Her skin was pale enough to be blue. She didn't smile or wave, but neither did I. I thought I must've looked like a crazy person. Schizo began to whine.

"Hello," I said, waving. I had trouble finding words. "I need help. A phone. Things have…happened."

The woman didn't move right away. Then she opened a hand and let her briefcase fall to the ground. Schizo's whine became a low growl. I grabbed his collar, maybe too roughly, and reprimanded him. I didn't want to scare the woman off.

"He's harmless. I promise."

The woman put her hand forward. It hung in the air for a few seconds before returning to her side. She spoke. "There's a phone inside. Come in, please."

The woman was holding keys, and she jingled them at me. Something in that movement set Schizo off, and he stayed true to his name. Muscles tensed under fur, and Schizo dragged me toward the woman. He spit and bared his teeth from around the chewy cross. His strength was incredible. Nothing stopped him. I yelled and dug my heels into the grass as the woman cowered on her front step. I wrapped my arms around the dog and used my entire body to pin him to the ground like a wrestler. I dragged him to a tree, unhooked his leash, looped its clip end around the tree's base and through the handle, and reattached it to the dog's collar.

"Bad boy! *Very bad!*" I screamed. "I'm taking Jesus away."

I pulled the cross out of Schizo's mouth and tucked it in my back pocket. I turned to the woman. "I am so sorry. I don't know what's gotten into him."

The woman shushed me and spoke, this time with a drawl. "Don't worry, honey. But give the poor dog back his toy. Takin' a toy from a dog is takin' away the one thing it cares about most in this world."

I looked at Schizo. He had settled down, but he was still growling.

If we were going to make this work, he had to learn.

"I think I'll keep it for now."

"Do what you like," the woman said, sounding truly disappointed. She reached the top step and turned around. "I don't got all day."

A large crow swooped in.

It flapped expansive wings above the woman and brought the point of its beak down on her head. The woman punched fists in the air. She reached into her coat pocket and took out a silver canister. She fumbled with the top as the bird managed another bite and flew off with a clump of the woman's skin and hair. The woman swore and shoved the canister back in her pocket.

"Are you okay?" I asked, collecting her briefcase from off the ground and rushing up the stairs.

"Damn birds," she said.

Our double feature had attracted several onlookers. I couldn't imagine where all those people had been before. The traffic was still light, but it was picking up as we stood there. People milled in front of their houses. One man started yard work across the street, shoveling soil from several large holes in the ground. Probably for shrubs or trees.

Had I made it all up in my head?

Maybe the sleeping aid I took on the plane was bad? Maybe I was still asleep? Dead? I felt dizzy. "Am I dreaming?" I asked the woman.

"Why you asking such a stupid question? They do something to your head at the farm?"

"I'm not...I never said I was from a farm." The woman shrugged.

The crowd we'd attracted with our commotion was still lingering. The woman whipped around to face them.

"Go away!" she yelled. She punched at the air erratically, like she had done with the crow. I stepped aside to give her room.

Her head wasn't bleeding, from what I could see. I looked at Schizo. He had turned his attention to the gathered people and was making like *Cujo*. I felt bad for leaving him, but I wouldn't be gone long. If the police wanted to come by and talk to me in person, I'd go and wait outside with him.

~

We entered a long hallway. There was a blinded window next to the front door, and the woman creased a section to look out. Without a word, she started down the hallway. The floor was wooden and creaked beneath her like the hull of a ship in a storm. I put down the woman's briefcase and followed.

The hallway opened into a large, empty room and that room into a larger room, filled up with many things. The woman had disappeared, and I didn't see which direction she went, so I waited. Her voice coming from behind made me jump.

"Phone's in the kitchen," she said, pointing. "Two doors that way on your right." She had a little boy next to her no older than four. He had her skin. I waved.

"Hello there," I said.

The boy stared at me, looking excited...eager...like I was swinging a large lollipop in front of his face.

"Thanks. Uh, I won't be long. I know you've got work."

I looked down at the boy again. No more than four years of age, and ill. His head was triangle-shaped, his cheeks not plump like they should be at that age but drawn tight over the bones underneath. Was there someone else in the house I hadn't met yet, or did she plan on

90

leaving an ill child home alone?

It's none of your business, Emma. Just do what you came here to do.

"Two doors that way, on your right," she repeated, pointing again in the same direction.

"Okay, yep."

In the kitchen, the only light cast was from behind a blue stained-glass globe. It gave the room an underwater quality to it, which, instead of being calming, was quite claustrophobic. The table against the far wall was set for two. Strange black flowers yawned and stretched, stems deep in an oriental vase.

The woman hadn't mentioned where the phone was, but there were only so many places it could be. I was guessing it was a landline, and people didn't keep them in drawers. I started right and worked left. A friend once told me most women turned left after entering a room. Since then, I'd done everything in my power to go right, even when it was most inconvenient.

This time it paid off. The phone was hanging on the wall to the right, next to the sink. I picked up the receiver: *beeping*. I poked the hang-up. Same damn beeping. *No!* It was broken—just like the phone and the television at the pink house and the radio in the cab. I tried again and dialed zero for the operator. Nothing. I was so wrapped up in the concept of something else not working that I didn't see the drink carton on the counter next to me. My elbow hit it, knocking the carton on its side and sending its contents, a thick dark liquid, over the counter's edge and onto the floor.

"Oh *no*," I whispered. "No, no, no."

I recovered the carton and grabbed a sponge from the sink. I worked quickly, wiping the sponge back and forth over the countertop and then the floor. Whatever it was *(juice? fruit smoothie?)* was thick and hard to clean up *(so red)*. I dropped the sponge into the sink and took some paper towels from off a roll. They did a better job at soaking up the liquid. Once I had gotten it all, I located the trash bin under the sink and threw away the used towels.

I looked at the carton. I had left my bag and the bottle of tap water outside with Schizo, and I was regretting it now. My mouth was dry. I felt dehydrated. A glass of juice would be wonderful. And fruit smoothies had a ton of antioxidants. It was just what my immune system needed.

I found myself a glass one cabinet over, put it down on the counter, and picked up the carton. Each of the carton's sides was blank, except for one which had a black and white picture of a forty-something woman on it. *Must be a missing person's ad.* The woman was white with teased hair bound in a scrunchy. Underneath the photograph, it read:

(O+) Odorless
Chico, CA
Farm-raised

That's odd, I thought.

"It's just horrible," the voice said, behind me.

I yelped and nearly released the carton onto the floor. I turned and faced the woman in the doorway. Her arm was around the boy.

"Sorry…you scared me," I said. "I was just going to have a glass of juice." I shook my head. "I was hoping you wouldn't mind? But it's

92

not good?"

The woman laughed, and the boy looked up at her and laughed too. I hadn't noticed their teeth. Something was wrong with their teeth.

"They make us drink that cheap, processed crap. It used to be good. In the beginning, it was good."

I smiled uneasily. "What is it?"

"When we were reborn," the woman continued, "things were different. We got the fresh stuff. Always the fresh stuff. They'd come in the fancy trucks and let them out by the hundreds around the neighborhood." The woman smiled with those teeth. Those fucked-up teeth. "You know, it wasn't really all that long ago. Times change fast." A deep crevice formed between her brows. "Which farm you say you escape from?"

"I never...listen, I'm from Boston. I never said anything about a farm."

Things were getting uncomfortable, and I needed to leave, but they were blocking the doorway. I put the carton and glass on the counter and braced myself to push by them. The woman looked down at the boy.

"Boston is on the coast of *Mass-a-chu-setts*."

This was my chance.

I rushed them and pushed out into the hallway.

The little boy fell onto the floor, but the woman stayed on her feet, retreating back a few steps to the far wall. I jogged toward the front door mumbling something about the phone not working, and thanks very much, I'd be leaving. Whatever was going on there wasn't right. I felt that, but I didn't know for sure and I was just trying to save face following an extreme act of rudeness. *But those teeth*, I thought. They were wrong. Very wrong. I reached the front door and heard the little boy speak.

"Can we have fun now, mommy?"

"Yes. Yes we can."

The floorboards groaned.

I didn't look back. Not right away. Doors were meant to be easy to open from the inside, and the woman and her boy were still safely at the other end of the hall. I had plenty of time to get out of there. At least that was what I thought, but the damn door wouldn't budge.

From behind me came the jingle of keys. I turned around.

The hallway was now empty.

Schizo barked outside. What I would've done to be out there with him. I pressed myself against the door, before taking a step deeper into the house. The door wasn't opening without those keys, so either I got a hold of them, or I found another way out.

The floor showed no mercy. Each step on those boards was an announcement of where I was and where I was going. The bare room was first. It wasn't completely bare. A large, round rug was in the middle with a window opposite. I darted toward the window.

The floor fell out from under me.

I was stuck.

In a hole beneath the rug.

And the rug now held me like a cocoon with my feet dangling somewhere in the bowels of that frightful house.

I can't move!

The floor was at my chest, the room at my back.

"This is fun, mommy. I don't want it to end."

I screamed. They were in the room with me. I squirmed and

struggled in the trap. I positioned my hands on the floor in front of me and tried to lift myself out, but I wasn't strong enough.

"Oh, the end is the best part," the woman said, her voice followed by a series of telltale creaks.

I pushed down on the floor again in another attempt to free myself from the hole. I yelled—halfway out. My arms weakened, and I fell back in. I tried a third time, and this time I freed myself. I whipped around and scurried against the wall.

"Get away from me!"

"It's been so long. Too long," the woman said, wistfully.

Outside, Schizo had gone hoarse. I felt regret for taking his chew Jesus away from him. This crazy, fucked-up woman was right about the one thing. She didn't want me to take it from him.

She never wanted that.

I could feel the cross pressing into my backside. I fumbled for it, got a grip on it, and held it out.

The woman hissed.

The little boy's eyes fluttered, and he rubbed them like it was way past his bedtime. He turned and ran into the stuffed room, making squeaks that got further and further away until they were gone.

I stood. "Give me the keys...*now*."

I moved forward. The woman hissed again and covered her eyes with spread fingers. She backed away into to the next room.

"I *mean it!*" I gripped the cross harder. My arm ached.

The woman gave a half hiss, half laugh. "Humans are always so full of meaning."

"You need help."

"I think it's *you* that needs help."

The woman laughed and shook her head. Her hair fell out of her office up-do. I stepped over the door jamb and followed her. I moved the cross into my left hand.

"I'm going to give you one last chance—give them to me."

"Let me and my child drink."

"*Drink what?*"

I had lost my patience with this woman. Next to me on a bookcase was a bronze statue of a girl dancing. She stood long and thin and almost two feet tall. Her arms were raised above her head, and both hands came to a point. I was afraid the statue would be too heavy for me to lift, but it wasn't. Aiming for the woman's ear, I swung and hit my mark. Her face distorted, her head and neck snapped sideways. Her body dangled midair before collapsing on the floor.

I choked down a sob and dropped the statue. I knelt and took the woman's wrist to find a pulse.

There wasn't one.

"You stupid, crazy bitch!"

Visit L.A. and become a serial killer. I hadn't meant to kill the woman. Myers was dead, but that was different. He'd had a weapon. This woman had tried to trap me and was threatening, but she never attacked me. *Was it because I didn't give her the chance?* I'd never know.

I patted the woman's jacket and found the keys. Four total attached to a ring: three ordinary ones and a tarnished skeleton. I poked my finger through the ring and stood.

The woman moved. A twitch…

…before her eyes opened and she grabbed my ankle with her bony hands.

I kicked her off and ran.

I ran down the hallway to the front door. I tripped over the woman's briefcase. I regained my footing and applied the skeleton key to the lock with shaky hands.

She was behind me.

I turned and saw her thin shape at the end of the hallway, silhouetted by the blue light from the kitchen. She approached slowly at first but then picked up speed.

Her limbs flailed, appearing to multiply so that she looked like a big, dark spider. I stabbed at the lock with the skeleton key. *Please.*

It wasn't the one.

I tried another, well aware of the chances.

It fell in.

~

Schizo was still barking. I slammed the door shut behind me and stuck the same key back in to lock the door from the outside. A loud bang erupted on the other side, and the door shook.

I ran to Schizo and knelt to detach his leash from the tree. My body was shaking. I unhooked the leash from his collar, pulled it free, and then hooked it back on. I held the chewy Jesus in front of his nose, and he took it. He continued to whine, but the barking stopped.

I retrieved my bag, and we ran. We hit the sidewalk full throttle. The dog was much faster than me. I thought about detaching the leash, but I was afraid he'd run off and I didn't want that. I needed him.

Things were so much different now than they were before. There was activity in the city. The road was busy. Cars sped by us. People busied themselves in the houses we passed. Pedestrians weren't in abundance, but I wasn't surprised by that. I'd heard that nobody walked in L.A. Someone had even written a song about it.

I looked behind us. There was no sign of the woman or her son. I didn't slow my pace though. I contemplated knocking on a door or flagging down a car, but I didn't have the greatest track record with that. As far as I was concerned, strangers weren't to be trusted. I needed to find a police station. Somehow.

Several cars beeped as they drove by. A white van with a black stripe down the middle drove through the intersection ahead of us and then pulled up onto the curb. Approximately eleven yards separated us from them.

I slowed to a walk. A man with long, dark hair got out from the passenger side, closed the door, and leaned up against the van. He crossed both his arms and legs and watched us.

"I don't like this, Schizo," I whispered. The dog gave a low-growl affirmation.

Another door slammed shut, and the driver came around the front of the van, fat and bald. Cars were slowing down as they drove by, passengers taking more of an interest in me than they should have.

I turned right into a driveway and ran. Behind us, more cars screeched to a stop. We sprinted across a plush lawn. I let go of Schizo's leash to give him that chance to save himself.

I cornered a garage with a plastic reindeer on its roof. Tall, thick shrubs lined the side of the garage. Before I could react, an arm stuck out from behind all that green to level me. I hit the ground and lost my breath.

I struggled for air as the arm dragged me backward into the bushes. Branches sliced my face. I pushed away an oncoming haze and started to punch and kick. The stranger's hands tensed around my arms: "Be quiet if you want to live."

I did want to live, but what do you do when every person you meet is trying to kill you? *You fight.*

"You fight," I mumbled. The voice shushed me.

CHAPTER SEVEN

I BREATHED IN.

Above me, a virgin mourned her dead son.

I coughed. Wherever I was smelled of wet, burnt wood. I sat up, and the back of my head throbbed, sending my surroundings spinning. My stomach clenched. I dry heaved, no food in me to come up. I wiped spit off my mouth and waited for things to settle. Several feet away, a fire came to life, and light acrobats danced around the space.

I was in a church, or what was once a church in body, but was now mostly a church in spirit.

It had been torched.

The outer structure appeared intact, but the inside had gotten it good. The pews were skeletal, charred and collapsed, leaving no place for sitting. Bibles bitten by flames were strewn about the floor, some open, some shut. The walls had been white but were now black, with wallpaper peeling like skin and hanging down in long strands. Six beautiful stained-glass windows had avoided damage.

By the fire, a guy about my age sat petting my dog. He was thin, but perhaps just lean, with brown hair and a square jaw. Both dog and guy looked at me. Schizo got up and trotted over to give me a kiss.

"You're awake," the boy said. He had a nice, scratchy voice. "Sounded like you were having a bad dream."

"I always have them," I said. "Why does my head hurt?"

"You fell. Hit it on a rock."

The guy stood up and dusted his pants off. He reached down to collect something and came toward me.

"What do you want?" I backed away.

He stopped and held up a bottle of clear liquid and a white rag. "It's alcohol. I wrapped your head in gauze," he said. "I'm just going to check it...if you want?"

I put my hand up to my forehead and felt the fabric. I nodded at him and looked away as he knelt down next to me and removed the bandage. I could feel his breath on my neck. It was strange being this close to someone after having no human contact for such a long time. Well, no normal human contact. I felt jumpy but tried my best to relay calm.

"I'm sorry about this," he said, removing the gauze slowly. "You were really booking it and I didn't know how else to stop you without being seen." He placed the old gauze down next to me. There wasn't a lot of blood on it, but there was enough and it was fresh.

"I remember now. You hit me." It came out more accusatory than I meant it. I tried again. "But you saved me. Thank you."

He nodded, then removed the cap from the alcohol bottle and put a clean rag against the opening. He turned the bottle upside down and the liquid fell to meet the cloth. "This is gonna hurt a little."

He applied the wet rag to my head, dabbing. I closed my eyes. It felt like he was doing arts and crafts with razor blades on my scalp. I shut my eyes tighter and forced a grin.

"You won't need stitches," he said. He pulled a new strip of gauze from his pocket, like it was second nature.

"How do I look?" I asked, when he was done wrapping my head.

"Good. Like a pirate, maybe. Without the hook." He made a sorry hook with his right hand, then looked embarrassed and put that hook

101

away.

"Give the hook time. Injuries have been coming in abundance these days." I laughed but didn't mean it and wondered if he could tell. "So, what the hell's wrong with everyone?"

The guy replaced the cap on the alcohol bottle, put the bottle in his pocket, and gathered up the dirty rag and gauze. He stood and walked back to the fire. It danced as he approached and shadows twitched across the ceiling. He sat on the first stair of three leading up to the remains of an altar and began feeding the rags to the flames.

Schizo lay by my side with a moan. He put his chewy Jesus down in front of him so his nose stayed touching it. The guy sat slumped over the flame with his hair falling down over his eyes. He spoke, and the silence had been so long that its interruption seemed unnatural.

"I've been following you since your taxi broke down at the intersection," he said. "I had to make sure you weren't one of them."

"You've been *following* me?" *Oh no.*

"You seemed panicky, and you were covered in guts, which looked like it bothered you." He shrugged. "Both good signs, but I had to make sure before I approached you. They're smart. You have to check and recheck or you're dead."

"They who?"

"The vampires."

"Vampires? You mean the blood-sucking kind?" I thought of the carton and the thick liquid that had spilled from it.

"Do you know another kind?"

I snorted a laugh. Schizo looked up at me and whined. "I know the imaginary kind," I said. "Stop pulling my chain. I'm really not in the mood."

He didn't respond. He gave me nothing—no smirk or wink or finger gun. I crossed my arms. "You know, this is really typical of the past 24 hours. I have crazy people surrounding me. I guess it serves me right for being a psych major, right? I should be eating this stuff up, right? Well, I'm not. I'm just…not."

My eyes were welling up, and I concentrated on petting Schizo to push the tears back. He didn't seem to mind being used. I spoke again only when I was sure my voice wouldn't waver.

"Vampires don't exist. They are a product of folklore made up by early people to explain what is understood today as the natural processes of disease and dying. Period." A fly buzzed near my face. I brushed it away. "No, this is something else. Terrorism or…or some kind of, like, mass hypnotism."

I put my head in my hands. Something was knocking at the door to my brain, but I kept that door shut and threw the deadbolt. I hugged myself and ran my hands up and down my arms. It was cold. I thought about moving closer to the fire but didn't want to risk it. Definitely not now.

The guy got up to dig through several bags tucked near the crumbling altar. I glanced around for mine, found it under a pew, unzipped it and removed the bottle of water. I unscrewed the cap, took a few gulps and poured some in my hand for Schizo. I did this three times, and he lapped it up. I wiped my hand dry on my pants. I was about to put the water away but thought I should offer some to the guy, crazy or not.

"No thanks," he said, without turning around.

"You're wrong, you know. You just have to step back and think about how crazy it sounds. Because it is…crazy."

I didn't think he was going to respond because he seemed preoccupied with finding something in those bags. I lay down and rested my head on Schizo's stomach.

"That woman whose house you went into...did she have strange teeth?"

They were enormous.

"In situations of stress, people in a certain state of mind can will things to happen. Like the mother who lifted an SUV to save her child. Have you heard that one? There have been lots of studies done. It's a heavily debated topic, but what happened today has really opened my eyes to it."

The guy grunted. I closed my eyes, then couldn't resist myself. "Hey, man, maybe you can *will* yourself some sanity." It was mean, but I couldn't help it. I didn't really think he was crazy. But he was having a laugh at my expense, so wasn't I allowed some fun too?

"My name's Cooper—not man. And you?"

I opened my eyes. "Emma."

Cooper turned around and chucked something at me. It was a blanket tied in a tight roll.

"Have a blanket, Emma."

I muttered a thank you, untied it and wrapped it around me. The warmth made me sigh. Cooper came down from the stairs with one of the bags. He cleared some floor space of debris and dropped the bag in the center. He got down and stretched out, putting his head on the bag and closing his eyes.

"What are you doing?" I asked.

"I thought it was obvious. Us crazy people need our sleep," he said, without moving.

"Oh, no. You need to tell me why you were following me."

Cooper ran his hand through his hair. "Like I said, I had to make sure you were okay."

"Okay for what? Obviously, I wasn't a vampire because vampires can't go out during the day, right? I learned that from watching a *fictional* movie about vampires."

Cooper sighed. "They have humans who work for them. Herders. They help catch other humans."

My stomach turned. I was about to ask why a person would do such a thing, knowing full well that some people will do anything to anyone to get what they want. I was about to ask this, when a loud crash sounded from outside.

Another crash followed, similar to the first but louder and more painful to the ear. Metal crunching metal. Something was hissing and moaning outside the church. It quieted, and I released my breath.

Then the pounding started. Someone wanted in.

I got on my feet in a panic. Schizo put his nose in the air and gave a quiet growl but stayed where he was. Cooper didn't move either. He didn't even open his eyes.

"*Hey*," I whispered. "What is that?"

"It's men willing themselves fangs and a thirst for your blood."

"I'm serious, Cooper! Shouldn't we get out of here?"

"If my theory is correct, we have nothing to worry about," Cooper said. "Vampires don't do churches. They don't like them. If your theory is correct, we'll be dead by morning." Cooper rolled over so his back was to me. "Sleep tight."

The sounds from outside did stop. I wasn't sure how much time had passed until they did, I was too scared to keep track. Cooper fell asleep with the noises still going, and Schizo soon followed. From there, both competed in a snoring match.

I took my sweatshirt off and used it as a pillow. The bump on the back of my head was sore, so I turned on my side and watched the fire. Whatever was outside didn't come back, but the strange noises stayed with me, a soundtrack to my sleep.

~

I woke up sad.

The invading sun pulled me from a restless sleep. Light came through the windows in beams, and dust particles floated serenely in those beams.

A pigeon cooed and peered down at me from a rafter far above my head. Schizo was lying next to me, watching me with one eye open. When I looked at him, he opened the other eye and rolled onto his back with his legs in the air. Chewy Jesus was still in immediate reach, more worse-for-wear.

I reached over to rub Schizo's stomach and sadness was replaced by another feeling that made me want the sadness back. I had felt this feeling before—too much, recently.

Cooper was gone. His bags were gone. The church was void of any sign that he had ever been there.

I forgot how to breathe and inhaled too quickly and choked on something in the air. I coughed it out. "He saves me," I said aloud, throwing my hands in the air, "tells me vampires have taken over, and then leaves me to my own vampire-fighting devices. Doesn't he know I have no devices?"

I jumped to my feet and ran to the door with Schizo on my heels. Maybe I could catch him if he just left? I could apologize for being rude, for doubting him. As I reached for the door, it flung open nearly knocking me down.

Cooper stepped into the church.

He stood about an inch taller than me, strange because in the dark he was shorter. He had been clean last night, but today he sparkled in a stark white undershirt, crisp jeans, and new black Cons. Compared to him, I must've looked like an ogre after a day at the swamp spa. I looked down at my clothes.

I was dirty.

Blotches of mud stained my tacky shirt. A stream of dried blood cut between the sequined letters making "BITCHIN" look more like "BIT CHIN." I must have bled on myself when I fell, or maybe the woman had bled on me when I hit her. I threw my hands up.

"Will people *stop* bleeding on me!" I said, addressing Cooper, as if it had been his fault.

Cooper's bottom lip quivered before his mouth spread into a smile. I had a feeling it had been a while. He looked down at the floor, and when he looked back up the smile was gone, as if it hadn't had very good adhesiveness. He pointed at my shirt.

"Better get used to that," he said. He scratched the back of his head and held up a set of keys. "I've got clean clothes in the car. The pants probably won't fit you, but they'll do for now. It's locked...habit."

I took the keys from him. "You have a car?"

He just nodded and edged by me. I thought of apologizing then and there. I did feel bad for calling him crazy. But what did he expect? If he was so quick to share the "V" word with people, I imagined he had to be pretty used to the "C" word. *Nonetheless*, I thought, *I owe him an apology*. He had saved my life and found us a safe place to crash for the night. And he had wheels. That bit of knowledge made me giddy. Besides, we just met. The arguing was meant to come later in a relationship.

I glanced back at him. He was feeding Schizo something. Cold cuts. Bologna, maybe. My stomach growled loudly, and both Cooper and Schizo looked at me. I pointed at my stomach.

"*Aliens*," I said. Cooper was not amused.

The apology could wait, I decided. At least until my breath was less offensive and I got some food in my stomach. Never start an apology on an empty stomach.

Angels sang when I passed through the doors of the church to the outside. I had never seen a car so beautiful.

I wasn't a gearhead, but when I saw Cooper's car, I wanted to know everything about it. I wanted to prance toward it, making grand sweeping gestures, and once there, I wanted to slide my fingers playfully along its glossy red finish.

It was old—1960s, I was guessing, and there was that forwardness to the design that said, "I go really fucking fast."

"Nice metal. What's a California Special?" I said, reading what was written on the car's tail.

"It's a Mustang GT. Same basic design as the Shelby, but it was made exclusively in California."

"Is it yours?"

"I borrowed it," Cooper said.

"Yeah," I said, pointing at Schizo. "Same deal."

Schizo glanced at me from a far corner of the church. Cooper had stopped the edible handouts so what followed was playtime. His tongue dangled out the side of his mouth as he stalked a flitting moth.

He bounded after the insect, tried to stop, and skidded headfirst into a pew.

"I like yours better," I said.

I closed the door behind me and took a deep breath of fresh air. It seemed like Los Angeles had finally found a solution to its smog problem: vampires taking over equals no daytime traffic equals less air pollution. And who would've thought it could be so easy?

I refused to accept Cooper's theory even though what he said made an awful kind of sense. The puzzle pieces wanted to come together in my brain and form the BIG PICTURE. But I wouldn't allow it.

Not just yet.

I was ready for crazy. I wasn't ready for vampires.

I walked to the car and squinted in the sun reflecting off its surface. A warm wind blew in from the west, dragging dead palm fronds (L.A.'s version of tumbleweed) down the street.

Crows watched me intently, and I was ready to run back into the church at the first sign of flight. I liked birds, but I had my limits, the main one being letting them feast on my scalp. By the time I was halfway to the vehicle, they seemed to lose interest, focusing their beady eyes elsewhere.

At the car, I slid the tips of my fingers along the tailgate to the passenger door. The finish was mint and as soft as a baby's bottom. I caught a glimpse of my reflection in the cherry red paint and looked away so as not to ruin the experience. I wondered if red was its original color. The car had to have been worked on. Unless it was stowed in a garage and under a cotton blanket for 40 years (*a selfish, selfish act*), there would've been scratching, denting, fading, cracking, rusting, and all those other things that time and use does to a beautiful piece of machinery.

The inside was black and also perfect. I unlocked the passenger door and got in. The bags were stacked in the backseat, separated by a neat pile of clothes resembling a folded Cooper. The pile included: a white tee shirt, blue jeans, black socks, and black sneakers. Not Cons, Nikes.

"I guess these are for me," I said, picking them up. "I've always wanted a twin."

I changed in the car to keep my modesty even though there was no one in sight to bear witness. The shirt was big but because it was a tee it would do, the jeans slid down to my knees if I wasn't feverishly clutching at the waistband, and my size ten feet swam in Cooper's shoes. I kicked them off and put mine back on, carefully placing my fingers to avoid all the stains and bits that had been left behind. *Ugh.* I'd get a new pair as soon as possible, but until then, these ones could serve as a reminder to expect the unexpected.

I found a cloth belt in one of the bags, put it on and cinched it past the last hole, then poked a hole of my own. There was toothpaste too, and I squeezed a greedy amount onto my finger. I returned everything to the backseat, along with my old clothes—which I folded and put on the floor—and locked and closed the door. The act of hygiene had lifted my spirits, and I had a hop in my step on the way back to the church.

Cooper startled when I came in. Schizo, who had either given up on the moth or eaten it, ran to my side and slid his tongue fanatically over my toothpaste finger. Cooper gave me a quick once-over.

"Good fit. Let's go."

I scowled and followed him out the door. Schizo took the rear.

When we arrived back at the car, I realized I had no idea where we were going and wondered if Cooper did. Besides his vampire theory, he seemed to know what he was doing.

I handed Cooper the keys before unlocking my own door and had to wait to get in. He went around the front to the driver side. I looked down the street. Parked, empty cars as far the eye could see. I knew all of them wouldn't have keys waiting in their ignitions, but some would. Crazy people didn't bother with the minutiae of protecting their cars from theft. So, what if I thanked him and apologized and then went my separate way?

But there was the issue of getting gas, I thought.

My door unlocked.

Plus I didn't know my way around. And nighttime comes fast in winter. Cooper got out of the car and looked at me from the other side.

"Are you coming?"

I glanced down at Schizo who glanced up at me. "Where are we going?"

"A safe place—where there are others like us."

Others like us, I thought, with a sick feeling in my stomach. The phrase implied few, and I didn't like that at all.

I opened the door, put the seat forward, and directed Schizo into the backseat. He got in and settled on top of the bags. I kept a hold of my bag, returned the seat to its upright position, and got in too, closing the door behind me.

Cooper turned the keys in the ignition, and my body vibrated. The car snarled and growled, like the soul of a fighter had been trapped in the engine. I rolled down the window and looked out at the church. The doors had stuck open, and the badly charred interior was visible from the car.

"It's a shame." I said, "Such a beautiful building. Do you know what happened?"

"The fire department," Cooper said, sliding a cassette into the player. The tape was swallowed, and drumming started through the speakers.

I nodded. "The fire department couldn't save it."

"No, the fire department burned it down."

The music increased in volume, and I was left with one more unanswered question. I thought Cooper might turn it down to let me speak, or to explain himself, but he didn't. My hygienic high was gone and I had a headache and everything around me vowed to make it worse. I put my seatbelt on and scooched down to try and get comfortable. I took a stab at nice thoughts: Cooper would bring me to a working phone, I could call the police and home, and everything would return to how it should be. First and foremost, I was getting far away from those crazy people—the ones with the big teeth and the abnormal strength.

Let me and my child drink.

The distance we made in that fast car was a blessing.

A blessing.

For the sake of my new "nice thoughts" trend, I told myself that. But I couldn't shake the feeling that Cooper was taking me closer to the freak show and that mine would be a front-row, non-refundable ticket.

~

We continued on La Brea.

It was turning out to be a beautiful day—the kind that people flock to Southern California for. The sky turned so blue that it felt like a Hollywood set, and I was sure, at any second, men in overalls would appear to roll my blue sky away.

We passed a large supermarket that was boarded up. The parking lot was empty, and square yellow signs warned against loitering. My stomach growled, and I dug into my bag for the granola bars I had taken from the pink house.

Schizo's interest was peaked. He had spent the entirety of the journey thus far with his nose against the car window, but now he put himself between Cooper and I and made his presence known. I shaped a bowl out of the dog food bag and placed it on the seat next to him. He needed no encouragement. I took two granola bars out of my bag and offered one to Cooper, who just shook his head, to which I replied that I was more than happy to eat them both. Though, my desire to devour them whole lost out to my desire to not be sick for a second time in front of the same stranger. I ate slowly, chewing fully and swallowing small amounts. The first taste sent my mind reeling. I hadn't eaten anything since the chips, and my mind, not realizing that it wasn't by choice, was letting me know that food was AMAZING.

I finished the bars and repositioned myself, as my bum was going numb and becoming one with the Mustang's upholstery.

I had a count going in my head. We had passed 12 coffin retailers in just a few blocks. Like Starbucks in most major cities in the United States, there seemed to be one on every corner. Displayed in the front windows were coffins of all sizes, but generally in the traditional, six-sided shape.

I turned my head to read a passing sign and had a chuckle figuring I must have misread it. I thought it said:

MAHOGANY MODELS

FULLY-EQUIPPED

BAR & PLASMA TV

Then underneath, in smaller letters:

100-year SAT contract available

It must have been a sign for a neighboring store, I decided. It was too late to check. The plaza was long gone.

I looked over at Cooper who was staring straight ahead, concentrating on his driving. I thought about mentioning it to him, but I already knew what he would say and it wasn't because I was psychic. The damn "V" word. He would say very matter-of-factly that there were lots of coffin stores because there were lots of vampires. I shook my head and secretly hoped Cooper would notice and ask me what was wrong, but he just kept on driving.

Out of boredom, I began to toy with the idea that I was psychic, and with a little effort, I could get into Cooper's head. I thought of how nice it would be to have the answers to all the questions nagging me. I closed my eyes and massaged my temples and waited for the fortuitous pictures to come. It was silliness, really. I didn't expect anything to happen. The pictures did come but were taken from my own life and the strange and horrifying events of the past two days. And they all pointed to one thing:

IT IS VERY POSSIBLE WE'VE BEEN TAKEN OVER BY VAMPIRES.

I started to sweat—a cold, uncomfortable sweat. When I opened my eyes, Cooper was looking at me sideways. "Are you alright?"

"Tell me, Cooper." I strained against my seatbelt to turn and face him. "How bad is it?"

Cooper returned his eyes to the road. He didn't need me to clarify what I meant. "It's bad, but we've got a plan."

I nodded. A plan was good. Very good. "Is there a phone where we're going? I need to call people...warn them. My mom. She takes the real-estate exam on Thursday. I need to call my mom." I could hear Cooper's hands tighten around the steering wheel. It sounded like strangling.

"They're dead. They're all dead," he said. "The sooner you accept that, the sooner we can get done what needs to get done." His face was stone.

My heart ached. I could feel the bomb about to go off inside me.

"Screw you," I said. "Don't you dare even begin to think you know anything about my friends or my family. They are 3,000 miles away from here. You know nothing. *Nothing*." I shook my head. Tension prickled up my neck. "I feel like..."

I felt like killing him. I wanted to threaten him and make him feel how he just made me feel. I wasn't the type to resort to threats, but I was a firm believer that when the time came, a person needed to be able to back up their words. It was never the threat itself that scared people, but the chance of the threat being carried out that made them quiver in their shoes.

Every school has a bully, and when I was in the fifth grade, the bully was Tommy Reynolds. His mother was a guidance counselor at the school, and Tommy had apparently overheard her discussing my home situation. When you're young, having a runaway, Elvis-impersonating father got you picked on, and the freckled inferno that was Tommy Reynolds pulled out all the stops. Sometimes he got physical, but mostly it was words and name-calling. I was a girl bastard. My dad was a fruit loop. I was often informed to hurry up and open a box of Fruit Loops because my dad was in there and he couldn't get out. One time at recess, I gathered up the courage for the following threat: I would buy twenty packs of Hubba Bubba, go to Tommy's house, climb up on the roof, and wait for nightfall. I'd spend that time filling my mouth with gum and chewing every piece in every pack. Then, by the light of the moon, I'd sneak through his window and siphon the gum into his ears while he slept. I told Tommy that a child in Estonia had had it done to him once and it took twelve surgeries to remove the oozing gum from his eye sockets.

Of course, it was a bluff, and Tommy knew it. My threat was rendered powerless. You think things were simpler when you were four feet tall and everything in your life revolved around sweets, but it was never simple. Only different.

"If you say something like that again, I'll sic Schizo on you," I said. Schizo barked in the backseat.

It wasn't a threatening bark, just a bark of excitement that his name had been mentioned. He was so much more convincing as a force to be reckoned with when we first met. I looked out the window to distract myself, which seemed to work for the dog. They weren't dead, because they couldn't be, and it was as simple as that.

"Listen," Cooper started. "I didn't mean what I said. I mean, it just came out wrong." Cooper paused, then took a deep breath. With the exhale came what sounded like an apology. "You're right. I have no idea about your family."

We turned right off of Sunset onto Laurel Canyon Boulevard. The car revved uphill, past tall, leaning trees.

"We don't have a phone at the base," Cooper continued. "There are payphones nearby, but calls can be traced. It's not a good idea."

It just keeps getting better. "How did it all happen, Cooper? You have to give me something, I'm dying over here."

THEN:
COOPER

Cooper Knox was drained.

The day was only dawning and he had been up for three hours already.

He sat on the stoop in front of his parent's house, his hands around a warm cup of caffeine. Rojas was late again, which meant they wouldn't get to Burbank until seven-thirty, which meant another late night on site, which meant Mel was going to kill him. And he couldn't blame her.

It would be the second date night he missed that week. Since date night only happened twice a week, he was batting below average. It was an idea his girlfriend proposed when Cooper moved back in with his parents. The two of them had done things backward. They met, dated for a year, lived together for two, and then started dating again. Not that either of them wanted that. Things had been good.

Not perfect.

But good.

Cooper graduated Mission Viejo High at the top of his class. His parents were so proud that Cooper saw camera flash in his vision for an entire week. He deferred a full-ride to Berkeley to earn some extra cash and help his dad out with the family business, which was construction. It was just meant to be for a year, but Cooper always had a problem with the word *meant*. After all, it was just a word, and words were interchangeable and too easily replaced. Mel used to say that the two of them were *meant* to be together, but after so many silences from Cooper, she stopped.

The day before he was to leave for school, his father was diagnosed with leukemia, and everything else became not so important. He had the choice of starting his pre-med req. courses (and maybe tripping over a miracle cure first semester), or staying near home to run the business and assure that enough money was coming in to get his dad the best treatment. Without it, the doctors gave his father a few months, and they were being kind. The decision was simple, and he stayed, and it was when his mom had a breakdown that Cooper moved back into his old room upstairs with the cowboy wallpaper, because before his girlfriend, before school, before his life, came his parents.

Cooper heard Rojas' VW bug before he saw it. The car appeared around the bend at the end of the street, and he was sure he spotted another dent in the thing. It was bright orange, and Cooper thought it looked like a deflated pumpkin, but he would never say that to Rojas. The car was his baby.

Cooper glanced at his watch and the bright side: Rojas had showed up.

Flu season had been brutal that year and incapacitated five of his team over the past week. That put the Broitman property way behind schedule. Fortunately, Broitman Senior's daily progress calls had stopped, so Cooper didn't have to continue with the stream of lies that began as just one. Cooper hated lying, even when it was necessary, and did everything he could to avoid it.

Rojas pulled into the driveway. His car chattered away like a pleasant, rotund man with too much to say. The muffler spat out a cloud of black fumes, and Cooper wondered when the car was last inspected.

Rojas started his apology through the driver side window, holding his hands crossed over his heart. "I'm sorry," he said, his words muffled by the glass.

Cooper smiled wanly. Rojas was the kind of person it was hard to be mad at, which was tricky for a boss. It was true Rojas was doing Cooper a favor by driving him to site every morning while his car was in the shop. The favor had its fringe benefits in the form of two extra Franklins a week, but Cooper liked to think he'd have done it anyway.

Cooper opened the passenger door. "La Guitarra" played quietly through the car's speakers. Cooper recognized the song because Rojas played it every morning and every time he would tell Cooper that "La Guitarra" was the story of his life. Rojas turned to Cooper.

"Mi hermanita está muy enferma."

"I'm sorry to hear that, Ro," Cooper said, "but you know we're behind schedule as it is, and at this rate, the drywall isn't going up until the end of March. That's only if Smithy and the rest of the guys come back. Last I heard from them was on Friday." It was Thursday.

Cooper closed the door and put his seatbelt on. He took a sip of coffee. He was going to let Rojas off but not right away. As to whether his little sister was really sick, it was likely. Everyone was sick. Cooper rarely got colds when they went around, but he was doing all he could to fend off this one, short of injecting vitamin C directly into his veins.

Rojas reversed down the driveway. He started to speak Spanish again, but Cooper stopped him. "English, Ro."

He understood Spanish, but there were gaps in his knowledge. As a native speaker, Rojas spoke fast, and in the time it took Cooper to translate, entire conversations had come and gone.

"Sorry, boss," Rojas said. "My grandma hits me when I speak *inglés* in the house. Just a little smack upside the head to remind me where I came from, you know?"

Cooper nodded and looked right to make sure no cars were coming. "You're okay this way."

"Thank you, boss." Rojas pulled into the street. They both winced as he grinded the gears.

"I can't drive when I'm nervous, boss," Rojas said, apologetically. "Are you really mad?"

"No, it's alright, Rojas," Cooper said, feeling bad for making him sweat. "I'm sorry your sister isn't feeling well."

Rojas smiled sadly and nodded. "Thanks, boss."

The VW drove down the block, past neighboring houses looking dark and empty. Most residents of Alderbrook were of retirement age, like his parents. They appreciated their mornings. Cooper, a five o'clock riser, was used to being the last one outside every day. Mr. Schwartzman across the way, with his pruned skin and gangly legs, was out at the crack of dawn "loosening up the joints with a brisk walk," as he would say. He'd tell anyone who'd listen that a morning slept in was a day wasted. Cooper wondered why older people were so good at saying things that made you want to change. Today, there was no sign of Mr. Schwartzman. Things were different today.

They got to the end of Cooper's street. Rojas turned up the music. "You know, boss, this song here," he said, pointing at the radio, "is the story of my life."

"Why's that?" Cooper asked, feigning interest and trying not to smile. Rojas must have told the story a thousand times, and Cooper would listen every time like it was the first.

"Can you believe it, boss?" Rojas asked, after finishing. Cooper shook his head. "Man, those were the days. I was good, real good. Had some talent." Rojas chuckled to himself, then looked cautiously at Cooper. "How are things with you, man? How's Mr. Knox doing?"

Rojas and Cooper's father were very fond of each other. Rojas had worked for his dad for over ten years, and despite the tardiness, his father always spoke of Rojas as someone you could depend on.

"He's the same," Cooper said. "Spends the day in bed. This third round of chemo really took it out of him."

"I'm sorry, dude," Rojas said. "Your dad's a good man. Last person on earth deserve something like this. My grandma prays for him every day."

Cooper nodded. "Thank her for me." He didn't believe in God, but he thought that saying thanks was the right thing to do. Besides, it wasn't God he was thanking, it was Ro's grandmother. He felt the need to change the subject, but Rojas beat him to it. Cooper was relieved. He didn't like talking about his father's illness. Not talking about the cancer was like it wasn't there. Work had become a sweet vacation—a badly needed break from the hell that had been dropped on his family's doorstep.

"It's lucky your dad has that nurse coming in to look after him,"

Rojas continued. "My grandma called the doc this morning for my lil' sis and they're booked all day—can't send anyone 'til tonight." He paused to stop at a light. "But that's okay. They just said to have her stay in bed and keep her comfortable and everything. My grandma, she knows what to do."

"Your sister will be okay, Ro. It's just the flu. She's young and healthy. She'll be back on her feet in a few days."

"I know. I know, you're right, man. It's just my lil' sis. I'm protective and everything, you know?"

A clear tape ejected from the player, and radio static came on. Rojas turned the dial. Where he stopped, Miss Molly was rockin' at the house of blue lights.

"*Oh yeah*," Rojas said. "I like this stuff. You like this stuff?"

"It's good," Cooper said, just as the song was interrupted.

"Stupid DJs. Don't they know people just want to hear the music and not—"

"Wait, hold on...turn it up."

Rojas rolled his eyes and turned up the volume. "You and your news, man. So when you gonna put all that knowledge to good use?"

"Shhh."

"*...in downtown Los Angeles. This marked the end of a tough week in law enforcement which have many asking for the resignation of Police Commissioner Anthony Harris. In a late night press conference, Mr. Harris stated that this year's epidemic had most of the force on sick leave, but he wants to assure the city that his officers are now back, feeling better than ever, and ready to enforce the law. This is Christine Watts reporting for ROX ninety-five-five.*"

"Wow, interesting stuff," Rojas said, changing the station quickly.

"Glad we didn't miss that."

Cooper laughed. "No, but don't you think it's weird?"

"What, man?"

"Look around," Cooper said, making a point of looking around. "There's about half the cars on the freeway than there usually is. Everyone's resigned to their beds with some new strain of the flu. Violent crime in the city has doubled."

Rojas was getting irritated with the radio. He found something with a heavy beat, smiled, and made a sound like a preacher exorcising demons.

"I don't know, man," he said. "What I do know is that upstanding citizens like you and me need time off when we get sick. Criminals, they don't. They've got better immune systems or some shit."

Cooper smiled. "Yeah, I guess."

"But my grandma would agree with you."

"Why?"

"Grandma, as you know, is a deeply religious woman." Rojas crossed himself. "As you are not." He looked at Cooper for confirmation. Cooper gestured for him to get to the point. "Anyways, she's always talking 'bout the end of the world, but this time she seems pretty sure. She says that blackout a few weeks ago let the darkness in or some shit like that."

"What does that mean?"

"Beats me, and I didn't ask. I love my grandma and I love God," Rojas said, crossing himself again, "but when she starts talking 'bout religion, it's time to leave the room, you know?"

They were getting off the freeway. Just past the off ramp, a tall man in a nice suit slept face down on a bus stop bench.

"It's funny, though," Rojas continued. "My grandma said that Magda who organizes the annual bake sale at St. Paul's saw firefighters burning down the holy center behind her house Tuesday night."

Cooper snorted. "Why would firefighters burn down a church? Does Magda like to tip the bottle?" Rojas gave a shocked expression. "Okay, then maybe it was kids fooling around. Did she say she got a good look at them?"

"Well, it was dark," Rojas said, "but she claims she heard a loud noise, and when she went to her window, there was a fire truck and a bunch of men throwing *bombas de fuego*...or um—" Rojas flicked his forehead "—you know...the bottles with fire attached?"

"Molotov cocktails?"

"Yeah, Molotov cocktails...through the windows. I drove by the next day, and the building was dust, man."

"Why didn't she call the cops?"

Rojas shrugged. "Scared, I guess. Old Magda likes to have a look-see, but that's as far as it goes."

Rojas took a right on Valley Street and then another right onto the site.

The product of his father's genius sprawled ahead of them. It was an eight-bedroom, five-bath mansion yet to be finished, but already a jaw-dropper, with cathedral ceilings, numerous patios, hand-pounded ironworks throughout, and a Roman-style pool in the back. There were twenty rooms total, and Cooper figured the Broitman family of two would only ever use about a quarter of them.

The day's roofing supplies were waiting for them, as they had been for two weeks. Tar paper leaned against the side of the house in tied rolls, and stacks of wrapped shingles sat under a large pine tree. Sawhorses, ladders, and other materials that wouldn't be damaged by the elements were strewn about the lot. Cooper kept his tools and the company's expensive machinery locked in the house. It was Burbank, but you never know.

Rojas turned off the radio, and they got out of the car.

High in the sky, at least a hundred crows were flying eastward. They created a massive shadow on the earth below that made the two young men shift uneasily. The air smelled like rain, even though Cooper hadn't seen anything about rain on the Weather Channel. *I'm going to finish this house whether you like it or not*, he said in his head, not sure who he was speaking to.

Over the past couple of weeks, the odds seemed stacked against him. But Rojas was a hard worker, and with any luck, they'd have the roof shingled by the next afternoon. Then the siding could be put up, the house would be dried-in, and they'd start on the inside, which was always Cooper's favorite part.

The inside of a house was its heart and soul. Most of the work was done by the contractors (except for laying the insulation), but Cooper was in charge of everything coming together. He had his finger on the pulse, so to speak— it was like bringing something to life. He figured it was the closest he'd ever get to being a doctor.

Cooper dialed the plumber to ask him to come in the following week. He got voicemail and left a message. Rojas grabbed the toolbox and his portable CD player from the back of the VW and went to search for an extension cord, which eluded them every morning. Cooper started unrolling the tar paper. When Rojas returned with his player plugged in to the cord, the music went on, the ladders went up, and their day began.

~

Cooper had never seen rain like that before.

It came down in long, cold spears to tear at his flesh and clothing.

They had managed to get all of the equipment back in the house before it really came down, but the rain had soaked them to the bone and they were feeling it.

With five hours spent on the roof, they had made some progress, but not enough. That put them an extra half day behind schedule, in addition to the two weeks they were already behind. *I hate you*, Cooper thought, again not knowing who he was addressing, but knowing it was whoever let his dad get sick and whoever took his men away that week and whoever let the rain come down that day to lay one last kick to the dead horse that was his father's company.

"You alright, boss?" Rojas asked. They stood next to each other, watching the rain from the shelter of the house. "Tomorrow's another day, you know." Rojas put a solid hand on Cooper's shoulder.

"Yeah, Ro," Cooper said. "Let's just get out of here."

They jogged to the car and got in. Rojas blasted the heat, which helped a little, but the VW was old and airy. The ride back was in silence. There was no traffic so they made good time. Cooper called Mel to let her know that date night would still be on. He wasn't really in the mood, but the alternative was spending the whole night with his parents. Mel sounded excited to see him, and it cheered him up a bit. She was already in the vicinity of his parents' place for work and would probably arrive before he did.

"I brought that DVD for your mom—the one she's been wanting."

"Oh yeah?" Cooper said, having no idea what she was talking about and feeling too tired to ask.

"You have no idea what I'm talking about, do you?"

"No."

"It's the DVD on Alaska. She told me she's always wanted to go and I've had this DVD forever. I think I got it in the mail with some magazine...my daddy's National Geographic or something."

"That's right, I think you told me that."

"Okay, so I'll see you at your place? Hey, maybe we should go to Alaska...I hear it's beautiful. Maybe we could go live there one day—you know, live off the land."

Mel would never like Alaska, and Cooper knew that. She wasn't a wilderness girl, she was a Cooper girl, and her suggesting plans was her securing a future, at least in her head, with the one she loved.

"See you soon, baboon," Mel said.

"You, too."

Cooper sat back and relaxed for the rest of the trip. When they arrived at Cooper's parents place, Mel's silver Jimmy was parked in the driveway.

"OK, man, say 'hi' to Mel for me," Rojas said, putting his hand out the window.

"Will do. Six tomorrow? Don't be late." Cooper took Rojas' outstretched hand.

"Me late? Never, man. You've got yourself confused with another Rojas." Cooper gave him a look. "Six o'clock, boss. Bright and early."

Cooper waved at the orange VW as it reversed down the driveway. The rain had subsided slightly.

Cooper shouldered his stuff and walked around the front of his parents' place to the side entrance. The kitchen door was unlocked, and he let himself in. The kitchen was dark. He flicked the light switch and deposited his wet things on the table. He took off his coat and hung it on the rack.

"Hey, I'm home. It's a drag out there," Cooper called, into the depths of the house.

The house smelled funny. *Have to put the trash out before we leave*, Cooper thought. He wasn't sure what Mel had planned. Usually it was a movie down at the Cineplex or sushi at the Saloon. He walked through the kitchen and down the hallway toward the living room.

"Hey, where are you guys?"

"In here."

It was his father's voice coming from the living room. Cooper stopped in his tracks. He hadn't seen his father out of bed in weeks, and his voice sounded strong.

"Dad?"

He found his feet again. The smell was getting stronger. It hadn't been the trash, after all. Cooper entered the living room.

His father sat in the old rocking chair with his back to Cooper. The chair had been passed down three generations on his mom's side. It had belonged to Cooper's great-great-great-grandmother who was run over by a timber train in North Dakota. Cooper hated the thing. It whined whenever someone sat in it.

It was sure whining now. His dad, still dressed in his sleeping clothes, did not turn around to face Cooper but kept rocking back and forth.

"Dad? How you feeling? Where is everyone?"

"I need to talk to you about something, son," his dad said, in that strong voice, "and I don't want you to be upset."

Cooper got closer. "What's wrong, dad? Where's Mel?"

"She's in the laundry room," his dad said, standing up. "I got her tied to a chair."

Cooper took a step closer. "Dad, what are you—" Cooper's dad turned around. "Dad, whose blood is that?"

His dad looked down, as if unaware that his entire front was covered in blood, and looked back up at Cooper. "It's your mother's," he said, with a smile and his voice booming like he was a television presenter talking about a fantastic set of golf clubs. His dad stepped away from the chair, toward him. There was a lump in the rug. A pale, bejeweled arm stuck out from under it.

"Mom!" Cooper yelled, moving toward her.

His dad blocked the way. "Don't, son. Your mother was left to feed me."

"What have you done? I don't understand."

"No, you don't...not yet...but you will."

The creature that had been his dad, but was now very much not, stood tall. Cooper's father had gotten to slouching as the illness took its toll. The thing before him seemed to pulsate with life, and behind all the blood and craziness, there was a younger, healthier version of his father.

"When they came to me," the creature continued, "I was in a bad way, Coop. But now, it's like I'm 20 again. I feel like buying myself another motorcycle to go *crrruuuizin'* for chicks." Mr. Knox gave his son two thumbs up. "They want us to build things. They like our work. We can be a father and son team, again. Live forever, build forever. You can take the insides, how you like. What do you say?"

Cooper turned and ran toward the laundry room.

129

The door was open. Mel was there, bound to a chair with electrical tape over her mouth. She was crying and black mascara streamed like two polluted rivers down her face. Her eyes widened when she saw Cooper. He knelt to untie her. He peeled the tape off of her mouth, and she screamed.

"Did he hurt you?" Cooper asked, as his girlfriend clutched at him, sobbing uncontrollably. She didn't answer so he asked her again, pushing her away from him and taking her chin hard in his hand. "Mel. Did he hurt you? Can you run?"

The girl's fingers went to her neck. She shook her head. Between sobs, she spoke. "No, I'm...not...I'm okay...*oh God, get me out of here!*"

She screamed at what was behind him. Cooper turned and swung his arm around.

His fist hit the creature's face. Cooper drew his arm back and swung again. He ran at it, shoving his right shoulder into the thing's ribs. He pushed it into the next room. They landed on the table, and the table's legs snapped, releasing them onto the floor. The creature grabbed at him, but Cooper tore himself away. He ran back to the laundry room to get Mel. They escaped to the kitchen and the front door.

The thing called after him. "Don't do it, Coop. Don't leave your old man like this."

Cooper stopped. His dad pleaded behind them. "I'm sick, Coop. I'm really sick. After all I've done for you—don't leave."

Mel grabbed at him frantically. "Don't listen to him, Cooper. *Let's go!*"

Cooper knew better. He knew that his father was gone; he just never imagined it would happen this way. He always thought it would be the cancer that took him. This was something else. Something evil in intent.

Cooper tightened his hand around Mel's and they burst out the door. They started for her car, but Mel shook her head. "The keys are in the house," she said, her voice competing with the rain that was coming down strongly again.

They headed up to the main road, neither of them slowing their pace once. What was behind them was far worse than anything that could be ahead of them. A car drove by and blared its horn. Up ahead, the corner 7-Eleven had all the lights on inside, shining as bright as a million halos. They ran to it. It was all they had.

The door announced their entrance with a loud *ding*. No one was at the front counter. The store appeared empty. Cooper checked the aisles with Mel in tow. He went to the back and cracked the staff room door. "Hello? Anyone there? We've got an emergency out here."

It felt all too familiar. Mel tugged at his shirt sleeve. "Coop, I don't like this," she said. "Let's go. I want to go. Let's just go, okay?"

"Where, Mel? Where do you want to go? Got any *ideas?*" Cooper asked. "Huh?" Mel started to cry again, and Cooper regretted getting angry with her.

"I don't know." Mel wiped at her face, making a good effort to stop what had started. Her mascara smudged across her cheeks and came off on her hands. "Somewhere safe. My parents' place? We can get a bus from here."

"And what if they're like my dad? What do we do then?"

Mel shook her head. "No...no, they won't be—why would they be?" She smiled reassurance. "Your dad was...well he was...I don't

131

know, Cooper. I don't know, it could've been...maybe it was the chemo that made him like that?"

Cooper laughed. Mel winced. "Um, were you there, Mel? Did you see him? Chemotherapy doesn't make a person's teeth grow like that—it doesn't make people *kill*." Mel threw her hands in the air and started to yell.

"Of course, I was there you shithead! Your dad bit me! He *bit me!*"

Cooper moved toward her. She slapped him. He tried again, and she let him take her this time.

"It's okay, I'm sorry." Mel was shaking. They stayed like that for a couple of minutes before Cooper pulled away slowly. "I'm going to look behind the counter for a phone. It'll just take a second, okay?"

Mel nodded and released him reluctantly.

Behind the counter, a puddle of blood shaped like an amoeba stretched across a dirty floor. It didn't look fresh. Cooper felt relief. He spotted the phone, a big black clunker, next to the register and stepped around the puddle.

He picked up the receiver and dialed nine-one-one. The line was busy. Cooper slammed the receiver against the counter. The counter dented, but the phone stayed intact. Mel looked at him but said nothing. Cooper returned the receiver to his ear and dialed the operator.

"Hello, operator?" said the voice at the other end. The voice was nasally. Cooper pictured an old-school operator with orange hair pinned up in a tight bun, red lipstick, and square glasses balanced on the tip of her nose.

"Hello, I'm trying to get a hold of the police, but their line's busy. It's an emergency."

There was a long pause on the other end. "Hello?" asked Cooper.

"Yes, sir, where are you calling from?"

"We're at a 7-Eleven by my house. Can you connect me to the police?"

Another pause.

"We're coming to get you, sir. What is your location?"

Cooper was silent. He could hear whispering in the background.

"We've got your location. We're coming to get you."

The line went dead. Cooper replaced the receiver. *I didn't tell them what the emergency was,* he thought.

Cooper had forgotten about the blood, and a quick step forward nearly had him on his ass. He caught his balance, jumped the puddle, and rounded the counter toward Mel.

"What happened?" she asked. "Are they coming?"

"They're coming, but I'm not sure that's a good thing."

"What do you mean?"

"I mean we need to leave. Right now."

Mel began to question him, but he took her hand and they were out the door before she got the chance. They had just arrived at the main road when a dark van drove past them, braked, fishtailed, and veered onto the sidewalk in front of them. The side door opened, and a man about Cooper's age with blonde hair and a torn jacket hunched in the gap. "Seen some vampires lately?" he asked, smirking.

"What?" Cooper asked, situating himself between his girlfriend and the van.

"Get in. We're here to help."

Cooper took a step back. "Who are you?"

"It doesn't matter."

133

"It does to us."

"We take care of what you're running from."

"How do you know we're running from something?"

"Oh, out for a jog in the rain? As much as I love the conversation we got going here, man, we have places to be." He started to close the door.

"No, wait." Cooper looked at Mel.

"We can't trust them," she said.

"What are our choices?"

Mel glanced at the bus stop across the street. It was empty. The rain bounced off the structure, and the stop's lights cast a funny haze, making it look not-of-this-world. She searched down the street for an approaching bus. The 89 would take them directly to her parents' place. The trip would take 25 minutes. Her daddy would hug her when she arrived and tell her everything was going to be alright. She could faintly smell his tobacco pipe.

No bus was coming in either direction.

"Okay."

~

There were no seats in the back of the van.

Large panels of wood reinforced the van's floor and walls. With the addition of Cooper and Mel, it was a tight fit. Four of the strangers were in the back with them, with one up front driving. The blonde guy sat down opposite Cooper and Mel, and the door slid shut automatically behind them. They took seats where they were.

No one spoke. The rain beat the living hell out of the outside of the van, and on the inside, the battle was amplified. The four strangers eyed them. A young girl and a woman (the girl's mother?) were in a state of disarray. The pair huddled at the back of the van. A girl about their age was seated across from them, next to the blonde guy. They were both dressed similarly in dark clothing. The driver had graying hair but a young face, and he kept his eyes where they should be—on the road.

Mel was in tremors. Cooper wanted to say something to her, and was about to, but the blonde guy spoke first.

"What's that on your neck?"

Mel brought her hand up to her neck and looked at Cooper nervously. There were two holes there. Cooper hadn't seen them. Mel always wore her hair down and long, and date night was no exception. The holes were neat and red, and there was no stray blood. Mel's fingers touched the wound and then came away quickly as if the bite itself had bitten.

"I was bit. His father…he bit…me." Her words faded.

"She'll need medical attention," Cooper said, resting a hand on Mel's knee.

The blonde guy's face fell. "*Bite!*" he yelled.

Before Cooper realized what was happening, the girl opposite them had taken hold of his arm and was pulling him toward her. The door behind them was open again, and the complicated soles of the blonde guy's boots came forward, hitting Mel square in the chest.

She flew backward, out the door.

There was skidding, several horns sounded. A *thump*. Cooper thought he heard Mel scream, but he couldn't be sure.

He was never sure.

CHAPTER EIGHT

NOW:

I NEEDED A CIGARETTE.

I wasn't an addict. I was someone who appreciated.

I felt like Cooper could use some time, so I gave it to him. The road beneath us curved and rose. Street signs warned of crossing deer and fire.

With what Cooper had gone through with his parents and his girlfriend, I could understand his outburst earlier. It seemed the crazies weren't just following me. As far as I was concerned, his friends had murdered his girlfriend. That's if she had even been killed in the accident. I wondered if Cooper had made them go back for her.

His story didn't get me any closer to an explanation—especially the one that had vampires taking over the country. What I'd seen and been told thus far didn't prove anything except something very strange and violent was going on, and it had to be stopped.

Cooper slid a hand over his face. He looked like he could use a bed and a good 15 hours. I contemplated offering him another granola bar, for some energy, but I didn't want to force the topic. He had already declined, and I was no granola pusher.

Tall trees blocked the sun, and my heart fell into my stomach with the very idea of night. But it meant nothing, and I silently repeated that to myself, just to get it in there.

Night means nothing.

Though there was something to be said for the day without people that I had experienced and the one very active night. We had yet to pass another car on the road. Reminiscent of my drive from the airport, all life seemed to have taken leave.

Cooper cleared his throat. "They came in the blackout."

Two weeks ago, lights went out in major cities across the country. Syracuse wasn't one of them, but Boston was, along with Los Angeles, New York, San Francisco, Las Vegas, DC, and others. The blackout lasted three days, and what was first blamed on terrorism, ended up being caused by a massive, sudden overuse of the country's electricity.

Cooper continued. "Before the first day of the blackout, statues were delivered overnight to government buildings, military posts, police departments, news stations, and universities. A letter was attached from the president to each addressee, thanking them for their part in getting the "Youth of America" bill passed. It was a Trojan horse. They put vampires in those statues, small ones…mostly children. When the lights went out, the vampires left their statues, which were really just coffins, to bite anyone with influence. And when the lights came back on, many powerful people were looking paler, and their priorities had changed."

"The media and the military," I said absently. "That's how they were able to take over cities without people realizing."

Cooper nodded. He braked at a stop sign and looked both ways.

"Okay, okay," I said. "If what you're saying is true, then why? Why did they do it? I mean, these creatures have existed for a long time, right? Yes. So after all these years of hiding their existence…why come out now? What changed?" Cooper started to speak, but I wasn't finished. "And okay, so they feed on our blood because they need it, right? But what happens when they run out of blood? Eventually, they'll kill or turn all of us, right? So, what then?"

Cooper shrugged. "Look, there's someone you're going to meet…Scott…he can explain everything and do a much better job. But I don't know—" Cooper turned off the main road onto a narrow, dirt drive "—I think they got tired of living in the shadows. They wanted what we had, so they took it. There are other things. Like I said, Scott will explain. But as far as running out of humans, they have procedures meant to prevent that. Breeding farms and kill quotas. Any human found has to be reported to the UVF. A lot of them don't do it but—"

"The UVF?" Those were the letters on the airport soldiers' armbands.

"United Vampire Front," Cooper said.

My tongue throbbed recalling Myer's threat. My stomach turned. I rolled down the window. Schizo nearly tumbled out in excitement, and I grabbed his collar and pulled him back into the car. He whined as I rolled the window up to a three-inch crack, but he still managed to fit his whole head through. He sniffed and sneezed convulsively.

Cooper looked at me. "You okay?"

"It's just my stomach. The fresh air will help."

Cooper stopped the car. I looked around. Nothing but trees and a wooden sign up ahead. My eyes focused.

"Welcome to Sleepy Storage," I read aloud. *"Your stuff will love the stay."*

Cooper undid his seatbelt and opened the door.

"Are we getting out?" I asked, with a tinge of desperation. I really needed to work on my desertion issues. "I mean…is this it?"

"Nope," Cooper said, casually taking the keys from the ignition. "I need to get something out of the trunk."

Cooper got out of the car, and I turned in my seat to watch him. His feet crunched the ground. The trunk opened silently, and Cooper disappeared into it. There was rustling, before the trunk slammed shut, and Cooper got back in the car with a walkie-talkie. It was green and bulky and looked ancient. He switched it on and spoke. "Cooper to base, come in base."

"This is base," said a broken voice at the other end.

"I'm on approach with one and a canine, do you read?"

"I read, how's protocol?"

"Good. I checked her," Cooper said, glancing over at me.

"Drive up. Base out."

"Cooper out." Cooper put the walkie-talkie on the dashboard and stuck the keys back in the ignition.

"You checked me, huh?" Cooper glanced at me. His skin was darker than mine, but I thought I saw a flush rise up his cheeks.

"I checked you for bites," he said, "when you were passed out. Just your neck and arms. Vampires can bite in, um...other places...but you've been fine today. It's a full day or so before someone who's been bitten turns, new-bites we call them. New-bites can take daylight, but they don't like it very much. They look ill, fall asleep frequently." Cooper took the car out of park and continued up the road. Tree branches fell low to high-five the mustang's side mirrors. "You look fine," Cooper repeated.

I thanked him, not knowing why. Maybe for saving my dignity by not doing the thorough check that someone had wanted. Or it could've been him saying in so many words that I didn't look like death, even though I really really felt like death.

We drove deep into the forest. The road was heavily potholed, and Cooper did his best to dodge the craters that gladly would've eaten the car's undercarriage, if given the chance.

Two miles in, trees parted and a concrete fortress appeared. It was Sleepy Storage in none of its glory. A rocky slab in a woody world. Whoever designed the building should have been shot on the spot, but it was never meant to be called home by anyone and here we were. I undid my seatbelt and moved closer to the windshield for a better look.

The building was tall. Several robust columns protruded from the concrete structure. In between, multiple green squares made the façade look like a massive checker board. Moss crept up from the forest floor to the roof. SLEEPY STORAGE was painted in red block letters at the top. The paint was fading, and the "L" in sleepy was all but gone, making SLEEPY look more like SEEPY.

"Did you forget your toothbrush?"

The car dipped into a pothole, and the world rose around us. "Are you always this sarcastic?"

"No," I said. "Yes. Sometimes. Come on, you're a bit sarcastic too."

Cooper shrugged. "It's not much, but it's perfect for what we needed. It's a good distance from the main road. It has a rear entrance that is the only way in or out of the building. Top floor's got windows to keep a lookout—lots of space. This place has been out of business for years. No one's coming here."

You did, I thought. I looked up and noticed the windows at the top floor. They were tinted green and just looked like more squares of concrete at first glance.

We drove on in an encapsulation of dust. The dirt drive ended, but our journey didn't and Cooper veered right, bumping over a small mound and crashing through a tangle of grass and shrubs. Miscellaneous items were scattered on the ground and broke for the umpteenth time beneath the car's tires. I wondered why no one had felt the need to return and collect them. We drove over an old record player with a 45 still in it. Both items were one now, pressed into the ground and split into many pieces so it looked like an abstract tiling of a record player.

There were lots of books, mostly paperbacks. Ten or so hung from the branches of a tiny tree next to my window. *What a well-read tree*, I thought. A book with a burly man on the cover kissing a woman with heaving breasts and flowing locks disappeared under the car.

I couldn't believe the massive amounts of debris until the car finally ambled around the back of the building and there it was: more massive amounts of debris. Two mountains of rusted metal, chewed wires, broken glass, cracked plastic, mildewed cloth, torn paper, and splintered wood reached its ugliness into the perfect blue sky. The junk mountains sat in the middle of an average-sized parking lot, land that had been taken away from the forest but that the forest was now taking back. The pavement was cracked, and giant roots curved in and out like exploring sea creatures.

"It was all here when we found the place," Cooper said, following my gaze. "I guess they didn't know what to do with everything leftover after the facility closed. We've taken things from it, refrigerators, furniture, but it never really makes a dent."

I wondered if I could find a soccer ball and found five. The brain stimulation was good for keeping me awake. We pulled up in front of a large, metal door. Another door was next to it, our size. Cooper leaned over me, and I jumped.

"I just need the door opener," he said, slowly pulling the glove compartment open.

"I just need a warning," I said.

We had only met a day ago, and I was never that person who trusted people right away. If in my old life it was a good approach, in this one it was the only approach. Of that, I was sure.

Cooper took a brown cube with a rectangular button out of the glove box. He pressed the button twice. After the second time, the door in front of us opened. When the door was halfway open, lights blinked on inside. Cooper took the Mustang out of park and drove forward.

~

I had trouble coming to grips with what I saw.

The space was enormous—the kind that held alien crafts, in a different story. Silver track lighting was suspended from long, thick wires. And there were cars.

Oh, were there cars.

But calling them that seemed to do them an injustice. They weren't cars—they were Super Cars. Mobile Art. Beauteous Transport.

There were at least twenty, large and small, mostly black. In the old world, they had hefty price tags, but in this world with so many costs, they were free.

Tail ends bragged as we drove by: Ferrari, Alpha Romeo, Aston Martin, BMW, Mercedes, and others. Cooper drove slowly, either for the cars' benefits, or for mine. You could paint me impressed, and when I managed to look away, Cooper had an answer ready for the question barely formed on my lips.

"They're all borrowed," he said. "Like the Mustang. We keep track of what we take. All data goes in the same book. We need the cars, but we're not crooks. It's all a means to an end—everything you see and learn at this place is all a means to an end." Cooper's voice trailed off. A fathomed guess was that he was thinking about that end, and I let him, in silence. When I thought enough time had passed, I asked my next question:

"Isn't it a bit much, though? I mean, won't these cars call attention to you?"

Cooper pulled into an empty space next to three purple motorbikes. "Vampires, like humans, appreciate nice cars. We blend driving one of these. Driving a Kia would get us noticed."

Sure vampires. Whatever you say. My mind was as decisive as a ping pong ball. It seemed a vampiric takeover wasn't so easy to swallow. Schizo whined in the backseat. I turned to look at him, and he landed a wet one on my face. Then he directed both eyes at the exit. Cooper switched off the engine, and I opened my door. Schizo bolted, and I lost sight of him.

"I hope he's not doing what I think he's doing," I said.

Cooper removed the keys from the ignition, replaced the garage door opener in the glove box, and got out of the car. From not too far away, the sound of fluid hitting pavement. I looked at Cooper.

"Sorry."

Cooper shrugged. "He's a dog. It's been a while." He went into the back for a handful of bags. "At least he didn't go in the car."

Schizo returned looking lighter. I gathered the remainder of his food from the backseat and put it in my bag. I thought about scolding him but didn't. He had been through enough, and I was proud of him for holding it. My bladder was ready to burst at the church. I could have asked Cooper to stop somewhere and let me out to relieve myself, but there was no way I was ready to venture out alone again. Even though it was daytime and things were meant to be okay when the sun was shining. If I was a dog, I would've gone in the car.

Cooper threw a bunch of bags over each shoulder. I offered to help, but he declined. Inside those bags, hard objects shifted making hollow banging noises. He started walking, and I followed after attaching Schizo's leash to his collar. We headed toward a door in the far corner of the garage with a circular window like the door of a ship. Cooper tugged a chain from his pocket, and at the end was a key. He opened the door and motioned me through. I noticed I was standing on a welcome mat and moved my feet to read what it said:

GO AWAY.

That mat lacked manners. I wiped my feet on it. *If there was any place else I could be*, I thought. The mat responded with "GO AWAY" and I concluded that conversing with something that had such a limited vocabulary was pointless. I gave both shoe bottoms one last wipe. Cooper held the door open for us, and I went through with too many second thoughts to count.

We entered a wide hallway with numbered storage units on our left and right. There were twenty in total. All were closed up and secured with padlocks. A desk was at the end of the hall, and behind that desk, a slouching boy no older than sixteen.

"Is there still stuff in these?" I asked.

"No. This floor's empty. We checked the whole building when we got here. Broke open all the locks and replaced them with new ones. Seven hundred units."

"You locked them again because it would've been like living in a big house with seven hundred closets to check every night."

Cooper nodded. "And we have better things to do."

Better is a tricky word and never as good a word as I feel like it should be. Cooper's hard footsteps sounded like the soldiers at the airport, and I shivered. When we got to the desk, the skinny kid stepped out from behind it. He was tall, but the slouching made him shorter. His hair was sandy brown, combed neatly, as if his mother had just come by to fuss. Zits formed constellations across his forehead. The boy's wide eyes went from Cooper to me to Schizo.

Cooper to me to Schizo.

Schizo, very interested in the boy, met his stare and shook his stub of a tail every time it came back around.

"*This* is your security," I whispered to Cooper, aware that the boy could hear me, but not minding.

I inhaled quickly when I saw what the boy's hand quivered over: the butt of a gun.

The freckled hand wavered in and out with indecision and a bit of rhythm. However unintentional that rhythm was, it reminded me of my father making Elvis. That was what I called it as a kid, *making* Elvis. Every Saturday morning, he would put the needle on the record and dash into the middle of the living room, his fancy white jumpsuit unique against a backdrop of bargain-basement furniture.

He'd stand there with his head down and his body still and his little girl waiting anxiously on the couch. He'd stand there until the music started, and the first thing that moved was his right hand—just a twitch. It would twitch more and more with the crescendo of the song. There were moments when I was sure that his hand would twitch right off his arm and out the door and we'd find it hours later being fought over by the neighborhood dogs.

My mother worked Saturday mornings, and my father only made Elvis when she was away. She'd tell me years later that she hated his obsession. I never knew any better. At the time, I thought all kids had dads who dressed like Elvis.

"Where you been, Cooper?" the boy asked. "Everyone's been worried. You go away for two nights, and we don't hear anything. Now you're back with a girl and a dog." The boy looked down at Schizo, who was ready for it. His butt wiggled. "It's not *pro-to-col* and you know it."

The boy said *protocol* like it was a word he wasn't used to saying but one he thoroughly enjoyed saying when he got the chance. The tips of his fingers brushed the handle of the gun.

I am not dying here. It was not going to happen at the hands of some pimply faced, gun-toting spastic.

"Hands off the gun, John Rambo," Cooper said calmly. "I ran into a problem." He looked at me.

I was that problem.

Cooper continued. "We have new guests. They're tired and hungry, and we're going to help them. Sam, this is Emma and Schizo."

I presented my hand, slowly, and Sam moved his hand away from the gun to meet mine. His eyes stayed low. His grip was like margarine, and his hand slid from my grasp and fell limp against his thigh.

"When was the last time you got some sleep, Sammy?" Cooper asked.

"Haven't been sleeping much, Coop," Sam said. "Nightmares, you know?"

I did.

A *buzz* sounded behind me, followed by more *buzzes*. The boy lifted his eyes now. They were wide and full of veins.

I turned around to see darkness approaching.

A solid, impenetrable black came nearer as the lights blinked off, one after the other. Already half the hallway was swallowed.

The last light buzzed and flickered over us.

Cooper lunged for a panel on the wall next to Sam. He swiped at it, and the hallway was illuminated again. A bead of sweat trickled down Cooper's cheek. "I hate it when that happens." Schizo whined agreement.

Sam massaged the back of his neck with one hand. "Lights have...have been acting up all night. I've got them on regular...but it doesn't want to stick."

"I'll come down and check it out after I get these guys settled."

Cooper walked by Sam and put a hand on his shoulder. They made eye contact. An understanding passed between the two—an understanding that only those who have been through something very bad together could grasp.

Sam nodded and sat down. As Schizo walked by, he leaned in for a quick pat. The dog responded by licking Sam's hand as if it was the last hand on earth. The boy's demeanor changed in less than a second. It was remarkable.

I held the door open for Schizo and led him through. I leaned down and whispered in his ear. "You did good, boy."

Sam called out behind us.

"Coop, who's John Rambo? Should I be expecting him?"

Cooper and I exchanged a smile. "No," he said. "Unfortunately, no."

The next hallway was much like the first. The door shut behind us.

"Sorry about the lights," Cooper said. "They're motion-sensored. It's only on this floor and the fifth that they're meant to stay on all the time. We've got a quality generator running in the basement but a limited supply of fuel to work with."

"Why is a 16-year-old guarding the entrance?" I asked. "Do you really think he could take on one of those…crazies…if one or two got in?"

"It was Scott's idea," Cooper said. "Sam's sister was just killed. Scott thought work might get his mind off things. He's young but usually pretty dependable." We arrived at an elevator. Cooper hit the up arrow. "Besides, day's easy."

The elevator opened. I hesitated, remembering the airport and the last time I had been on an elevator. The carriage had gone down instead of up like I wanted it to—like I needed it to. I had thought something was waiting for me.

I could have sworn something was waiting for me.

I got in with Schizo, refusing to let the past two days set a precedent for my life. In my twenty-one years, I had been on plenty of elevators, and nothing else bad had ever happened.

Button five was lit. We ascended.

"What happened to Sam's sister?" I wasn't sure if it was my business, but was any of it? Cooper was giving me a lot of information I never asked for. What was I meant to do with it all? He knew I wasn't sold on his vampire theory. Everything that had happened so far could have another explanation. No, as far as the existence of vampires was concerned, my jury was still out and deliberating. *Maybe the jury's dead*, I thought. As far as all the information sharing, Cooper was either simply being a good host, or he was preparing me because he needed me for something.

"She was bit," Cooper said, taking the bags off his shoulders and resting his back against the wall. "A group of us went to catch a movie down the road. We wanted to do something for the kids. Let them be kids, I guess. It was daytime, with hours before sunset, but Cara...she wandered off." Cooper looked down. He fidgeted with a loose thread. "When we found her a couple hours later, she was scared but seemed fine—said she had gone to check out the store and gotten lost. Two days later, she was at her brother's throat. I think he knew. He knew, but he hid it. She was his sister, after all."

The elevator jerked to a stop. Cooper held the doors open for us to exit. We were now in a small lobby. A "5" with a circle around it was painted on the wall. It smelled like Thanksgiving. Someone was burning cinnamon incense or candles. I felt warm and fuzzy inside. For a second, I wasn't in a dark, concrete storage facility but near a roaring fire. People weren't trying to kill me. The moment couldn't have lasted long enough.

More units were up ahead, one with its door open. I tried but it was too dark to make out anything inside the room, even with the lights bright in the hallway. It's strange how darkness commands things.

"The stairs," Cooper said, pointing at a door across from the elevator. "One more floor's above us, with a kitchen and common area. There are windows up there, so lights stay off on six. Flashlights and candles can be used after sunset, but we'd rather you just stick to the lower floors. Feel free to make a late-night snack and come down here. There's a lounge, and we've got a television and movies. Twister."

149

The open unit was now directly in front of us. More open ones were further down. The other end of the hallway looked pretty locked up.

Cooper continued: "This is the residential floor. Living units that way—" Cooper pointed to the left "—storage units that way—" he pointed to the right. "You'll find extra furniture, blankets and stuff in those units."

Cooper approached the open unit in front of us. The door was rolled up with the handle just above eye-level, and Cooper gripped and shook it. The noise was loud and unforgiving. "Rise and shine, Rudy. Sam needs replacement up front."

A deep moan came from the room.

"Get over it, Rudy."

"I didn't sign up for this shit."

"None of us did." Cooper motioned me forward. "I'll introduce you two later."

Cooper continued the tour, offering up more names outside of several closed units. Cooper's unit was right next to Rudy's, and I thought maybe close proximity was the reason for the tension I had sensed. Maybe it went deeper. Seven more names followed. An army, it wasn't.

Schizo was whining and gnawing at his leash, so I took it off him. He ran ahead and disappeared into an open unit. Cartoon sounds *banged*, *whammed*, and *boinged* from inside.

~

The girl, Bugs, sat with her back to us.

She was a tiny thing with long blonde hair that touched the floor when she sat. A television was in front of her, resting on the woven seat of a wooden chair. A DVD player balanced on top of the set. The player's lights blinked.

On the television screen, The Roadrunner ran circles around The Coyote.

A square pink rug covered a small area of the concrete floor. Astronaut Barbie did a pants-free split in the middle of the rug. Posters of unicorns and pinup pages of young faces I vaguely recognized were taped along the wall, crooked but equal distances apart. A twin mattress dressed in white sheets and a *Bugs Bunny* comforter occupied the right side of the unit. A painting of a window was behind the television set, painted directly onto the wall. The window's frame was fluorescent orange, and beyond the imaginary window, an imaginary outdoors. The sky was blue, the sun was yellow, and the trees were purple and green. A smiling stick figure with an enormous head and black hair filled up the right pane.

Schizo glanced at us for permission, and then jumped up on Bugs' bed without waiting for it. The young girl took no notice of the dog. At that moment, television was her world.

"Hey, Bugs. This is Emma. She's going to be staying with us."

I looked at Cooper. I had never said anything about staying at Seepy Storage. In my head, things were confused, but I had no desire to remain in that place for an extended period of time. *Maybe one night to figure out my next move.*

"Hi," I said. "And that's Schizo on your bed."

Bugs turned around to look at Schizo and then at me. She had an apple in her hand. She bit into it and studied me. "I don't think I like dogs. They bite." A piece of hair fell across her forehead, and she brushed it away with the apple.

"Oh, he doesn't bite, honey. He's a good boy," I said. *Well, kind of.*

151

Bugs seemed satisfied with my answer and turned her attention back to the cartoons. I decided it was okay if Schizo stayed on her bed, as long as I was going to be close by. He was tired, and neither little girl nor canine was very interested in each other.

Cooper was busying himself with the padlock on the unit across the way.

"Are there any more televisions around? We should check the news—they'll know something, right?"

"I've caught the news...*their* news," Cooper said, undoing the lock and disconnecting it from its latch. "It's nothing you want to see."

He handed me the lock, its dial set on seven, and bent down to pull open the door. It sounded like an earthquake. Inside the unit was a naked mattress, a thin beige rug, a bedside table (more of a bed-over table), and a tiny lamp, tiny enough that if it disappeared while you were staring at it, you wouldn't notice.

"We don't have anything that uses a signal here, besides the walkie-talkies, but those are low frequency. No cell phones, pagers, radios, or computers."

I sighed. "I don't have any of those things. Not anymore."

"I know."

"Let me guess, you checked my bag?"

"It's—"

"Protocol. I know."

"There's extra furniture and linens in unit 504 just down the hall. You'll need sheets. Always close the door when you leave, but not when you're in. That way we don't have to bang on it and guess. Are you hungry?"

I imagined closing myself in that cold, dark unit. *What sane person would do something like that?* It was like a tomb.

"I won't be staying long enough to need extra furniture. A day, at the most. Maybe two."

"Talk to Scott. Then, do what you want."

Was talking to Scott an order? I felt like saying *Okay, take me to your leader* but what came out was, "Hungry."

My stomach was eating itself, having given up on my ability to send food its way. Despite the unwelcomeness of my new surroundings, my legs gravitated toward the bed. I started to feel like I was in one of the little girl's cartoons. Nothing made sense. My mind reeled. I rubbed my eyes to see if that would help, but it just made Cooper blurry.

"I'll go get you some food from upstairs," Cooper said. "Check out Unit 504—take what you want." He turned. "Bugs, help Emma out if she has any questions."

"Em," I said.

"Huh?"

"*Em.* No one really calls me Emma, except for my professors."

"Em," Cooper said, smiling uncomfortably.

Bugs turned around to give me a suspicious look. The apple remains sat on top of the television. I waved, and she swirled back around.

Cooper left, and I stood there with a lost feeling like someone had gone inside me and taken something but I would never be allowed to know what. I looked at my new accommodations and wondered how anyone could muster the inspiration to decorate a concrete storage unit. I shrugged, put the lock in my bag and my bag on the floor, and went shopping.

I passed Rudy's door, now closed and padlocked. I dragged my feet with the fleeting worry it might annoy someone, but I couldn't garner the energy to pick them up.

At the unit, I pulled the door open and found a light switch behind a coat rack.

Stay a while. Stay forever.

Most of the stuff crowding the unit fulfilled basic needs, no frills allowed. There were things to place things on and hang things on, and things to sit on, sleep on, and stand on. I found a new sheet set in a trash bag and took it. A pillow was in the same bag, and a rolled rug, and I shoved the items under my arms.

An empty bookcase made me feel sad. I focused on a nice-looking sofa made of a silky material and dark wood. I sat. Defiant springs buoyed me. I pictured myself dragging it down the hallway. *Why would I do that? I'm only staying the night.* I had the thought that I could pretty up the unit for its next guest, but shook my head and left.

Back at my temporary digs, I sheeted the mattress and pillow and walked around holding the rug spread out between both hands. It was forest green with bits of yellow, brown, and red.

"What are you doing?"

I jumped.

"Bugs, you scared me half to death. You can't sneak up on people like that."

"I just did."

"No, I mean...uh, never mind. I'm figuring out where to put this rug. It's a big decision, you know." I smiled. "If you put a rug in the wrong place, there are serious consequences. Not sure I can handle the pressure all on my own."

The girl yawned, her little mouth an oval. I was trying to engage her, but it didn't seem to be working. Schizo brushed past the child's bare legs, stepped up on my bed, and circled himself into a tight ball on my clean sheets. He deposited his chewy cross. I picked it up and wiped at the gray saliva stain left behind. I put the cross on the floor.

"Car turned into a vampire, and now she's in hell," Bugs said.

"Oh, I'm sure she's not...in hell, Bugs."

"That's what Mary told me."

"You mean Mary, uh...the mother of Jesus?"

"*No*," Bugs said, like I was the biggest idiot on earth. "*Mary*. Scott's wife."

"Oh, I haven't met her yet."

"My pop's a vampire. And my grandma, too."

"That's too bad, honey," I said, not really knowing what to say to that. Children tend to believe what adults tell them.

"That's okay. They get to live forever. Unless Rudy or Cooper find them. Then they'll die for sure and go to hell."

I wanted out of the conversation, and my escape came in the form of a Christian revivalist named Mary. She appeared outside my unit. She looked like Bugs and could've been her mother, but wasn't, to my knowledge. Mary wore a brown dress that rose to her chin in a high ruffled collar and fell stiffly against her ankles. Her mouth was set in a straight line, and her dirty blonde hair was loose with not a single strand astray.

"Come with me, child," she said to Bugs.

"Hello, I'm Emma."

"Yes, I know." She nodded and took Bugs away.

"Nice to meet you, too," I whispered. Schizo opened one eye and looked at me. "Never mind. Go back to sleep."

Sleep.

I took the old rug off the floor and rolled it up. What I thought were decorative orange dots were stains, and I avoided them as best I could. I dropped the old rug outside the unit and placed the new rug next to the mattress, presumably where my feet would land in the morning. The room looked more livable with my minor touches. I thought about Cooper and the food he was meant to be bringing. I stretched out on the mattress, minding Schizo, who moaned despite my carefulness. The bed was comfortable, with no revolting springs or offending firmness. I wanted to shower before I slept and eat before I showered, but you can't always get what you want. Cooper hadn't shown me where a bathroom was, and I wasn't about to go wandering around without a flashlight or a clue.

I closed my eyes, and a nightmare came knocking.

~

He's a man in black, his thoughts and his clothes.

A long time ago, the act of another put the dark in his veins, and it's been there ever since. The night he lost his true love, his heart and his brain became one, so that his heart was scheming and his brain was loving. *That doesn't sound so bad,* my dream-self thought, but suddenly I could feel it, and it was very bad indeed—for when a brain loves, it is only out of obsession, and when a heart schemes, it does not mean well.

My dream soul shivers, and I understand that the only way the Man in Black can ease his pain is to find the one he loved and lost and stir up much madness and mayhem along the way.

I force myself from the Man in Black's thoughts and am surprised to find my arms swallowed up by an enormous brain. Pink, blubbery layers are tight up to my armpits. I twist and tug, and my arms are released with a sickly *squoish*. I hurry through an ear canal and tumble out into a void, before grasping desperately at a pale, pierced lobe. The Man in Black plucks me off his ear and dangles me in front of his face like a mouse.

Only the lower half of the Man's face is showing, with the rest disappearing into tumultuous purple clouds. He opens his mouth wide, and a billion maggots jerk from it like possessed fried rice, until his chin is completely covered. *This doesn't scare me*, my dream-self thought. But the teeth.

Those teeth could drive a person mad.

I kick out of his grasp, and he bids me farewell with a flutter of skeletal fingers. I fly fly away, over the city of angels, through Bug's painted window, and into my sleeping eyes.

Peter fucking Pan.

CHAPTER NINE

IT WAS AN OFFERING FROM HEAVEN...

...for the hell I had just escaped and the one I had just reentered.

I sat up and feasted my eyes.

The most perfect sandwich was in front of me on a round white plate. Turkey cuts stuck out from between four thick, toasted slices of wheat bread. The sandwich had been sectioned into triangles, and each section was tooth-picked and garnished with an olive. A generous amount of chips bathed in the juice from a nearby pickle.

Next to my sandwich plate was a smaller plate of assorted meats, I guessed for Schizo. Even if the extra meat hadn't been for him, his nose and tongue had already claimed it as his own. The short stack was mostly bologna, but there was some turkey and a couple of uncooked hotdogs. Schizo was overjoyed.

I made sure to eat slowly, though my taste buds screamed *GO!* I was just finishing when Cooper showed up. I wiped my mouth with the backside of hand since I didn't have a napkin. I put my plate down, and Schizo jumped to action, inhaling what little was left. The plate rattled against the floor with Schizo's tongue lapping against it.

Cooper stood in the doorway, looking freshly showered and rested.

"Thanks for the sandwich," I said. "It was fantastic. Schizo says 'thank you' too."

Cooper looked down at his feet. "Well, I didn't make it, but no problem," he said. "Get some sleep?"

"Enough," I said, standing up.

There was something about sitting on the bed and talking to Cooper that made me uncomfortable. I felt the same way standing. Cooper anxiously shifted his weight in the doorway, as if passing the unit's threshold might catapult him into another dimension.

"You decorated," Cooper said.

I didn't think adding sheets and a rug was decorating, but I let him have it. We seemed to be struggling for conversation and any was better than none. Cooper continued: "I know it's not a huge selection to choose from, but there's some more stuff up on six. You can add personal touches later…if you decide to stay."

Personal touches? I thought. The place needed a personal smack upside the head.

"Okay," I nodded. "Yeah, so I met Mary." I saw a slight panic wash over Cooper's face.

"What'd she say?"

"Oh, nothing. She didn't have much to say…to me."

Relief. "Mary's kind of had a hard time of things. Scott's busy, so she spends a lot of time by herself. When she's not alone, she's with Bugs. Her room's just there." Cooper pointed to the right. I remembered from the tour.

"She's into religion, huh?"

"It's a new thing. We got some books from a local library—mostly research stuff. But the Bible was one of them, and Mary became *attached* to it."

"She's not going to strap me to a tree and burn me alive, is she?"

"Not today."

I laughed. "Good to know."

Cooper returned my smile, but like the ones before, it was quick.

159

Here today, gone today. "So you ready to meet everyone?"

It was time for my smile to falter. I didn't think I was ready. Meeting people under such odd circumstances was difficult. What would I say? I could start with the usual:

"Hi. I'm Em."

(But then?)

"How 'bout those vampires?"

or

"You stabbed a gynecologist? Me too!"

or

"Crazy thing"

(and they'd say) "What's that?"

(and I'd say) "Absolutely everything."

I wasn't sure what I was doing. These people thought what they thought and they'd go on thinking it. They would want to talk about vampires, for sure. Probably a lot. I decided I would listen and nod when they brought up the "V" word, but not say anything. Besides, not long ago, they had gone through what I was going through—the doubt, the suspicion, the fright. *It won't be so bad*, I thought. It was just talking, after all.

"Mind if I take a shower first and change my clothes?"

Sweet, sweet procrastination.

~

Cooper led me down a flight of stairs. A weak bulb messed with our shadows.

Above, fourth floor lights buzzed on and accompanied us on our walk to the bathroom. The motion-sensor lighting made me feel as if we were heading somewhere of great importance, controlling light like gods as we went.

The bathroom was snug between two locked units. Inside were three toilet stalls and a single shower, sink, and urinal. I wondered if many people had taken advantage of the shower when the place was in business. In a way, it was brilliant idea:

Get a little grimy ditching old memories? Scrub yourself afterward and really finish them off.

Cooper opened a cabinet next to the sink and tossed me a towel from it. "I'll leave some fresh clothes outside your door," he said and was gone. I was quickly learning that he wasn't much one for goodbyes, and I wondered if this was a habit from youth or something much newer.

I noticed a mirror above the sink and ran by it without looking. We were not on good terms. I got in the shower and stripped off my clothes. I winced pulling my shirt up over my head. I had forgotten all about my injury, and the bandage, too—the one I had been wearing since my arrival, like a wounded soldier returning from battle. I felt myself blush. *No wonder why everyone was looking at me strangely.*

I carefully undid the bandage and slung it over the curtain rod with my clothes. This time, it wasn't bloody. I turned the water on and let the spray beat my skin. I rode through the pain of the water on the back of my head.

There were two travel-size bottles of shampoo and conditioner in the stall. No soap, so I used the shampoo on my hair and body. I finished washing and stood watching the water and suds get swallowed by the drain. I imagined the water was my worry being sucked down underneath the shower floor to spend all eternity nestled in a slimy snarl of hair.

The lights in the bathroom flickered and turned off, and I waved my arms back and forth, feeling the pressure of the dark on my chest.

"Damn lights," I said aloud, only after they had come back on.

I dried and got back into my clothes with big exaggerated movements to keep the bathroom lit. I could have wrapped the towel around me and made a dash for my unit, but I wasn't feeling comfortable enough for that. The clothes Cooper gave me at the church were still relatively clean, and I felt I could make it back to my unit before any dirt from the clothes settled onto my skin.

I bolted past the bathroom mirror to the door. Reconciliation would have to happen at some point, but not today.

~

A change of clothes was waiting for me outside my unit. Everything fit. Not perfectly but better than before.

There were no shoes this time, too big or otherwise. My old sneakers were a nauseating sight. It was the dried blood—a grisly union of Myers and his victims. I felt bad that the poor girls were being forced to mingle with Myers after death, on the surface of my sneakers. A stringy pink substance stuck to the toe of my right shoe. It looked like chewed bubblegum, but I knew better.

I glanced around the room for something to scrape it off with, but I had no possessions, which made starting a search pointless. I honed in on Schizo's chewy Jesus but rid my head of the thought. It was wrong in every way, the main being that scraping a funky substance off my sneaker with a cross had to be some sort of sacrilege. Schizo *was* using it as his chew toy, but as a canine, he was protected. He didn't know any better. I was human with a human mind and would have to deal with any moral consequences.

I wasn't religious but thought better safe than sorry.

Schizo peered at me through one eye, like he knew what I had just considered and very much disapproved.

"I wasn't going to *do* it," I said.

I went into the hallway. Bugs' door was closed, as was Sammy's and the rest. I knelt down and scraped my shoe along the sharp edge of the doorway. The pink matter came off without much fight and fell quietly to the floor as if compensating for its offensiveness.

"Everything fits?"

Cooper appeared from out of nowhere and scared the crap out of me, like Bugs had earlier. It seemed the residents of Seepy Storage were very good at sneaking.

"I was just cleaning my shoes," I said. "They're dirty." *Nothing like stating the obvious.*

Of course, the scraping hadn't gotten the stains off and Cooper looked down at my blood-covered shoe and didn't ask whose blood it was or how it ended up there. Apparently, blood was the new accessory.

"The clothes?"

"Oh, yeah, they fit fine. Where'd you get them?"

"Sammy's sister was about your size. She was tall for her age."

I was wearing a dead girl's clothes.

All of the items still had the tags on and looked like they hadn't been worn, but they were taken for Cara to wear one day and that meant something. I suddenly felt like tearing them off my body. It was ridiculous thinking that a dead girl's clothes could kill you, but you can't help what you think.

Cooper was looking at me expectantly. I put my carnage sneakers

163

on and called Schizo. He came, slipping the cross in his mouth along the way. I still didn't feel ready for any meetings, but all good procrastination must come to an end.

"Okay. I'm ready."

"You'll meet Scott first," Cooper said. "His office is upstairs." I remembered Scott being the one who knew things, the one who could explain everything.

"Let's go."

~

Upstairs, dark curtains revealed slivers of a blue starry night.

Actual offices, and not units posing as offices, lined the hallway. Cooper knocked on a door, which was ajar and pulsed in response. Soft light from inside spilled through the door crack and onto Cooper's face, marking it like war paint. A voice told us to enter.

A man, presumably Scott, was sitting at a square, wooden table. He looked a young forty, with thin eyes and pepper hair that also covered his chin and circled his mouth. Ivory candles with molten wax feet dressed the table, and flames on top hopped on wicks. Several books and a tape recorder were nearby. When we entered, the man rose from his seat and walked toward us.

He was shorter than me by a few inches but stood like he got all the height he could ever need. He smiled a real smile, and Cooper made introductions. "Scott St. Martin, Emma Spade," he said. "Emma Spade, Scott St. Martin." Our hands met halfway.

"Mr. St. Martin," I said.

"Please, call me Scott."

Schizo whined, feeling left out. Scott knelt down to ruffle his fur. Schizo was a dog and licked him.

"Who's this guy?"

"Emma's dog Schizo," Cooper said.

"Unusual name. Doesn't seem to fit him," Scott said.

"Oh, it does," I said. "He just likes to pretend to be normal."

Scott laughed and gestured at two empty seats. "Please. Sit. Sit. Emma, I'd like to say I've heard so much about you, but it's actually been very little. Cooper and you had a quick first meeting under strange circumstances."

"Yes," I said. "They were...strange." I sat after Cooper did, taking the seat next to Scott. I looked around.

The office was double the size of the residential units. The walls were papered white, and tightly blinded windows ran the length of the room. Three large pieces of furniture dominated the space: a desk, a wooden screen, and a bookcase. On the desk was a silver suitcase with a combination lock. Behind the screen was a twin bed, the rumpled end of which could be seen from where we sat. In the bookcase were some novels I recognized, others I didn't, packed horizontally and vertically.

I found the room to be cozy, with candles surrounding us in varying stages of melt and a carpet that made me want to be barefoot. Paintings hung from the walls, mostly landscapes. They were Monet knockoffs and I suspected paint-by-numbers. A plastic fire clicked on the floor behind us, its orange light making me sleepy.

"Found that at a thrift store," Scott said. The plastic fire must have been leaking warmth because Schizo went over to settle by it. Scott continued: "Never had a house with a real fireplace in L.A. I do miss that sound—the crackling. You don't get that sound with candles much...or fake fires." He smiled. "Where you from, Emma?"

"Boston."

165

"Ah, got the cold winters there."

"Yeah, plus I go to school in Syracuse, so I guess I have a penchant for torturing myself."

"Don't we all?"

"I guess."

I liked Scott, so far. He was easy to talk to, and when he smiled, it was with his mouth *and* his eyes. Most people wouldn't see the importance in such a thing but meet a stranger and know it's a good sign.

Scott offered us drinks, and I said water would "do me fine." I'm not sure why I said it like that—like I had just sidled up to the bar at a Wild West saloon. Scott stood and went to a fridge next to the bookcase. It was small and brown and identical to the one I had in my dorm room freshman year. He pulled out three bottles of spring water. My mouth went dry, and I hoped no one would ask me anything until I had gotten a sip. Scott handed Cooper and I a bottle each and poured the third into a bowl for Schizo.

"If you don't mind, I'm going to help myself to a bit of scotch? It's been one of those days."

I shook my head and cracked open the bottle of water. I was sure that every day in Seepy Storage was one of *those* days.

Things settled. Scott sat with his scotch. The room was comfortably hydrated. Silence set in, and business was at hand.

"Do you know what's happened, Emma?"

"Just what Cooper told me."

"So you haven't seen them? The vampires?"

"No, I've seen *people*," I said. "Disturbed people suffering from some sort of...of dementia." Scott held his hand up.

"Please don't call them people. They're so far from human you couldn't possibly imagine." Scott took a sip of his scotch. He rolled his lips inward. "Accepting such misconceptions will get you killed...or much worse."

A candle extinguished. I didn't think the others noticed.

Scott continued: "That's why by the time you leave this room you'll know the truth, Emma. And then we can take it from there."

I nodded. My heart forgot to beat. I looked at Cooper, he looked back.

"It's time," Scott said, "to forget everything you know about the history of your country." Scott leaned back in his chair until I was sure it would topple. "Because it's all wrong."

THEN:
SCOTT ST. MARTIN

Scott St. Martin was a patriot.

Like his father before him, and his father before him, Scott believed that protecting the country like it was your own child was every citizen's duty. Scott's great-grandfather had fought in World War I, his grandfather in World War II, and his father in Vietnam. In hindsight, each man was weighed down by their medals and their pride.

Scott's parents had him late in life. Both died when he was just a boy at the hands of an alcoholic named Henry Ryan who swallowed down one drink too many and took them out going the wrong way down I-95. His father's head was knocked clean off and found the next day in the forest fifty feet from the scene of the accident. At least that was what Scott read years later.

His parent's house was sold, and Scott went to live with his aunt and uncle a whole state away. He loved the name of his relatives' street and said it over and over when the car first pulled up to his new home and later that night to lull himself to sleep in a strange bed.

Whisper Lane. Whisper Lane. Whisper Lane.

His aunt and uncle lived on a farm and made enough to get by. They had one child, a girl two years younger than Scott. After his aunt squeezed out Beth Ann, his uncle became infertile, and they blamed it on the television. The "devil box" was thrown out, replaced by an old radio that got one station on a good day.

Scott did well in school. Lots of people have their things. His dad's was the military. Getting good grades was his. He graduated high school first in his class and four years later With Honors from Georgetown. Life had been bad after he lost his parents, but books became his surrogate guardians. They told him what he could expect from the world and what he was meant to give back.

Scott stayed at Georgetown to pursue a master's in international relations. He was starting his final year when he met Mr. Frank. It was at a bar he never went to and over a drink he never drank. It just made sense that a complete stranger would take the stool next to his and introduce himself.

"I'm Mr. Frank," the man said, his hand extended.

"Okay," Scott said, not looking. He thought the guy was hitting on him, and although he was fine with the existence of homosexuals, being hit on by one was a whole other story. His books hadn't taught him how to handle that.

"I'm giving you my hand," Mr. Frank said. "You might want to take it."

Scott looked at him. He had shaggy blonde hair and perfect teeth. He wore a black pea coat, collar up.

"That's not a threat, is it?"

"No. Just friendly advice."

Scott wasn't sure how friendly it was, but he took Mr. Frank's hand anyway. The shake was firm. On the stage, the lead guitarist played a riff that made Scott's ears hurt.

"*Mr*. Scott," he said, over the noise.

Mr. Frank smiled big. "*Scott St. Martin*," he said, like Scott was the next contestant on the Price Is Right. "Let's get down to it."

"Wait, how do you know my name?"

"We've been watching your progress over the years, and we like what we see. We want you to work for us." Mr. Frank caught the bartender's attention. "Johnny Walker. Neat."

"Who's *we*?"

"The government. You've got what it takes, kid."

"I do?"

"Yep."

Scott had heard about things like this happening. Recruiters tapping the university to get the best of the best. Despite his exceptional grades, Scott never viewed himself in such high regard. Though, he did recognize an opportunity when one was presented and could turn the confidence on at a moment's notice.

"Thank you, sir. I've been working hard. I've got one more year, but I expect the offers to be coming through soon. Can I ask what division?" Mr. Frank's drink arrived at the bar.

"The Central Intelligence Agency, kid," he said, standing. He took a sip of his drink, squinted, and put it down. "That's real good. You should get one."

A business card landed in front of Scott—a wad of bills on the bar. "Give me a call. You've got a good future with us."

Scott picked up the card and read it: "Special Services Director, Mr. Frank." The emblem with the eagle's head was in the left-hand corner. It looked official, Scott thought, but how many professional business cards didn't display a person's first name?

"You scare easy, kid?"

"No, sir," Scott replied, but when he looked up Mr. Frank was already gone, making his way through the crowd to the exit. His glass was still on the bar, full.

Scott went home and propped Mr. Frank's card against the phone. It was Friday night, so he waited until Monday to call. Mr. Frank answered on the first ring.

"Mr. Frank, Scott St. Martin. How are you?"

"Scott, I was expecting your call. Have you decided?"

"I'm very interested. Should we schedule an interview?"

"No interviews, kid. Just a couple tests. Pass those and you're good as gold. I've got faith in you."

"Okay. Thank you, Mr. Frank." Scott paused. "I did tell you that I'm still studying, right? I'm in the final year of my master's program."

"You've got to quit that, Scott. We need you now. Think about it. Call me back." The line went dead.

It took two days for Scott to accept Mr. Frank's offer. He looked at it like this: he was going into the family business. He'd been born to serve his country and serve it he would. So it wasn't as overt as serving in the military, but it was service just the same. There would be no medals, but Scott didn't feel like he would need them.

"Service to my country is reward enough," Scott said aloud after closing the door to the cab. Scott looked up. The building in front of him was a dilapidated hovel. He flipped open his notebook and read the scribble:

"One-Nineteen Tracy Street."

The numbers on the building's front corresponded. Scott climbed the stairs. The door was unlocked. He took the elevator to the second floor. When the doors opened, a large rat squealed and scurried under a broken armchair.

The second floor was an open room with surrounding windows. Some were broken, letting in the cold from outside. Scott could see his breath. Besides the armchair, there was no other furniture. A gray carpet under his feet looked fire-damaged, and the room smelled like smoke. A man who wasn't Mr. Frank was standing in a corner when Scott got off the elevator. Now he approached him. He had mottled skin and a thick head of hair.

"Hello," Scott said. "I'm here to see Mr. Frank."

The man handed Scott a folded piece of paper. Scott opened it. An address was written in purple ink.

"Mr. Frank will meet you at that address in 20 minutes," the man said.

"Twenty minutes? This is across the city. It won't be enough time."

"Twenty minutes," the man said, again.

Scott, accepting that the man was just a messenger, made a dash for the elevator.

NOW:

"I made it there in 22 minutes," Scott said. "To this day, I have no idea how." Scott laughed and looked down at his glass, empty except for a few ice cubes. He shook it. "Of course, he wasn't there—Mr. Frank. It was just another messenger who told me to come back the next day."

The door to the office opened. Mary, Scott's wife, stood there. Her face was red and swollen. Her hair had gotten unkempt since last I saw her. There were three of us in the room, and two looked very worried. Cooper stood.

"You okay, honey?" Scott asked. "Need me to get you something?"

Mary made a sound like a growl and charged toward us. Cooper moved but not fast enough. She raised her hand and brought it down in a fist on the table. The candles' wax bodies separated from their feet and jumped to attention. Her fingers came out of the fist separated and curled like a cat's claws.

"You can get us back our *son*," Mary said, "instead of sitting up here telling your stories."

She rushed at Scott, and Cooper stepped in to hold her back. He put an arm around her waist and moved her toward the door.

"He's alive, Scott," Mary said, over her shoulder. "Our son is alive and I'm going to be with him. I'd rather be one of them and be with my son than spend another day in this place with you!"

Cooper got her into the hallway and closed the door behind them. I was alone with Scott in the aftermath. He had stayed silent the whole time and didn't even stand to defend himself when his wife came at him. He just sat staring at a spot on the table that I was sure would start to smoke. Scott finally raised his eyes and spoke.

"My wife and I lost our son. He was taken. We're pretty sure he

172

was part of the first stage. Cooper told you about the statues?"

I nodded. He nodded.

"Yes, well...my wife...she hasn't been the same. The religion seemed to sedate her for a bit. I guess being with the CIA for so long helped prepare me for something like this, but my wife...she never had any training. She was just trying to be a good mother."

Scott stood and went back to the fridge. He unscrewed a bottle of Glen Fiddich and suspended the bottle's opening over his glass.

"She never knew about my employment with the CIA until it all went down and I finally revealed the truth," Scott continued, still holding the bottle but not yet pouring. "I had to tell her that I knew about the vampires for 12 years. I had to tell her that our son was taken because of what I did."

Scott upended the bottle and poured the remainder into his glass. He grinned grimly before reapplying the cap to the empty bottle and placing it back on top of the fridge. He sat down next to me, a tsunami in his glass.

"That monster couldn't deal with me leaving him."

THEN:
SCOTT ST. MARTIN

Scott St. Martin relocated to Los Angeles and worked as an undercover operative for five years, with Mr. Frank as his handler. He saw the world and spent time in its shadows. As Chance would have it, he fell in love and started to think about a life without the burden he'd so readily accepted half a decade ago.

Her name was Mary, and she was what he'd been missing. He met girls over the years, committed to a few short-term relationships. Scott found it unfortunate that the question of what he did for a living was generally asked within the first few minutes of meeting a person. Sometimes he lied. Mostly he said his goodbyes early. With Mary, his desire to have her around was much stronger than the guilt of lying to her about what he did. Every morning in the mirror when Mary slept, and at that split second before he blew a man's brains out, he said:

For the sake of my country.

They married after six months of dating. It was a small wedding with the groom's side suffering comparatively in numbers. Mr. Frank attended as Scott's best man. Scott looked over at him during the ceremony and saw a spy, which made him wonder how many people recognized something strange about the man but couldn't quite put a finger on it.

Mr. Frank gifted the happy couple with a blender. For most, a blender was not an unusual gift. For Scott, the appliance, with its sharp blades and puree setting, reminded him of a particularly distasteful job in Salzburg. Mr. Frank had been with The Company too long, and killing had turned comical. Maybe it was how he coped. Whatever it was, Scott knew the moment he opened that gift that he wanted out. A card was attached:

Congrats to you both.
Scott, you've been promoted.

Mary was ecstatic for him. If only she knew. He had it in his mind to quit the day he got home from his honeymoon and arranged to meet Mr. Frank at the office. He had it in his mind, but it would take much more than that.

~

"I'm promoting you to handle, kid," Mr. Frank said, putting a match to the chunky end of a cigar. He'd disemboweled the smoke alarm in his office years ago. It sat above them with its guts hanging out.

"I'm leaving, Frank," Scott said, determination in his voice. A couple years earlier, he would have jumped at the chance to handle. It took ten years minimum for an operative to even be considered for the job.

His boss puffed on the cigar. He exhaled. For a moment, smoke hid his face. "You'll stay in L.A. You'll be traveling less so get used to spending more time with that lovely wife of yours."

"Did you hear me, Frank?"

"An extra 30K, plus a new company car. They've got the VarioRam on the Nine-Nine-Three."

Scott stood. He placed the envelope containing his resignation letter on the desk in front of his now ex-boss. He turned to go. Mr. Frank cleared his throat.

"Your father would've wanted you to know."

Scott stopped. He felt like he had just been hit in the stomach with a giant fist. He turned around.

"You knew my father?" Mr. Frank motioned for Scott to sit down. Scott stayed standing. "You *knew* my father and you've never said anything? All these years?"

"It's the CIA, not Disneyland, kid. Lock the door and take a seat." Scott did as he was told. Mr. Frank waited. Only when Scott was seated did he continue: "I want to show you something," Mr. Frank said, smiling. When he smiled, he looked like Jack Nicholson. It was the eyebrows. "It's pretty fucking amazing."

Mr. Frank gripped a remote in his thick hand. He pressed the red power button, and the television in the wall turned on. It went from a blue screen to a room Scott had grown all too familiar with. The orange walls were a dead giveaway.

CHAPTER TEN

ORANGE MAKES PEOPLE CONFESS THINGS.

If that doesn't work, there are other ways.

When an agent had the luxury of time, they took the silent types to an orange room. These rooms were all around the world, supposedly for convenience, but Scott knew better.

The Company liked to keep tabs.

Most of the orange rooms had cameras installed, but the picture on the screen now was shaky which meant a handheld was being used. Either the installed camera had broken, so a handheld was being used as a last resort (highly unlikely since technology was the CIA's forte), or the installed camera was turned off against regulation and a handheld was being used possibly for nefarious reasons. The recording could have been taken for an agent's personal collection—Scott had heard of that before. Sick bastards are out there and some are working for the government.

The lens focused.

A man was tied to a chair. Scott didn't recognize him. It could've been anyone, but it was someone who knew something. Usually.

The man looked like he was of South American descent. He was well-muscled and his chest bulged under his shirt. He stared straight ahead. Scott knew the look in the man's eyes. He was going to be a tough one to crack.

Scott felt tense and wanted to leave. He had seen this type of thing a million times. To rephrase that, he had participated in this type of thing a million times. But he was staying for the information Mr. Frank had about his father.

"Is it on?" said a man's voice off-camera.

"Yeah, we're rolling."

According to the voices, two men were in the room with the prisoner. One stepped into the frame. He was tall and lean, with black hair that fell to his shoulders. He wore a black suit and tie. Scott marveled at the paleness of his skin. The man stood in front of the prisoner. The camera captured a side view.

In zero seconds flat, the prisoner went from tough as nails to panic-stricken. He started to scream. Scott couldn't understand what was happening and thought there might be a third agent off-screen threatening the man. Scott leaned forward for a better view. The camera zoomed in, which was when Scott saw it.

"No," he said. "That can't be."

The interrogator's teeth were growing.

He opened his mouth wide and two teeth poked out from beneath his upper lip. They looked as sharp as razors. The camera zoomed out.

The prisoner screamed and fought against his ropes. Terror ruled him. Tears, snot, and spit drenched his face. His neck muscles strained. He said something, but Scott couldn't say what. Then he spoke again, this time louder.

"MONITOR!" he said. "It's in my...my computer monitor. I beg of you...get him away!"

The interrogator took a step back. The prisoner calmed down but continued to weep. The interrogator looked into the camera and smiled, "This is just too easy."

"Is he telling the truth?" asked the voice behind the camera, calm.

"What do you think?" said the interrogator.

He chuckled, then turned back to the prisoner and straddled him. He bit into his neck, wrapping his whole jaw around it. When he took his mouth away, the prisoner's head fell back like the top of a Pez dispenser. His throat had been torn out.

Blood was everywhere.

Mr. Frank pointed the remote at the television and the screen went black.

"Is this some kind of joke?" Scott asked.

"No joke."

"What was that thing?"

"That was a vampire. He works for us. Decent guy."

"He just ripped the prisoner's throat out," Scott said, raising his voice.

"You've done worse than that, kid. In fact, we all have. If anything, killing their way is better than killing our way. They kill for food—the bodies don't go to waste."

Scott felt sick. Not because of the blood or what the thing in the video did. He could handle that. It was the sudden realization that he wasn't leaving the CIA and it would be his thirst for knowledge that kept him there.

"How was my father involved?"

"Your dad worked for us as Mabon's handler for ten years," Mr. Frank said, pointing at the TV screen. "He and your dad were pretty close." Mr. Frank stubbed his cigar into a brown glass ashtray with a palm tree on it.

"It's Project Sunset, Scott. The Company's best-kept secret. We've got five suckers—Mabon was the first. He brought the others along later. They joined the OSS during the Second World War. Word has it that Mabon approached Donovan in a bar much like I approached you."

William J. Donovan was the creator of the Office of Strategic Services or OSS, the CIA's predecessor. It was established in June of 1942 to counteract American intelligence deficiencies. Donovan was a war veteran, a Medal of Honor recipient, and an overall well-liked man.

Mr. Frank handed Scott a folder and continued: "We employ them like we do our human operatives. They gather intelligence and earn a salary." Mr. Frank's cell phone rang. He picked it up, looked at the number and then put it back down. "You see, what you've got to understand here, kid, is that vampires and the CIA are a perfect fit. We're the real dream team."

"Because they like to kill?" Scott asked.

"No, it's not just that," Mr. Frank said. "They're born hunters, good at tracking prey and smelling fear. They don't use weapons, which is great on the budget and, in turn, easier on the American taxpayer. They're pretty tough to kill, and let's be honest, how many of our enemies are expecting monster spies?"

Scott had read about vampires in books and seen them in movies. He racked his brain. A stake through the heart killed them, along with sunlight. They didn't eat but needed blood to survive. Holy water was like acid, garlic repulsed them. They could hypnotize with their eyes. They slept in coffins. They could control wolves and turn into bats. Bad breath. Pointy ears.

Scott opened the folder on his lap. Mabon Blackwell was at the top of the pile and looked the same in his photo as he did on television. He was smiling. His teeth were normal size. No pointy ears. His date of birth was listed as June 3, 1840. Birthplace: Savannah, Georgia.

Four others followed. Three males and one female. They originated from different places, all in the States, all born well before both World Wars. All meant to be long dead.

"Can they fly?" Scott asked. It was such a surreal question. He doubted anyone had ever asked that about an operative before.

"Don't be an idiot, Scott," Mr. Frank said.

Scott's face felt hot.

"They can't fly, and they can't turn themselves into fuzzy, little animals. They can't control people with their eyes, but they're damn good lie detectors. They fry in sunlight, work at night. They don't mind garlic so much, but crosses and holy water can be bothersome. Stake through the heart kills. Crows are a nuisance."

"Crows?"

"They've acquired a taste for vampire flesh. We've made a spray similar to mosquito spray, just more pungent."

"Are there any more of them…out there? Besides the five?"

"Plenty more—but we've got the patriots."

"They're patriots?"

"As true as you and me."

Scott looked down at the file photo of Mabon Blackwell. Vampire. Patriot.

"When can I meet him?"

Mr. Frank grinned from ear to ear.

NOW:

I felt like I had just dropped my lunch tray.

When I used to eat at the cafeteria up on the hill my freshman year, it would happen a few times a week to some poor student: the loud crash, the clang of silverware, the dish that got away, rolling off on its edge and settling noisily. And then there was that second afterward—when everyone waits.

The tray dropper pauses in dread for a reaction, including but not limited to, clapping or laughter from the crowd. The crowd waits for a person to rise among its ranks and react first.

Cooper had returned. The three of us, including the dog, were now staring at Scott St. Martin. When Scott finished, no one moved. We all just waited. The air was thick. I jumped in my skin when I realized the attention had shifted from Scott to me. Against all odds, I had become the tray dropper.

What to say evaded me. Scott told an unbelievable story and that was just my problem…believing it. There was something bad going on out there, and I wasn't about to debate that. But vampires? They weren't real. They couldn't be.

Crows are a nuisance.

What Scott's boss had said would explain the amount of crows in the city and their strange behavior. The woman with the little boy had had a spray can.

No.

It was more like Waco, Texas. I was being trapped in the sticky fingers of a cult. Things went aslant and these people holed themselves up in some dead-end storage facility to talk about demons and the end of the world.

Scott got up from his chair. I thought he was going to pour himself another alcoholic beverage, but instead he put his empty glass on top of the fridge and pulled open the door to grab a bottle of water. He held one out for me and I accepted.

"You think we're crazy," Scott said.

"I didn't say that."

"I can read it on your face."

I slackened my face.

"That doesn't help," he said, with a smile.

"I'm not sure what to think. Maybe I need more information?"

"Fair enough."

"Project Sunset," I said. Scott nodded. "Did those vampires have something to do with what's going on now?"

"Everything."

"That's not very patriotic."

"I agree. Mabon hated this country. He hid it well. I tried to warn Frank before I left, but he wouldn't listen. Stubbornness got him. Mabon got him next."

THEN:
SCOTT ST. MARTIN

Scott met his first vampire at a Krispy Kreme.

His newly acquired operative had picked the place, and at the time, Scott couldn't think of a reason not to meet there. It would be crowded—more children, fewer spies. Good donuts. He worried about putting innocent civilians in harm's way but decided to put his foot down and snub any preconceptions.

Scott got there early and sat at a table in the corner, watching donuts on the path to cardboard boxes and salivating mouths. He wasn't one for sweets but thought he might bring a few back for Mary. He had told her he was working late at the office. He was always working late. International banking proved a demanding career.

"You look like your father."

You look like your father. It was the first thing Mabon Blackwell said to him, and Scott realized then why he had taken the promotion after being so ready to quit. He knew very little about who his father was, what kind of man he had been. Scott's curiosity was never fully fed by the boxes of photographs, letters, and newspaper articles; those things did not make a man. They gathered dust and created a flawed picture of someone who had once been alive.

Mabon knew Scott's father for longer than Scott and from an adult's perspective. His father had had few close friends in his life. Scott found that out when he got old enough to go looking. In the end, his father's job had been his life. His life had been the CIA.

It explained everything. Scott should've known.

"Do I?" Scott had asked. His memory failed him, but he had seen plenty of photos and never came to that conclusion.

The vampire sat across from him. Tall. Lethal. He looked like he did on the recording, but his skin was less translucent, even rosy, like he had just been exerting himself. His blue eyes were pale, but cloudy. Scott wondered how old he was when he died. Early twenties?

Mabon observed him, smirking. He wore a similar suit to the one on the recording. Scott knew it couldn't be the same one. It was too clean.

"How are things, Scott St. Martin?" he asked, a Georgian accent playing up. Scott hadn't noticed it before.

"Good. Fine. I wanted to meet and get acquainted before we started working together."

"That's not very CIA."

"I guess I'm not very CIA, then."

"Neither was your father."

"No?"

"I was sorry to hear about the accident. He was a good man. I didn't hold it against him."

"Uh...thanks," Scott said, feeling at a loss for words for the first time in his life. "So Mr. Frank tells me you're a patriot?"

"God bless the United States."

"I wouldn't think of you as the blessing kind."

Mabon shrugged. "Some people see me as a monster, but I've been serving my country for over 60 years. Longer than you've been alive."

Scott didn't feel he could argue with that. "Where did it come from...the patriotism?"

"My father was a soldier."

"Oh, in which war?"

"The Civil War." Scott choked on some spit. Mabon waited until he recovered to continue. "My father fought and died for the Confederacy. I guess that gives us something in common—both our old men being taken away from us while in service to their country."

"That gets me to my point. I was hoping you could tell me about him...about my father."

Mabon wasn't looking at Scott anymore. He followed his gaze to a woman crossing the street. She was tanned and curvy with long brown hair and dimpled cheeks.

"I hate to cut this short, but my date has arrived."

"Your date…uh, so soon? I really wanted to talk—"

"All we got is time, Scotty," Mabon said, holding his arms out as if ready to wrap them around all that time.

Scott wasn't appreciating his new nickname, which to him sounded patronizing. He looked at the woman approaching and wondered if she knew what she was getting herself into. He thought the same might be asked of him. Scott leaned closer to Mabon who still had his attention on the woman.

"You're not going to drink her blood, are you?" he whispered.

Mabon laughed. It was loud, and people stared. He leaned in, so their noses were nearly touching, and Scott jerked upright. His eyes were all pupil. "I didn't ask if you were going to go home and fuck your wife. Spare me the same courtesy."

They said goodbyes, which was no more than a nod from Mabon. Scott used *I'll be in touch* which was what Mr. Frank would always say to end their meetings. On his way out, Scott brushed by the vampire's date. She smiled at him.

It was the sweetest smile he had ever seen.

~

The meeting that night with Mabon was strange, and there would be plenty more like it to follow.

Scott left feeling empty-handed except for the knowledge that Mabon was a cocky son of a bitch and he possibly murdered innocent civilians in his spare time. Scott couldn't see his father having a close bond with someone like Mabon. He knew it was possible Mr. Frank had lied about the closeness of their relationship in order to convince Scott to stay with The Company. It was possible, but Scott's father had been Mabon's handler for ten years. A long time—for a human.

Mr. Frank was telling the truth about one thing that day: vampires made good operatives.

And Mabon was the best.

Over the years, Scott kept a close eye on his vampire. He arrived at the understanding that he only ever knew what Mabon wanted him to know. With the human operatives, this kind of deceptiveness would be seen as a liability, but with the vampires, The Company simply accepted it as a part of the package. To them, the package was glorious, and Mabon, a golden boy.

During Scott's time as Mabon's handler, every mission assigned was successfully completed. Intel flowed like blood. Scott accepted the way Mabon did things because it worked, but when he found himself at one of the vampire's interrogations, he usually made a quick exit. Watching it on the television screen that day in Mr. Frank's office had been different. Violence displayed on a screen is easier to dismiss than live atrocities.

Out of the five vampires, Mabon had the record for getting people to spill their secrets the fastest. Prisoners were offering up their firstborns in four seconds flat. When Mabon or another one of the Project Sunset operatives was brought in, prisoners had one-way tickets to dead. The Company implemented the vampires when a situation was dire and things needed to get messy before they could improve. It was something Scott could never hold against Mabon. After all, he was just doing his job. But it was the glee plastered across the vampire's face when he killed that made Scott uncomfortable. Mabon thrived on people's fear of him. In the orange room, he never walked, he'd strut. Maiming was grand. Blood was his everything. It dripped from the ceilings when he was done.

The mess drove up cleaning costs, and what Sunset saved the American taxpayer on weapons, it made up for in dry-cleaning alone. The vampires had a crew, the Sweepers, on call twenty-four-seven. They followed the vampires in an unmarked van filled with bleach, mops, and freshly laundered suits.

Though Scott tried, the battle with his conscience never ended.

He knew the bloodbath had become less for the good of the country and more for the good of Sunset. The vampire was the U.S. government's ultimate secret weapon. Behind closed doors, the CIA, together with the NSA, cultivated its crop of natural-born killers with plans to recruit more vampires and create an army of undead that would devote their immortal lives to the United States of America.

The day Scott decided to get out was the day he re-sorted his priorities. Deep down, Scott had been fascinated by the vampires and remained so right up to his last mission on November 29, 2002.

It was the day Mary told him she was pregnant and the day he read the manuscript.

THE MANUSCRIPT

Scott and Mabon were waiting.

They stood quietly outside of writer Stanford Smith's ranch house in Simi Valley, California. The place was dark except for the yellow light emanating from the study window. Stanford was home alone, whacking out the second draft to his new book. A printed copy of the first draft was tucked away in a Guardwell safe, above the desk, behind the Robert Mapplethorpe. Tentatively titled *Fangs of the CIA*, the manuscript was very Stanford Smith, and because of that, Stanford

Smith would soon be very dead.

Scott had wanted to go alone. Begged Mr. Frank even.

The Company disagreed.

The copy in the safe was the only printed version of the book, and Scott had instructions to burn it along with Smith's hard drive. The mission had to go smoothly. The Company, including Mr. Frank, was adamant that they go together, and his boss said that the ying and yang of Scott and Mabon's working relationship would only guarantee another success. Scott was to handle the finer details and keep his vampire operative in line, and Mabon was to do the second thing he did best—scare. The first, of course, being killing.

Stanford Smith was a high-profile conspiracy theorist, with several of his books in the 1980s making it onto the *New York Times* bestseller list. The writer's popularity got him a get-out-of-death-free card.

At least that was the plan.

Stanford being killed would raise too many red flags and, according to the top minds at The Company, would be riskier than *Fangs* hitting the shelves at all the major book retailers. Their instructions were to nuke the manuscript from orbit and relay a warning to Stanford to stop all research on Project Sunset.

Scott was worried about Mabon's ability to follow these orders, which were very different from his usual ones, but Mr. Frank wouldn't listen to Scott's reasoning. Stanford had a journalist's stubbornness, according to Mr. Frank, and he thought Mabon would be more convincing. "All Stanford needs is a good scare," Mr. Frank had said.

The two agents walked right through the front door that night.

It was left unlocked for them. Stanford's 17-year-old lover was in the country illegally which made him very easy to bribe. He disabled the security alarm and left without locking the door behind him. He'd be found dead in Hollywood the next morning from a heroin overdose, his rainbow boxers down around his ankles.

"Remember—you talk to Stanford, I'll take care of the manuscript," Scott whispered, after entering the house. "Just talk."

"Pleasure, Scotty," Mabon said.

"*No* killing."

Mabon put a finger to his lips. Scott took out his gun. *Cocky bastard.*

Stanford was startled when they entered the study but remained seated behind his desk. His eyes locked on Mabon and widened as the vampire pulled a plastic tarp out of his bag and began unfolding it on the floor. Scott kept his gun aimed at the writer.

"I knew you'd be coming for me."

Mabon walked around the desk. At this point, Stanford tried to stand, but the vampire was behind him with that quickness Scott had witnessed many times before. It wasn't anything magical. The Company described it to Scott as learned speed. Supposedly you pick up these things after a century of being alive. Mabon took the writer in a fierce hug.

"Where you going, *Stan?*"

Mabon rolled the chair with the writer still seated in it out from behind the desk and onto the plastic. Stanford started to breathe heavy, his hands clenching the chair's arms.

"Remember, Mabon," Scott said in warning, as he holstered his gun and moved toward the desk.

"Yes, yes." The vampire petted the writer's bald head. Comb-over strands of Stanford's hair released reluctantly from Mabon's long fingers.

Scott reached the laptop. He turned it upside down to unscrew the hard-drive cover. Stanford whimpered. He glanced up as Mabon's teeth were sliding out. He thought about warning the vampire again, but he had already warned him plenty. He needed to focus on what he was doing.

He released the hard drive and put it on the desk. He took the thermite grenade out of his bag and put that on the desk, too. Then he turned to the safe. It was hidden behind a large photograph of a naked man. Scott took the photograph down and placed it on the floor. He rotated the safe's dial to the first number in the combination: thirty-two.

"Mr. Smith. Are there any more copies of the *Fangs* manuscript besides the one on your laptop and the one in your safe?" Scott asked. He spoke in an authoritative voice—slow, loud, and clear—one of the many tricks of the trade. Sometimes the captive's fear was so thick that it became like a wall around their senses. An interrogator, in turn, needed to be able to break through that wall because desensitization was very counterproductive in their line of work.

"No...no," Stanford said, whimpering again. At the safe, Scott had his back to the action. "I *swear* it."

"Well, then I guess it's true," Mabon said, mockingly.

"*Tell* me, Mabon."

"That's it—just the two."

The number 16 opened the safe. A black metal box was inside

along with several sealed envelopes and a brown worn-leather portfolio that looked manuscript thick. He took it from the safe, put it on the desk, and unwound the strap that bound it. Four hundred and fifty pages were tucked inside. On the top page, halfway down in Courier font, was the manuscript's title:

Fangs of the CIA: The True Story of Vampire Operatives

Scott looked up at Mabon. "Got it," he said. Mabon was now kneeling in front of Stanford, leering at him.

Scott put the hard drive and the manuscript case together on the desk and then placed the AN-M14 thermite grenade on top of the pile. He pulled the magnesium strips from his bag and dug for the matches. "I know you," he heard Stanford say.

"And I know you," Mabon said.

"I know why you're doing all this. You hate us," Stanford said, before turning to Scott. "You're all a bunch of idiots. Got your heads up your asses—every last one of you." Mabon hit him.

It was a bitch slap. Stanford's nose began to bleed.

"Speaking of heads up asses, your lover boy is dead. And it's the unfortunate kind of dead, not my kind of dead, which is of the best kind."

Mabon was taunting the writer, and it was getting on Scott's nerves. Yes, it was all part of the routine. Stanford had to agree to stop writing the book and to keep quiet about the discoveries he had made. But the vampire was dragging it out, taking pleasure in every bit.

"Get to it, Mabon," Scott said.

Scott looked down at the manuscript, underneath a device that would rid it from the world forever. He glanced over at Mabon, still occupied with Stanford, and held a vote in his head. Then he slipped the manuscript from out of its portfolio and into his own bag.

It was never part of the plan. The Company would have severely disciplined him for doing it, if they ever found out, but Scott had to know what was in those pages. As the manuscript settled at the bottom of Scott's bag, the writer let out a gut-wrenching scream.

Mabon was kneeling between Stanford's legs. Blood smeared his lips and chin. The vampire's cheeks were puffed out, giving Scott the impression of a killer chipmunk. Stanford was going into convulsions. His eyes bulged out of his head, and his body shook uncontrollably. Scott came around the desk and ran over to them.

"Oh, shit!"

Stanford's crotch was a mess. His trousers had been torn away and a fountain of blood spurted from the area.

"*What did you do?*"

Mabon stood up. He gripped his stomach and walked uneasily to the far corner of the study. He spit something out, which thumped against the hardwood floor, and brought his arm up to wipe his mouth. He shook his head.

"Ever had penis in your mouth," Mabon asked, spitting again. "I really wouldn't recommend it."

Scott ran to his bag and retrieved one of two Company-issued stakes from it. The stakes were 24 inches of titanium metal with a spear's aerodynamic design, a sword's comfortable grip, and no distinguishing markings.

Scott moved fast, returning to plunge the stake through Stanford's chest. It went in smoothly and the tip came out the back of the chair.

193

Stanford's body tensed, before slumping. Post-death, blood continued to spurt from between his legs.

"We were told to keep him alive," Scott said angrily. Mabon was bent over in the corner like a drunken schoolgirl.

"I wasn't the one who just drove a stake through his heart."

The vampire was trying to get a rise out of him. Mabon was well aware he had signed the writer's death warrant when he bit him. From first bite, a person was either a meal or a fanger. There was no in-between. Stanford's cells would have already begun degenerating when Scott staked him.

"I wasn't finished."

"I don't care," Scott said. "This isn't snack time. Your orders were to convince him not to talk."

"He looks pretty convinced." Scott could hear Mabon smirking.

"*Damn it.*" Scott ran his fingers through his hair. He looked from Stanford to the thing Mabon spit up in the corner. It had slid and left a thin trail of blood across the floor. "Call the Sweepers."

"Sure, Scotty."

Mabon grabbed a cell phone from his jacket pocket. He pressed a button, put the phone to his ear, and waited. Scott went back to the desk to focus on destroying the hard drive.

"Come. Now," Mabon said into the phone.

Mabon returned the phone to his pocket. He leaned over Stanford's body, wrapping his left arm around the writer's lower back and gripping the stake in his right hand. He pulled and the stake slid out of the back of the chair but stayed in Stanford. He picked the body up and placed it on the tarp.

Scott ignited the thermite and both agents looked away as the white fire brightened and sparked. Mabon was paler than Scott had ever seen him. He wondered if the vampire had eaten before the job like he was supposed to. Through the window, Scott could see a van pull into the drive.

"They're here. Pack it."

Scott wasn't worried about being seen. Stanford Smith, who had made a living snooping into other people's business, liked his privacy. There would be no nosy neighbors because there wasn't a house for miles.

The agents grabbed their bags. Scott's felt heavier and for 450 good reasons. He had never double-crossed The Company before, but he just had to know. It was as simple as that. He shut the safe and eyed the small pile on the desk, still consumed by a white glow. It would be taken care of, along with the emptied-out laptop. Scott's guess was that the Sweepers would either incinerate the place or make it look like a robbery, with Stanford's lover involved in some way. The writer's body would never be found. It was the stink his boss never wanted, but one he got because he chose not to heed Scott's warnings about his own operative.

Before leaving, Scott aimed his gun at Stanford's chest and squeezed off two. Just to be sure.

They left the way they came, through the front door, and went in separate directions. The Sweepers' van waited in the drive. There, Mabon would get a change of clothes and a rubdown. He'd give them an update if they needed it, but generally, somehow, they just knew. Scott called Mr. Frank on the way to his car to inform him of the mishap.

He was not pleased.

~

It took Scott under an hour to get home.

It was late and Mary was asleep. He went to his office, opened his bag, and removed the manuscript. He put it on the desk. Some of the corners creased upward. He stared down at the title page.

I know you, Stanford had said. *You hate us.*

Scott undressed, opened the closet door, and leaned down to lift the loose floorboard. He stuffed his clothes in one of the plastic bags he stored there, then sealed the bag and reached to put it far back. He put the duffel he had brought on assignment in there too, replaced the floorboard, and slid the closet door shut. His study had a full bath attached and he went there to clean.

After showering, he put on his bathrobe and padded barefoot into the office where the manuscript was waiting for him.

It began: "I know a secret. It's a secret I'm about to tell you, but be warned. Mind what you do with your new knowledge...because it is DEADLY!"

Stanford Smith wasn't reputed as the best writer, but he was known for his research which was always thorough. Scott started on the manuscript when the clock on the wall glowed midnight and turned over the last page at four. He returned the book to his desk and rubbed his eyes.

Although it contained very fantastic homoerotic overtones, the manuscript seemed factual overall and was heavy with information. Scott wondered where Stanford had found his sources and was willing to bet The Company already made whoever it was go away. Several chapters detailed Mabon's early years in Georgia—things Scott never knew.

Scott's phone vibrated on the table, startling him from his thoughts.

"How's the reading?"

Mabon knew. He must have seen him slip the manuscript into his bag. Or maybe he noticed the portfolio was empty when Scott set it aflame. He refused to be intimidated by the vampire. *I have the upper hand*, he thought.

"It's late, Mabon."

"Late is *my* time. So, how is it?"

"What?"

"Don't play. I know you have Stanford's manuscript. Any good?"

"It's fine. Lots of information."

"You know what they say."

"What do they say?"

"Don't believe everything you read."

"Then it's not truthful?"

"No, it is. Even the vampire orgies. They were a barrel."

"How did Stanford get this information?"

"Just like humans sell each other out, so do vampires."

"I'll need to tell Frank."

"He already knows."

"He knows about the girl you killed...when you were still human?"

"I didn't kill Sarah. It was that decorated heathen. Her daddy got the fire in him when he drank. Guess he didn't like the idea of his daughter running away with a nigger lover." There was a short pause before Mabon continued: "After they let me out of jail, I ran. A few days later, I was bit, and I went back to Savannah to let the general pay his dues. Then I left for good. There was nothing in that town for me—not anymore. My parents, my land, my true love...my unborn child…all dead and gone, thanks to this sweet land of liberty. As a child, I would never have thought it possible to truly despise where you're from. But I was wrong."

"You're not a patriot."

"No," Mabon said. "I'm the anti-patriot."

"Why the CIA?"

"It was a way in."

"I don't understand. You want revenge? After all this time? Up until tonight, you've been a good agent. You get the job done."

"Time doesn't heal wounds but it makes revenge that much sweeter. I'm a patient vampire. Besides…I've played a little."

Scott didn't like the sound of that. "Don't do anything stupid, Mabon."

"I wouldn't think of it." The vampire paused again, this time longer, and Scott thought he had hung up. Then he spoke: "We have a lot in common, you and me. Just a couple farm boys, our fathers killed by the very government meant to protect them."

Scott felt things crashing down around him. He tightened his grip on the phone.

"We farm boys need to stick together. I know you're thinking about leaving The Company, Scott. *Don't*."

Scott didn't reply.

"So I'll see you when I see you," Mabon said, and hung up.

NOW:

"I quit the next day," Scott said. "Part of me didn't want to warn Frank. It was the part of me that thought he had something to do with my father's death. I was going to leave without saying a word about my conversation with Mabon—let them deal with the mess. Let Mabon have his revenge on the government. I tried not to care."

Scott got up off his chair and started to pace, back and forth past the table. Guilt wore him. He opened a book on the table and flipped absently through its pages. He continued: "It didn't work—the not caring. But where did it get me? Mr. Frank refused to listen. The Company had its blinders on when it came to the vampires. Mary and I bought a new place just outside the city. There was no point in going far. The Company had their ways. If they wanted to find us, we would be found."

Schizo stretched from his lying position in front of the plastic fire and meandered over to me. He jumped up and put his front paws on my lap. He investigated the tabletop, vacuuming it with his nose. Flames jerked in sync with the dog's breathing.

"It was that Mabon guy that started all this?" I said. "Out of revenge for the death of his father?"

"Yes, for his father, his fiancé," Scott said, "and his unborn child. When everything started to happen, I knew what it was. Effectively, The Company delivered death to the doorstep of every American citizen. Mabon came to mine. He took my son." Scott pulled a small envelope out of his pocket and put it on the table in front of me. It had a red smear on it that looked like a partial fingerprint. A card was inside and I pulled it out.

"*How sweet it is,*" I read aloud. "What is?"

Scott shrugged, looking like half the man I had only recently met. "Revenge. For me leaving him. The card was attached to a box of Krispy Kreme donuts."

I returned the note to the envelope and handed it back to Scott. I wondered if he kept it on his person for easy access—a close reminder of his life purpose. Revenge is a funny thing. People misinterpret it as a cure.

Scott sat back down in his chair. The mechanical fire clicked away behind us while the real fire danced on the wicks of waxy stubs. Schizo had gotten comfortable half standing, half sitting on my lap. His eyes were closed, but I doubted he was asleep. I had the feeling he was faking it—for whatever reason dogs did such things.

I found myself again considering the idea of vampires existing and knew it was the company I kept. *Time for new friends*, I thought. Realizing it was my turn to say something, I chose my words carefully.

"It's all so unbelievable."

The idea of vampires existing was unbelievable and they couldn't hold that against me. But the word didn't mean I didn't believe, even though I didn't. Well, not really.

Both men stared at me like I was in the process of growing an extra head, and I half wanted to check. Scott glanced at Cooper. Cooper nodded, and they stood.

"I want to show you something," Scott said.

He exited the room. Cooper followed, not waiting for me. I gently nudged Schizo off my lap and stood. I contemplated blowing out the candles but didn't. They weren't mine to blow.

The two men led me along the sixth floor corridor. The floor had fewer storage units and more open space than the others. Rooms like Scott's flanked one side of the building. We turned a corner and passed a row of cubicles, each cubicle having an adjacent window. A lounge area was further along with a flat-screen television and cushioned chairs. A big guy with a shaved head stood next to the TV. He had a dragon tattoo that curved down his neck and disappeared beneath his shirt. He was looking out the window, a pair of binoculars in his lowered left hand. When we passed, he turned and nodded.

I noticed a gun holstered at his side. No introductions were made.

At the elevator, Scott hit down. Inside, he pressed **B**. The doors closed.

"There's a basement in this place?" I asked.

"Yes," Scott said. "What we have to show you...it's down there."

My heartbeat quickened. It was my understanding that unless you were a treasure hunter, being *shown* something in the basement was not a good thing.

"What is it?"

"You'll see," Cooper said.

"*No*. I don't accept that as an answer," I said, glancing at the panel for an emergency button. *If they were going to kill me, they would have done it by now*. It was possible they first wanted to determine me a nonbeliever before burying me and my naysaying in the bowels of Seepy Storage.

"You don't believe in vampires," Scott said. "That means we need to show you one."

"You've got one? In your basement?"

"It's a hermit," Scott said.

Cooper must have seen the confusion on my face. He explained: "About 34 percent of people bitten become hermits. They're like handicapped vampires. Something goes wrong in the process...I don't know...maybe their bodies don't handle dying and coming back as well."

"So, what? They get special parking spaces?"

Cooper looked at me annoyed. "They're deformed. They've got shorter lifespans and poor regenerative skills. Most can't speak. They still feed on blood. And they die the same way."

The elevator made its descent. My newfound phobia returned. I wondered what the name for it was—there was always a name. Just when you think you're the only person alive scared of bottle caps, you discover there are others like you and groups to help in your time of need. I knew a fear of elevators was probably more common. In the end, it was just a fear of what was waiting for me. The elevator stopped abruptly.

We'd arrived.

The doors opened. The light from the elevator fell on stacked chairs and cardboard boxes. Something hummed in the dark. Cooper got out and reached along the wall. The rest of the basement became lit.

It looked like the mountain of junk from outside, only more organized. Besides the furniture, most items were boxed up. Similar to the sixth floor, there were no storage units and the space was open, but unlike the top floor, there weren't any windows.

The humming was coming from a large generator to our right. Several barrels marked DIESEL lined the wall behind the machine.

Scott took the lead, with Cooper, me, and Schizo following along a cleared path. The sheer amount of stuff made the clearing through it minutely less miraculous than the parting of the Red Sea.

Schizo growled. I looked down to shush him and walked into Cooper's back. The two men had stopped.

There was an opening up ahead. The stacks of things ended and something I couldn't make out yet had begun.

Scott and Cooper went through the opening and took a right around a stack of boxes and free-floating books almost seven feet high. They disappeared behind it. I walked through after them…

…and finally saw the truth.

CHAPTER ELEVEN

THE CAGE WAS ENORMOUS.

It was the kind zoos bought to keep dangerous, pacing animals in. At first glance, this one had a man inside.

The man sat hunched over in a chair with purple upholstery. A coffin sat kitty-corner a few yards away from him. It was wooden and looked like it had been thrown together with some spare plywood and a couple of nails. It reminded me of Schizo's cross and the idea of creation from necessity.

The lid was on.

I couldn't see the man's face because his head was down. The parts I did see of him suggested severe malnourishment. His brown hair went missing in clumps, letting pale scalp show through. His blue-tinged skin stretched thin over jutting bones. He wore a *Barney the Friendly Dinosaur* t-shirt with holes and red stains, several coming together to look like a handprint.

I felt pity and fear and my mind racked ways I could get that man out of the cage and away from the people who had mistreated him.

"What have you done?" I asked.

The man in the cage raised his head at the sound of my voice. "Oh my God," I whispered.

It was no man.

His teeth were too big for his mouth. They were sharp yellow blades. His face was disproportionate, with a tiny chin and widened forehead. Pupils filled his eyes to the edges. He rushed the bars and stuck his arms through, desperately reaching for me. I screamed.

Schizo jumped up and seized the hermit's arm in his jaw. The thing grabbed Schizo's nose with its other hand and pulled the dog hard against the bars, as if trying to force him through the small space between them. Schizo yelped.

I ran forward and got hold of the hermit's other arm and pulled, smashing the thing's body against the bars once, twice—three times. It let go after the third, and so did I.

I got my fingers under Schizo's collar and pulled him back, away from that cell and the monster inside. I looked at Schizo's face. It seemed unharmed. I ran my hand over his snout and wondered where his chewy cross had gotten to. The dog never left home without it, and now I knew why. I felt a hand on my shoulder. It was Cooper. Scott knelt down next to me.

"You okay?" he asked.

I didn't think so. I wasn't sure any of us were going to be with monsters like that existing in our world. But I did know one thing: I wanted to live or die trying. The country was not theirs to take.

"You were right," I said. "Tell me what I have to do."

~

Unit 504 had the guns.

But not just guns. Every space was occupied by an object that could help you kill or maim someone or something in one way or another, or transport you to a place where you could kill or maim someone or something in one way or another. There were screwdrivers, swords, chainsaws, lanterns, blowtorches, knives, stakes, guns, bullets, nails, screws, machetes, ropes, pulleys, oil, flashlights, a bicycle, bows, arrows, matches, a pitchfork, a sickle, nail guns, rolls of wire, lighters, gasoline, holy water, a lawnmower, poison, binoculars, a flamethrower, crosses, hammers, baseball bats, spears, bricks, grenades, night vision goggles, wrenches, a nonstick frying pan, and a partridge in a pear tree. And it was one badass partridge.

An American flag draped the ceiling. I thought of a song but only knew the one line: *It's a revolution, baby!*

The boys were proud of their toys. It was obvious. They wore wide smiles. Even Schizo seemed impressed and he was still just a dog.

Everything was arranged neatly on tables. One table was strictly vampire, and I was drawn to it.

There were mostly stakes and crosses. Several bottles of water were labeled HOLY. I was strangely disappointed to not see the kind of stakes Scott had described in his story. I fathomed a guess they were confiscated when he quit. I picked up one of their stakes, which was wooden, plain, and uncomfortable to hold. It looked like a converted table leg. I put it down.

Next to the stake pile was a large box filled with smaller black boxes. I glanced at Scott and Cooper, and they nodded. I pulled out one of the small boxes and opened it. Six bullets were inside. They had brass casings and black tips.

"I didn't think bullets worked on vampires."

"Most don't," Scott said. "Those do. Winchester Black Talons—high-performance hollow-points. They expand on impact to three times their diameter. Six razor-like claws." Scott brought his hand up and curved his fingers.

"We use them in our VP70 semi-automatic pistols. The 'M' Variant." Cooper said. "It's one hell of a combination. Just aim for the heart. A head shot will confuse them and really piss them off, but it won't put one down." Cooper took a gun off a table and handed it to me. I surprised myself by taking it.

The gun had the same fast-forward look as Cooper's Mustang. Things that look like that mean business. They kick ass and take names.

The gun felt right in my hands. It was lighter than I thought it would be. "So, regular bullets don't work?

"No," Cooper said. "A spray of regular bullets might slow them down." Cooper made a face like he would never choose such an option. "That's about it. With proper aim, the Talons kill for good."

I handed the gun back to Cooper, who replaced it on the table. "Where did you get all this stuff?"

"I procured a hefty arsenal after I left the CIA," Scott said. "I chose to not run away, but I wasn't going to be stupid about it. I bought a sporting goods store down the street from my house and kept it all close but not too close."

I focused on one of the bricks. "I remember reading somewhere that people used to shove a brick in the mouth of a corpse if they suspected it of being a vampire. It was meant to stop them from feeding. How do you know what really works?"

"Experience. Stories from the others. Everyone here has killed one, including Bugs. At The Company, I got the basics. They knew more, but they weren't divulging. They didn't want me killing the vampires. I was more of a babysitter and babysitters don't kill the children. They just learn how to control them if they misbehave."

"Books help, too," Cooper said, "but you never know, do you?" He looked at Scott who shook his head in agreement. "Most books about vampires are novels, and novelists take liberties. But hell, a few weeks ago, vampires were just fantasy. They could've gained strength from strawberry milkshakes and shapeshifted into armadillos, for all anyone really knew."

My eyes fell on a large knife with a serrated edge. It was a horror movie knife.

"The hermits have provided us with a lot of information," Scott said.

"Like the one downstairs?" I asked. "How?"

"We use them to find out what works, what doesn't. We take them from the forest. That's where most of them are. Hard part is getting a hold of one."

"You mean this forest?" I said, pointing at the walls and beyond them. From inside Seepy Storage, the outside was beginning to feel like an illusion. Like beyond the facility wall was just more wall—drab, gray, forever.

"Yes," Scott said.

"But we're surrounded by forest," I said.

"Yes," Scott said, preoccupied with a box in the corner of the unit.

Cooper stepped forward to explain. "They're not smart enough to get in, Em," Cooper said, "and most are too weak to fight. The UVF has a kill policy on hermits...they're considered an embarrassment to the species. They take refuge in the forests, in abandoned buildings, and underground. They feed on what they can find, which usually isn't a lot. Most die from starvation in a matter of days."

"You say they're not smart," I said, "but they're smart enough to hide."

"That's just instinct," Scott said, still crouched in the corner. "Everything has a basic will to survive, even ants. It doesn't mean

208

they're intelligent."

"What about the other ones...the normal vampires?" That had to be an oxymoron. "Are they smart?"

"Some of them," Scott said.

"Then what makes you think we can beat them?"

"I'm not sure we can. We've just got to do our best."

Scott stood suddenly and excused himself. He gave a curt goodbye. I wondered if he had found what he was looking for.

Cooper invited me to the lounge to watch a movie, and I accepted. My watch said nine o'clock, and with my mind now set to information overload, I was no longer tired. Cooper closed the weapon unit's door but didn't lock it. The hallway outside was lit and quiet. We walked past the furniture unit where I had found my rug, pillow, and sheets. We turned a corner into a dark stretch of hallway. Cooper got out his flashlight and switched it on. He promised me mine soon. In such little light, I thought of the thing downstairs and shivered. I asked myself what on earth it could be and answered back rudely, *It's a vampire, stupid.* And it was. A real-life vampire. A real-life, blood-sucking vampire.

Further down the hall, almost to the end, laughter spilled from an open unit. The sound tugged me from my bad thoughts, and I was drawn to the space like a moth to flame. Schizo trotted next to us, tail wagging.

The fifth floor lounge was more furnished than the residential units, which shrank the room but gave it a homey feel. There were chairs and sofas covered with big cushions and soft-looking fabrics. Several hardcover books were tucked into a small bookcase. Crayons and a drawing pad sat on a child's desk. The overhead lighting was on, dimmed by bed sheets that draped the ceiling. The smell of pine burned my nostrils. I sneezed the trees out of my head, and everyone turned to look.

I recognized two faces: Mary and Sam. Scott's wife sat in the corner of the room, a bible open on her lap. Sam was on the couch between two other guys. On the television, a girl with feathered hair screamed. My body tensed.

Cooper made introductions. The guy to Sam's left was Rudy. He had spiked blond hair, wore a muscle tee and sweats, and looked like he was in a passionate affair with gym equipment. On Sam's right was Charlie. Tall, skinny, with light brown hair. He was wearing a Ramones tee-shirt.

Rudy looked me up and down. "Nice to get some fresh meat in here. Charlie's kept the good stuff for himself. No offense, Mary." He hit Charlie on the arm. Charlie rolled his eyes.

"Don't listen to this guy," Charlie said, smiling. "He's the self-proclaimed leader of the Sexual Harassment Movement."

"Proud of it, thanks," Rudy said.

Another loud scream. Schizo whined. The girl on the television was now running through the woods. She fell and started to sob.

"Shut it, Rudy," Cooper said.

"Nice manners, beautiful," Rudy said.

Those two had a history and the tension had nothing to do with me. I knew guys like Rudy before. There were plenty at my university. I held up my hand and stuck out a curved pinky finger.

"What other club are you the leader of, Rudy?" I said.

Mary glared at me from her corner. The others laughed. Rudy's face reddened.

"Very funny," he said. He turned to Scott's wife. "Can you believe that shit? I think she's going to hell, what do you think, Mary?"

"Leave her alone," Cooper said.

"I can't help it if she's crazy," Rudy said, shrugging. Everyone stared at him. "What?"

Mary returned her attention to the bible, bringing it up close to her face so it was almost touching her nose. She read aloud in a quick whisper.

Charlie offered me his seat. I thanked him and took it, not wanting to cause another scene. Schizo hopped up and settled on my lap while Cooper dragged two wooden chairs away from the wall, one for Charlie, the other for him.

The girl on the television screen was still running and falling. She stopped to rest against a tree, and a hand holding a giant cleaver came out from behind the tree. The girl's eyes widened as the cleaver punched into her neck. Rudy laughed.

"Pretty sick, man," Charlie said.

"What are you watching?"

"*Friday the 13th*—one of the sequels," Rudy said.

"We raided a video store," Charlie explained. "Grabbed a box in a hurry. It ended up being mostly these types of movies."

"That would be a cool way to kill a vampire," Rudy said. "Sneak up on it and slice its neck open."

"You know that wouldn't kill it," Charlie said. "You'd have to take the whole head off."

"I *know*," Rudy said. "I'm just saying it would be cool…if they did die like that."

"No shop talk in the lounge," Cooper said.

Sam stood. "I have to go to bed now."

"Hey, sorry, man," Charlie said. "We can stop."

"Nah, I'm just tired," Sam said, leaving the lounge.

Mary closed her Bible with a *smack*. "Sinners," she said, her eyes sparing time for each of us. She shuffled out of the lounge after Sam.

"Loon," Rudy said under his breath.

Cooper offered the group beers from a fridge, and I accepted. I wrapped my hand around the cold can and thought, *I deserve this*, and I did. The world had gone to hell in a hand basket and I wanted to be sedated.

We watched the rest of the movie in silence, except for the occasional comments from Rudy that included "Cool" and "That would be a cool way to kill a vampire" and "No one with an ass like hers should die so bad." By the end of the movie, I was ready to cut my own head off. I felt woozy after only my third beer and figured it was time for bed.

"Great movie, guys," I said, standing. "Very realistic. Come on, Schiz. Time for bed."

"Can I come, too?" Rudy asked.

"Do I *know* you?"

"What does that matter?"

I smiled and not because I was finding him endearing. He was ludicrous, which is funny when you're tired and drunk. "Good night, everyone."

"Wait, take my flashlight." Cooper handed it to me. I wasn't about to face the dark hallway without some protection, so I thanked him and took it. From outside the unit, I heard the conversation continue.

"She'd sleep with me if I was the last man on earth," Rudy said.

"You realize you just insulted yourself," Cooper said.

Someone laughed. Maybe Charlie.

"Oh boy," I whispered to Schizo. He looked up at me with perked ears. My light cut the darkness ahead of us as we made our way back.

~

Bugs' unit was open and dark inside.

Mary and Scott's unit, too. The others were closed tight. Schizo jumped up on my bed. I stood in the middle of the unit not quite knowing what to do. When it seems like you're living in a real-life nightmare, it's hard to adjust. You can't just wake up. *Maybe*, I thought, *I'll go to sleep and dream I'm on my interviews.* Fat chance.

"You don't look like Frankenstein any more."

Bugs' voice came from out of the dark in her unit. I squinted to make out her shape. My hand went to feel the back of my head. I wasn't wearing the bandage anymore, but I had been last time I saw Bugs. The bump was still there. Big. Like a separate entity, except for the pain. I winced.

"Thanks. Very flattering."

"Sure. Goodnight."

"Night."

I didn't have pajamas, so I took off my shoes and fell into bed as is. Schizo hogged most of the mattress, but without a blanket, I was grateful for the body heat.

I pulled the sheet over me and closed my eyes. My plans had been to leave—the next morning or the day after. But it seemed my plans had changed. I was now a believer, like it or lump it. That thing five floors below us was not human, I was sure of that.

I would stay and help.

I had no idea what the days ahead had in store.

CHAPTER TWELVE

DREAD.

It's an ugly thing to wake up to.

There's that deluded half second of happiness first—the confused state that comes before the dread. This is proof that we're programmed to be happy, but memory plays the BIG BITCH and nullifies our original settings and the state of *now* sinks in like cement in the gut.

Vampires had taken over my country. I was living in a rundown storage facility, surrounded by a forest of special-needs undead, with a group of people who had high plans to reverse the order of things when they couldn't even stand being in the same room as one another.

I moved, and my body screamed, *What do you think you're doing!* I rubbed the sleep from my eyes and sat up on my elbows. Schizo was snoring quietly next to me, his warm doggy breath a gale on my face. He was on his back with his legs stuck in the air. He had a smile on his face, and I wished I was him. Fur and all.

I rubbed my hands together to warm them. My room hadn't undergone any changes while I slept. It was still a sad combination of three cement walls, one small rug, one mattress, and one pillow. I would've traded my soul for a potted plant.

Seepy Storage was quiet. I looked at my watch: *9:35.* I wiped a smudge off the glass face. Besides my sneakers, the watch was the only other possession that had crossed over from my old life. The mucked-up sneakers would be gone once I found a pair to replace them, but the watch would stay.

215

While scanning my dim surroundings, I did notice something new just beyond the unit. It was a box. I got out of bed and walked tippy-toe to the hallway. The less foot on the concrete floor, the less sole the cold could permeate. Several items were in the box, and a note was on top:

Meet me in the lounge at 10
Don't be late
Cooper

There were books. I counted twelve. A yellow Post-it note attached to the top book said, "Read Me."

I wondered where Cooper thought the spare time to read twelve books would come from. What with the job of saving the country and all. I saw the title of the top book and understood.

"*Vampires,*" I read aloud. "*Dwellers of the Night.*"

The cover was black with two white fangs in the middle. One of the fangs had red on it. The red was metallic, so when I moved the cover up and down, it glinted. The pages were yellow inside and smelled like library. Dust and sweaty palms. Sentences had been highlighted or sometimes just a word. The other books were the same. "Cross" was circled in one. There was an equal amount of fiction to non-fiction. The day before, I would have found that funny—vampires being written about in a non-fiction way. Today, not so much, and the noise in the closet…well, it *could* be a monster.

May want to go check.

I carried the books over to an empty corner. I set them down stacked before placing them so they were leaning against each other but standing individually. I stepped back to look and nodded. Books were substance objects, and although they weren't mine and I hadn't picked them out myself, the feel of the unit improved with the books in it.

I looked at the time. I had ten minutes. I returned to the box and pulled out my clothes for the day: a pair of orange sweats, a black tank top, and a fresh pair of socks and underwear. Probably more of Cara's clothes. I wondered if this would become a routine. Every morning, I would have a dead girl's clothes placed outside my door by Cooper.

I took a mental note to ask Cooper if there was a washer/dryer on one of the floors. It was at the bottom of a very long list of things to ask Cooper, none of which had anything to do with vampires. I knew that that information would come whether I asked for it or not.

Happiness filled me when I discovered a new toothbrush and tube of toothpaste in the box. The last item was a journal. The cover was blue fabric with a gold maple leaf in the middle. A pen was attached to the binding rings. I opened it. *Too many blank pages*, I thought, dropping the journal on my bed.

I left the empty box in the hallway and changed quickly in the corner of the unit. It was now 9:55.

Time, it does creep.

I summoned Schizo into the hallway. He stood and stretched. He moaned as he came out of the stretch. It made me want to be a dog. Again.

"It can't be *that* good," I said to Schizo when he arrived at my side. He looked up at me with a drowsy smile and his eyes half lidded, as if to say, *Oh yeah. It's good.*

I shut the door to my unit, leaving it unlocked, and ran down to the fourth floor, gripping my toothbrush and toothpaste like they were keys to the universe. I paused outside the bathroom. Schizo ambled past me, setting off the lights. The mirror inside brightened, reflecting its life partner—a small section of blue-tiled wall across the way. I was in a standoff.

It's been a long time since I seen you ' round these parts, Mirror.

I recalled renting *The Good, the Bad and the Ugly* with Sullivan just a couple weeks before I left for Los Angeles. We had found it on some list on some blog that implied you were less of a human being if you didn't watch the recommended movies.

We were sucked in.

At the video store, Sul had confessed that until the age of ten he thought all Americans were cowboys. Big-hat-wearing, lasso-throwing, gun-toting cowboys. Then it was surfers. The post-teen him still living in Britain had believed us all to be war mongers.

I preferred cowboys myself.

He told me that moving to the States had changed his opinion of Americans for the better, and I replied that actually meeting the people you generalize sometimes does that. In the end, the movie had not been very good, was pretty bad and partially ugly. It put me off westerns and movie shame lists for life.

As I stood there in the bathroom doorway, I imagined a camera POV shot on my face. My eyes squinted, sweat on my brow, whistling and howling in the background. The camera then zooms in on the mirror. Reflected lights, spit marks on the glass, yodeling.

I walked up to the mirror and looked.

After more than 24 hours of not seeing my reflected self, I was starting to feel MIA in my own head. You go through a day and it's the mirrors and other reflective objects that give you proof of your existence. I wondered if it was true that vampires didn't cast reflections.

I sighed. My condition wasn't as bad as I thought it would be. The swelling in my cheek had gone down, but a bruise on my neck from Myers' dart had come up. I got closer and ran my fingers over it, gently. It could have passed as a hickey from an industrial-sized vacuum cleaner. If I were into that type of thing. Of course, the residents of Seepy Storage didn't know me from, say, Virginia Wolfe. I liked the kink, for all they knew.

Purple bags had come up to settle under my eyes. The curse of fair skin. They shared the same shade as the bruise on my neck, and I was glad to be, if anything, color-coordinated. My hair needed a severe brushing. I hadn't used a blow dryer after either of the showers yesterday and frizz had taken over. I raised my right arm and flexed my bicep.

"Emma Spade. Vampire killer," I said aloud. Schizo tilted his head at me. *Emma Spade. Hero?* I dropped my arm and made a face at myself.

Scott had pulled out all the stops with his story, serving up even the incriminating details. Then they had introduced the thing downstairs to convince me, and it wasn't about egos—who's right, who's wrong. They wanted me with them...on their side...fighting.

Schizo settled at my feet. He wagged his tail when I squeezed the toothpaste onto the brush.

"It's just toothpaste," I said, through suds and bristles. I spit and wiped my mouth. I glanced at my watch. It was five past ten. "Oops."

I leaned over to splash my face and then blindly reached for the towel cabinet. I found a small cloth inside, which I used to dab the wet away. My cheeks had pinked. I completed a confused rotation, wondering what to do with the facecloth, before tucking it in my pocket. I stuck the toiletries in my other pocket, clapped to rouse Schizo, and we were off.

~

Cooper balanced on the edge of a chair in the lounge with his elbows resting on his knees. I felt like I was at a zoo observing him through glass. The tour guide would say, "Here we have man waiting for woman. Notice the way he's not fully seated, his eyes are focused on the floor. The foot is tapping."

I approached Cooper with an apology, which was accepted, and he led Schizo and I to the kitchen for some much-needed breakfast.

The kitchen was two doors down from Scott's office. It had a stove, a microwave, a refrigerator, a sink, and a pantry for dry goods. Additional food items, including vast quantities of bottled water, were kept in the adjoining room where two bonus fridges hummed in contented unison. Cooper told me that the UVF was in the process of accounting for the city's fridge supply and destroying or locking up extraneous fridges, making the task of finding one difficult.

"Vampires can't eat food like us," Cooper explained, arranging another meat plate for Schizo. His fingertips glittered with grease, and he brought each to his mouth for a quick in and out. "And only the lower classes refrigerate their blood—given that the rich are supplied it fresh—so the UVF is trying to cut off our food supply and essentially annihilate anything that could help the resistance. Supermarkets, pharmacies, churches...most of these places are being emptied or demolished. Only some are being left intact for monitoring."

Cooper put the plate down for Schizo who nearly knocked it out of his hands. The dog snorted as he dug in. "Luckily we've done well to stock up. We know all the untouched places like the Albertsons out on Crenshaw. Plus, there are the houses. The abandoned ones are still packed with food, and the occupied ones…well, the vampires haven't gotten around to spring cleaning yet. Here, sit."

Cooper pulled out a bench for me. I sat. The table was as long as the room itself. The sun came in through the wide windows and left narrow sun windows on the tabletop. I had the idea it would be a nice place to eat with a large group.

"Where is everyone?" I asked.

"The hunters are out."

"Hunting an appliance?"

"Hunting an appliance," Cooper said, amused. "Except for Charlie. He's watching the front. And Mary took Bugs and Sammy out back for a walk."

"Is it safe? With those things in the forest?"

"Yeah. Vampires, hermits included, sleep during the day. Sunlight can kill them. There are servant patrols, but they're rare in these parts. Mary and the kids know to stick to the property."

Cooper went to the pantry. Cans and boxes inside sung their product's praises. *Fifty percent less fat! Real fruit! Whole Grain Guaranteed!* Cooper gripped the pantry door and absentmindedly moved it back and forth. A strand of my hair flew across my face, encouraged by the draft. I blew it away.

"What do you feel like?" Cooper asked.

"Lobster."

"Other than that."

"Cereal's good."

"Cheerios?"

"Yes, please."

"Okay," he said, pulling out a box. He went deeper for bowls, disappearing into the depths of the pantry. When he spoke again, his voice was hollow, like he was Abe calling out from the cavernous belly of Moby Dick. "We've only got powdered milk. Is that okay?"

Ewwwww. "Sure, fine."

~

Breakfast was short but sweet. And the milk wasn't as objectionable as I thought it would be. It's only after you've been starving that you can truly appreciate the food put in front of you.

After eating, we left the kitchen and Cooper led us to a conference room. We passed Scott's door on the way, which was partially open. He was sitting at the table we met at, reading a book. The blinds were open, and sunlight revealed his age like a mean friend. Both hands were combed through his graying hair, so it stuck out like the feathers in a voodoo headdress.

I wondered about the layout of the top floor and thought maybe the building's former owner had occupied a couple offices for storage business and then rented out the rest of the space.

In the conference room, a table much like the one from the kitchen was surrounded by eight metal chairs and covered at the far end with weaponry that included a gun and a bow and arrow. A podium was in front of a white board with the word "vampire" scrawled on it in black incursive. I never thought a word could look so threatening—like each letter was about to pounce.

Cooper invited me to sit. He walked to the front of the room and stood there. He shoved both hands in his pockets and looked from me to the word.

"Tell me what this word means to you," he said, freeing one hand from a pocket to point at the board.

"Vampires. Smell like death...big teeth," I said. It was an *Austin Powers* reference, but I didn't think Cooper got it, and if he did, he wasn't letting on. Humor was my defense mechanism. It came with artillery force. "Sorry, okay...um...immortal beings that drink blood."

"There," Cooper said, pointing at me now. He took a marker from off the board, removed its cap, and wrote out the word "immortal", saying it out loud like a teacher might. The marker squeaked like a frightened mouse.

"Immortal," he repeated, once he finished writing. "It means to live forever." Cooper replaced the cap on the marker and used the marker as a pointer, tapping the word on the board. "I don't want you to be confused about this, Em, okay? Vampires can live forever...yeah? But more importantly they can be *killed*. Any human can kill one. Quite easily, if you know what you're doing." Cooper's arms went into the back of the podium. He pulled out a notebook and a pen and placed them in front of me. "For notes."

I opened the book and poised the pen like an obedient student.

"Garlic doesn't work. Vampires have reflections. They don't have to be invited. They can cross running water." I wondered how they tested that one and pictured Cooper and Scott catapulting Barney over a stream. "They can't control humans with their minds, levitate, or turn into animals."

"How do you know that?"

"What?"

223

"Scott said he believed he only knew what Mabon wanted him to—that vampires are good at hiding things. Maybe they have powers but are keeping them secret?"

"By all accounts, they don't. We've got governmental records going back as far as the OSS, and our own observations, here and in the field. We go with what we see."

I thought that that was a dangerous approach. Underestimating an opponent was a good way to lose. But I let Cooper continue.

"Alright...on the flip side, vampires *do* drink blood, human and animal, they *are* nocturnal, holy water and crosses don't kill them, but *irritate*. What does kill them is—" Cooper popped off the marker cap again and started writing "—sunlight, fire, decapitation, and *violent* penetration of the heart." Cooper stopped writing and thumped a fist against his chest, making me feel like I was looking through the glass at the zoo again. He put the marker on the podium and walked to the end of the table where the weapons and other items were laid out, motioning for me to follow.

Besides the bow and arrow and the pistol, there were two cartridges, a wooden stake, a Zippo lighter and a small tin of lighter fluid, a spray can, a metal cross, and a knife like the one from the weapon unit.

My eyes were drawn to the spray can, which was similar to the one the female vampire had tried to use on the crow. Small. Silver. But unlike hers, this one had a white label with a drawing of a black cross. I picked up the spray can, held it close to my ear, and shook it. Liquid sloshed inside.

"Holy water," Cooper said. "Pepper spray for vampires."

I nodded and put it down. I owned a canister of actual pepper spray but had left it at home because I wouldn't have been allowed to take it on the plane. My mom gave it to me for protection, but I always felt that when and if the time came to use it, I wouldn't be able to locate it in my purse. The cops would observe my dead body, the tips of my stretched fingers just millimeters away from the yellow canister that could have saved my life if only I had been more organized.

Cooper continued: "A violent penetration involves an object and the person behind that object." Cooper picked up the stake and tossed it to me, sharp end back. I caught it but fumbled, sending the wooden weapon clambering to the floor. I blushed, feeling the weight of a million pairs of eyes, with just one on me. I picked up the stake.

"So you want me to stake you?" I asked, smiling.

"Yeah, that's it," Cooper said, with a crooked smile back. "No, just show me. Show me how you'd do it." Cooper stepped out of my way.

I was never very good on the spot. I clutched the stake and jutted clumsily forward with simultaneous leg and arm action. I could've killed an insect. Maybe. Cooper was fair. He didn't laugh or smirk, though hysterical fits would have been justified.

"That was good—like a fencer," he said, "but here's a better way." Cooper took the stake from me and put some distance between us. He lunged forward in one giant step, swinging the stake up and over, and stopping abruptly where the chest of an average-height male would be. "You need to think of yourself as a force to be reckoned with. When you move to kill, there can't be any second thoughts. No pauses. Momentum is the key and you get it with *forward*, *downward* motions. Not straight out or down up. Understand?"

I did and nodded, "Yep."

"Of course, sometimes luck is on your side. Your opponent falls and you can use their downward motion. *Bam.* We call that vampire-on-a-stick."

Luck—that thing that happened to other people. The only time I ever won anything was in the summer of 97. It was a goldfish I won with a ping pong ball at the local carnival, and I called him Pong instead of Ping and had my reasons. He was my life for one whole day and one whole night before his untimely death to the song "Wannabe" by the Spice Girls. Auditory epilepsy. I never forgave the Brit-pop group and wrote a letter to advise the use of warning labels on their next album. I included suggestions: a picture of a goldfish wearing headphones with a big red X over it or a simple "WARNING: THIS MUSIC KILLS GOLDFISH. PLEASE USE CAUTION." A month later, I got a letter thanking me for buying the album.

Winning Pong had been a brief blip in my 21-year luck drought. At a young age, I came to the conclusion that I would have to work hard for the things I wanted, and that moment with Cooper was no different. I vowed to listen closely to what he and Scott told me, train hard to become a good fighter, and never ever expect vampire-on-a-stick.

~

Hunter training was divided into three phases, and after the successful completion of all three, I would get to kill things.

Over a week, I trained in weaponry (WT), fear (FT), and consumption (CT). On my first day, I woke at 8:30, went for a jog around the building, showered, and met Cooper in the kitchen for breakfast. Mary, Bugs, Sam, Rudy, Cooper, and Seven, the girl I was yet to meet, were there when I arrived.

Seven was on the shorter side. Her long brown hair moved like expensive silk in its swept-up ponytail. She had darker features, maybe

Mexican, and a perfect nose, characteristic of ancient royalty—Caesar, Cleopatra, Mark Antony. She and the others spared me a quick glance, before getting up from the table and heading to the sink to deposit their dishes. Then they streamed by me like salmon. I felt leprous and was sure it showed.

Seven observed me once more, then elbowed past as if Seepy Storage wasn't big enough for the two of us. I was willing to shrug it off. Some women hated you before you even spoke. You would never be anything but competition to them. So much for the Women's Movement.

Rudy lecherously wiggled his tongue at me as he passed.

"Into the cocktails already?" he asked. "Don't worry. On the sixth day, it tastes like Kool-Aid." He laughed and patted my back.

"You're so funny," I said, not having a clue what he was talking about. I was ready to dismiss it, before the door closed and I spotted the elephant in the room.

CT:

"Um, Cooper. What's that?" I asked, pointing at the glass of fizzy clear and red liquid.

An empty bucket was underneath the table. Cooper leaned against the counter. He scratched his head and fought a smirk. "This is consumption training," he said. "Look, I never said it was going to be easy."

"What is it?"

I kind of knew. I kind of knew but didn't want to know and hoped that I was wrong. I had to be wrong.

"It's a B&T...uh, blood and tonic."

"You're joking."

"I'm not."

"You don't expect me to drink that?" I asked, stabbing the air with my finger. "Because not on your life...not in a...in a million years am I going to drink blood! Are you crazy?"

"Em, it's not human...it's deer. And I wouldn't ask if it wasn't necessary. We've all done it. None of us liked it, but we did it. You're going to need to build up a tolerance."

"Why on earth? I don't get it." Then I did. "Wait...*no*." Cooper folded his arms and looked down at his shoes. "We need to pretend to be them? That's it...right? We're going to go out there and *pretend* to be them." Cooper returned his eyes to me.

"Yes. We need to be them. What did you think...we, uh, waltz in? Slide off a couple coffin lids? Stake a couple vampires, and then *presto*...the country's ours again?"

"Well, no, but—"

"Everything revolves around information, Em. Information and knowledge. Without these two things, we're shooting blanks in the dark."

I recalled dressing up like a vampire once for Halloween. The plastic teeth that you can't talk through, the acrylic cape, the curved purple fingernails, and the red face paint around the mouth. I thought I looked scary at the time.

"You want me to be a vampire?"

"Once you're trained, you'll be ready."

"To be a vampire?"

"Yes."

228

"But I don't look like a vampire."

"After a vampire has fed, they look like you and me. A couple dental caps, some Terinols for sweating, since vampires don't sweat, and a tolerance for this stuff—" Cooper took the glass off the table and held it up like he was toasting me "—and you'll be a regular *Nosferatu*."

I sat down on the bench and accidentally kicked over the bucket. Cooper placed the glass in front of me. I slid it away without looking.

He shrugged. "You don't have to do this, Em...but know that we need you."

I nodded. "So we go into their homes?"

"No. Bars and clubs, mostly. These operations are few and far between but very necessary. We've got someone on the inside who sends us snitches, and they like the busy places. We've gotten great intel so far, which means if we need to arrange a meeting at the top of the Eiffel Tower...we're gonna do it."

"He's a hunter?"

"Who?"

"The guy on the inside?"

"No, he's a vampire. His name's Leech."

"A vampire? Why is he helping us?"

"He's an old friend of Scott's."

"And the snitches...are they his buddies too?"

"No, we give them blood. Good blood. Black market stuff."

I shook my head. Cooper sat on the bench across from me, resigned to explain. He moved the glass away from us, and from a distance it looked lonely and stricken.

"The rarest blood type is AB negative," Cooper said. "Also rare, the blood from a person of mixed origin...let's say Samoan and Russian, or Finnish and Thai. Combine both factors and you've got one hot vampire commodity. It's like tiger pelts or ivory...in our day."

In our day.

"Seven?" I asked. Cooper nodded.

"AB negative. Her mom's Mexican. Her dad was from Greece."

"Our blood tastes different?"

Cooper nodded again. "Yes. We wouldn't be able to tell but..." He stopped, his thought derailed.

"You can't keep taking her blood? She'll die, won't she?"

"We extract about 30 milliliters each time, enough to fill a small syringe. Her blood is a delicacy. Even that small amount goes for hundreds of thousands on the black market. The UVF keeps the good stuff for their members and sells what's left. Only the wealthy can afford it. Anyone caught with unregulated blood is sentenced to death, which in my books is a good thing. Less of them is always a good thing."

Listening to Cooper, I understood. I understood that the others had had more time for everything to sink in. To them, all this was like a thin film covering their bodies. It was thin enough to obscure and make things dismal, but it could be torn through with some targeted pressure. For me, it was a thick layer that kept getting thicker—like an energetic stranger was circling me with cellophane. I was suffocating.

A bit of vomit came up, and I swallowed it back down. I looked at the full glass at the end of the table and remembered the vow I had made.

Cooper continued: "Like I said Em, it's not hu—"

"Shush."

"Did you just shush me?"

"*Shhh.*"

I tucked my hair behind my ears and tried to calm my breathing. I leaned to get the glass and drag it over. It was a highball with a gold rim. From the top, the drink could've passed as a Tequila Sunrise, except with tonic water instead of orange juice. And blood instead of grenadine. Red swirls threaded through the clear liquid. From memory, I called up the recipe:

Ice

1 ½ ounces of tequila

2 dashes grenadine

Freshly squeezed orange juice

Fill a Collins or highball glass with ice. Add the tequila. Add enough orange juice to come almost to the top of the glass. The amount will vary depending on the size of the glass. Gently pour the grenadine into the glass and serve.

DO NOT STIR!

It's supposed to look like the rising sun: thin pink clouds twisting around a flaming star.

I glanced down at the top of the drink again and saw a bleeding silver moon. Bubbles rose from the bottom and burst at the surface. I smiled and it must've looked crazy, but I didn't care. I was willing to try anything and smiling is meant to make you feel better.

I seized the glass and drank.

Two different textures filled my mouth: dry effervescent fizzy and thick salty oily. I tried continuously swallowing but only choked, so then I went for a more assembly-line consumption. Drink, fill mouth, pause, swallow, swallow. Drink, fill mouth, pause, swallow, swallow. This was difficult, too. It gave me time to taste and think. My swallowing took on a sound, and I wondered if it was all in my head, or did blood really announce itself as it slid down a person's throat?

Swallow, swallow.

Blood, blood!

I finished the drink off and held the glass upended against my lips for a good minute before realizing it was empty. I was shaking. I slammed the glass down on the table. It teetered, then toppled over and rolled to the edge. Cooper stopped it just in time. He stared at me, looking lost for ways to make the situation better.

"It's all going to be okay, Emma." His hand reached for mine. I pulled away before we touched.

"I don't think it is." The inside of my mouth was coated and sticky. My stomach tensed. I stood up from the table, nearly knocking my seat over. "I don't think it is."

I turned and ran out the kitchen door. Cooper called after me. I was trying to swallow but had no more saliva, so the blood stayed, painting the inside of my mouth and tickling my tonsils.

I went left and ran past dusty, abandoned cubicles. I could almost see the ghosts of the people who had worked in them. They tapped on keyboards, stared at family photographs, and shifted paperwork. They watched me as I ran by. *Save us*, they said.

Save us.

The sixth floor lounge was on the other side of the building, and I would avoid it at all costs. I didn't want to see anyone, especially people who would take pleasure in judging me. What I needed was fresh air, and now.

I took the elevator down to the first floor. Charlie was reading a book at the security desk and startled when I ran past. I pushed through the exit into the garage. The second door was trickier: four deadbolts and a heavy metal bar that needed to be lifted up. I managed them and finally got outside. The sun was bright. I sucked fresh air into my lungs like a junkie. I stopped running and slowed to a walk.

The corner of the building was straight ahead, with Mt. Stuff looming at my back. I shot a glance behind me to make sure it wasn't following, brought to life by the human memories that filled it. Objects broke and shifted under my feet. I stepped over a mix tape labeled "LuvU4Eva 86." A doll head stared as I passed, sticking out of the ground as if planted there for the purpose of one day growing a doll-head tree.

I found a piece of wall free of weeds and junk, and sat. I felt better but not as good as I would've felt with a large bottle of mouthwash. I closed my eyes and enjoyed the sun on my face. I thought of the 7-dehydrocholesterol in the stratum basale and stratum spinosum layers of my skin being spurred into Vitamin D3 production from the UVA rays—a relatively useless tidbit from high school science class. I heard someone approaching and opened my eyes. Charlie. He waved. A gun was holstered under his armpit.

"Hey. Mind if I sit?" he asked.

"No, go ahead," I said, putting on a smile. I wanted to be alone, but sometimes that was the best reason to have company.

"God, it's nice out, huh?" He gave me a squinty smile. "You know, you can actually find some pretty cool stuff out here. I found a UK first edition *Harry Potter* the other day, over there behind that bike wheel."

He pointed to a rusty tire in the distance. "It was sealed in a box and bubble-wrapped. Not bad condition. Could've gotten some decent money for it on eBay."

"Yeah?"

Charlie nodded and leaned forward to pluck a long piece of grass. He put the root in his mouth and chewed. "CT training, huh?"

"Word gets around."

"Actually, I recognized the look on your face. It's the same for everyone. Well…and you got a bit of…" Charlie rubbed his top lip.

"*Oh*." I wiped my mouth with my sleeve. "That's *awesome*," I said, speaking through my shirt so the words were muffled and barely comprehensible.

"Don't be embarrassed," he said. "We all went through CT at the same time. We'd joke about our moustaches. A bit morbid, I guess, but it helped. It must be hard going through it alone."

I shook my head, keeping my mouth covered. "It's fine."

"Let me see," he said. I moved my hand reluctantly. "Yep, you got it."

"Thanks."

"So where you from?"

"Outside Boston."

"Oh yeah? The Boston Tea Party, huh?"

"What about it?"

Charlie shook his head and laughed. "I have no idea."

I laughed with him, and it felt good. We both looked up as Cooper made his way over to us. He had Schizo on a leash and the dog strained against it, batting the air with his paws as if he was trying to climb an invisible ladder.

"Someone missed you," Cooper said.

I stood, wiped off the seat of my pants, and took the leash from him. Schizo jumped up on me once, before finding something more interesting on the ground.

"I'm glad I can hold his attention," I said.

Charlie stood. "Back to post. Catch you two later."

"Bye, Charlie...and thanks," I said.

"I didn't do anything," Charlie said, smirking. He turned and sauntered back to the entrance. Cooper and I stayed, watching Schizo, who proved less exciting than it would seem.

Cooper reached into a messenger bag and pulled out a bottle of water and a small cloth. "I brought you these."

I took the bottle first, cracked the top, filled my mouth, and spit. Then I chugged until the rest was gone and in my stomach. The cloth was warm and damp, and I ran it over my lips and eyelids which were dry and sore.

"Better?" Cooper asked.

"Yeah," I said. "Sorry I spazzed out. I've been through a whole lot of firsts over the past couple days but none I want to relive." I handed him the cloth, and he returned it to his bag.

Cooper smiled sadly. "Life doesn't always give us a choice."

"Gee, thanks, but I don't need a lecture."

"No...I'm not...That's not what I meant." He paused. "I meant to say that right now you *do* have a choice. You don't have to continue with the training, and if you back out, I give you my word that no one here will look at you weird."

"Oh, I'm already getting those looks." Cooper shook his head and shrugged.

"It's just because you're new. They're curious."

"If they were curious, they'd introduce themselves."

I could hear the cringing self-pity in my voice. It was like having a white-gloved hand hovering above my head to pet me when I spoke.

"Everyone here's been through some bad stuff, and we all deal with it differently."

Cooper shoved both hands into his pockets and kicked at a blue pen cap half buried in the ground. The cap became fully unearthed, and he nudged it along a path with the tip of his boot. Schizo watched with perked ears, before pouncing and eating the cap and a mouthful of dirt. I knelt and coerced his mouth open.

"No pen caps, Schizo. You'll choke."

I retrieved the cap from his mouth and stuck it in my pocket. Schizo sat and stared intently at the fabric bulge in my sweatpants, his nose powdered with dirt. I looked at Cooper, and we met eyes.

"It's just that the odds seem stacked against us. I need to know the *how* part, Cooper."

He nodded. "Okay. We think that there are three vampire clans. Three clans and three masters. Information that we've gotten so far says that if we can get to the masters, we can turn this war in our favor."

"The *how*, Cooper."

"We don't have all the facts yet, but you're just going to have to trust me. What we do know is that the masters' identities and locations are kept secret, for obvious reasons. We think that they stay mobile, moving back and forth between different locations. Only a few higher-ups at the UVF are privy to this knowledge, and any uncovered deception is grounds for execution, but for the rare blood that we've got, most will risk it. Blood is the here and now for vampires—feeding is more important than considering the future of their species. I can't tell you everything right now…but like I said, you just need to trust me."

I think I did trust him. He believed we were on the right path, and that made me feel better. Suddenly my posture straightened. My sore muscles felt on the mend. Schizo's gaze shifted from the pen cap bump in my pocket to my face, as if he had noticed the lift in my attitude. When I spoke, my voice came out strong.

"Okay. Let's get on with it."

CHAPTER THIRTEEN

DRINKING BLOOD GOT WORSE…

…before it got better.

That gray bucket became my friend, and I fed it a lot. Every morning, I was greeted with a tall glass of hemoglobin. Just animal blood, as Cooper kept reminding me.

If Schizo only knew.

The sessions progressed, and the mixer amount lessened as the blood levels increased, until the last few days when I became very aware that the mixer was gone from the glass entirely. It never did taste like Kool-Aid, as Rudy had joked, but one day it tasted like nothing. I was talking to Cooper in between sips, and before I knew it, the glass was empty. A glass of nothing.

Cooper patted my back. "Looks like you're a vampire now, Em." I would never forget that. I was a vampire.

WT:

Fight Training was called Weapons Training because abbreviated it was FT and Fear Training already had that abbreviation. Setting the record straight (if there was a record being kept somewhere), before killing Myers, I had never gotten in a fistfight, let alone used a weapon on someone. My first day of WT, Cooper started me on hand-to-hand combat. Scott had taught him strategies from varying disciplines, which, when combined, were very effective in matters of self-defense and could be deadly when it came to other humans. To kill a vampire, of course you needed a weapon.

HTH was anticipatory and reminded me a lot of poker. It was about knowing your opponent's next move by observing slight motions and tics. It also dealt with likelihoods by means of carefully measured percentages, for instance, if you swiped a person's ankles with your leg, coming in from the left on a right-handed opponent, there was an 84.3% chance they'd land on their back, giving you a 93.2% chance at a successful kill. There was a notebook with hundreds of these combat percentages written by some long-dead statistician. I figured there was a 98.6% chance that said long-dead statistician had murdered all of his friends and family to make that tedious book of numbers.

"So did this guy test on vampires?" I asked, slowly deflecting a punch from Cooper. We started fight sequences in slow motion, step by step.

"Of course not," he said, taking a practiced step back.

It was all very beautiful, but I was starting to feel like we were dancing, which would be great if waltzes killed vampires. I didn't think waltzes killed vampires.

"Well, I wasn't sure if he worked on Project Sunset—with Scott."

I took a step, copying the move Cooper had just completed by bringing my right arm forward. It was hot out, and a bead of sweat sped down the bridge of my nose and then clung to the tip, as if it had been on a suicide mission and was now having second thoughts. I wiped it away.

"Then aren't all those numbers meaningless to us?" I asked. "Those percentages are based on human-to-human combat—not human-to-vampire. Am I wrong? I mean...aren't vampires stronger or something?"

"They're like you and me," Cooper slow-deflected my arm, "with different strength levels. Some are stronger and some are weaker…especially if they haven't fed. The trick is to keep them away from your neck and to…*concentrate*." Cooper grabbed my arm, twisted around, and flipped me over his back. I thudded.

In my line of vision, the blue sky became Cooper's smiling face which was red and sweaty from exertion.

"You suck," I said, from the ground. "What happened to slow mo?"

"It ends when you stop concentrating."

Cooper reached down to help me up. He blocked out the sun completely and became a looming shape with vague features. My heart fell instinctively as the light level went down a notch.

"What's wrong? Did I hurt you?"

"No, no, it's nothing."

Nothing except my newfound fear of the dark. My phobias seemed to be multiplying and attaching themselves to me like lampreys. They sucked out my courage when it was the one thing I needed most. I grabbed Cooper's forearm and felt the muscles work as he pulled me to my feet. "In case you hadn't noticed, I was asking a question. A rather important one."

"Ask later, do now," Cooper said, letting go of my arm and getting into a fighting stance. I stood there.

"Catchy. Mind if I put that on a tee shirt?"

"As long as I get fifty percent of the profits," he said.

"Thirty percent."

"Forty."

"Twenty."

"*Hey*, you're supposed to go up," Cooper said, seeming genuinely irked.

"Really? Well, you being difficult makes me want to give you less. Remember that."

~

It was my first training day, and we sparred until just before the nighttime pushed the daytime behind its big black curtain. In the days to follow, WT sessions involved a bit of hand-to-hand in the morning and practice with a weapon of choice in the afternoon.

Stakes and semi-automatic pistols were a hunter's keepsakes. Scott picked the USP45CT for the hunters. The gun, developed for use by U.S. Special Op forces, was small and easy to conceal, had a decent recoil system, and kicked ass at getting off a lot of shots in a short amount of time. Known for accuracy and stopping power, the .45 cartridge was larger, and as a hollow-point, could create a substantial wound channel, or as Cooper put it, "a big fucking hole."

My targets were cheap Halloween decorations collected from the back room of some boarded-up store in Santa Monica. In reality, they were perfect for what we needed them for, these life-size cutouts of the monsters that haunted American cinema until one arrogantly stepped out of the screen.

Dracula was in there, along with the Wolf Man, the Mummy, the Swamp Thing, and a generic zombie. About 20 of each. They were constructed out of thin cardboard, their limbs attached by pegs to enable movement. We nailed them to trees at varying distances from the shooting point. With the wind just right, the cutouts arms and legs would swing wildly up and down, making them look like members of a demonic cheerleading squad.

241

A red paper circle was taped to each chest. The .45 bullets ripped through the paper hearts and lodged into the tree bark behind, sending out a violent spray of wood chips. After I shot through the Draculas, I moved on to the Wolf Men, which were just as scary looking as the vampires, if not as realistic. Funny enough, of all the creatures, werewolves were the ones whose existence I would have more readily accepted. I'd heard stories in the past about people being raised by wolves and seen a documentary about a man with hair covering his entire body. It was an affliction, and he certainly didn't go around eating human flesh, but it had made the legend more believable somehow.

When it came to target practice, I was a good shot and surprised both myself and Cooper. My instructor's voice went an octave higher after I emptied a magazine into the paper hearts of five Draculas swinging from far-off trees, in only my second hour of practice.

Holding a gun was like nothing I had ever experienced before. Holding a knife was different. People hold knives every day. Knives serve multiple purposes like spreading butter, slicing bread, cutting meat, opening packages, and carving wood. Guns have one purpose, and the first time you hold a gun that message gets sent through every inch of your body like an electric shock.

You can kill something with this!

I could have turned around and shot Cooper point blank, and he would've been DEAD. In a box. Food for worms.

Overnight, Cooper had become my murder guru, and it was funny 'cause he was such a nice guy. Scott, too. What it was was getting down to business. Spreading lethal knowledge so that what had to be done got done. It was the means to an end—the end of our grisly means.

Cooper taught me to think of the weapon I was holding as an extension of myself. The weapon and I would see the same things, move the same way, and share the same goal. It was a dangerous limb that could protect me from harm.

Standing there outside of Seepy Storage and loading and reloading that gun seemed like a rite of passage. It was different than killing Myers, which was in self-defense, and drinking the blood every morning, which made me feel sick or nothing at all. Loading that gun, I became the aggressor. I was the one with power. I swam a torrent river and climbed out on the other side with an extra set of guts.

Watch out vampires. I'm coming.

FT:

Similar to the small amounts of blood served to me in Consumption Training, Fear Training started with slight frights.

As a psychology major, I understood, and even believed in, the concept but didn't appreciate being a guinea pig. Did anyone ever, really? *Emma Spade...guinea pig.* It had no ring to it. Not even a twang.

Despite my apprehension, the systematic desensitization of me went ahead as planned. That was what it was called in the professional world. Systematic desensitization or graduated exposure therapy. It involved taking someone with a phobia, teaching them relaxation techniques, and then exposing them to a hierarchy of their phobic object—in our case, vampires. The idea was that I could conquer my fear of the creatures through gradual exposure (pictures, video) and meditation. After completing the tests successfully, a former patient can roam the earth without fear shackles and a hunter can go undercover and come out from under alive. For the hunters, conquering fear meant the difference between life and death because...

...vampires could sense fear.

As predators at the top of the food chain, they had acquired a heightened sense of smell. I wondered what fear smelled like. Sweat? BO? A roast dinner? Vampires didn't experience fear in everyday life like humans did. As far as they were concerned, there was nothing for them to fear.

FT at Seepy Storage assumed that anyone with or without prior vampire experience would be frightened of them, and not just frightened, but pissing-in-your-pants, *oh-my-God*, for-all-that-is-holy frightened. From personal experience, I knew this assumption to be dead on. Since my vampire revelation, nightmares plagued me like never before, in my sleep and in my wake. I discovered that my previous dreamtime had been a cakewalk. Comparatively, a real joy.

Every night, thousands of teeth bit into me and sucked me dry like I was a drink pouch. Every morning, I woke up desperately running my hands over my body, afraid of what I might find. An Emma suit minus its fillings.

The basement was in those dreams.

After my meet-and-greet with Barney, I never went down there, and when I got in the elevator, I'd check and recheck to make sure the **B** wasn't lit up. That I hadn't hit it by mistake. That the elevator wasn't malfunctioning. My heartbeat would quicken as the carriage descended to the first floor.

Are you sure? The elevator would taunt. *Are you sure you don't want to go down to the basement?*

Are you sure?

Yeah, I was sure. I didn't have plans to see another vampire until I had to. Unfortunately, that time came sooner than I would've liked.

CHAPTER FOURTEEN

BARNEY SMILED AT ME.

He licked his pale lips.

Cooper had fed him before my session. Filled his stomach with deer blood. His cheeks were rosy, but he didn't look stuffed. No, on the contrary, his eyes told me he was ready for dessert.

Cooper and Scott were outside the cage and what a nice place that was to be. Thick steel bars separated me from them. I was in the third phase of Fear Training. I figured it had to be the final one because what was worse than being locked in an 8x8 cage with a hungry hermit. Sure, I had my gun. I was told to keep it holstered until I needed it. I asked them to clarify.

"If Barney is on top of you," Scott had said, "and you can't fight him off, use the gun."

From Scott's answer, I understood that there were no plans for an intervention. If the shit hit the fan, I was on my own.

I straightened my posture, crossed and uncrossed my legs. I couldn't get comfortable. Fate had it that the vampire was in the comfortable chair. Mine was hard plastic that revolted against my curves. I came close to asking Barney to switch.

I brought a hand up to massage my shoulder. Barney took a keen interest in the movement. Too keen for my liking. My new watch beeped and flashed at me with fit-inducing fervor. It had taken my pulse and sincerely disapproved. The watch had been going off like that since the elevator, and I felt a headache coming on—one of the bad ones that make you feel like your brain is bruised. I glared at the contraption before caressing my temples

"Relax, Emma," Scott said, from outside the cage. "Practice your meditation."

"When can I get out of here?" I asked.

"When you show us you can sustain a safe heart rate."

"For how long?"

"I don't know Emma. It's best you don't think about that."

Not the answer I was looking for.

I started breathing like Scott had showed me: short breaths in, long breaths out. He said it was a common misconception that deep inhalation relaxes the body, when in fact deep breaths only let more oxygen in, accelerating panic. I kept my eyes on Barney, whose black eyes were on me, and counted backward in my head from ten.

When I hit one, I was on the island of Martha's Vineyard. My mom had a friend who lived there, and we'd go for daytrips when I was little. We'd sit on the beach and watch the ferries come in, brimming with happy tourists. I heard birds singing, water lapping the shore, and distant voices speaking in lazy, summer tones. Scott, the host of my meditation, told me about the fluffy cloud that would eat my worries when I was ready, and I was, and I fed Barney to that cloud and the cloud turned black. Then the sun shone down on the cloud until it began to break apart and soon was no more.

I was back in the cage. I had never left, really. On my beach, there had been an awareness of Barney and his movements. A total disconnection was far too dangerous and would defeat the purpose of the exercise. The meditations were meant to relax but also to build up a reserve of tranquility that could be dipped into when needed.

Eventually, it would be like flipping a switch. Instant calm. Until then, force-feeding would be necessary.

The beeping had stopped. I was proud, as were my two watchers.

"*Good*, Emma," Scott said. "Now stay with it. Your worries are gone…your mind is free."

Scott had gone through fear training at The Company. The transition from college kid to assassin had to have been tough. Appropriately, Scott was the one leading me down the path from fearful to fearless.

~

It started with a picture and a watch.

The picture was a color photocopy of Edvard Munch's *The Scream*. The watch was a Seiko that mainly monitored heart rate, but told time on the side. I studied the photocopy, which was furled at the edges from age but still vibrant. The painting had always entranced me with its long, sweeping strokes and that poor, poor person on the bridge so consumed by a mystery horror.

"Fear," Scott had said, holding the picture up, "is debilitating. It's a disease that can be spread to others. In the business of hunting, you have to know that your fear will kill you, if given the chance, and probably others around you."

Each FT session started with meditation practice. Then, Scott would inundate me with photographs and drawings of vampires. It was a presentation of death and destruction. Scott allowed time for each picture, dangling them in front of my eyes until I vocalized a number from one to ten on my fear barometer, ten being uncontrollable fear.

My heart monitor did most of the telling and I figured Scott had the hunters rate their fear out loud to encourage participation and maintain interest. The pictures included scenes from films, paintings by famous artists (including another one from Munch called *Vampire*), and anonymous sketches. I wondered if a resident of Seepy Storage had made the drawings. Perhaps the place offered an art-as-therapy class. *Don't fear vampires. Draw them!*

I found most of the pictures scary, and all of them made my heartbeat quicken and skip like a girl with curls. Pictures of *Nosferatu* scared the hell out of me. But there were others even more frightening.

Polaroids were taken of a group of actors backstage at a vampire play, probably *Dracula*. The decade was the eighties; telltale signs being banana clips and crimped hair. The actors didn't have their makeup on yet, but the teeth were in. A few posed casually, while others turned up the drama for the photographer.

A quick look at one of these pictures and it was as if my soul were scraping its fingernails up and down my spine. The monitor would scream. In the end, vampires weren't 18th century lords in castles. They were mothers, daughters, fathers, sons, grandparents, and neighbors, and they looked like us because they were us.

Whether Scott understood my reaction to the actor photographs, I didn't know, but in time, I learned how to ride my fear and the beeping stopped. The next level of FT was one of suggestion: *Barney's next door* (lights on). *Barney's next door* (lights off). *Barney's in the room with us* (lights off). *Stay very still* (lights off). *Did you hear that noise* (lights off)? After a few hours of this, I was a bundle of nerves and failed to sleep a wink that night.

I learned to hate my heart monitor. It became the bane of my existence, second only to vampires. It was my own personal tattletale. Always with me, always shouting out my weaknesses from the depths of Seepy Storage.

~

Barney sneezed, and I jumped, screeching my chair along the floor.

I didn't think vampires could sneeze, and I nearly blessed him. He stood, scratched his nose, and eyed a smudge of blood on the front of his shirt. I wasn't sure why that particular one got his attention, there were so many to choose from.

My watch started to beep. I stood, too, taking a step so my back was against the cage bars.

"Guys, what do I do?" I asked, not moving my eyes off the vampire. I liked him sitting better. Sitting was good.

"Stay where you are. Don't do anything right now," Scott said.

"Cooper?"

"He's right, Emma. You have your gun if you need it. But just try to stay calm. Control your breathing."

Barney's eyes moved to me. He walked forward, a limp in his step. He looked at my watch and tilted his head. "I like scare," he said. His voice came out gargled.

Another step.

I moved a hand closer to my holster. My watch beeped faster.

I tried to slow my breathing. My chest ached. I thought of a big sun. A big sun blowing Barney to pieces. Martha's Vineyard. Water lapping. *Calm. Calm.*

"I like scare," he said, again.

He lunged at me.

I scrambled for my gun, but it was too late. The vampire was on top of me.

He smashed into me with the force of a tornado, all legs and arms.

My body hit the floor. The smell of old blood permeated. I had forgotten everything Cooper taught me. I was a child being attacked by the closet monster. If only I had a blanket to hide under.

Cooper shouted my name.

I was pinned. Barney wasn't just a bag of bones like I had thought. *You live, you learn.* But sometimes you lived, you learned, then you died.

I heard the door to the cage shimmy. Was that a key in the hole? I couldn't turn my head to look. Someone said, "No." Not with urgency, but with authority. Scott.

They really weren't going to help me.

Barney's mouth, those sharp teeth, moved closer to my face. His eyes rolled back in his head in anticipation of my blood in his mouth. My right arm was the only thing between us, wedged in against my chest and his. I squirmed and kicked. My other arm floundered for my gun and...

I felt it—the cold metal of the gun's handle.

So pleased to meet you.

No more beeping, now. Only stillness.

Barney stopped his descent toward my neck. His head tilted, his forehead furrowed. "No scared?"

"No. No scared," I said.

I drew the gun and shot the vampire point blank in the head. The hole was massive, and I could see the other side of the cage and Barney's comfortable chair through it. I got my legs underneath the vampire and catapulted him backward.

Another shot to the heart, and he was dead.

Bits of everything that had been in Barney came out. The blood would have been deer blood, but the other stuff was all him. I wiped my face, making eye holes, and spit.

Barney lay dead on the floor of the cell. Now just a bag of bones.

Cooper jiggled the key in the cage lock. He swore. I sat up calmly, the sound of lapping water still in my brain.

Cooper finally managed the door open, and it felt like the end of an eternity. I holstered my gun and noticed slime on my weapon catch on the edge of the leather holster. He rushed toward me. I put an arm up to keep him away. I ached from my fall, and everything was sticky, but I could get up on my own. I stood and moved past him through the door. Scott remained outside the cage, where he was when the hermit was about to take my life.

I left that cage with a grudge.

"Good job, Emma," Scott said. "You'll be ready soon."

"Fuck you," I said.

Scott smiled grimly and looked down at the floor. "What did you want me to do?" he said. "It was part of your training."

I stayed silent and made my way through the maze of boxes. I got in the elevator without them. They were both watching me as the doors closed.

"I'm saving your life in the long run," Scott said. The doors clamped shut.

~

Back on the fifth floor: I still had my gun, but that was okay.

Once I passed basic WT, I was allowed and encouraged to have it on me at all times. I turned the corner not expecting to see anyone. I had learned that at that time of day the hunters were on errands and Mary was tutoring the kids in the upstairs lounge.

I turned the corner not expecting to see anyone, but saw everyone because they were all there. Except for Cooper and Scott, who hadn't made it upstairs yet, and Charlie, who must have been on watch. The rest were lined up on both sides of the hallway outside the residential units. When I appeared, covered in Barney, there were no shocked faces. No *tsk*ing over my appearance. They clapped and smiled and gave me congratulatory slaps on the back as I passed. Rudy, first in line, gave two thumbs up.

"Looking hot," he said. "Red's your color."

The guy called Topps tipped his cowboy hat at me. He had a shaved head and was covered in tats. No one had made introductions that first night, after I saw him standing guard upstairs, and we had yet to officially meet. Seven was clapping, too, but I felt she was under duress. Her mouth was tight, and her head was stuck arrogantly to one side. Mary raised her bible in the air as I passed, and I was half convinced she was going to hit me over the head with it, but she didn't. She closed her eyes and prayed, her voice strangely louder than the celebration. Sammy and Bugs stood next to her. Bugs jumped up and down and said *yay* over and over again, and Sammy congratulated me with a real smile. He had Schizo on a leash, and the dog seemed to be the only one reacting logically: he was growling.

It appeared that I was in the middle of my killer graduation.

I stopped outside my closed unit and turned around. That was when I heard the music.

"Is that circus music?"

"Yeah. It was my idea," Rudy said, laughing. "The speakers are crap. Otherwise, I'd have it blasting."

"Well, thanks," I said. "It really makes me feel like a freak."

Rudy nodded and smiled, as in mission accomplished. "Speech" was being uttered amongst the crowd of six. *Speech? About what?* My watch started to beep, and everyone laughed. I turned it off and felt my face flush under the grotesque blood mask.

"Um, okay...a speech," I said. Cooper and Scott came around the corner. Cooper looked concerned while Scott was floating in a dull air of anger. "Thank you for this. It's great. I, ah...just blew a hole in Barney. I hope none of you were close." *(Laughter)*. "This is an honor I never asked for. I never wanted to be a hunter, but I guess...well, I guess none of us did. I only hope that all this makes a difference. Thank you, Seepy Storage. I'm going to bed."

The crowd had turned somber, except for Rudy, who shouted for an encore. I knelt to open my unit door and vaguely heard Bugs say something about my going to bed so early and during the day of all times and that people would start to think I was a vampire. Schizo followed me into the unit, still growling.

"Be quiet, Schizo," I whispered. "It's *me*."

I sat on the bed and called him over. He became persuaded only after I pretended to have food in my hand.

I couldn't bear touching myself and needed to take a shower, but felt too drained, emotionally and physically. I contemplated crawling under the covers as is, but couldn't get myself to do that either. So I just sat. Cooper appeared in my doorway.

"If you ask me how I am, I will shoot you," I said.

He came over and sat on the bed next to me, and it was okay. It even felt comfortable. It's funny how relationships can take leaps and bounds in a short amount of time. The noise outside the unit was dying down. The circus music had been turned off, and voices grew distant.

"I just wanted to tell you that I'm leaving," he said.

"Leaving?" I felt a tug at my heart and was glad my monitor was turned off.

"A few of us are going out for some supplies," he said. "Gas for the generator, some more water, and other stuff. Mary, Seven, and Charlie are staying behind. And the kids."

"Can I come?"

"Not this time," he said. "Training's over, you should relax. Do some reading...get some sun. You might have to watch the front for a couple shifts, but it's easy. Just coordinate with Seven and Charlie."

I nodded. "When will you be back?"

"We'll be gone today and tonight and back on...uh...Wednesday day, I think."

"Have you been holding out on me?" I narrowed my eyes. "You don't have a calendar, do you?"

Calendars were hot commodities at Seepy Storage. The facility closed its doors in 2003, which meant the calendars at our disposal were useless. Although one would have been nice to have, hunters had more important things to collect on supply runs. Consequentially, we never knew what day it was. When someone asked, days were suggested, but they were just guesses and we often found ourselves choosing between two. Everyone still liked Friday.

I thought a calendar might be good for me—that planning and making goals would help me to feel real again. I could even cross off days.

"No, but I heard it was Monday," Cooper said.

"Oh."

"Scott seemed pretty sure about it."

"Oh, okay. Well, that's good. Maybe I'll write it in my journal…so we can keep track. I mean, even if it's wrong, we should start somewhere. We could post it in the kitchen too."

"Sounds good," Cooper said. He looked at me, and I looked back. He brought his hand up and hooked my hair behind my ear. Rudy's voice popped into my head.

Red's your color.

I remembered I had Barney all over me and looked away. Then it was Cooper's turn to look away. He scratched his head before standing.

"Guess I should get going."

"Yeah, okay, bye."

Neither of us was looking now. It had become a competition of whose eyes could avert the best. Of course there could be no winner without a third party present, and Schizo didn't count. Cooper was nearly out the door.

"Hey, Cooper." *I lose.*

"Yeah?"

"Be careful, okay?"

"Sure." He smiled. "See ya."

He waved, then left. I counted his footsteps down the hall: twenty before there were none.

I felt horrible and I wasn't sure whether it was about Cooper leaving, or well, everything else. I decided to really take it easy over the next couple days, like Cooper had suggested. I'd get some reading done and maybe socialize a bit, though my options were limited.

I had dubbed Mary and Seven "The Shun Sisters." Mary ignored everyone except the children, and Seven ignored just me. Charlie was someone I could hang with, but I had learned from Bugs that Seven and Charlie were *special friends,* and the news made me wary of overstepping my bounds. Though a giant rift already existed between Seven and me, of her own making, I had no desire to decimate the chance of building a bridge one day.

Schizo deposited his chewy cross on my lap. He had lost it for a while, and I was convinced Mary had taken it. I picked up the cross and threw it to the other side of the unit—just another act that would probably buy me a one-way ticket to hell. Schizo fetched it and returned it to my lap. I threw the cross again and began gathering up a change of clothes. I had found the motivation for a shower.

~

The next two days passed like snails in honey.

After my talk with Cooper, MONDAY got written down in my journal. It was the only thing in there, and the other pages were beside themselves with jealousy. I was never much of a writer. I probably could've kept track of the day in my head, but I didn't want to assume. Head injuries seemed likely. I still wasn't sure it had been Monday, but whatever. Like I said to Cooper, it was a start.

I tried to relax, which was easier said than done. The state of relaxation usually preceded thinking, and thinking in the day of the vampire usually preceded panic.

I kept up with the meditation and jogged the facility grounds once in the morning and again in the afternoon. I guarded the front entrance a total of two times. They were long shifts, going twelve hours each, but I could read and had found a book that had nothing to do with vampires or killing. It was about a boy who loved a girl.

To my surprise, Mary asked me to babysit Bugs on Tuesday. She said she wasn't feeling well and wanted to lie down. Bugs herself was looking pale, so I gathered Schizo and some of Bugs' toys and we headed outside. I knew Sammy was on guard, and hanging out front would be a good way to put my mind at ease. Since our first encounter, the boy had been taken off watch permanently, but being short hunters meant Sammy got a shift. He wasn't too pleased about it, either.

"How goes it, Sammy?" I asked.

"Okay...I guess," he said. He slouched over the desk with his head heavy in his hands. His palms pushed his cheeks up, squishing his eyes and making him look like an Asian version of Sammy.

"We'll be right outside if you need us," I said, over my shoulder.

"Yep."

Bugs blew Sammy a kiss as we walked by. He was twice her age, but to a little girl with no other kids around, he was her one true love. Sammy sighed and rolled his eyes. Bugs kept smiling, simply delighted to see her crush. I stifled a laugh.

Outside, it was overcast, but the sun made an appearance every few minutes which was good enough for me.

I found a nice spot, cleared it of some obstructive weeds, and laid a blanket down. Bugs dropped her toys, and they looked at home in the jumble encircling us.

I removed my sweatshirt and straightened my tank underneath, making sure I wasn't flashing skin in front of an eight-year-old. I sat down, satisfied. Schizo curled up next to me, but his eyes were on Bugs. He tilted his head and perked his ears every time she touched a toy.

Bugs seemed content to play by herself, so I read a little and then closed my eyes. A breeze blew past, carrying far-off memories—ones from happier times. Bugs' voice rose and fell as she put on a melodrama starring Barbie and friends. They were all naked, and I was amused by my earlier concern of showing too much skin.

From what I gathered, drifting in and out, Barbie and her *special friend* Ken were going to a birthday party. Ken turned into a vampire at the party, and Barbie ran away and hid behind a rock. Ken walked by the rock several times and spotted Barbie when she poked her head out.

"I found you, Barbie," Bugs said, putting on a deeper voice as Ken. "You can't hide from me."

"Oh, *no*," Bugs said, raising her voice for Barbie. "Leave me alone, Ken. I don't want to be a vampire. Vampires go to hell."

Ken: "No, we don't. We live on earth forever and ever. You can be my bride."

Barbie: "Okay. I love you, Ken."

Ken: "I love you, too, Barbie."

Bugs pressed the dolls' plastic bodies together. Barbie screamed.

Ken: "You're a vampire now, Barbie."

Barbie: "Okay. I don't like it."

Ken: "Too bad. Let's go back to the party."

Barbie: "Okay."

I watched as Bugs put their hands together and walked them toward Schizo's big head. *Little did Barbie and Ken know*, I thought, *there were greater troubles on the horizon...like giant, drooling dogs!* Schizo went for Barbie's head, but Bugs moved the doll away just in time.

"No, dog," she said, with a warning finger. She pouted her little pink lips. Schizo gave a half moan, half bark as if resisting eating Barbie's head was the hardest thing he ever had to do. I ruffled his fur.

"I know, buddy," I said. "Hey, Bugs...how about Barbie and Ken go to the beach? Maybe do some surfing? I don't think there are any vampires there."

Bugs gave me a look that she had mastered. It said, "Someone is being completely illogical, and it's not me."

"Der, Emma. Vampires are at the beach. Vampires can go anywhere...'cept mass."

"Church, you mean."

Bugs nodded. "Church," she said, with her bottom and top lip sticking out in careful pronunciation. A fly flew at her face, and she swung her head back and forth, using her hair as a swatter.

I wondered what was ahead for the girl. A life of hiding in cement hovels, being tutored by a religious zealot, and playtime with Vampire Barbie? It was no life to lead. If anything, I could say that I had experienced a childhood and even an early adulthood without vampires, and that was a lot. Mine was a good life and it wasn't over and I'd be damned if this little girl in front of me wasn't going to have a good one, too.

"Want to raid the kitchen for junk food?" I asked.

Bugs' eyes lit up. "*Yes.*"

"Come on."

We gathered up our things and headed back inside.

We managed to squeeze every bit of sugar from the kitchen. I collected a couple of Disney DVDs from a stack in the sixth floor lounge. Bugs wanted to watch the movies in her room, so I obliged. I hated leaving the sun spilling unappreciated through the top-floor windows, but I felt sorry for Bugs and had a new urge to give the girl whatever she asked for. She spent practically every day with crazy Mary, and I was determined to let her have a fun time away.

Charlie and Seven's door was open. I snuck a peek walking by and saw them sleeping on the bed entangled in each other. Charlie was lightly snoring, which made Bugs giggle. Both hunters had worked the late shift the night before, with Seven upstairs and Charlie downstairs.

Bugs' room was next door. When we arrived, she and Schizo plopped themselves on the bed. She opened her arms like a crane and released the junk food, and it spilled onto the comforter in a bright assortment of colors. In fifteen minutes, boxes and bags were emptied and wrappers licked clean. Bugs reached a sugar high halfway through *The Little Mermaid* and came down hard at the beginning of *The Incredibles*. I liked the movie, so I covered a now-sleeping Bugs with a blanket and kept watching.

My eyes were heavy lidded when the scream came from next door. Bugs awoke, her face stricken. Schizo stood on the bed, muscles tensed.

"Emma?"

"It's okay, Bugs," I said. "Stay here, okay? Everything's okay."

I was on my feet and around the corner in two breaths.

Charlie and Seven were sitting up in the bed. Seven was crying. Charlie had his arm around her and was repetitively, but gently, running a hand through her hair.

"Are you alright?"

Seven looked at me, her face stained and puffy. She slapped her tears away and folded her hands on her lap.

"Get *out* of here, Emma," she said, focusing straight ahead.

"But I— "

"*Now.*"

Charlie looked at me, his face full of worry and apology. "She just had a bad dream, that's all. She'll be fine."

Bugs peeked around the corner of her unit and called to me. I couldn't get over how small she looked standing there. Everything was so big. Everything happening was just so *big*. I went to her, took her hand, and led her back into her room. We sat on the bed, and I tucked her in. It was early still, but she looked tired and I thought another 20 minutes or so would do her good.

"Is Seven okay?" she asked.

"Yes, she just had a scary dream," I said, pulling the covers right up to her chin.

"Do you have scary dreams?"

"All the time."

"Me too…I think," Bugs said. "Sometimes I can't remember them."

Small blessings. "Well, you don't have to worry any more, Bugs. I'm here to protect you."

"Promise?"

"I do."

I said it and meant it. I had a newfound attachment to Bugs. I wasn't sure what it was. No one could deny the girl had spunk, but I thought it might be something more. Possibly something maternal was trying to break through the strong female shell I had built up over the years.

Bugs' eyes were closed already. It was as if my promise had opened a window and summoned sleep in.

I turned down the television volume and heard the voices next door in a low buzz. Charlie and Seven were talking about her dream, no doubt. What I did next didn't make me proud, but in the grand scheme of things, I thought it was forgivable.

None of the residents of Seepy Storage seemed willing to share their stories with me. I had heard Cooper's and Scott's, but the others kept silent. Granted, I had never come right out and asked, and I couldn't claim to be any more open, but I felt ignorant as to what was happening beyond the walls of the storage facility. When I started to go out on missions with the others, I could do without surprises. Realistically, I had to expect a few, but the more revelations now, the better.

I took another look at Bugs to make sure she was still sleeping, then tiptoed to the corner of the unit that opened into the hallway. I grabbed my book along the way, for a prop in case someone came by. I got right up to the edge and turned my ear to the voices. The buzz became words.

"...feel better," said Charlie. "You can't just shut yourself off. It'll come out in what you do and who you are."

"Well, I can't help that, can I. And if you don't like it...you should leave."

"Please, Seven. I beg you. *Tell me*."

There was a long pause. Sheets made noise. Seven sighed laboriously.

"Alright."

CHAPTER FIFTEEN

THEN:
SEVEN

SOMETHING DRIPPED ON HER FACE.

It was warm, and it slid down her cheek and into her ear. Seven opened her eyes.

Wherever she was, it was dark, and as she waited for her eyesight to adjust, she heard an odd noise—a grunting—and things felt...

...not right.

Seven started to panic when she realized her eyes weren't adjusting. Things brightened a little, but stayed fuzzy, as if she were wearing someone else's glasses.

She tried to gather herself. She was lying down. And moving slightly. She squinted and a shape appeared above her—moving with her.

"What?" she heard herself say.

The shape moved faster, and so did she. She became aware of a pressure between her legs. *Inside her*. She reached up to touch the shape but didn't feel anything, like maybe it wasn't even there.

More dripping. Whatever it was went in her mouth and tasted distantly of peppermint.

A man screamed out. "*Oh, fuck!*"

Warmness inside her.

"Who are you? What are you doing to me?" Her voice echoed.

The movement slowed, then stopped completely.

Seven tried to move now, but couldn't, like she had been stuffed with rocks and thrown into a lake and she was...

...*sleeping with the fishes.*

She was in a murky underworld where strange creatures stared at her with big, hollow eyes. She was suffocating, before the vagueness that had offered her so little extinguished.

~

"Rise and shine, sleepyhead."

Seven felt hands on her. Her eyes jerked open. "*No!*" she screamed.

She was in a bed. A woman wearing a white uniform was applying a cotton ball to the crook of her left arm.

"Shush, honey. Don't get your panties in a twist," the woman said.

She was of medium height, with her hair pinned in a bun, and cheeks like a cherub. She was rotund, and the buttons of her uniform strained to hold her in. A nametag said Nurse Hobbs.

Nurse Hobbs slung a Band-Aid over the cotton ball. She held Seven's arm up and rubbed with one pudgy hand.

"There, there." The nurse walked to a window and threw open its curtains. "Let there be light!" she exclaimed, as suffering light filtered through dirty glass. She smiled back at Seven. "How do you like that?"

Seven tried to speak, but her throat and mouth were much too dry. Nurse Hobbs went to fetch a pitcher of water by the bed, and Seven glanced around. The walls were yellow—the brightest yellow—as if the happiest person on earth had chosen the color. The room was sparse and sterile. The smell of bleach engulfed. Machinery hung limp and silent behind her.

The nurse handed her a tall glass of water, and Seven grabbed it.

Without reason, she had it in her mind that this was someone who would take things away from her. Seven gulped the water, and some of it went down the wrong tube, making her cough.

"Silly girl. You should know how to swallow at your age."

Seven talked through the scratchiness in her throat: "Where am I?"

"You're at Sisters of Mercy Hospital," she said. "I'm your attending nurse...Nurse Hobbs. Anything you want, you just holler."

"What am I doing here?"

"Your doctor will be by shortly to go over everything."

Pain shot through Seven's head. She spoke through gritted teeth. "I need to know what I'm doing here."

Nurse Hobbs stared at her blankly. "I don't have the auth—"

"Listen, *bitch*. If you don't tell me what I need to know right now, I can't promise you you won't end up in one of these beds real soon."

"My, *my*," Nurse Hobbs said. "Someone's got a filthy mouth. Okay. You got the flu. Avian Flu. You're in quarantine. Sorry 'bout that." Seven could tell she wasn't sorry and knew it was her fault. She had a way of turning people against her within the first few minutes of meeting them. Nurse Hobbs headed for the door.

"Avian Flu? Wait. *Please*."

The nurse stopped.

"Please...I'm sorry. Really. I didn't mean it." She had, but all too often she found herself severing the hand that fed her, and that was no way to get ahead in life. "Can you please tell me how I got here? I don't remember."

Bits and pieces were coming back to Seven. Last she remembered, she was sitting in her gynecologist's waiting room over in Studio City. She'd gotten a notice in the mail saying she'd missed her yearly, and even though she called them to say they were mistaken—she'd already been in—the woman on the phone had asked her to stop by anyway. "Everything's easier face to face, don't you think?" she had said.

"Poor old Dr. Gibbons," Nurse Hobbs said. "You gave him quite the fright. Hot as a potato you were by the time we got you."

"Have I had any visitors?" Seven asked.

"Your parents. They got immunized, like myself. Near peed my pants the needle was so big." Nurse Hobbs chuckled.

"When can I see them?"

"Oh dear. You know quarantines are very specific about people coming and going, and I'm afraid your parents have used up all their passes. But I'll check with the doctor. Might be able to get you a special circumstance seeing as you've been out like a light the whole time."

"How long have I been here?"

"Going on a week, if I got my thinking cap on straight."

A week! That meant she had missed a week of work which meant she wouldn't have her rent on time which meant her landlord would be pinning her door with that pink eviction notice. He'd probably make her that offer again. The one involving dirty deeds in his office while his wife was away. Last time, she told him to beat it and that he'd be very sorry if he tried it on with her again.

Nurse Hobbs waited in the doorway. She shrugged, extending her uniform to its brink and making the exposure of her gigantic breasts seem imminent. "Is there anything else?"

Seven felt horrible, like her limbs were detached from her body and floating around the room, flipping each other off. She knew very little about Avian Flu. She thought it was contracted from being around birds, and she couldn't remember the last time she'd been around a bird, or any animal, for that matter.

"Am I going to die?" Seven asked, feeling vulnerable and hating it.

"Oh, almost certainly. The nurse closed the door behind her.

"Is that a joke?" she asked aloud. But Nurse Hobbs didn't return to answer her question.

Seven lifted up the Band-Aid and observed the tiny, crusted, puncture wound. She stuck it back. She had never thought of herself as someone who was scared of dying, but when it all came down to it, living had much more appeal.

A clock in the room said 10:30. She waited for her body to feel less unsure of itself before carefully swinging her legs out of the bed. She was wearing a teal johnny, and when she stood, pervy air caressed her bare backside. She walked to the window.

Outside, the hospital grounds were vast. A picnic-table area was spread out across bright green grass, stopping at a tall chain-link fence. She was high up, and she pressed the top of her head against the glass facing down and guessed there were at least ten floors below her. In the distance, the skyscrapers of downtown Los Angeles went missing in muddy skies.

Seven came away from the window and noticed the television for the first time. *I bet I'm on the news*, she thought.

"Finally made it to the big time," she said sourly. After three years, seven months, 13 days, five hours, and 42 minutes of auditions and only scoring a bit role as Bike Messenger #2 on a sitcom that was canceled before it could breath, her big debut would be made in real life, as a person of ethnic origins dying from a rare virus. She was sure that they would mention she was Mexican, and maybe they would even imply that she had brought the disease across the border with her, even though she had been a legal resident of California for over 18 years. *That's what we all do*, she said in her head. *We all work on farms, steal, and carry diseases.*

The television was suspended by brackets in the corner of the room. She reached up to turn it on, but nothing happened. She pressed all the buttons to no avail. *That figures*, she thought. A camera above the television had its red light on. Apparently, she was starring in someone's movie.

She eyed the camera and walked to the door. It was locked, and she wondered if that was normal. *Of course, it's normal, girl*, she thought. *You're contagious*. She felt restless and looked around for something to do. She settled back on the bed. She was tired and fell in and out of sleep as the sun moved across the room.

She woke up with Nurse Hobbs standing over her.

"Up and at 'em, Sleepyhead. The nurse took the liberty of throwing the covers off of Seven. The clock said 6:30.

"What's going on? Are my parents here?"

"No no, Silliness. We're going to move you into your new room, and then we're going to get some food in that nice, flat stomach of yours."

"New room?"

"Yes. You didn't really think you'd be staying in this lap of luxury forever? Born with a silver spoon in your mouth, I see."

Seven was surprised by *that* assumption. "It's just that I've been here a while and no one's told me much of anything."

"Aw, poor baby." Seven tensed at the nurse's patronizing. "Well, what I can tell you is you're getting some roommates and then you'll probably get some more."

"Roommates? But I'm contagious."

"And so is everyone else. You didn't think you were the only one, did you?"

Seven could have gotten into it again—the fact that she had been told a whole lot of nothing so far. But she thought *why bother* and hoped the look on her face said it all. Nurse Hobbs didn't seem to notice. She went into a closet and pulled out a folded pair of pants that matched the johnny Seven was wearing.

"Put these on." Seven rolled her eyes. "Unless you're interested in flashing your wares around?"

That was a point, and she slipped the pants on while Nurse Hobbs bustled around the room, not settling on any particular area or accomplishing anything noticeable.

When Seven was dressed, the nurse went for the door and she followed.

The lights were very bright in the corridor, making it seem like everything they passed was revolting against its current state. Seven didn't feel well at all, and she dragged her feet behind a waddling Nurse Hobbs.

They walked by a lot of people, some dressed in teal, like her, but the majority wearing white uniforms and nametags. They all smiled at Seven which made her uncomfortable. She had never been in a hospital before, but she was distrustful of such a large number of friendly people in one area.

Maybe it's because I'm dying, Seven thought.

It occurred to her that people might be friendlier when you're dying which annoyed her to no end because she would feel much better leaving the world she had known than leaving a world in which people were accommodating.

"Move your tush," Nurse Hobbs said, over her shoulder. "We haven't got all day."

There was always Nurse Hobbs.

Two bulky men walked by them, pushing a girl on a gurney. The girl looked to be about Seven's age, and Seven felt a strange emptiness as she passed. It was nothing like she had ever felt before and nothing like she would ever want to feel again. The feeling went away as soon as the threesome was around the corner, and Seven breathed a sigh of relief.

They traveled through a set of double doors into a long room with beds lined up against the walls. The doors buzzed as they opened and buzzed as they closed. Nurse Hobbs stood aside for Seven to go ahead of her.

"Cot number eighty-three," she said. "Down at the end on the left." She handed Seven a towel, a bathrobe, and a small zippered bag. "There are two bathrooms. You can pick one and freshen up, if you like. I'll be back in a jiffy." She left.

Seven proceeded slowly down the center aisle. The room reminded her of war hospitals she'd seen in movies, without the bloodied, moaning men. Some of the beds were filled, and shapes shifted restlessly as she walked by. The faint smell of vomit caught her nose. She noticed buckets next to several of the beds.

Each bed had a number, and she found hers. The bed was freshly made, with the linens tucked tight around the mattress. She sat and opened the bag Nurse Hobbs had given her. A small black comb, a toothbrush, a tube of toothpaste, bottles of shampoo and conditioner, a bar of soap, and a box of cotton fingers were in it.

Seven tugged at her nose ring, a habit she had picked up hours after getting the piercing. It hurt initially but was painless after the wound healed. She suspected the act looked very similar to nose picking, but she couldn't help herself. It comforted her.

Three beds down, a girl of about 13 thrashed, before settling into a curled position. Seven went to the bathroom and washed her face. There were no mirrors, and Seven wondered why and decided that maybe hospitals didn't have mirrors so people couldn't see the mess their bodies were in.

Seven brushed her teeth and returned to the main room. With perfect timing, Nurse Hobbs came through the doors at the far end. Seven deposited her stuff on the bed and met the nurse halfway. Next stop was the cafeteria, where girls all around Seven's age, give or take a few years, chatted and nudged large servings of colorful foods across plastic plates. A few eyed them, and Seven felt her guard go up.

None of the girls looked sick to Seven. If anything, they just looked sleepy. A few slept seated and bent over the tables with their trays pushed aside. A Chinese girl with dyed orange hair was passed out and drooling on an open magazine. Seven found it hard to believe that all these young women were dying. There must have been a hundred beds in her new room, and that wasn't counting the private suites. The situation was grim.

Seven caught the remnants of an idea floating around in her head, but it was gone in an instant, and trying to recall what she had been thinking was giving her a fat headache. Nurse Hobbs was in the middle of a spiel:

"—from 4:30. Don't arrive beforehand 'cause they'll boot you out. We encourage healthy eating habits. At Sisters of Mercy, you are what you eat. Vegetables and fruits are mandatory. Cafeteria closes at eight o'clock. Don't get here late 'cause they'll boot you out." Nurse Hobbs kicked up her right foot. The movement seemed to require a lot of effort, and she brought her foot down with a breathless chuckle.

Seven was led through the cafeteria to the game room, the most appealing room so far and very un-hospital-like. The artificial lighting was soft, and large windows promised lots of natural light in the daytime. Hanging evenly spaced from the baby blue walls were at least twenty framed romantic comedy posters, including ones from *When Harry Met Sally* and *Serendipity*. Cushioned lounge chairs with personal reading lamps and tables flanked both sides of the room. At the front and back of the room, a giant sofa and plasma television with surround-sound speakers. Shelves teemed with games, books, magazines, and DVDs. Four treadmills offered an amazing view of the city while you worked out. Yoga mats filled a wooden chest.

The room was crowded. Besides a couple of orderlies, the rest were female patients, again about the same age as Seven. Most were in groups, with a few curled up alone, sleeping or reading.

Nurse Hobbs started on another spiel, and this time Seven caught most of it.

"Here we have the game room. It opens at 10:30 in the a.m. and closes at 8 in the p.m.. You eat in the cafeteria. Food is not allowed in the game room. If you are caught with food in the game room, you will be given a warning. Three warnings and you will no longer be allowed to enjoy the game room. There is no cable or internet access. We here at Sisters of Mercy find today's news too stressful for sick individuals.

We got lots of games: Parcheesi, Monopoly, Life, Candy Land, Trivial Pursuit, Checkers, Chess, Operation, and more. We recently acquired an Xbox, which the girls really enjoy. Other than that, pill time's at 8:20 sharp. Be here or you'll be served a warning. Bedtime's at 8:30 on the dot. Any questions?"

Nurse Hobbs looked concerned. "My dear…are you feeling okay? Here, take a seat." The nurse led Seven to an occupied chair and made a plump black girl wearing headphones get up. Seven sat. Nurse Hobbs stood over her with folded arms.

Seven felt ill, but she wanted the nurse to leave more than anything. It was all just too much. She looked up at Nurse Hobbs and put on her best strong face. "I'm fine. I think I just need something to eat. Is the cafeteria still open?"

Nurse Hobbs raised a thick arm to look at her watch. "Oh, yes. With 15 minutes to spare if you move your tush. Mind pill time at 8:20." The nurse shook a warning finger at her.

"Okay." Seven got up from her seat feeling like she couldn't be away from the woman fast enough. She tripped over nothing and almost walked into a wall, and she couldn't recall a time in her life when she was so clumsy.

In the cafeteria, she got a tray and slid it down the line. There were a few stragglers, but most of the place was empty. She had the choice of chicken, pasta, or fish. She asked for chicken "minus the Bird Flu" and got a breast with a heap o' unidentifiable greens. Seven wasn't a big vegetable eater, but there was no refusing them. She tried. The cafeteria lady with the large mole on her cheek shook her head and gave Seven an extra scoop just for asking.

"Bitch," Seven mumbled, loud enough to be heard.

Seven found an empty table and sat, smacking her tray down. The Chinese girl who had been passed out over a magazine was still there, a few tables away. Seven stared at her, wondering if she was dead. For a whole minute…nothing. Then the girl scratched her nose, and Seven jumped. *Jeez, calm yourself,* she thought, but decided to give herself a break. *You're dying,* she reasoned. When the time came, she'd go with honor, but until then, she was allowed a break from perfection.

Seven shoveled the food into her mouth. It wasn't bad after all, and she was hungry. A licorice aftertaste lingered in her mouth at the end of the meal, and she went up for another Coke. She wasn't sure where to deposit her tray, so she left it on the table and returned to the game room in time for pill dispensing.

Three nurses circled the room like sharks with blue trays of Dixie cups. Nurse Hobbs wasn't among them, and Seven was relieved. One nurse announced, "Pills here!" every time she arrived at a patient, which made Seven think of city newsvendors.

Seven observed the process, and it was the same for each girl. A nurse approached the patient, the patient would take a cup from the tray and upend it into her mouth, the nurse would take the cup and check the patient's mouth, and then the nurse would record the patient's number off of her ID bracelet. Seven's number was eighty-three, same as her bed number.

Seven waited for her turn, and the nurse who approached her was the vocal one.

"Pills here!" she shouted, and Seven reached into the middle of the tray for a Dixie cup. Two pills sat at the bottom of the cup, one large, oval, and beige, the other quite small and blue.

"What are they?" Seven asked.

The nurse's nostrils flared. "The large one is a multi-vitamin, and the small one is a sleeping pill."

"What if I said I sleep fine?" She was generally a very good sleeper.

"Then you can take it up with Nurse Hobbs."

Seven downed the pills and showed the nurse that everything was empty. The nurse smiled smugly and recorded Seven's number on a small notebook pulled from her pocket. Seven wasn't afraid of Nurse Hobbs. She just didn't have it in her to see the woman again, so soon. *Besides*, she thought, *what's the harm?*

After pill time, patients were herded back to the sleeping quarters. Seven thought her turn in the bathroom would never come, but it did and she washed up quickly. She could feel the sleeping pill kicking in, and she wanted to be in bed before it took full effect.

Seven arrived at her bed and folded over the covers. Others did the same around her. There was a low chatter, but most of the girls seemed dazed and occupied with getting to sleep. Seven glanced up and down the aisle and immediately felt annoyed to be in front of so many strangers at such a vulnerable time in her life. Seven liked keeping her business to herself, which had been her only qualm about getting into acting. But the money she could make was always the sugar sweetening that ride.

In reality, the business that now separated her, number 83, from number 21 or 62 or 89 was minuscule, if any existed at all. They had become dead girls walking.

There was a tiny table next to the bed, the top as big as a paperback novel, and Seven put her towel and toiletry bag on it. As she slid under the cold, crisp sheets, someone spoke up next to her:

"New here, huh?"

It was a blonde girl in the bed next to Seven's. She was about 15, with big brown eyes and a chipped front tooth.

Seven felt her eyelids getting heavy. She rubbed at them. "Yeah...yes." Nurse Hobbs had told her she'd been there a week already, but Seven wasn't about to get into all that with the girl.

"Two weeks for me," the girl said. "It's been, like, insane."

"Yeah, has it?" Seven said, closing her eyes and hoping the girl got the hint.

"Well, not really, I guess. I just mean, like, being away from my parents. I've never been away from my parents—not even when they wanted me to go away. Cheerleading camp was meant to be all the rage last summer, but I said, 'No go,' and my mom and my brother thought I was completely whacko. I guess I'm kind of a nerd. I like being at home. What's your name? My name's Heidi."

"Seven."

"That's a cool name. *Seven.* I wish I had a cool name. Heidi's not cool. I'm always like, 'Mom, so did you want me to be a goat herder or something?' Seven's kinda my lucky number, but sometimes it's five, too. It depends, really. Maybe you'll bring me luck, ya think?"

"I have no idea," Seven said, becoming amused. "So aren't you tired or something?"

"No, uh-uh. My mom always says when I was little it would take me forever to get to sleep, and it still does. It used to annoy her. They could give me 80 billion of those pills, and it would still take me forever. Plus I'm sick. Well...sicker than the rest. I can't keep anything down. I'm like a big vomit monster or something. It's gross."

The girl looked sad, but Seven wasn't much of a consoler. Even when she cared enough to try, like where her family was concerned, it all came out sounding false. So she never bothered. She gave the girl a minute before asking some questions that were needling her.

"How did you end up here?"

Heidi's face brightened, and she seemed pleased that Seven was now participating in the conversation.

"Oh, I was at the school nurse for shots. I was talking to Tommy Dillon when they called my name over the loud speaker. I was like, '*Great*, shots. Just what I always wanted.' I hate needles. There's nothing I hate more, except for maybe spiders. There was a Daddy Longlegs in my bathroom once when I was taking a show—"

"So the school nurse noticed that you were sick?"

Heidi didn't seem to mind being interrupted. Seven imagined it happened a lot. "I guess." Heidi shrugged. "I blacked out or something. When I woke up, I was here. Why? Are you doing a survey because I'm really good at surveys. In Mrs. Montag's class, I did a survey on where my classmates see themselves in 20 years, and I got an A plus. I could help you, if you want?"

"It's not a survey. What about doctors...has a doctor seen you since you've been here?"

"No, not doctors—just nurses—which is fine with me because doctors always seem like more serious people, don't you think? I do. Really serious people make me nervous which is why when I go to college I'm not majoring in law or medicine, except maybe veterinary medicine because I really like animals."

"That's good. Listen, Heidi, I'm really tired so I'm going to go to sleep now, okay?"

"Oh, *sure*. Me, too. I'm tired, too. And sorry ahead of time if you

278

hear me puking. It's usually just in the mornings, but sometimes it hits me at night right before I pass out. It's pretty gross. I really don't like vomiting even though it can make me skinny like you. Anyways. Sorry, okay?"

Seven had closed her eyes already, and she put a hand in the air to give Heidi a thumbs-up. Heidi muttered, "Okay," again, before a raucous of springs and sheets and then silence.

The girl can talk an ear off, Seven thought. Her body felt heavy, and she went with it, pleased to have the weird day be gone. It was surprisingly noiseless in the room, and the occasional snore, creak, and rustle were finally strong-armed by insane quiet.

Seven thought (as well as she could) about what Heidi had told her and reasoned things away, as it was human to do. But she was also naturally suspicious of others and her suspicions would remain.

~

She was back in that dream again...

...the moans and the dripping on her face. Things were no clearer this time around, but in her head, she thought it was a good thing she was dreaming because it was all kind of frightening. Even for her, a girl who prided herself on fierce courage. Then she wondered if she'd think about being in a dream, in a dream, because she couldn't recall ever doing that before.

Seven tried again to reach up and touch the shape, and this time there was contact with a warm, slick surface. She gathered the effort and the mind to form her hand into a claw and swat at the shape.

A man's voice: "Ow!"

Seven's arms fell back. She was just a blob, heavy and unable to feel any separateness to her limbs. She was moving, like the last time,

279

but it was another entity's movement that moved her. Blackness crept in.

~

Seven heard a bell.

Slow and hollow, like a death toll. It quickened, and when she opened her eyes, she realized it was the Sisters of Mercy wakeup call. Two nurses walked down the center aisle swinging bells at the end of long handles.

Seven sat up and her head throbbed. Girls around her stretched, rubbed their eyes, held their heads, and looked awkwardly from one to the other. The smell and sound of vomit were acute. Seven pinched her nose and tried to think of other things. There was no retching coming from the neighboring bed, which made Seven happy despite herself. *Heidi must be feeling better*, she thought, but when she looked, the girl's bed was empty.

Others were making their way to the bathrooms. Seven grabbed her bag and towel and pushed past the girls already in line to a chorus of annoyed *heys*.

"I'm just looking for someone," she called back, not caring one bit whether they believed her or not.

The bathroom was fogged from steam. Seven checked out the girls at the sink area, waiting around for some to lift their faces from the porcelain basins. No Heidi. She called her name outside the showers and the toilet stalls. No answer. She went to the second bathroom and did the same. Still nothing.

Seven didn't understand her determination to find the young girl she only met once the night before. It was just there and she couldn't deny it.

A lanky nurse who Seven hadn't seen before stood in the center aisle, still clanging her bell even though most of the girls had risen and were out of bed at that point. Seven approached her.

The woman's nametag read NURSE SANDERS. The nurse's facial skin was slack and her hair stuck outward, as if both things were making a getaway from her body. Seven smiled. She needed information that the nurse might have and she'd be smart about it.

"Excuse me," Seven said. "I'm number eighty-three, and I noticed number 84 was not in her bed this morning. She was feeling sick last night, and I'm a bit worried she might be passed out somewhere."

"Number 84 was released," Nurse Sanders said, "into the custody of her parents this morning." She turned her back on Seven and started with the bell again. Seven winced as the noise split through her ears.

"Excuse me," Seven said, tapping the nurse on the shoulder. "Hi, me again. Um, you said she was released. Does that mean she was all better?"

"Yes. Clean bill of health. Someone else will be taking her bed today." Seven nodded. "If you're done washing, you need to get to the cafeteria for breakfast and pills."

"Sure. Great," Seven said.

She was confused. From what Heidi had told her last night, the girl was not in good shape. She even referred to herself as a vomit monster. That didn't sound like someone who was ready to be released after being quarantined for a deadly virus. Also, besides the multi-vitamin, no treatment was going on that Seven had noticed. Heidi said she hadn't even been visited by a doctor.

Seven made her way back to the bathroom and got in line this time. She showered, walked back to her area dressed in a towel, and slipped into a new hospital johnny that had been left on her bed. It was the same as the last one, and she was grateful, having seen grown women walking around in yellow sleeping gowns with tiny clowns on them.

She felt no different than the day before. No better. No worse. She wasn't feeling nauseous yet, and, assuming that was one of the symptoms of the virus, she was luckier than most.

It was a chorus of heaving around her. All of the bathroom stalls were occupied by those fortunate enough to make it there in time. The other girls got the buckets and the prying eyes. A few were ushered away by nurses, with worried expressions and vomit still on their faces. *It's okay, though*, Seven thought, *because it's not me*. She had fleeting thoughts of Heidi before they flitted away for good and she headed to the cafeteria.

Breakfast consisted of a vegetable omelet with a gargantuan orange and a side dish of strawberries. After that came the pills. It was the same beige pill, but the other one was different: small, round, and white.

"What's this one?" Seven asked, shaking the Dixie cup so the pills jiggled at the bottom.

"A multi-vitamin and the first course of your treatment," the nurse said.

"Treatment? Is it a cure?"

"It's treatment. You can address any questions you have to Nurse Hobbs."

"What about a doctor? Can I see a doctor?"

"When one is available—we're short-staffed at the moment."

"Short-staffed," Seven repeated, procrastinating. Her mind went back and forth. Either she took the pills that could potentially make her better, or she waited until she got more answers. Instinct told her something wasn't right, but refusing to take the pills would raise alarms.

"Bottoms up." She raised the cup and then emptied it into her mouth.

The nurse checked both Seven's mouth and the cup, jotted down her patient number, and nodded her head. "Very good."

Seven waited until the nurse was well away before coughing the pills into her hand and hiding them in the carcass of her omelet. She noticed the tray deposit this time and walked casually there, thinking light thoughts. Kittens and snowflakes. *Besides, what's the worst that can happen*, Seven thought. *A slap on the wrist?*

After emptying her tray, Seven went against the flow of girls heading into the game room and made her way to the bathroom. The stalls had been occupied all morning, and she was close to exploding urine all over the shiny floors of Sisters of Mercy Hospital.

~

She saw *him* on the way back from the bathroom.

He was dressed like an orderly, and he smiled at her as they passed each other in the hallway. He had brown skin, frizzy black hair, a bit of a belly, and three mean-looking scratches down the side of his face.

Seven's heart picked up speed. She stopped short, causing a pimply girl to knock into her. They both tumbled to the ground. The pimply girl apologized profusely even though it had clearly been Seven's fault.

"Did you see that man?" Seven asked the girl.

"Um, I'm sorry...what man?" the girl asked, trying to untangle herself from Seven and get up off the floor.

"The man...there...there," Seven said, pointing at where the man had been but wasn't anymore. "He was just there. He had scratches on his face." Seven touched her own face.

"Um, I don't think so." The girl talked through braces and had a bit of a lisp. She was standing now, and she started to back away from Seven, slowly, as if Seven had just gone nuclear.

"*Fuck*," Seven said, taking off in the direction the man had been heading. She stopped at the end of the hallway, where it turned, but didn't see him. She went back to where she had passed the man and began peering through windows and open doorways.

"Can I help you, Seven?"

Nurse Hobbs was standing behind her. The nurse's makeup was on heavy today, fire-engine blush decorating each cheek.

"Yes. Yes, you can," Seven said, continuing with her search. She went up on tiptoe to look through a door window. Beyond was a room much like the one she had first woken up in. It was unoccupied. "Your hospital is in heaps of trouble, Nurse Hobbs. *Heaps*."

"Well why don't you tell me what's going on in that head of yours," Nurse Hobbs said. "Come join me in my office."

CHAPTER SIXTEEN

NURSE HOBBS STARED AT SEVEN.

The nurse's hands were folded, and her thumbs twiddled. Bobby pins stuck out from her hair like tiny swords.

Seven could feel her temper boiling over and there was nothing that the yellow walls or the rainbow pictures or the lollipop treasure chest could do about it. "I already told you that I don't really remember it because those sleeping pills you give us make us *retarded!*"

Nurse Hobbs tsked. "Are those mean words necessary?"

"*Yes!* I'm telling you I've been raped by one of your orderlies and all you can do is sit behind that desk on your fat ass and criticize my choice of words."

"Sticks and stones, Seven," Nurse Hobbs said, standing. "I hate to say this, but my hands are tied. We run a very safe ship here at Sisters of Mercy. I know everyone who works on this floor personally—I even know their kids and their kids' kids—and no one matches the description you gave me."

"It could be that he doesn't work here? Maybe...maybe he's a visitor or something?"

"It's a quarantine, and we have very strict visitation rules. If this gentleman were here...well, I'd know about it."

Speaking of choice of words, Seven thought. Nurse Hobbs calling the rapist a "gentleman" made Seven madder. She felt helpless, a rare thing for her, and she despised it. Even with all of her past money problems, Seven always felt in control. She always had the upper hand, even when no one else saw it. Sitting in front of Nurse Hobbs, she had no idea what to do next and that scared the shit out of her.

The nurse turned to a filing cabinet behind her. "What's your number again, dear?"

"Eighty-three." Seven eyed a pencil holder filled with miscellaneous items on the desktop in front of her.

"Oh, let's see." Nurse Hobbs bent at the knees to reach a lower drawer, and her joints popped under the strain. "Oh *my*," she said, with a chuckle.

Seven spotted a letter opener in the holder. It was metal and smudged with fingerprints, long and sharp for a tool with such an innocent day job. *There you go,* she thought. There was something that could make her feel more secure—something she didn't object to using, if the need arose.

Eyes on the nurse, Seven brought her hand forward and got a hold of the letter opener between her thumb and index finger. She airlifted it from the holder, worried the various items around it might shift and make noise.

"Voilà," Nurse Hobbs said, except it was more like *voyla*. She straightened and half turned. Seven's arm jolted, nearly sending the pencil holder and its contents over the desk's edge. "Oh, wait...that's not it."

The nurse turned back, not lifting her face from the folder in her hands. Seven freed the letter opener and stuck it in the cinched waist of her hospital pants. Not sure it would stay, she applied some pressure with her lower arm.

"Here we go," Nurse Hobbs said, removing another folder from a different drawer. She opened the folder and looked the contents over briefly. "Oh, yes. You see, you'll be out of here in no time. Two months or so." She stuffed both folders back in one drawer and slammed both drawers shut.

"Really?" Seven asked, doubting the folder wasn't filled with a bunch of blank pages. "You mean I'll be cured?"

"Oh yes."

"Like Heidi?"

"Heidi?"

"Number eighty-four. A nurse told me she was released this morning."

"Well, then...yes. *Just* like Heidi."

Nurse Hobbs stared at Seven, and Seven stared back. The air in the room changed. It seemed to thicken, like it was becoming something she'd have to struggle to get through.

"So, what about the rapist, Nurse Hobbs?" Seven asked, sneering. She had half a mind to use the letter opener now.

She pleasingly pictured puncturing the nurse's big belly, but even her imagination couldn't rid the woman's face of its plastered grin. The nurse's entrails and black lies would be spilling out onto her regulation shoes, but that damn grin would remain. *No*, Seven thought. *I have to keep my wits about me.* She would escape, but the planning would take some time and she'd need her roaming privileges. *Kill the nurse and kill your chances*, Seven concluded.

"We'll look into it, but I'm sure we'll find nothing 'cause there's nothing to find. In the meantime, I'll lower your dosage. The treatment can make you drowsy...you may see things kinda funny. That's probably what happened, Seven—you're just seein' things funny."

Seven stood, careful not to lose her new prized possession. "Maybe

287

you're right, Nurse Hobbs. I don't feel well." Seven pressed a hand against her stomach and the concealed letter opener. "I'm going to go lie down for a bit. You know...rest up so I can get better."

"That's the spirit, honey. I'm glad to have cleared things up for you."

Nurse Hobbs accompanied her to the door. Their journey was but a few steps that felt like miles of torturous terrain. The nurse put a hand on Seven's shoulder, and she felt a chill penetrate her. Out of the office and down the corridor, the nurse's eyes stayed on Seven, and she felt them on her back, like two laser beams.

Seven stopped to catch her breath around the corner. It came in shaky and went out the same. Apparently her new tool didn't help her feel secure at all. If anything, the fear of losing it and being found out made things much worse. She beat feet back to her bed, grabbed her toiletry bag, and made her way to the bathroom and into one of the stalls. There, she slipped the letter opener out of her pants and into the bag. Seven covered it with the bag's other contents, then zipped the bag shut.

Seven returned to her bed and replaced the bag on the side table. Anywhere else would have been suspicious, but it took an effort not to hide the bag. Forces wanted her to slip it in her pillowcase or under the mattress or deep inside the layers of bedding. *Plainly not in sight*, her doubts warned her. *It'll be easier for them to take it from you.* She determined the best hiding place was no hiding place at all. Besides, whatever she did, she had to consider herself watched. At bedtime, when the lights went out, that letter opener would be in her hand.

~

Seven tried to nap, but the idea was almost absurd.

She had to have her head on straight over the next few days, making ample sleep necessary, but after what she had just discovered, it was the furthest thing from her mind. After a few minutes of excessive tossing and turning, Seven sat up and decided on a bit of recon. She stood, stretched, and observed two cameras in each corner of the room down at her end. Both red lights were on. She walked slowly to the windows, yawning. She tried the handle of one with a relaxed smile. *Some fresh air would be nice*, she thought, hoping to relay a feeling of calm to anyone watching. The handle wouldn't budge. Neither would the next, and she guessed the same went for the other two. She looked out the window.

Business as usual outside: birds, bees, flowers, trees. There was a peculiar amount of crows perched along some electrical wires, before one flew off and the rest followed in a heaving mass.

Seven looked down on a recently tarred parking lot and car roofs reflecting the sun. It was a long way down, and even if she could open the windows, jumping from them was not an option, and neither was abseiling. Without a rope on hand, she'd have to undress at least forty beds. Besides, they only did that stuff in the movies.

The parking lot was enclosed by the same perimeter fence that she had noticed the day before. There was no way through that Seven could see, and tangles of barbed wire looked threatening at the top. She knew if there was a way in, there had to be a way out. Somewhere.

Seven walked to the other end of the room, observing four more cameras—one at each bathroom entrance and two sandwiching the main door. In the hallway, cameras watched the elevators and the exits. Lots of staff milled about, taking notice of Seven but not dangerous amounts. They carried white cards that they'd swipe to enter most of the rooms, except the main ones frequented by patients. *I'll need to get me one of those*, she thought, not fully embarking on the thought just yet.

In the cafeteria, girls were finishing their lunches and heading for the game room and another day of distraction. From what she could see, all the silverware was plastic and wouldn't do as a replacement if the letter opener was taken from her. Virtually everything in the caf and the game room was harmless, except for one item. Seven had played a video game once that involved beheading zombies with thrown CDs. It was a stretch, but DVDs could be broken into shards that would be just as effective as her letter opener. Seven spotted just one camera in the game room, also by the entrance. Out of the windows, the parking lot cornered the building wide, like a giant lazy river. Seven still couldn't see a break in the fencing, and, frustrated, she slumped into an armchair.

Around her, girls occupied themselves with stuff people did on vacation: movies, books, and exercise. But unlike vacationers, the girls were peaked, lackluster, and carrying around vomit buckets. An Indian girl sitting next to Seven hugged a bright red bucket between her knees. She was halfway through a wilted copy of *Anna Karenina*. Seven recalled the ending and shuddered. Seven never liked the idea of mistakes that couldn't be fixed, which was why she gave every decision the thought it deserved and avoided one-way streets at all costs.

Seven knew Sisters of Mercy Hospital was somehow *wrong*. Something was going on and it didn't sit right with her and it wasn't just the rape. Seven had dealt with stuff like that before. Guys were horny bastards. It didn't mean that if that man tried to take advantage of her again, she wouldn't cut off his dick. Because she would. Nurse Hobbs couldn't turn a blind eye to the culprit after that. Seven would say to her: "See the guy running down the hallway without a dick. Yeah, that's your rapist."

No, there was something Seven couldn't quite put a finger on. Nurse Hobbs' reaction to the rape, Heidi's disappearance, and the hospital's lack of doctors were all arrows pointing to some secret horror.

There was no doubt in Seven's mind that many of the girls around her were ill, but she felt fine. Surely she wasn't sick. Since skipping her pills that morning, her energy level was up, her mind clearer, and her muscles felt less like soggy boards. *Maybe it's the pills making them sick?* Then the possibility occurred to her that the girls could be victims of a kidnapping scheme to test experimental drugs. It seemed farfetched, but Seven didn't want to rule anything out, even for its illogicality. *Stranger things have happened.*

Seven stayed reading in the game room. Through the window, the sky changed outfits. Pill time came and Seven gave a repeat performance from the morning, since it could not be said that the questions she had were answered to her satisfaction. After the nurses made their rounds, the patients were moved like cattle out of the game room and into the sleeping room. Although the vomiting had tapered off, the occasional sound of distant retching came like alien birdcalls.

~

Seven washed up and entered the bathroom stall with her bag.

Out came the letter opener.

It glinted in the light, and Seven caught her reflection, blurry behind fingerprints. She wiped it on her shirt and looked again. She was not past saving. Her dark gray eyes were clear, and her olive skin was without a blemish. She pulled the opener away from her face and focused on the point. She felt her eyes cross. *A point like that wouldn't take much effort*, she thought, uncomfortably. She was glad she had a weapon, but she wasn't looking to kill anyone unless they gave her a reason. Seven sometimes talked big, to others and in her own head. She used to get into fistfights a lot when she was little, but murder was leaping into unfamiliar territory.

Seven stuck the letter opener down the front of her pants, careful not to stab herself, which would be choice. She zipped up her bag and tucked and straightened, making sure no proof of dangerous intent was visible. She left the bathroom and swam through a gathering of girls to get back to her bed. When she got there, she noticed two new girls in the beds on either side of her. They looked nervous and she felt the societal pressure to spew comforting words, but had neither the knowledge nor the desire. If they forced dialogue upon her like Heidi had, maybe she'd end up feeling differently, but they didn't.

Seven got into bed, way down deep under the sheets, and touched the tips of her toes to the footboard. She remembered thinking as a young child that her bed was a safe-zone warding off harmful things. When she would hear a noise in her room, she'd pull the covers up so that only her eyes were showing. Eventually she'd escape into sleep, leaving whatever had made that noise far, far behind.

Lying there, Seven longed for those days—when cheap Kmart sheets were a force to be reckoned with. Even with the cold metal of the letter opener pressing against her belly, Seven knew that sleep would not come easily that night, or the next, or maybe even the next. That she'd reacquaint with sleep only after she was away from Sisters of Mercy Hospital.

Lights were turned off, the door buzzed shut, and soon, settling noises quit. Seven stared up at the ceiling, which was white and painfully uninteresting. Her mind began to wander, gripping thoughts she wanted to avoid. She thought of the man with the three scratches and wondered if he'd pay her another visit. The tough Seven challenged him to do so, wanted him on top of her so she could avenge herself. The real Seven wanted that man far away. *With any luck he's had a nasty fall.* She wished him on some other girl, even though she, armed and not sedated, would be the one girl most prepared.

The newcomer to Seven's right mumbled in her sleep, asking Joseph to take the dog out. Seven rolled onto her side and closed her eyes. *Just for a second.*

~

Seven's eyes slapped open. She wasn't sure how long she'd been out but thought it couldn't have been too long. She didn't feel rested at all and hadn't changed her position on the bed.

Low voices had woken her. Quiet squeaking, too, with a rhythmic pattern: *squeak, squeak, squeeeeak* and a couple seconds of silence before the next *squeak, squeak, squeeeeak.*

Seven didn't move, thinking it best to play dead. Two women were speaking somewhere out of her view.

"This here says it's numbers one to ten, excluding eight. Then 13, 24, 52, 68, 79, 89, 90, 91, 93, and one hundred and six," one of the women said. Her voice was deep and not familiar to Seven. "They're nearly a month along, so we can take them to the other floor. The ones being processed tonight are marked...right...here. Yep, you see—it's right here. Clipboard doesn't lie."

"I'm so sorry," the other woman said, her voice much airier. "I thought those ones were already processed last night. I *am* sorry. I'm just new to all this."

"They were processed last night and they'll be processed every night until we get results. I'll tell you, though. Some of these girls couldn't get knocked up if they were screwed by a stork." The other woman giggled. "But you didn't hear it from me, okay?"

Giggling, again. "Sure."

The squeaking resumed and got further away, as did the women's voices. Seven's heartbeat had quickened and she couldn't drop the worry that the two women might hear the beating and come by to discover her awake. At this point, as the troublesome thought was burrowing itself into her brain, the entrance door at the other end of the room swung open, and dueling light beams and silhouetted shapes appeared. They poured in with gurneys, and their numbers filled the center aisle. Then, they waited.

Seven observed two shapes per gurney, one at each end. The shapes got more human as they neared. They were wearing white, which distinguished them as staff. Most were women, and each had a small, circular light strapped to their head that cast a beam barely strong enough to penetrate the room's darkness.

The gurneys were empty but not for long. The figures abandoned the gurneys for the beds, one at the head and one at the foot. Covers were thrown off. Girls stirred. But not enough to save themselves.

They can't even open their eyes, Seven thought.

Then, she blinked, and each gurney was full up with a sleeping girl and the trail of them was leaving. The gurney with the squeaky wheel was the last to go. The girl on it had long dark hair that cascaded over the sides and rode the stirred breeze like waves. The two women she had heard earlier were still in the room. They were near her, speaking in whispers. Giggling in whispers.

Seven was sweating. Her hand rested on the waistband of her pants, and, more importantly, what was underneath. If those shapes had come to take her, she was sure she would've used the letter opener and ruined any chance of escape. There were too many of them. She wouldn't have made it out the door. But what she had heard those women say made her crazy. So crazy that she didn't think she'd be able to resist using any means necessary to not go where they wanted to take her.

Processing?

Seven didn't have to think too hard for the answer. It was right there waiting for her to turn over in her head a billion times. *Some of these girls couldn't get knocked up if they were screwed by a stork,* Seven recalled the woman saying. She attempted to make something else out of it, something innocent, but she was only fooling herself.

They're trying to impregnate us!

Seven wanted to scream.

The situation had gone from strange to unimaginable, moving her need to get out of that place from desperate to dire. Her body was shaking, feeling like it was already heading for the exit without her. Keeping still was becoming impossible. She wished those women away—pictured them walking out the door and stating loudly that they were done for the night. *All done here,* they said in her head, and then they giggled because it seemed to be something they did a lot. *All done here,* they would say, before closing the door and leaving Seven and the remaining girls alone.

But it didn't happen that way. The dark train came back.

It started, again, with the squeaking wheel.

Seven closed her eyes tight as the gurneys reappeared through the door. She prayed for the first time in her life. Seven had always hated asking for favors, even from someone who supposedly liked doing them. When the moment came, it was nothing eloquent. She had never learned anything official and she hoped God wouldn't take offense at her simple go at it. Just two words: Please, God.

She kept her eyes closed, faking sleep. The hand pressing against the letter opener stowed beneath her clothing stayed where it was. Whether she would use it or not, she didn't know. Maybe the best plan was to stay still and go where they took her. Somewhere along the way, staff numbers could dwindle, increasing her chance of escape. Seven knew it was easier said than done, and her mind was enticed by the idea of running, *now*, and not ending up on one of those gurneys.

Minus sight, her other senses were tweaking. Rubber soles screamed against the linoleum floor. The noisy wheel passed her, along with clipped stories: Barbara was left at the club, Sonia dumped Michael, a bass put up a fight, and a friend had back problems. Someone's stomach growled. A repetitive, hollow knocking noise in the room seemed to sync with her heartbeat. The letter opener felt hot against her skin, and Seven feared that it was glowing through her hospital gown and the bed linens and would soon give her away.

A woman cleared her throat near Seven. Footsteps approached from her right. A breeze chilled the sweat on her forehead.

The covers were thrown off of Seven's body. It took all that she had not to move, not to defend herself. Hands slid under her shoulders and around her ankles. Strong grips. She was off the bed and being carried now. Only a few seconds passed before she felt the hardness of the gurney beneath her.

Seven had played a dead girl in high school. Her French teacher, Madame Renée, advised her at the time not to think about death but to think about nothing, which was what she did now. The nighttime dose had put the other girls into an unreactive state, and Seven needed to mimic it to pass undetected.

After a few minutes, her gurney started backward. She hadn't been strapped in and Seven had the quick thought that a higher power might be paying attention after all. A breeze kicked up by the gurney train shoved hair across Seven's face to tickle her nostrils. Seven's hand twitched.

The gurney took a sharp corner, and Seven wondered if a four-foot fall was enough to wake someone from a drug-induced slumber. Would she be able to fake sleeping through something like that? They took a right, before stopping abruptly. Seven heard someone sigh.

"Damn elevator," a woman's voice said. "It sure does take its time, doesn't it?"

"Does," a man's voice responded. "Broke down a week ago. Had to carry them up and down the stairs. *That* was fun."

"Where was I?"

"Night off, I guess," he said. "Lucky bitch."

"Better believe it." The woman lowered her voice to a whisper: "Rumor has it I'm being turned."

"What? You're joking."

"No way, man," the woman said. "I've done my duty. My time is now."

"Whatever."

"Aw, don't be like that. You'll get there."

"As long as you let me in on what it's like then maybe I'll speak to you again. I'll live vi…vi…shit, what's that word?"

"Vicariously?"

"That's it."

"*Psht*. If you think my ass will still be working here, you are seriously mistaken."

There was a *ding* and Seven heard an elevator door slide open. They moved forward.

"Hi Harold," the woman said. "Give me your card."

"What happened to yours?" a new male voice responded.

"Lost it. Sue me."

The first guy laughed. "Maybe you'll be better at keeping track of your things when you're one of them. Ya think?"

It was the woman's turn to laugh. "Get out, Jay."

"Be quiet you two," Harold said. "You'll wake them."

"We ain't wakin' nothin'," the woman said. "Have you ever seen one of them wake up?"

"Well, no but—"

"Well, there you go. Now quit your whining, Harry, and give me the damn card."

There was no comeback from Harry. Rustling. Plastic swiping. The elevator jerked up. Seven couldn't be sure of how many floors they passed before stopping. The gurney was on the move again.

"Adios, *Harry*," the woman said. Jay snickered.

"Hey, what about my card?"

"I'll look after it for ya, *Harry*. But I know you got more, don't lie."

298

"Sure, okay," Harold said, sounding defeated.

"What a geek." They took a left and traveled a bit in silence before the woman spoke again. "Hey, go get the papa. I got it from here."

"You sure? We're not meant to separate."

"I'm sure, I'm sure. Christ, all you doubters are gonna get in my head."

"Alright. *Chill.* I'm going."

Another swipe, a beep, and the sound of a door giving way. The gurney hit something and jarred beneath Seven. She heard the door close behind them. The woman started to hum. Seven tried to stabilize as the gurney spun around.

"*You think you're hot, but you're not,*" the woman sang. "*You think you're cool, but you're a fool.*" Seven felt a hand brush the hair off her face. "Aren't you pretty. Not for long, though. Soon I'll be on to bigger and better, and you...well, you'll just be big."

The woman took her hand away from Seven's face, and Seven heard her yawn. It was a *now or never* kind of moment, and she moved. Seven shot her hand into her waistband and grabbed the letter opener. Before the woman knew what was happening, the duplicitous office tool was at her throat.

"That's what *you* think," Seven said.

The woman was black with a short, stylish Afro and penciled brows. A nametag said NURSE WALKER. She held both hands up. Her eyes were wide and watery. "Okay, girl, I see where you're coming from...I won't hassle you."

"Do you see? *Do you really?*" Seven pushed the blade in further. Nurse Walker screeched.

"*Yes.* Yes, I do."

Seven swung her legs over the side of the gurney and jumped off, being mindful her hand didn't slip. She was barefoot and the floor was freezing, but she passed the test, making not a peep. "Get out your key card."

Nurse Walker stared blankly ahead. Seven pushed her into the wall and scraped the tip of the letter opener against her neck. Her skin split and bled. It was a small, shallow cut—just enough to scare her. "I want you to get out your key card."

She nodded frantically and brought one hand down to reach into her pocket. Seven pictured the nurse pulling out a giant hypodermic needle and jabbing it into her stomach. Seven started to rethink her demand until she saw a corner of the key card in the nurse's hand, and her body relaxed as much as it could under the circumstances.

"Good," Seven said. "Good. Now hold onto that."

Seven looked around. The room was like the first room she had woken up in with the yellow walls, the single window, the mounted television, and the bed. A camera eyed this room too, but the red light was not illuminated, leading Seven to believe that either the light was broken, or the camera was off. She hoped for the latter but had to assume the former. Things had happened so fast that she hadn't even thought about the cameras. They were everywhere, and they'd track her progress.

Seven looked up at it and wondered if her newfound enemy was looking back. Regardless, she knew she didn't have much time before the guy named Jay returned and her chance of escaping would once again slim. Seven eyed the gurney pushed up against the hospital bed.

"What's going on in this place?"

Nurse Walker looked at Seven and smiled. She had thick lips, and the smile did nothing to thin them. "We're harvesting humans," she said. Seven felt her face falter and she saw the nurse noticing and she shoulder-slammed her against the wall to stop her from getting any ideas.

"Tell me why."

The nurse spoke, her voice strained after Seven's last incoming. "To...feed the...the nightwalkers."

"Nightwalkers?"

"The *vampires*."

Seven couldn't believe the nurse, in her position, had the gall to tell such a blatant lie. She experienced a moment of reverence for the woman's *cojones* before bringing a clenched fist into her stomach. "Bitch, stop lying!"

Nurse Walker's body slackened, and she became dead weight. Seven tried to hold her up, but the woman slid to the floor, letting out a cackle when she reached it. "I'm not lyin', girl. You're in some deep shit."

Seven pointed the letter opener at the nurse's eye. She was just a few millimeters from penetrating it. "Get up," Seven said. "You're showing me out."

Nurse Walker struggled to her feet. She winced and cradled her stomach. It made Seven feel good. *This is going to happen.* She would escape from that place and leave behind whatever screwed-up experiments they had going on there. And she would to tell people. Lots of people. Anyone who would listen, in fact. Sisters of Mercy Hospital would pay.

Seven positioned herself behind Nurse Walker, gripped her bicep, and reacquainted her jugular with the letter opener. She pushed the nurse forward, and they shuffled like Siamese twins to the door.

"You scream, I kill you. You run, I kill you. You do anything besides what I tell you to do, I kill you."

Nurse Walker nodded, convinced. The woman had an attitude, but Seven could now see that she valued her life enough to keep the pride in check.

At the door, Seven noticed the panel at eye level on the wall. It had a vertical slit down the middle and a pinhead-size red light on it that shone brightly.

"Open it."

Nurse Walker positioned the key card at the top of the box and then slid it downward. A green light replaced the red and beeped at them politely. Seven nudged the door open. She squeezed the nurse's arm before peering into the corridor.

It was empty and maybe darker than a hospital corridor should have been. Rooms stretched out in both directions. At each end, the hallway turned. Seven recognized these turns as her blind spots. For all she knew, Sisters of Mercy was having a staff party around one of them. She pictured Nurse Hobbs wearing a big party hat and blowing a noise maker. She was cutting into a cake with a picture of Seven on it.

"Which way to the elevators?"

"That way," Nurse Walker said. Seven had the nurse close enough to feel the woman's breath on her face and smell the hazelnut coffee she drank that day.

She pointed left with a hot pink nail. It had a butterfly on it, as did the other nine, and Seven wondered how such an innocent adornment could be worn by someone who participated in pure evil. She thought about the Catholic priests who wore crosses and molested children and knew it wasn't about what people wore on the outside but what they wore on the inside. That part was always harder to see.

Seven was no angel. She did for herself and never did for others. But she saw that more as being smart than anything else. If she didn't look out for number one, who would?

Seven glanced both ways again. Still, the hallway slept. She wasn't sure she could trust the nurse. In fact, she knew she couldn't. Those lies she had told about vampires. Did she think Seven was an idiot? No, the nurse had said it to make her feel foolish. Seven pressed the tip of the letter opener against the woman's neck. She didn't break the skin this time but didn't intend to. Nurse Walker cried out.

"I swear! You can go both ways, but that way's the quickest."

Seven shrugged. "Fuck it."

They abandoned the doorway and entered the hall. The hairs stood up on the back of Seven's neck. Her heightened nerves had her feeling like some sort of addict. Escape was her drug, and she was jonesing for it.

Seven hurried her hostage forward. Each door they passed brought a pang of guilt. She knew what was going on, or about to go on, behind those doors. *Processing.* Seven convinced herself that there was nothing she could do. That the girls were drugged and even waking them would be a feat. That if she even managed to do that, there would be explaining to do before they would agree to go with her. Tick tock. Time would be consumed, any chance of escape would be lost.

No. Get out now. Save them later.

Up ahead, an exit sign buzzed above a blue door. Seven veered toward it.

"Where we goin'?" Nurse Walker asked. "The elevators are further down."

"New plan. Give me the card."

The stairwell seemed safer. As far as Seven knew, the hospital staff was still using the elevators to transport girls. That would make the stairs the path of least resistance. It was a quick decision, but Seven believed it to be the right one.

The nurse handed Seven the key, and Seven opened the door. A camera looked down on the two women, watching them enter. This one had its light on. *All systems were a go.*

"I think you should take the elevator," Nurse Walker said.

"I don't care what you think," Seven said.

"Then what am I here for?"

"Collateral."

"You be trippin' if you think they're gonna risk losing you, for me."

"Why am I so special?"

"You got that blood up in you."

"What do you mean?"

"You got the blood they all want." Nurse Walker paused, as if giving Seven a moment to let what she just told her sink in. Not for Seven's benefit, of course. The nurse was the type to enjoy a good stirring of the pot. She continued: "And you know they're countin' on your babies havin' the special blood, too."

There were voices in the hallway. Seven ran, leaping down the stairs and dragging the nurse with her. They descended one flight and then another. Floors fell away. Nurse Walker flailed beside her like a rag doll being held out the window of a fast-moving vehicle. Each step was precarious at full speed ahead, but falling progressively was better than falling behind.

Because darkness ate the ones left behind.

Heavy footsteps sounded below them, and they froze as if someone had just shouted, *Red light!* The floor numbers were marked out on each landing, and two stairs down put them on the fourth floor. Seven gave Nurse Walker a warning look and drew her close. Instead of fleeing from the noise, they moved toward it and down the remaining stairs. Seven inched up to the door panel and slid the key card.

The light blinked red. The door stayed locked.

"What's wrong with it?" Seven whispered. Nurse Walker shook her head. Seven tried it again, with the same result. There was a chance the hospital had deactivated the nurse's card. *They'll catch me for sure. I'll never get out of this stairwell.*

The footfalls and voices grew nearer. She needed to think of something and quick.

Nurse Walker beat her to the punch, bringing her arm up to knock Seven's hand and the letter opener away from her throat. The nurse brought her other arm around in an attempt to smack Seven's face with a loose fist. Seven blocked it and grabbed a chunk of the nurse's hair. The nurse screamed. Seven got her in a chokehold and brought the tip of the letter opener to her cheek.

Movement nearby.

Three men wearing slate gray uniforms appeared on the platform below them. Two nurses watched the action from behind the men. Seven thought she recognized one of the nurses, but she hadn't seen the men before. Two of them beat batons against their palms. The middle guy, who had a flurry of black hair on top of his head, raised a gun to point it at her.

Seven tightened her chokehold on Nurse Walker, so she was now lifting her off the ground. The nurse was almost her size. Seven brought the letter opener to the nurse's neck and twisted it where her big vein bounced.

"Make another move and I'll kill her," Seven said. "Don't make me kill her." If the middle man had been bothered by what she just said, he hid it well.

The gun fired, and Nurse Walker collapsed. A small amount of air escaped from her mouth in a hiss before she fell—like that air had been the only thing keeping her standing.

"Tranquilizer gun, number eighty-three. Don't look so sad," the middle man said. His voice was monotone. No dips or elevations. Just words serving their purpose as is.

Seven got her feet out from under the body of the nurse. She appeared dead, but Seven wasn't about to check for a pulse. If she looked sad it was because she had just lost her collateral, which meant she either had to make a run for it, or find new collateral. And it wasn't like new collateral was just going to walk up to her and say, "Use me."

Or was it?

Seven turned the letter opener on herself. She dug the tip into her jugular enough to hurt. Seven didn't know these people from Adam, but she knew fear and was pleased to see it flash across their faces.

"Shoot me, and I fall," Seven said. "Just make sure I don't fall on this here letter opener. Because if I fall on this here letter opener, my precious blood will spill and be wasted."

Seven had them. The middle guy lowered his gun. She started to back up toward the stairs, and they followed her with their eyes but not their feet. She wasn't sure the key would work on the next floor, but she would try. She'd considered the possibility that the key card in her possession didn't allow access to the fourth floor, which was why it hadn't worked—that that particular floor could only be accessed by staff with better security clearance. *What horrors?* Seven thought, quickly pushing the question away.

Seven climbed the stairs, keeping the letter opener on her throat and the middle man in her sight. She stayed away from the railing, as to not encourage sneaky hands, and used the wall behind her for support. When eye contact between the two parties was interrupted by the ascending stairwell, Seven lowered the letter opener from her own neck and ran.

The fifth floor entrance was up ahead.

She didn't bother with delusions. She knew that the second she had made a break for it, her pursuers had too. She could hear them advancing, closing in. She could feel their silent determination to get her, like a heavy cloak descending.

Seven reached the door and slid the key in. If it didn't work, they would have her.

She'd be done.

She thought she could feel time reversing.

The green light illuminated.

Seven shoved through the door and sprinted down the hallway. She came to a turn and dared a look back, just as her new friends were arriving. She continued her full-throttle pace before stopping outside a room. The door was closed and no sign displayed the purpose of the space behind it, but she needed a place to hide and this one was as good as any.

She unlocked the door with her card and crept inside.

What she saw made her momentarily forget the men chasing her and threw a new obstacle in the path to her escape.

CHAPTER SEVENTEEN

BABIES.

Loads of them.

Seven had never seen so many babies collected in one area.

Some slept, others waved their little arms and legs as much as their bassinets and Mother Nature would allow. Hurried footsteps approached from outside, and Seven moved away from the door. A voice she recognized as the middle man's shouted to check the other stairwell.

She was safe, for now.

A quick scan of the room brought up no cameras. Seven found it odd and stayed wary. If she spotted one with its light on, it would likely be too late. But she'd rather know. She was the type of person to take the bad news first. She challenged life to send its worst, and she supposed now that life had listened.

Seven wove her way around the cribs. The babies in them looked healthy, for the most part. They wore clean white frocks and slept under pink and blue blankets. Not all of them were newborns, and a few looked to be outgrowing their current sleeping arrangements. Each crib was numbered, and each baby wore a corresponding numbered bracelet with blood type and several mysterious letters on it. An Asian baby with a full head of hair slept quietly, and Seven leaned in to get a closer look: *35 B+ AU-CN-US-US.*

Looks like country codes, Seven thought. Australia, China, and the United States. Seven moved on to another baby. Number 45 was awake. The baby directed its blue eyes at Seven before something not apparent caught its attention. The bracelet read: *45 A- unknown.* Another baby, number 58, bald and tiny: *58 A- US-US-IRE-US.*

Seven checked a few more. She tried but couldn't think of a reason for putting country codes on the bracelets. Blood type, yes. But country codes, no. Ruling out the parents, since there could only be two biological, she determined the four countries might be the grandparents' origins. *But why would that be so important?*

Nurse Walker told Seven that she had the blood *they* all wanted and that her offspring might have it too. Seven wondered if the *they* were sick people with rare blood types who would go to any lengths to find a match—including harvesting newborns? *No,* Seven thought. There was no real blood crisis that she knew of. She saw the Red Cross television advertisements for blood drives in her neighborhood, and sometimes she heard a tinge of desperation in them. But that was just a ruse to pull at the heart strings. Rare blood types did exist, but Seven noticed no concentration of one type among the babies.

No, Seven thought. It was bigger than desperate, sick people. Seven knew that whoever was behind this operation was very wealthy, very immoral, and not worried one bit about getting handed down a death sentence by a court of law. *How long?* Seven wondered, knowing at least nine months. Unless they had managed to snatch women who were already pregnant. And babies already born. Automatic babies in both cases but maybe not the ideal because not all of them would have the *special blood.*

Seven was sweating. More babies were moving in their cribs. Some reached out to her as she passed. She wasn't one to care but knew only a monster wouldn't care in this situation and she was no monster.

She wanted to strap a baby to each appendage and make a run for it. With luck, she'd make it to the stairwell, but luck was not a frequent visitor. She had the inkling that luck would throw its hands up when put to the task of an escapee wearing a live baby suit. *Yep*, Seven thought, *four babies is impossible.* And then came the afterthought followed immediately by action, so no time was left for reason.

But one isn't.

Seven picked up baby number 96 with no particular criteria in her head. Though this baby was already awake, and she figured that was good. Seven gathered the pink blanket from the crib and wrapped it around the tiny frame. Number 96 had dark skin, long lashes, and a drool bubble clinging to its heart-shaped mouth. The baby was at that early stage when determining sex was difficult. Seven would have taken a cue from the blanket color, but she knew better: a "program" like this wouldn't bother with tradition. It didn't matter, anyway. Boy or girl, Seven was getting it away from that place.

Snug in the blanket, Number 96 looked up at Seven like she was a wonder to behold. *Wait 'til I get us out of here, kid, before you start idolizing me.*

The room had two entrances, and Seven headed for the door nearest to her. She startled at the discovery of a desk tucked away in the corner, as if the piece of furniture had come alive and said, *BOO!* On top of the desk was a lamp, a neat stack of papers, a couple of pens with one saying, "Sisters of Mercy Hospital: Yes We Care!" and a cup of tea—still steaming.

Oh shit!

Whoever belonged to that tea would be returning soon. The question was when, and would she and Number 96 be safely away by then?

Seven didn't have long to wait for the answers to those questions. Footsteps approached from outside in the corridor, the knob on the door nearest to Seven turned, and a behemoth entered the picture.

~

The nurse was well over six feet tall with a thickness to her body that seemed to reproach the surrounding air.

Her black hair was twisted in a bun, her bangs sticking up, poised like a giant wave ready to crash hard on any baby thieves below.

Seven hid behind a cabinet storing various baby linens in transparent drawers. She held on tightly to the nurse's warm cup of tea. She had hoped the tea would be hotter since there was nothing like a cup of scolding liquid in the face to disorient. Now Seven was banking on the element of surprise to get her and her passenger past the giant.

The nurse walked to the desk and sat. The chair cried foul beneath her. She put on a pair of spectacles, which hung from a chain around her neck, and fingered the stack of papers in front of her. She looked up from the stack to where the cup of tea had been and sighed. Her big body slumped like the last straw had just been delivered.

"Forget your own head if it wasn't attached," the nurse mumbled.

She stood, to the relief of the chair. Seven tensed. The baby squirmed. The nurse walked to the door, opened it, and walked out.

Seven waited a minute. When she was sure the nurse had gone, she let go of her held breath and bounced Number Ninety-Six. "Looks like luck took pity on us, baby." Number 96 stopped squirming and stared at Seven, once again fascinated.

Seven replaced the mug on the desk and the letter opener in her right hand. She knew the nurse would be returning soon, so she was quick about searching the desk for anything that might serve as a better weapon. Coming up empty, Seven made a dash for the door.

The hallway was empty, just as she liked it.

She had a choice of routes: the now infamous stairwell, that stairwell's doppelganger on the other side of the building, or the elevators. The layout of this floor was similar so far to the layout of the floor she had been residing on. The exits were located at each end of the long corridor, with the elevators smack dab in the middle.

After quick thought, the chase stairwell was out. She refused to return to the scene of near-capture. And the elevators weren't an option, either—too much traffic. *The virgin stairwell it is*, Seven thought. Her pursuers had been on their way there, but she reckoned they'd be gone by now and on to newer pastures.

She ran, turned a corner, and spotted the exit door, as well as the cameras. The electronic eyes were a downer, but there was nothing she could do since the cameras couldn't be disabled without getting close to them. If she planned on leaving Sisters of Mercy Hospital via the few routes available, she'd have to get used to being a star.

Seven dreaded the many flights of stairs she needed to get down with baby, but she had made the choice to pick up the tiny passenger, so that was that. She would be careful but not too careful. Too careful was too slow and bound to get them caught.

As an added bonus, Number 96 didn't seem to like running very much and scrunched its face in disapproval.

"It's okay, baby," Seven said. "Just don't cry."

She arrived at the exit and swiped her card. The door opened, and she ran through, giving the middle finger to a watchful camera. She went down six stairs and then another six. Every door they passed had the potential to open up and release bad guys, but none did, and they reached the bottom without event. There were two doors at the bottom, and Seven chose the one with TO LOADING DOCK on it. She peeked before committing. On the other side was a narrow stretch of hallway before a bend.

Number 96 had gone from fussy to hysterical, and Seven could hardly blame it. She likened their descent to putting a newborn on a rollercoaster ride. The baby was flushed, with its eyes as big as quarters, but there would be no time for comforting. A door opened up behind them.

Her foe had arrived.

CHAPTER EIGHTEEN

JUMPING WAS A NO-BRAINER.

With bad guys at her front, more at her back, and a screaming baby giving away her exact location at any given moment, making that jump was the easiest decision of her life.

Seven approached it fast like a bullet. Ninety-six screamed bloody murder. Maybe it understood what was coming, but Seven knew the baby would thank her when it was old enough to understand. She wouldn't exaggerate the story in the retelling; she needn't have to.

They had taken that narrow stretch of hallway, which led to another hallway, and a storage room, and a loading dock stacked with bundles, and a drop of indeterminable height. Outside, a large truck idled with its open back pulled up to the dock. Seven felt the night air on her skin. Stars winked in the fast approaching sky, as if to say, "This is it, kid. You're home free."

Her feet left the edge of the loading dock. The pavement met her fast.

Seven's ankle twisted on the landing, and she fell to one knee. The momentum dragged her along the blacktop. Rocks and broken glass lodged in her skin. The pain was excruciating, but what was chasing her was far worse. She struggled to her feet and set her sights on the truck's open driver door. She could hear a tinny version of a Bee Gees song playing over the radio, which meant one thing:

Keys in the ignition.

She scurried forward, dragging her bad leg behind her. The inside of the cab smelled like vanilla and rubber. She tightened her one-armed hug of the baby, tossed the letter opener onto the passenger seat, and hoisted her and Number 96 up and in with one free hand.

Next to her, the side view mirror shattered.

She slammed the door and reached for the ignition. The Bee Gees song ended, and a radio DJ came on to send a shout-out to his girl Marcy in Culver City. *And I hope my night grooves got you dancing.*

Seven turned the key and pressed the gas pedal to the floor. Her twisted mess of an ankle protested with a searing pain that caused her vision to stutter. She held the wriggling baby tightly in the crook of her left arm and gripped the steering wheel with her right hand. A dart whizzed by her ear and hit the dashboard. Angry shouts were drowned out by engine noise as truck, baby, and Seven screeched forward into the night.

~

The hole was tiny.

Larger than an apple but smaller than a bowling ball.

Broken glass encircled the hole like flower petals. Seven couldn't feel anything, but emptiness echoed deep down inside her. She wiped debris off of her face and looked up at the truck seat looming above her like its time had come to do the sitting.

Seven slowly propped herself up on her elbows. The truck cab was dark except for the soft glow of the dashboard display. Beyond the broken windshield, a single headlight beam illuminated tall blades of grass and immense, twisted trees. Realization hit her like a freight train, and she sat up.

The baby is gone!

Frantically, she searched the truck's cab.

316

They were in an accident. Several ambulances had been chasing them. She gave them the slip but hadn't slowed her speed. She veered off the road, and the truck flipped.

Seven's eyes went to the small hole in the windshield. She scrambled to the door and grappled for its handle. She was sweating, shaking. The door wouldn't budge, so she maneuvered around and kicked it with both feet. She blacked out, for a moment, coming to with her legs still poised in the air. She kicked again, and the door gave way with a groan to match her own.

Outside, the grass was wet. A bird sang far away. A thick forest was spread out on Seven's right, and on her left, a road where no cars went, at least for the moment. Boxes from the upended truck littered the ground behind her. Besides the truck's windshield, little else was damaged. A headlight was out. Seven noticed that the edge of the road met a steep dirt incline.

Seven got to her feet and started searching the area in front of the truck. The sky was brightening, which helped. She weaved in and out of the headlight beam. She listened over the hum of the engine for crying or movement.

In her nightmares after that day, Ninety-Six's hand would crawl onto her shoe like a deadly spider. In reality, the baby's hand hadn't moved since his body was thrown through the windshield, landing many feet from the toppled truck. The hand was so small that Seven nearly missed it.

"It's okay, baby," Seven said, tearing away the long grass.

But it wasn't.

Number 96 was motionless, covered in a layer of dirt and blood. His neck had been broken, part of his face was...not there. Seven felt the rage building up inside her, but she kept it at bay. There were things to get done.

Seven wrapped the baby's body in the pink blanket, which she recovered near the truck, carried him a bit further down the road, and found a spot for burial. She dug the grave with her bare hands, placed the baby in the hole, refilled the hole, and piled rocks to serve as a marker.

"I'm sorry, baby," she said. "I don't know why bad things happen."

Seven then stood and limped toward the woods. The sun was coming up, and it was time for her to leave.

NOW:

I shifted my position, getting up on my haunches.

Only silence came from the room next door, and silence made me nervous. Everything about Seven made sense to me now. A person couldn't go through something like that and come out the other end unaffected.

Seven finished her story: "I traveled for a couple days. Got into the city and ended up on Wilshire. That's when Scott picked me up. You know the rest."

"Seven, I'm—"

"*Don't.* Don't say it. I don't want your pity, Charlie. That's not why I told you."

"I know. I know."

I pictured the two of them sitting on the bed, together but separate. Seven with her cement wall around her, and Charlie with his spoon.

Bugs was still fast asleep, and I got up quietly and moved over to her bed. She slept with her arms and legs stretched out in opposite directions. Her eyelids fluttered, but not enough to suggest a bad dream, which made me feel better. Bits of chocolate had collected at both corners of her mouth. Empty candy wrappers outlined the child, and I grabbed a plastic bag to get rid of the evidence.

I had the shift downstairs after Sammy but figured a bit of shuteye beforehand could be just what the doctor ordered. I lifted Bugs' arms and legs and moved them closer to her, then crawled in. The sun had made me sleepy, and my body welcomed the rest like a long lost friend.

~

A hand on my arm woke me. I started awake, and Cooper stood above me.

"You're back?" I said. "What time is it?"

"Just past six."

"Oh, no—my shift."

"It's okay, Rudy's down there. There's someone I want you to meet. Wash up, then come upstairs for dinner."

"What about Bugs?"

"I'll take her."

I did as I was told, like a good soldier. I wondered who our guest was. Someone the hunters had come across on the outside, I supposed. A new person to join our strange menagerie. If it was another hunter, Cooper would be pleased, as would Scott. Hopefully, she or he would be less eccentric than the rest of us. Maybe fewer chips in the shoulder area.

I washed, ran downstairs to take Schizo to relieve himself, then back up to the sixth floor with dog in tow. Schizo had been acting feisty since I woke up and was not in my good books. We had to stop halfway up the stairs for some reprimanding.

"Schizo," I said. "If you don't calm down, you won't be meeting the guest, and I know how much you like meeting new people."

The dog tilted his head and continued with his symphony of barking and whining. I was tempted to walk him back to the unit and lock him in there for the night, but I hadn't done that yet and wasn't about to start. The thought of being closed up in there made me uncomfortable. Granted, I was a human and he was a dog, but there was no doubt in my mind that sometimes Schizo was more human than dog, and sometimes maybe I was more dog than human. So it was settled. Neither of us would be locked up in the unit any time soon.

We arrived on the sixth floor and headed toward the kitchen. Schizo's agitation increased, making me wary. Schizo acted like *Cujo* whenever vampires were around. I stopped outside the kitchen door and heard laughter and pleasantries coming from inside.

"Schizo, what is your problem?"

The door flung open. Schizo tensed. I jumped.

Cooper stood in front of us, backlit by soft light. He closed the door quickly.

"What's going on?" I asked.

"Nice of you to join us."

"I know. I'm late. Sorry. Schizo's been holding true to his name. Something's gotten under his fur. I'm not sure what."

"Weird," Cooper said, not sounding particularly convincing. "Might want to put him in Scott's office then? We can give him his dinner in there?"

"Yeah, okay," I said, taking hold of Schizo's collar. "Come on, Mr. Annoying." Cooper cracked the door to go back into the kitchen. I eyed him. "What's for dinner, anyway? Something good?"

"Should be," he replied, giving me not much of anything, in that way that he did. He slid in and closed the door behind him.

I dragged Schizo to Scott's office and promised him leftovers if he kept the noise level down. My attempt at bribery had no effect. The dog had gotten into a fixed state of aggression, and I started to wonder if it was what was in the kitchen that had put him there.

~

Martha Stewart had exploded in the kitchen, and it was beautiful.

Candles filled up every corner and spanned the tabletop, felling the room in a dreamlike glow. Wax dripped from candle tips, down wine bottle candle holders, and onto a pretty blue tablecloth that shimmered when caught at the right angle. A vase full of yellow and white flowers was in the middle of the table. Loosely covered bowls and dishes released steam and pleasant aromas.

Whether it was the smell of well-prepared food or the company, everyone seemed happy. Even Seven whose story of personal horror I had just heard recounted. She was talking to Scott and laughing, dimples indenting her cheeks. I wasn't sure I had ever seen her smile. Charlie was absent, along with Rudy, who had taken my shift. If this would be the evening ahead, I didn't envy them.

The mystery guest stood in front of the stove with his back to me. Before him, contents jostled in four large pots of boiling water. The guest's arms reached out like octopus legs, dipping into herbs and other chopped piles and dropping pinches into pots. The man was of average height, his body stretching out more than up. What was left of

321

his strawberry blonde hair was being worn in a tight ponytail, a torture it could not possibly withstand for much longer.

Cooper was chatting with the mystery guest. He waved at me, and the others greeted me in unison. Seepy Storage—where everybody knows your name. Bugs got up from the table, leaving Sammy's side for mine. She took my hand as Cooper began introductions.

"Emma, I'd like you to meet Leech," Cooper said. "Leech, Emma."

That crazy name rang a bell, and now, face-to-face with our guest, I knew why. I had my hand out, but I pulled it back quickly enough for everyone in the room to notice. I didn't care. I didn't like our visitor.

Leech was the vampire informant Cooper had told me about. My interest in getting to know him stopped at pointy teeth.

Leech kept his hand out a moment longer. I was going to verbalize that he needn't bother, but I showed it on my face instead. His hand dropped almost immediately. "Emma, I've heard a lot about you."

"Me, too." I hadn't really, but I wanted to seem prepared.

"All good things, I hope."

"Yeah but I didn't believe them."

Leech laughed. His neck arched, his mouth opened wide, and his teeth became prominent. I had the thought he must laugh like he killed.

"Feisty," Leech said. "Reminds me of the missus."

"Oh, you haven't eaten her yet?"

"*Emma,*" Cooper said.

"Oh, not to worry, Cooper. No, Emma, the missus is alive and well. Went bowling tonight with a few of her gal pals. Besides, I'm a vegetarian. Only animal blood passes these lips." Then, in singsong: "*If it's rat, give me some of that.*"

"Charming." Leech's face faltered.

"I tell you, Emma, try my cooking and you'll look past my species. That's how I won the rest of 'em over. Of course, I don't cook for myself anymore, but watching humans appreciate my food is the closest I can get to my former diet. I do miss it. Well." Leech moved back to the stove and stuck a wooden spoon in one of the pots. He lifted it carefully, with a hand underneath for spills. "I need a taster over here." Bugs released her hand from mine.

"No, honey," I said.

"It's okay. He's nice."

I was resistant, but the others didn't seem bothered. Mary looked distracted. Her hair was greasy and flat on her skull. She clenched a bread roll in her hand, a long-distance smile lingering on her lips. Mary wasn't even in the room.

I eyed Leech with the girl. He blew on the spoon to cool its contents, then slowly brought it down to Bugs' mouth.

"Be careful, now, darling. Don't get it down your pretty shirt."

Bugs spoke through chewing. "Yummy. That's the best ever."

Leech took the spoon away and put it back on the counter. "Tell you what Bugsy-Girl. You can be my taster anytime."

"Really?"

"Really."

Leech ruffled Bugs' hair, and she skipped back to Sammy's side. The vampire returned to his duties, announcing that dinner would be served in five minutes. Cooper grabbed my arm and escorted me out the door. I had an idea what it was about.

"What's wrong with you?" he asked.

"What's wrong with me? What's wrong with you—with all of you? I mean, what next? You'll all be slicing your wrists and offering him hunter cocktail straight from the vein. I mean, *come on*. While we're at it, why don't we just have a big vampire party? We can invite all the vampires in the neighborhood. It'll be neat. As long as they can cook...I mean, they should bring something to the table."

I was raising my voice, but there was nothing I could do about it. I was mad. Who had spent the past week learning how to kill vampires? Me. Befriending these things was never on my agenda.

And talk about your complications.

How did you tell the nice ones from the mean ones? Could it be the mean ones were just having a bad day? The idea that some of these things had a conscience raised the whole question of morality. Not long ago, I had been set up to kill one downstairs, in the name of training, and I was meant to kill more. It wouldn't help knowing that some of them went bowling and abstained from human blood. And where did it all leave Cooper? Cooper whose girlfriend was thrown out of a speeding vehicle by his fellow hunters before she had even turned. Where did it leave him to know that maybe...just maybe...she would have been one of the good ones?

"Listen, Emma," Cooper said. "Leech was one of Scott's colleagues at the CIA. He got in contact with him after it all went down saying he wanted to help. Everything's checked out so far. The information he's given us has been good. Real good. The fact is we can't do this without him. We need him, Emma."

Schizo was barking his head off in Scott's office, increasing an already present tension.

"Sure, okay, but whose idea was it to bring him here...to compromise our hideout?"

"If he was going to turn us in, he would have done it by now. He's had many chances."

"Well maybe he's waiting for something."

"For what?"

"I don't know...something."

Cooper tilted his head, giving me an exasperated look.

"I'm not a miracle worker. I can't just figure it out right now. I need time."

Leech announced from inside the kitchen that dinner was served.

"Until then be civil," Cooper said. "Now, can we eat?"

Schizo's barks had become full, raging snarls. I walked over to Scott's office and tapped on the door.

"It's okay, Schiz. Calm down, buddy." Schizo responded with a whine, half a growl, and a moan before settling.

Cooper nodded at me when I turned to go back into the kitchen with him. Apparently he didn't hate me, despite the trouble I had caused. I wasn't the kind of person to act up without reason. Maybe Cooper could see that about me.

~

Dinner had not waited for us.

The table's occupants shoved food into their mouths like famished mongrels. Except the vampire, of course. He sipped nonchalantly from a tall glass of hemoglobin. Our eyes met when I came through the door, and he smiled. If there was anything other than kindness behind that smile, I couldn't see it. There were the teeth that could rip my throat out, but when it came down to it, everything could kill. Even humans, whether we had the right teeth for it or not.

I seated myself at the furthest possible point from the vampire. There was a potential seed of understanding in me for the vampire, but trust was a long way off. I would watch him and see. Cooper sat next to me. Mary was across from us and hadn't made any improvement since I last observed her. Her plate was untouched. The roll that she had gripped in her hand was sitting on the tabletop now, looking more like an apple core.

As we sat, Mary set her dark eyes on me and kept them there. Whether it was because I had just filled the empty space across from her, or something more, I couldn't tell. I found it ironic that, as a woman of God, she chose to stare me down with a real-life demon in the room. I wanted to shout "Look! Satan spawn!" and point a finger at Leech, but I started on my dinner instead.

"How's the better half, Leech my man?" Topps asked.

The hunter I barely knew sat big on the bench next to the vampire. His muscles were magnificent up close, and they flexed when he talked, as if conversing with each other. He wore a different cowboy hat than usual. It was dark blue and deep enough to hide half his head.

Leech dabbed at each corner of his mouth with a napkin. He was very good at staying clean, and I wondered if that was for our sake.

"Nancy's doing well, yes. Enjoying retirement and I have to say it suits her. You know, she's into the clubs. Just joined another one. It's a local meet-up group that's part of a larger movement called…" Leech scrunched his face and tapped a finger on his glass "…Back in Black, I think it is. The thing's spearheaded by some older vampire folk. They meet every Thursday to talk about us vampires going back to our roots. Back to the shadows. Back to the way it was before. You see, not everyone agrees with the takeover." He directed that last part at me.

"Back in Black. That's clever," Topps said. "That's a song, isn't it? Who sang it?"

"AC/DC," Cooper said.

"Right," Topps said. "Good song. Not country, but good."

"Country sucks," Seven said with a slight smile.

"You break my heart, girl."

"What do they do…this group?" I asked. "I mean, are they making any progress?"

"No, I wouldn't say. They chat and sign petitions, but they're part of a small minority. Besides, tell me how over a hundred million vampires are going to fit back into the shadows? A bit silly, if you ask me."

Over a hundred million! "Were you a vampire when you worked at the CIA with Scott?"

"Quit the inquisition, Emma," Cooper said.

"I'm just getting to know our guest."

"It's okay," Leech said. "No, Scott and I both worked for the CIA, but I was in Payroll. He left The Agency, and I continued my employment. After the blackout, my Nancy was bit by a boy in the neighborhood, and then she bit me. I don't think we were ever meant to be reborn. We're old with not much to offer. My Nancy cleaned houses for 30 years. Regardless, the UVF doesn't get rid of you just because you're useless. Might give you cheap blood for all eternity in hopes you'll take your own life." Leech chuckled. "Good thing we like the animal blood."

"So, Leech, do you enjoy being undead?" I asked. "I mean, don't tell me you're not bothered at all by the fact that we want to bring an end to your species." The rest of the diners shifted in their seats and stared intently at their plates.

"Why don't we change the topic?" Scott said. "I know you've just met Leech, Emma, and you've got questions for him. But for now, why don't we switch to a more appropriate dinner conversation?"

"Sure, whatever," I mumbled. "Pass the salt." I felt defeated, but I'd get my answers. If not now, then later. We just needed later not to be too late.

Seven leaned across Scott and Topps to get to the salt shaker. She handed it to me.

"Here you go."

"Thanks," I said, trying to mask my surprise at Seven's gesture by dowsing my meal in salt. It was a winter wonderland.

I excused myself before dinner's end to bring Schizo leftovers. I hated to say it, but my first meal prepared by a vampire was exquisite. It was hard for me to not finish every last morsel, but I had made a promise to a dog. It occurred to me that Leech might've laced the meal, and when midnight arrived, out we would go, following him through the night. But besides the pleasantly full feeling in my stomach, everything else felt the same.

Schizo seemed pleased to see me, but really, just pleased to see food. I put the plate in front of him and thought he might turn his nose up at it, smelling Leech's undead touch, but he didn't. When he was finished, I picked up the plate and put it outside the kitchen door. I brought Schizo the other way around so we were heading away from the kitchen. He turned his head and let loose a couple of snarls left over between his furry chops.

"Sure but you'll eat his food no problem." I directed the flashlight down the dark hallway, past the row of cubicles. I sighed. "I ate it too, Schiz."

He may not have understood, but I felt better for the confession. I let go of Schizo's collar once we arrived at the stairwell. Back on the fifth floor, I was happy to see lights again. For people who had every reason to be scared of the dark, we certainly traveled through it a lot. I spotted an object outside my unit. It was a calendar tied up with red ribbon. An attached sticky note read:

Found this. It's March 20th.
Cooper

I slipped off the ribbon and flipped through the pages. It was a puppy calendar. It was perfect.

I opened the door to the unit, and Schizo pranced in and hopped up on my bed. He yawned and began maneuverings to achieve ideal sleeping position.

"Don't get too comfortable, Fur Face," I said to Schizo. "I'll be back."

I put the calendar on the bed and collected my toiletries for a trip to the bathroom.

I shuffled past units, down the hall, down the stairs, and to the bathroom without batting an eye. It's funny how things become so regular so fast. Living out of a storage facility. *Regular.* Becoming a trained killer. *Regular.* Having vampires on the mind 24/7. *Regular.* Maybe it was part of the survival instinct: the human body and mind were adept at dealing with change, normalizing change, because otherwise the species would give up and cease to exist. The country had just gone through a major change, but I held out hope that there were others out there like us, adjusting and expediting a bite back.

The overhead lights buzzed on in the bathroom. In a far corner, one light flickered before finally surging on, brighter than the rest. The air was dank, and mildew caked the ceiling. There was a fan for ventilation, but it broke the week before and mildew was opportunistic.

I splashed my face with cold water, pulled up my shirt to dry, and entered one of the toilet stalls. I sat on the toilet, and after a moment of stillness, the overhead lights turned off. My heart thudded. *This happens all the time*, I reassured. I waved my hands in the air, like a shaman summoning spirits. The bathroom stayed dark.

"*Grrrr*," I said. "Stupid lights." I stretched my arms up high and waved them back and forth.

Nothing.

"It's okay, Emma," I said aloud. "Don't freak out."

I had a flashlight, and I dipped into the pocket of my pants to bring it out. I turned the flashlight's yellow head, and a beam appeared, weak but there. It was like the dark was a thick steak and I had brought along a plastic butter knife. I sighed. I had been meaning to ask Cooper for replacement batteries. Too little, too late. It was a phrase I'd need to get used to if I didn't smarten up.

I stayed seated with my hearing on high alert and my hands gripping the flashlight like it was a light saber. Something scurried outside the stall. Probably a mouse or a cockroach. I hadn't seen either around the facility yet, but stories of sightings were frequent. Guys loved to tell those kinds of stories. I lifted my feet off the ground.

I heard the bathroom door open and nearly fell off the seat. I waited for a flashlight beam to meet mine on the ceiling, or a noise—a voice announcing entrance, bare feet slapping against the tiles, running water—but there was no indication that anyone had come in, and I released my breath only because I couldn't hold it in any longer.

"Hello?" I said. "It's Emma. The lights aren't working. Do you know where the switch is?"

I was referring to the mythical switch that took the bathroom lights off power-saver mode and put them on permanent mode. I hadn't used the switch before but would use it from now on. When it came down to it, screw saving power. From what I had heard, acquiring gasoline in the new world wasn't difficult. Vampires used fuel too, mostly in their cars, and until they devised a plan to keep us from getting it, leaving the bathroom lights on was not going to make much difference.

I could hear footsteps now. Dragging ones.

"Cooper, is that you?" I asked. "Quit it, okay? I'm not even wearing my monitor."

I leaned down from my seated position to get a look under the stall door. I moved the flashlight beam across the floor. A small roach caught in the light froze, then scurried away, gone home to tell its family about a close encounter with one of the giants threatening their peaceful, dirty world.

Two ladybug slippers shuffled into the stall next to me. I had my light on them as they turned to face me.

"Cut it out. You're not funny."

I could hear something. A slight whisper and the words were so quiet that I

...can't quite make them out...

so I pressed my ear against the stall divider, but the whispering stopped. I waited with my ear suctioned against the chilly metal and my teeth chattering. My body started to shiver, as if someone wasn't just standing on my grave, but stomping and grinding fingers and feet into its dirt.

"*Emma*," the whisperer said, in a small female voice.

I stood up, quickly backing myself into the wall behind the toilet and accidentally entangling my feet in my downed pants. Bits of peeled paint from off the wall fluttered down to the floor. Only then did I realize who the owner of the voice was.

"Bugs, you scared the bejesus out of me," I said, pulling my pants up. "You have to stop doing that. Seriously."

I exited the stall and walked to the sink to wash my hands, checking the floor to make sure the roach was truly gone.

"Did you have fun hanging out today? I heard Cooper say something at dinner about another supply run. If I go, I can look for some new cartoons for you? Not promising anything, but we'll see. Might get you some new slippers, too. Ones that fit you a bit better."

I stood the flashlight beam-up on the shelf below the mirror. I leaned in close to the reflective glass. My head bobbed bodiless in the dark. The exercise and sunlight had done me good. The bruising was gone from my face, a rosy glow its replacement. I was beginning to recognize myself again.

I upended my bag, spilling assorted contents. I'd been able to acquire some toiletries from the other residents, and Cooper got me the rest, even a box of tampons, which I suspected he'd gotten Charlie to steal from Seven's stash. I perused the scattered mess for dental floss.

"Dental floss, *come on down*."

Bugs still hadn't come out of the bathroom stall, and no telltale noises were emanating from within.

"You okay in there, Sweetie? Bugs?"

I turned and walked toward the stall.

I reached a hand out to open the door. It flung open.

Bugs wasn't in the bathroom with me, after all.

CHAPTER NINETEEN

MARY HAD A GUN.

It was pointed at my head.

She stood half in, half out of the bathroom stall. She was dressed in a tank top and pajama bottoms with small red roses all over them. The crotch of her pants was wet.

She moved forward and I backed up until I had nowhere left to go. My butt pressed against the sink basin. I could've made a run for the door, but a bullet in the back didn't appeal to me.

"Mary, what are you doing?"

She took another step forward.

I glanced at my stuff spread out on the shelf. The dental floss was there, obvious—a joke by an invisible wiseass. I had no weapons. Nothing would guarantee me an escape from this mess.

"Please," I said. "Let me go get Scott. He'll be able to help you." I moved sideways, and Mary moved with me. "You're going to let me go find your husband, Mary…your husband who loves you very, very much."

Mary got close enough so that our knees touched and her body heat licked my skin. Her eyes were swollen as if she had been crying, but I was afraid that she was well past the LEAVING SADNESS sign and the WELCOME TO MADNESS sign was just around the bend.

"Mary, talk to me. I can't help you if I don't know what you want."

She smiled oh so sweetly, her lips slightly parted, bringing the gun closer to my face as if it were a prop, and we, the actors, in a beautiful romance. The gun was smaller than the ones I had trained with but no less capable of tearing a hole through my skull. From that proximity, the bullet would go clean through me, taking my brain on a brief, permanent journey to the outside.

Mary spoke again in that childlike voice that had had me mistaking her for Bugs. "What I want is my son, Emma, and God told me that I can get him back…with you. He wants you, and when he has you, I get my little boy."

Knowing that Mary thought God wanted me was not a good turn of events.

"Think about this, Mary. Why would God want me? And isn't it a sin to kill someone…it is…it's one of the seven deadly sins, and so why would God ask you to do that?"

I needed to find a chink in her armor and fast.

"Well, God did ask Abraham to kill his son." Mary shook her head. "But I have no intention of killing you. I'm going to bring you to him. What he does with you from there is none of my concern. He might just show you right. I could tell you were a sinner the second I laid eyes on you—walking with all that confidence. This place is full of sinners."

My moment was coming. I could feel it. *Patience.*

Mary continued: "Do you know what it's like to lose a child? Of course you don't. I'd rather have every bit of flesh ripped from off my bones than go through that again. I'm not going to lose him this time. So we're gonna go. *Now.*"

Mary took one hand off the gun and grabbed my arm. Her fingers were strong and I could feel early bruises sprouting. I pretended to concede and directed my eyes downward in defeat. She never saw it

335

coming when I brought my forearm up to shove the gun barrel away and my head forward for a direct hit to the bridge of her nose.

Mary stumbled backward. Blood spurted out of her nostrils in wet threads. She tried to grab onto the stall door, missed, and collapsed onto the floor, smacking the back of her head on the toilet on the way down. She had dropped the gun and now it was skidding into the neighboring stall.

I went for it. She did, too, but shock made her slow.

I grabbed the gun and moved back around the stall to aim it at her. The door was closing. I shoved it open and cocked the gun.

"Don't move, Mary."

She looked at me, eyes wide, still trying to come to grips with what had just happened. She cupped her nose in her hands, and blood streamed between her fingers as if it was coming out of something larger than two tiny holes. Recognizing the pointlessness of trying to catch the blood, she dropped her hands in her lap. A grim goatee formed around her mouth. Her eyes began to water before the hatches broke and tears and blood reigned supreme on her face. Mary spoke, but it was gibberish.

"It'll be okay," I said, feeling like a Judas.

I had just incapacitated one of our own. So the stress had gotten to her. Only a robot could carry on unaffected by what was happening. *Maybe I could've disarmed her with less force?* Mary lay sprawled on the dirty floor like a marionette whose strings had just been cut. Her sobs were followed by snorts, the pain of which contorted her face in an expression fit for Halloween masks. I lowered the gun.

"I'm going to get Scott. I'm sorry."

I thought about grabbing the flashlight but didn't want to leave

Mary in the dark. I was almost out the door when the sobbing stopped. There was a shuffle of limbs behind me, and I turned to see Mary up on all fours. She was still mostly in the stall, with just her head and arms sticking out of it. Her greasy hair was releasing from its updo in serpentine jumbles.

"God will get you, Emma. Whether you come with me or not. But if you do help me reunite with my son, he might show mercy for the good deed you've done."

From what Scott had told me, if their son was alive, he was vampire. God had nothing to do with that, and neither did I. How Mary had gotten it in her head that God would return her son in exchange for me, I didn't know.

"I won't be long." I sprinted out the door.

In the hallway, I welcomed the stale storage air and wished I had a tissue to rid my nose of the scent of blood and urine. *Not a scent to bottle.* I did notice Mary was in rough shape at dinner, but I was also prioritizing at the time. Maybe badly. Hushed mentions had Scott keeping her on a tight leash with a cocktail of sedatives and anti-depressants because of an earlier escape attempt. Scott had conveniently left out of our every conversation the danger his wife posed. As long as Mary had it in her head that her son was still alive, the residents, the base, and the plan Cooper had eluded to were at risk. The drugs weren't working.

I found Cooper in the kitchen where I had left him. The dinner party had halved, with just the men and vampire remaining. The dishes and food remnants had been cleared, flames licked at the last bits of wax. Papers, books, and searching hands covered the table. Leech and

Topps toked on large cigars, and blue smoke swirls decorated the air like dirty icing.

When I entered the room, all eyes were on me. This was something I had gotten used to at Seepy Storage. It came down to expecting the worst. Times being bad, everyone was in a subconscious state of limbo waiting for the bearer of bad tidings. Tonight, I would satisfy them.

"Cooper, can I talk to you?" I felt the gun tucked down the back of my pants.

"Emma, I thought you'd be in bed by now," Scott said.

"Nope. No such luck." I smiled politely, trying to hide any indication that I had just leveled his wife. "Cooper?"

"Sure, okay." Cooper stood.

I could have just run in there and announced it. In our home of ten, they'd all know sooner or later. But the idea was to tidy the situation before presenting it. Cooper could fix Mary, calm her down. Even though, apparently, Mary thought of Cooper as a sinner, they still had a rapport. He defended her from the others.

Cooper came outside with me. He left the door ajar, and I grabbed the handle to shut it tight.

"What's going on?"

"I beat up Mary."

"*What?*"

"No...it was self-defense. She had a gun. This one." I pulled it out to show him. Cooper took it from me, and I wondered whether it was a goodwill gesture to get it off my hands, or something more.

"Where is she?"

"In the bathroom."

I thought he might run in to tell the others, but he didn't, instead running for the elevator. I followed.

"How bad is she?" he asked, in a cautious tone, as if how he asked might decide the outcome.

I assumed he meant her physical condition, rather than her mental one, which was a disaster. In other words: *How badly did you beat her?*

"Could be worse," I said. It was honest. I didn't give him specifics, and he didn't push for them. He'd just see.

We squinted in the bright light of the elevator and were released into the blackness of the fourth floor. The lights did click on, but they took their time.

Cooper and I paused outside the bathroom door to listen. Cooper had his own gun holstered and Mary's tucked away in his jeans. Neither one was coming out. As far as we knew, Mary was unarmed. If she was still hostile, Cooper planned on using words to placate or strength to detain.

Cooper opened the door, motioning me to get behind him. Irrational thoughts seized me at that inopportune moment, *those fuckers.* I worried what Cooper would think of me when he saw what I had done to Mary. I wondered if Mary had gotten the chance to freshen up for appearance's sake. Mine and hers.

My flashlight was still there, propped up on the metal shelf. The light it radiated had dimmed even more, the batteries' souls ready to cross over to some power-source heaven.

"The lights are broken," I whispered, pointing at the ceiling just as they clicked on. "Oh."

There were small pools of blood on the floor from the stall to the sink. The liquid could have been anything in the dark but was very much blood in the light. Sometimes dark *was* better. I motioned to the first stall. The door was closed.

"Mary? It's Cooper. I'm here to help." There was no answer or movement. He gently nudged the stall door open. It was empty. Bloodied tissues littered the floor. Our eyes fell on the next stall. "Mary?"

She wasn't there either. On the other side of the bathroom, the shower curtain was wide open. No Mary. There was blood from the stall to the sink and in the sink but none beyond.

"She's gone," I said. Cooper turned to me.

"What happened?"

"She came at me with a gun. She said she was taking me to God to get her son back. She was delusional. She grabbed my arm and I just went for it, and I...head-butted her...and maybe broke her nose."

"Was she conscious when you left?"

"Yeah. She was still trying to get me to go with her. I said I'd find Scott. That's it. That's what happened."

Cooper looked at me, thoughts I wasn't privy to behind those green eyes. Then: "Go check the residence floor. She might be back in her room or with Bugs. I'll call Rudy and give him a heads-up at the front. After that, I'll get Scott. She's somewhere in here. We'll find her."

We had just left the bathroom when Rudy's voice came out of Cooper's walkie-talkie:

"Coop, what channel you on? Out."

"Rudy, channel three. What's up? Out."

"Mary left...I think she went into the woods. Out."

I flinched as Cooper tightened his grip on the walkie-talkie and threw his arm outward like a major league pitcher. I closed my eyes.

When I opened them, the walkie-talkie was still in his hand.

"Stay there, Rudy. We're coming down. Out."

Rudy: "Ten/four. Out."

Then: "Cooper, Charlie here. Is it my imagination or did I just see Mary outside? Out."

"You saw it," Cooper said. "Alert the others. Meet downstairs. Come rigged. Out."

Charlie: "Got that. Out."

"Another day in paradise," Cooper said to me. His voice was different. "Get to Weapons. The others will meet you there."

I tried to find something on his face that said he didn't blame me, but he turned and bolted for the stairwell before I could get a reading. I followed, heading up to residence and weapon storage.

Cooper left me in his wake.

~

The garage was filled with hunters.

Well, not filled. It's hard to fill a stadium with six ants.

We left Bugs sleeping. Sammy was woken up to keep watch from the sixth floor. All the hunters needed to be in on this one.

I felt lucky, in a way. Most of the bad attention was being directed at Rudy who was fast asleep at post when Mary snuck out. The door closing had stirred him. As he was wiping the last of the sleep away, Mary showed up on the surveillance monitor lunging into the forest.

Scott stood before us. His real age had given him a shakedown over the past half hour. His peppered hair had become less dignified, sweat from small exertions poured down his face, channeling through a pattern of twisted wrinkles.

Scott would stay behind to guard the front. Someone had to, and

Cooper insisted it be our leader. Essentially, his research and expertise were required to, putting it lightly, save the world. The rest of us were expendable. Scott could find other hunters to help him.

I had never thought of myself as expendable before, and it was a strange feeling. Like my past, present, and future had joined together for the sole purpose of bringing Mary back safely, and if I didn't, there would be no evidence of any three. Who'd have thought that being sent to your death could be so liberating? The moment was surreal. As I checked my weapons for the umpteenth time, I might have been invisible.

We were each armed with two wooden stakes and one semi-automatic pistol. There weren't enough night vision goggles to go around, so Cooper and Topps got the two available, as they would be leading the pack. My stakes were sheathed, one down my back and the other, my calf. I felt like Pinocchio, but I was a real girl.

Besides the weapons we had trained with, there was another weapon. If you want to guess, it's too large to fit in a pocket, but it fits in a coffin just right.

"I'd be honored to go," Leech said. "She's my friend, too, and Nancy...well, she'd be devastated to hear of any harm coming to Mary. Let's go bring her back."

Cooper spoke to us, now. Scott left him to it. Scott wasn't all there. "Okay, you know the drill. Tight line, stick with your partners. Mary entered the northwest side of the forest. As far as we know, she hasn't come out."

"Yeah, can someone explain that?" Rudy asked. "Mary knows as well as the rest of us that going into the forest at night is pure suicide. I mean, what did you say to her, Em?" Just like Rudy to pass the buck.

Everyone looked at me. "Nothing. I said nothing. She attacked me."

"Look," Cooper said, "none of that matters right now. Mary's gone and time's wasting. As I was saying, tight line, no Rambo tactics."

"But those are my favorite," I overheard Rudy whisper to Topps. Topps smirked. Cooper glared.

"Topps and I have the tranquilizers...for Mary." Cooper spared a glance at Scott. "If they're needed. Um, I guess that's it. The less time we have to spend out there, the better. Any questions?" Rudy raised his hand.

"Any *real* questions?" Cooper asked. Rudy put his hand down. "Good. Let's go."

The garage door opened, spilling six hunters into the night. "You're with me, okay?" Cooper said, nudging me.

I nodded. It was okay.

"Time to pop your cherry, doll," Rudy said.

~

The air was cool. Above us, a family tree of gods and mortals.

We kept a fast pace with a vampire on point. Our flashlights were upgraded from the cheap ones we used around the facility. The new ones were chunky with beams that could blind. They carved out a path in front of us.

Topps and Cooper had their goggles down over their faces. I thought of children playing spy when they first put them on and had to stifle a laugh. There was a small part of me that still refused to believe what was happening—that toyed with the idea that this was all some big, elaborate joke being played on me, and at any moment, a washed-up celebrity was going to hop out from behind a bush, donning plastic vampire teeth and holding a camera. I'd laugh, play the good sport, and go over in my head whether I had said anything incriminating me as a bitch. This small part of me was my comfort zone, and I wouldn't tell anybody about it, so it couldn't be taken away.

We only paused in our heads at the entrance to the woods. The others began to unsheathe weapons, and I followed suit, removing my gun. We slowed our pace once we were fully in. We weren't sure where Mary had gone and we didn't want to be moving so fast that we missed her. Twigs cracked like bones under our feet. Our flashlight beams and hushed voices crashed the silent gathering of trees and shrub.

"I knew a girl named Emma once." Rudy was next to me. It was the last place I wanted him to be. "I screwed her sister. It's a funny story, actually."

"Shut it, Rudy," Cooper said.

"What? I'm just lightening the mood."

"You and your stories," Seven said. "It's the same thing every mission."

"What do you mean?" Rudy said, laughing.

Topps turned his smirking, goggled face at Rudy, and it was all the encouragement Rudy needed. He leaned closer to me and continued: "So, this chick and I had just gotten back from a party, and we were fucking in my bed. This girl was a wildcat and she's on top and we're getting this real momentum going. We're bouncing and bouncing, faster and faster, to the point where we couldn't even stop if we wanted to. And the next thing you know, she's dangling from the freaking ceiling with her head sticking through the plaster. No lie. And listen to this: my bro upstairs...Goober...stoned off his ass...takes a lit blunt out of his mouth and puts it between the girl's lips. Yeah, yeah."

Laughter ensues.

"I swear it's true. You believe me, right Topps?"

"I love you man, but your stories are weak."

"Seriously, Rudy," Charlie said. "Where do you get this stuff?"

"Yeah—you forget we've all seen your penis, Rudy, and you'd be lucky if an ant could slide up and down it," Seven said. More laughter.

"Ha, ha...very fucking funny."

Rudy's massive sweaty arm flung over my shoulders. He had a stake in his hand, and the tip scraped against my breast.

"You believe me, don't you? Come to think of it, I even screwed her sister Emma, Emma, and you know, I was really out of it that night, so maybe it was you?"

Rudy liked to feed off of other people's irritation with him, but now was not the time or the place. Shadows were all around us. At any given moment, one could come alive and strike. The others had gone quiet, maybe understanding that Rudy had crossed a line.

"You know what," he continued, "I *do* think it was you. Come on, Emma, don't you remember me? *Rudy.* Should I drop my pants and give you a closer look?"

Cooper moved fast, pinning Rudy against a tree. Cooper didn't have his size, but he held him there like he was as light as a feather. "If you don't shut up, I won't wait for the vampires to take you out. I'll do it myself." Rudy nodded, and Cooper nodded to complete their transaction, before letting him go.

Rudy avoided glances but straightened his posture as a first step to recovering his dignity. "I was just joking, anyway. We'll be okay...we've got Leech with us. Leech will protect us, won't you Leech?"

Up ahead, Leech responded, "That's what I'm here for."

"See? It's all good."

I knew then that Rudy was acting up because he was scared, and it made it easier to dismiss the fact that he had just acted like a complete asshole. I wasn't sure what to think of Cooper defending me, but I filed the thought away for when I once again had the security of four walls around me.

The group pushed on. We traveled with Leech in the lead and Charlie and Seven taking up the rear. Topps was the first to spot the white pajama bottoms hanging from the tree branch. The empty pant legs were inflated by a breeze and looked like they were running. We got closer, and I noticed the rose pattern, confirming the pajamas as Mary's. I eyed the blood stains and the faint yellowing of the crotch area.

"Looks like she's hurt," Charlie said.

"No, she was hurt when she left," I said. "It looks like the same amount of blood."

"Why would she take her pants off?" Topps asked, addressing the question to me. Everyone looked at me. I shrugged. I had become the anointed expert on everything Mary.

"She really is a loon," Rudy said, making safe space between himself and Cooper.

I had a thought: "Maybe she wants to be found?"

"Let's hope," Cooper said. "That'll make our job easier."

The hunters affirmed. We found Mary's top further ahead, discarded on a rotten log. Nearby, a dark hole was in the ground.

"It's manmade. There's the cover right over there," Topps said, pointing to a round, rusted disc.

I put my light on the hole, exposing the first few rungs of a ladder. "Looks like some type of sewerage access...or maybe a bomb shelter?"

The other hunters directed their flashlights. The ladder was approximately ten feet in length. The bottom met a cement landing. I looked at Cooper who had his night vision goggles pushed up on top of his head. I knew what he would say before he said it. I think we all did, and we dreaded the moment for the short time we could.

"We go in."

"*What*?" Rudy said, backing up. "You're crazy, man. We all know what's down there. There could be hundreds of them. If Mary's dumb ass went in there, good fucking riddance, I say." Rudy looked around at the others for support.

"Yeah," Cooper said. "It figures you'd say that." He also eyed the others. "Mary has problems, but she's one of us and she's Scott's wife. We'd probably all be dead if it wasn't for Scott. Before we go back, we have to at least try."

Silence ensued.

"I'll go," Leech said.

"Yeah, cool," Rudy said. "Let Leech go. He can scope things out and report back."

Leech shook his head. "Don't get me wrong. I may be a vampire, but I'm not stupid. Hermits have no allegiance. They'll enjoy tearing me apart just as much as they would any of you."

"No," Cooper said. "We all go in." Cooper lowered his goggles back over his eyes. The others gathered close to the hole. I joined them. Rudy took a few more paces back.

"I'm not doing it, man. It's just not right."

Cooper looked at him. If looks could kill behind night vision goggles. "Fine, stay here. Keep watch." Cooper cocked his gun and then lowered himself first into the hole. I thought it was what we had the vampire for. In my head, I screamed at him not to go. Outside my head, only the crickets spoke.

Each ladder rung gonged. Eight hollow gongs before Cooper was out of sight. Leech went next. The rest of us followed. As each of us entered the hole, Rudy tried to look busy with his position as watcher. Topps tipped an imaginary cowboy hat at him.

"Thanks, partner," he said.

Rudy's face faltered, before his eyes returned to the surrounding darkness.

~

Going down that hole, I felt more like the tunnel was pulling me in than I was voluntarily entering. There was a smell, but wasn't there always? It came before most bad things, a first hello from the nastiness around the corner. I had been told by an old acquaintance that smelling something meant that the particles of whatever you smelled were actually up your nose. If I could return that little piece of knowledge, I would.

I pressed my nose against my sleeve and breathed in the blessed toxicity of detergent. The ladder rungs were rusted and wet. Grit pierced my palms. Someone below put a light on me as I descended. I squinted, "Hey get that light off me." A mumbled apology.

I was glad to put two feet on solid ground despite the location of that ground.

"Looks like an old shelter of some sort," Charlie whispered.

The hunters gathered around the bottom of the ladder, mentally clinging to the escape it offered. Our flashlight beams darted midair in a vacant, drippy room. Though at one time the room might have been a sturdy example of a bomb shelter, it was now in ruins.

What could only be described as muck seeped through the walls and ceiling and stretched green arms to the floor.

"What is that?" Seven asked. "It looks like sewerage."

"Don't touch it," Topps said.

"I wasn't planning on it."

Papers and canned goods littered the floor. Most of the cans were punctured or dented. My flashlight beam fell on a birthday card with Darth Vader on the cover. It looked new, as if it had recently been delivered via force field bubble to the dirty floor of that room. There were clothes, too, all unusable and some ripped in inappropriate places. Fabric crotches and chests were missing.

The stench was making me ill. My stomach turned.

Cooper, Topps, and Leech moved forward first. I gave a last longing glance up at the entrance. Dark trees and a midnight blue sky were framed in the hole. Insects hummed contentedly, perhaps feeling lucky not to be us. I had the thought that the exit was no place we were getting to quickly, if the need arose.

Last chance.

I wanted to be Rudy, all 250 pounds of crudeness and cowardice. If it meant I could have been where he was, I'd have made the sacrifice.

I touched the ladder, a reluctant goodbye, and moved further into the room.

CHAPTER TWENTY

THE BODY WATCHED US…

…eyeless in a corner. It was a woman. Cooper spotted her first.

"Is it Mary?" Seven asked.

"I don't think so," Cooper said.

It was hard to tell. The scene was one no light should ever illuminate. Ever.

The woman was naked, covered in dirt. Her hair was matted, slick with whatever was seeping through the cracks in that room. A large drop fell repeatedly onto her head—a sickly last diatribe. The face was the worst part: black sockets, not red as you might expect, and a mouth wide open, stretched slightly beyond capacity in an eternal scream.

The vampires hadn't just bitten, they had taken pieces to go. Holes in the shape of mouths covered every inch of her pale body. They wouldn't have eaten the flesh, but sucked the blood from each piece, like it was bread drenched in the finest balsamic vinegar.

The only one in the group who wasn't affected by the sight of that woman was Leech. He glanced at her like she was just another withered corpse in his corpse-full existence. I supposed she was. The chance was slight that all of his friends were vegetarians. He lived in a world of *meat eaters*. I also thought that if just a lick of blood had been remaining in that woman, his interest would've been keener.

"It's not her," Cooper said, coming back from a closer look. His face had gone pale.

"So, can we get a move on then?" Seven asked, motioning toward the next room. "As much as I love this place and all."

"Yeah," Charlie agreed. "Let's just check it and get out of here."

"That's the plan," Topps said, moving forward first without being asked. "Eyes open."

The room we were in opened into a bigger room. We first thought the smell had been coming from the sludge dripping through the walls.

We were wrong.

Bodies covered the floor like carpeting in hell. I counted at least twenty, but it was hard to tell where one body stopped and another began. Intact limbs mingled with loose ones. The hunters seemed to have lost control of their flashlights. Beams flew around the room, not stopping on any particular spot. Not daring to stop.

There was a young boy, face down, clutching a teddy bear with his severed arm. An old woman with a large nose, her neck wrung and stretched like a wet towel. Another woman, with dreaded hair, stiffened limbs locked in an unnatural position.

I felt the adrenalin rushing through my veins. *Fight or flight. Fight or flight.* I pushed it back down. Somewhere far off, a sea bell tolled.

"Easy with the flashlights, people," Cooper said. "Stay alert."

"Does anyone see her?" I asked. "Do you see her?"

"They're all face down," Seven said. "And I'm not turning them over to see."

"Hey, I thought we left Rudy behind," Topps said.

"He's *your* buddy," Seven said.

Our vampire wandered in first amongst them. He wove his way and leapt to and from limited floor space until he reached the center of the room.

"Do you see her, Leech?" I asked, raising my gun. "Do you see

351

Mary?"

Leech shook his head, "I can't be sure."

"Look, they're all dead," Seven said. "If Mary's here...she's dead, too. Let's *go.*"

"*No,*" Cooper said. "We stay and make sure. Topps, over there, Seven and Charlie, get the right side. Em, stay with me."

Cooper and I walked down the center, taking mental pictures of each dead face and running them through our internal database. *If this person had a nose, skin, hair, eyeballs, their left leg...would it look more like Mary?* It was the kind of thinking that did irrevocable damage. These pictures would not go away. Considering the dreams I was already having, these mangled bodies would stay in my head and be very comfortable there.

Cooper and I arrived at our last body against the back wall. No Mary. The others were nearly done with their search, too. Where we'd go now, I wasn't sure. There was the chance Cooper would make us continue our search of the woods. Maybe we'd wait until first light, but what was the point of that? Give Mary a few more hours and we were giving her more time to run into something she couldn't defend herself against. If she wasn't down here, she was up there, and if she was up there, she could still be alive.

I holstered my gun and wiped my face with my sleeve. *At least we haven't run into any vampires.*

"Over there," Charlie said, in an urgent whisper. We all looked at Charlie. He had his gun pointing toward the right side of the room. "It moved. I'm sure of it. The one that looks like...like the lead singer of the Ramones. He moved his hand."

"Which one's that?" Topps asked, waving his gun in the general direction.

"The guy with the long hair...I swear, I swear he moved."

"We believe you," Topps said, and we did because there was no reason not to and every reason to.

We were all pointing our guns and flashlights now. Our beams met on the seemingly lifeless body of a tall, thin man with pruned flesh and three missing fingers. He was shirtless, in tight black jeans. His eyes were closed.

The room was still.

If he moved, we'd know it.

"What's that sound? Do you hear it?" Seven asked.

We did. It was a wet noise—very quiet but coming from all around. Only holding your breath could you hear it. We eyed the bodies and aimed our guns.

"They're dead. We checked them," Seven said.

Leech was standing a couple feet away from Cooper and I. He leaned over one of the bodies, an older woman with a wide forehead and frizzy hair. He straightened up suddenly.

"It's their teeth, folks. They're coming out."

Quick movement somewhere.

A horrible screech.

A shot was fired, and other shots rang out in succession.

My hearing dropped out, but I still had my sight, and I saw the hermits, toothy and mad, rising up off the ground in shifting beams of light. The ones that had no limbs made do, shuffling, hopping, jerking, lunging toward dinner.

Toward *us*.

Someone screamed. It might have been me.

A hermit appeared in front of me. Its whole body was vibrating. I shot.

Missed.

I fired again and hit the hermit's chest, catapulting the vampire into the wave of violence behind it. A hand wrapped around my arm, urging me forward. Cooper. He was yelling something.

We surged ahead, torn mangled bodies we had just inspected for Mary-ness coming for us from all directions.

The little boy with the severed arm rushed at me, ducking and dodging. I emptied my gun, not able to get a mark.

I threw the gun.

It hit his head but did nothing to slow him. I pulled the stake from out of my back sheath and whacked him across the face twice. He rammed into me, making me drop my stake. I got a hold of his tiny ears and veered his gnashing teeth away from my stomach. I pressed my hands firmly against both sides of his head and yanked to the right. I felt a pop and let go.

The child hermit backed away from me, his head now lolling to the side. I retrieved my stake and heaved it into his chest.

Bull's eye.

Far away shots fired. My arm flared with pain. I looked down at a small circle on my bicep seeping blood. I'd been shot.

An arm, more bone than the other stuff, slid around my neck. The hand at the end of that arm forced my head to the side, stretching my jugular. Breath that promised no tomorrow slid across my cheek.

I struggled, but nothing was working in my favor. *Is this how it's going to end? After everything?*

Teeth, now, against my skin. I braced myself. *Is everyone else dead, too?*

All for nothing: such a sad thought to have in one's head the moment before death.

All for nothing.

The arm tightened around me before warmth spread down my neck. But not just there. It drenched my scalp and the side of my face. I felt no different. The grip loosened, and the arm slid away.

I turned. Leech stood over a fallen corpse, its head like a hole now. Bits of gore slid down his face into his mouth. He spat. For my benefit, probably. He had a gun, which he handed to me. His lips were moving, but I only heard ringing. I pointed to my ear and shook my head.

My stomach shifted. I felt lightheaded. The wound in my arm was emptying me. Not sensing any imminent danger, I shoved the gun into my pants and tore a strip of fabric from my shirt. Leech stepped forward to help, but I warned him off. Vampires attending to wounds seemed like a bad idea.

The strip wasn't long enough to make it around my arm twice, but it would have to do. I wrapped my bicep, gripped the fabric between my teeth, and pulled, making a knot.

The pain was excruciating. My legs weakened and my stomach did somersaults—two conditions that could prove fatal in my current predicament. I fought through it. Anger helped. It was a worthy emotion in the right situation.

Ahead of me, vamps brightened like bulbs, as if the pain I had just experienced was a doorway and on the other side was a 20/20 world. Things were clear. There was no gray area. Evil was black, and boy, did it stick out like a sore thumb. I knew exactly what I had to do.

Bam, bam, bam, bam!

It's the sound fired bullets make in comic books. Four bullets. Four vampires. No longer undead but dead. I looked around me, not knowing if I was the only survivor—the last one standing and the one who, at least in my head, had caused all this. I lowered my gun. The bodies that had risen were back on the ground where they belonged. Messier. I stepped over others that had stayed put, too dead to be undead. The lucky ones, in my mind.

I could barely contain myself when I saw the others. They had all seen better nights, but they'd live. Life was good.

~

I felt like I was being reborn when I crawled out from the manhole.

The cool air caressed my mucky face. I wanted to scream, but I held onto it, not letting it pass my lips.

Rudy looked us over, guilt and relief waltzing across his face. He was shiny clean. No hermits had ventured up here. I wanted to use his untouched skin as a rag to clean myself. Then he would be dirty and I would be less dirty and maybe it would help me feel better. Maybe. *It would probably turn him on*, I thought, and that was where my musings ended.

My arm hurt so much that it didn't hurt at all. It was as if my body couldn't quite register that level of pain, so it gave up trying. No argument from me. The wound hadn't stopped bleeding, though, and the thin strip I had wrapped around it was soaked through. With shaking hands, I cleared my sodden hair away from my face and grabbed a fistful of shirt. Cooper stepped up.

"Let me help," he said.

I could hear again, though Cooper's voice sounded distant, like I was underwater and he was safe on shore. I obliged and he peeled the wet fabric away. I winced.

"You were shot?" Cooper asked, shock on his face.

"Guess so," I said. "The team's already trying to get rid of me, huh?" I laughed. Cooper didn't. He eyed the others. "You could have been killed."

"Well, better by one of your own than, um...you know." He did.

Cooper moved his face closer to the wound. "It doesn't look so bad. Just a nick, no arteries." I became worried that my wound might spit at him, like an angry camel. *That would be embarrassing.* I inched away.

"Stop fidgeting," he said.

"Okay, I'll try," I said. "How are you? Are *you* okay?"

Cooper glanced up from my arm. "Fine. Got any bites?"

He asked this as casual as one would "Cream with coffee?", "Biscuits with tea?", "Change for that dollar?" *Got any bites with that bullet wound?* It was the furthest thing from a casual question, and both he and I knew it.

"Sure. I mean *no*. Definitely not." Cooper locked eyes with mine. "No," I said, again.

Satisfied, Cooper went back to my wound, discarding the used fabric onto the forest floor and wrapping the clean, new strip around my arm several times. He made a knot at the end.

"That'll do it. A couple stitches, you'll be fine," he said. "Good job down there."

"Sure...thanks."

Cooper moved on to help the others. We all conceivably could have just been in a fight with a butcher, but none of us were bitten and thankfully most of the blood had come from the enemy. Topps had a laceration on his forehead that had brought down a sheet of blood over his face, like Satan pulled a curtain. It was starting to dry but looked no less grisly. Charlie's lips were collagen implants gone wrong, and he casually mentioned twisting his ankle. I caught a glimpse of it, and the thing could have been the size of all the hunters' ankles put together. Seven was seated on a fallen tree, running her hands down her ponytail. She was the cleanest (apart from Rudy), and when and if the time came that we were friends, I'd ask her how on earth she did it.

Cooper moved quickly, finishing up and allowing Topps to inspect him for bites. The night was still upon us and we were vulnerable. I looked around.

"Where's Leech?" I asked Rudy, scanning the area.

"Oh...all the blood," Rudy said, pointing. "He's over there somewhere having a cat bath."

I looked at where Rudy had pointed but didn't see Leech. "That makes me feel real safe. I thought he was a vegetarian?"

"Blood is blood. It's just hermit blood, anyway." Rudy swatted a bug away.

"Yeah, I guess."

I would give the vampire the benefit of the doubt...for tonight. He had just saved my life.

I wondered what the consequences would have been if any of us were bitten. Cara was staked but only after she had gone for her brother's neck. Cooper's girlfriend was killed no questions asked, but that must have been before the group's introduction to Leech, your friendly neighborhood vampire.

"Listen up, guys," Cooper said. "We're heading back to base. Stay frosty."

"What about Mary?" I asked.

"Leech found her under some clothing in the first room," Cooper said, looking down at a small cloth bag he was carrying. Something round bulged from inside. "We're returning it...*her*...back to Scott. She'll be buried."

I covered my mouth and turned my head. My eyes welled up, but I didn't want anyone to see. Mary and I hadn't been close, but she was one of us and she had died a horrible death. I felt for Scott and the kids. I didn't envy Cooper who'd have to hand Scott that bag.

And there was the issue of blame. Rudy let her out, but I left her alone in a state. I wiped at my eyes and looked over at Rudy. He was adjusting a strap on his vest. I wasn't sure he could ever get his jock mind around it. Me, I was a guilt magnet.

We punched back through the darkness, blood as our new camouflage. Insects buzzed around us, playing tag in our flashlight beams. Mary's remains bounced inside the bag. Cooper had looped the closure around his belt in order to keep his hands free. I wondered what it was like having a decapitated head beat against your leg repeatedly. *Um, not nice?*

I picked up my pace to catch up with Cooper. He had his goggles down and his gun out. He moved like a hunter. Every step was a calculation.

"Cooper?" I whispered.

"Yeah?"

"Are you sure you want to go ahead with this?"

"With what?"

"Bringing it...that...*her*...to Scott."

"It's not something I want to do, it's something I have to do."

"Why? I mean...can't you just tell him she's dead? That you saw her body?"

"He'll need closure."

"Closure does not a decapitated head make." Cooper looked at me, goggle-eyed. I shook my head. "What I mean to say is that there are other ways to give Scott closure. You're his friend. He'll trust what you say, and if you say Mary's dead, he'll know that to be the truth."

"Why are you bringing this up?"

"I just think that something like this could really mess with a person's mind. I don't know Scott very well, I admit, but even the strongest person would have trouble getting past something like this."

Cooper sighed. "He's going to want to bury her, Emma. I know that much."

"Yeah, *jeez*, Em," Rudy said, leaning in, "he's not going to throw the thing at him."

I held up a warning finger. "You, get away."

~

Seepy Storage was quiet.

The hunters unstuck themselves and called dibs on the shower. As a newbie, I would go last. When and if more hunters joined us, I could get clean before them. Until then, I had to suffer in my stench and keep away from Schizo for an hour and a half.

First thing, Cooper locked Mary's head away in the trunk of a silver Audi. He didn't want Scott or Sammy becoming curious as to the contents of the bag. Scott knew the truth when he saw Cooper's face. His eyes didn't search the garage for his wife, his mouth never asked of Mary's whereabouts. He only stated, "She's dead."

Cooper went for Scott before I could. It wasn't my place, anyway. The other hunters busied themselves with things more comfortable:

weapons, buckles, and blood. Cooper walked Scott out of the garage and away from the head in the trunk. I wrapped an arm around Sammy.

Those remaining said their goodbyes to Leech. He made us promise to give his condolences to Scott since he hadn't gotten the chance. I was glad to see him go. His cat bath had removed any evidence of blood.

I could see my reflection in his skin.

~

The bathroom dripped and steamed. Rudy slipped by me at the doorway, wearing just a towel. I expected some sexual remark and got one.

"Enjoy yourself in there." He winked.

Oh, he wanted me to *enjoy* myself. I rolled my eyes. Rudy was innuendo central. It must be hard being taken seriously when most things out of your mouth relate to sex. Unless you're a porn star. Then only other porn stars take you seriously.

I shut the door tight behind him, peeled off my clothes, and wrapped myself in a towel. When we met, Cooper told me I needed to get used to being dowsed in blood and guts. I wasn't sure it was something I could ever get used to. Sure, it had become a constant, but I found having someone's guts all over me to be equally repellent every time.

My wound burned beneath its dressing. It was no longer bleeding. Cooper had done a good job. *He would have made a good doctor*, I thought. I wasn't sure if I should remove my makeshift bandage, so I didn't.

I went for a pee, when I noticed Mary's blood still on the floor of the stall. Someone had cleaned up outside the stall, but apparently hadn't checked the inside.

"That's just great," I said aloud. Guilt washed over me. It was like Mary was in my ear, insisting I wallow in the destruction I had caused.

I found a bottle of bleach next to the garbage, removed the cap, and poured. When all else fails, disinfect your troubles away.

Once there was more bleach than blood, I grabbed a few handfuls of toilet paper and started to scrub. I felt the door open behind me before it actually did. Sometimes it just happened that way. I got up on my knees and adjusted my towel for a PG-version. The door opened to Scott as I had never seen him. His eyes were bloodshot, his back curved, the weight of his dead wife on his shoulders. The smell of booze overpowered the odor of a half bottle of bleach.

"I was coming to do that," he said. "I was putting it off as long as I could."

He looked away and thanked me for cleaning up his wife's blood. I nodded because *you're welcome* seemed so wrong.

"Cooper just gave me her...body. I'll bury her under the big palm tomorrow." I knew the one. It was a magnificent tree. So big, I was sure it had lived many lifetimes. Scott continued: "I prefer to be alone, but anyone who feels like visiting her later can do so." Scott turned to walk away. Then, "I could have done more."

I looked down. When I looked up, he was gone. "We all could have."

I finished cleaning up the blood and dragged myself into the shower. I didn't use my injured arm during the cleanup, but even immobility pained it. I thought about Scott. He was a good leader, but I wasn't sure he could get through this. In crisis, love was a weakness. Cooper had been right to tell me my family and friends were dead.

362

Love could stick itself right in between you and what had to get done, which was reproachable when you had the task of saving the world.

Ice cold water spit at me. Going last meant arctic shower. I leaned down and worked on a resistant patch of muck on my ankle. After a quick, fervent scrub, I turned off the faucet, dressed in the towel, and hoofed it to my unit.

Cooper left a note to meet him in the lounge. It was early in the a.m., but understandably none of the hunters could sleep, so a movie marathon was born. Schizo was happy to see me. He jiggled his butt and nosed at my bandage, whining. He was a third clumsy leg as I made my way to the lounge.

"About time, Em," Rudy said. "We were ready to send out the cavalry."

Rudy, Topps, Charlie, and Cooper were in the room. A movie was paused on the television screen.

"Sorry," I said. "Just got the memo. What are we watching?"

"Well, it's got chainsaws," Charlie said, enveloped by the sofa with his leg wrapped in ice packs and resting on a cushioned stool, "more chainsaws, and rumor has it, Topps' second-cousin-twice-removed-in-law playing a stuntman."

"Wow, sounds horrible. No offense to your relative, Topps."

Topps winked at me, then took a large gulp of Heineken.

They all had beers in their hands, with empties teeter-tottering in a partial pyramid nearby. Cooper opened the fridge and came out with a fresh one. He popped the top before offering it to me with a long smile. He was drunk.

"Well, now I have to take it," I said to him.

"Looks like," he said.

I took a sip. "So, where does this endless supply of alcohol come from?" I asked the room.

"The wishing well on the third floor," Rudy said, smirking. "Jeez, would everyone *stop* wishing for booze." Various debris flew his way.

"Let's put this movie on before I pass out." Charlie said. Cooper aimed the control at the television, and the movie started. I was going to regret this.

"Be seated, woman," Rudy said.

Schizo made rounds. He stopped at Topps and proceeded to lick the condensation off his beer can. Topps brought a big arm around the dog.

"It's good, huh, buddy."

I took a seat near Cooper. We were the furthest ones from the television. I had gotten my share of violence for the night. Given the choice, I'd stay as far from it as possible. On the screen, a group of teenagers stopped for a shifty-looking hitchhiker. *First mistake.*

"Oh, they're gonna get it," Rudy said. "This is a good scene."

"Look at those roads," Topps said. "Only get roads like that in Texas." Topps had another hat on, and he nudged it up. Schizo curled half on his lap.

My eyes were straight ahead, but I was very aware of Cooper next to me. Too aware. I felt like I was in high school on a first date, with adults sitting between us. My mind raced for things to say. We both brought our beers to our mouths, taking sips at the same time. We spoke at the same time.

Me: "Where...?"

Him: "How's...?"

Me: "You go."

Him: "You go."

We laughed.

"Quiet," Rudy said.

I went. "Where are the others?" I absently rubbed my face and felt something sticky on my chin. *Damn*. Worrying about having guts on your face was the modern-day version of spinach in the teeth.

"Seven's up front. Sammy's bunked with Bugs. Scott's...around. How's your arm?"

"Good, fine. It stopped bleeding. Don't think I'll need stitches after all."

"Let me see." I moved closer.

Cooper unwound the fabric slowly. It was still damp from the shower. I forced myself to look and found that, not gushing blood, the wound was much easier on the eyes.

"Have you washed it out?" People were screaming on the television. I glanced up. The shifty-looking hitchhiker was attacking the teenagers with a razorblade. I looked away.

"No, uh-uh. I left the bandage on in the shower."

Cooper nodded. "I'll find you some hydrogen peroxide. Clean it before you go to bed. You might end up with a bit of a scar."

"That's okay," I said, smiling. "I don't plan on getting shot again, so I'll keep this one to show the grandkids." I nudged him and lowered my voice. "By the way, which one's trying to off me?"

He laughed. I was really curious who had shot me. I didn't think it had been on purpose, but I wanted to know for next time. That way, I could keep one and a half eyes on the vampires and half an eye on the person with the bad aim. Cooper tore a piece off his clean white shirt to rewrap my arm. My protests were futile.

"Don't worry, I can pick up a hundred shirts tomorrow."

"Tomorrow?"

"Want to go shopping?"

"Is this a trick question?"

Rudy shushed us. The teenagers were in a bad way now.

I leaned in and whispered, "Are you being serious?"

"We need gas. The mall is on the way. I'm really a clothes freak and seeing everyone in the same clothes day after day is pushing me over the edge."

"Really?"

Cooper smiled, scratching his head. "No, not really. But we're still going shopping."

"You told a joke. Nice one," I said.

~

We left the screaming.

Cooper had manifested a pack of cigarettes. He was fast becoming my miracle man. Neither of us smoked, we said, before he lit my cigarette and his.

Blank headlights watched us quietly. Cooper informed me that at night the garage became the smoking section. I had no idea. The cavernous room was always just the place I passed through to get to the outside. The cars that had stunned me when I arrived at Seepy Storage had meekly slipped into my background.

Cooper dragged an ashtray toward us along the surface of a wooden workbench. It was full and sprinkled a trail of old ash.

A shiny fender with a small dent took up most of the space on the bench. A red metal box behind it was filled with drawers filled with tidbits too tiny to be left out and too important to lose. Next to the box were tubes and cans of liquids, the contents of which could dirty a man's hands up to his forearms in half a millisecond.

A sudden *whirr whirr* erupted behind me. I grabbed for the fender.

Cooper was holding a yellow drill. At some point in his life, he had mastered the pleased but apologetic look.

"You scared me. I was about to end you with a fender. Managed to hold on to my cigarette, though." I held it up proudly. "Priorities. So which one does it belong to?"

"The fender? I'll show you." Beer replaced drill, and Cooper motioned me in amongst the beautiful cars.

I moved ahead carefully, almost worried that my many imperfections would trip an alarm and I would be eternally banned from that place where exquisite metal slept. We walked to the other end of the garage. I stopped and bent over a blue Porsche to look at my reflection in the paint job. Staring back at me was *Cousin Itt*.

We are our own worst critics.

My hair fell forward in bundles, brushing the hood. I smiled, two beers having their way with me. I got a mischievous urge to apply one finger to one unsullied hood. It was like staring at that big red button, surrounded by hundreds of signs that warned you against pushing it. None of them ever had the courtesy to tell you why.

I circled my index finger above the car before bringing it down for a landing. *One small step for man; one giant leap for mankind.* I surveyed my work. Cooper cleared his throat beside me.

"What?"

"Charlie will dream about that fingerprint tonight. It'll be like a pea under his mattress. These are his babies."

Honking, zooming, metal sperm. "I didn't know Charlie was into cars. He never said."

Cooper shrugged. "He hasn't worked on them in a while. Don't know why. I guess Seven's been occupying his time."

"Yeah, us girls. *Humph*."

"I didn't mean it like that."

"I know." I smiled to reassure him. "Is this it?" I pointed at a car covered with a black tarp.

"Yep," Cooper said, taking hold of a corner of the tarp and whisking it off. Underneath was a pumpkin-orange clunker minus its shiny fender.

"Well, it's got a nice...fender," I said. "I didn't think lemons were allowed in this part of town." I finished my cigarette and looked around for a place to stub it out.

"Here," Cooper said, taking a swig of beer, then handing me his empty can. I stuck the stub through the sip hole. The cigarette hissed at me from the can's bowels.

"My dad gave me this car when I turned sixteen. He was big into lessons." Cooper raised a finger and stuck out his chest in imitation of the elder Knox. "I refuse to raise a spoiled child, he would say." The driver's side window was open. Cooper jumped up, swinging both legs through. "Managed to get it back from the garage after settling in here. Couldn't believe she was still there."

"The car's a she, huh?"

Cooper sat balanced in the window frame, his arms resting on the car's roof. "Aren't they all?"

"Uh-uh. My friend had a car named Billy Bob."

"I stand corrected."

"What's her name?"

"I don't really have one," Cooper said. "She's just a she."

"A car named 'She.' I like it." My head swam. I put my beer and Cooper's empty on the concrete floor. Cooper disappeared through the car window. The passenger door unlocked. I breathed and opened it.

The interior of the car was worse off than the exterior. Seats and ceiling spewed dry yellow foam. The netting that secured the foam to the inside roof had frayed and hung low to tickle the top of my head. A crack in the dashboard ran its entire length, as if a Samurai had come by to pay respects with his giant sword.

"Nice. I like it," I said, and I did. It had character.

Cooper grinned at me. "*Come on.* It's always been a piece of shit. But..." Cooper's grin faltered.

"But what?"

"I guess it means something more now. When the war is over...this is the piece of shit I'll be taking with me. I'll start her up and drive her right out of here. Maybe head to the beach—stay there until the sun goes down. There'll be nothing more to worry about. This clunker right here...she's my freedom."

"You know everyone else will be leaving in the Mercedes and the Porches, don't you?"

Cooper laughed. "Yeah." He turned his attention to a black scuff mark on the side of the door. He scraped at it with his thumbnail. My ears tingled unpleasantly.

He had called this thing a war. I never thought of it like that. Didn't a war require an opposing side greater than nine?

"Is your plan going to work, Cooper?" The scraping stopped.

"I don't know. There's a chance."

Not the answer I was looking for.

Cooper continued: "It's all up to Leech. Once he can get us the head vampires' locations, then it'll be up to us."

I didn't like the idea of depending on a vampire first and humans second. I would have felt more confident without Leech in the equation. What can you do? Kill the vampire that has his hands on all the good intel—in fact, the only intel? *And he did save your life*, my inner voice prodded me. *You again? Go away.*

"So we need to get to the head vampires you said? Kill them, right? What happens after that?" I asked. Yes, I was crashing the party. These were just things I had had on my mind, and my slightly intoxicated state didn't allow for containment.

"The vampires in their lineage...they become human again."

I felt like I had just been sucker-punched in the gut. Since Cooper had told me about The Plan, I had been under the impression that when the masters were killed, the rest would die too. This news brought everything into a whole new light. A harsh light. Department store lighting. "That means we're murderers."

"Huh?"

"We belong in jail."

"Emma, you're not being reasonable."

I held up my hand and counted. "That means I've killed...two, three, four, *six*. *Six* vampires that had another chance to be human...another chance at life." I was having an attack of conscience. Throw in the guilt repercussions for the Mary incident and it was an all-out ambush.

I hadn't counted Myers. I had yet to tell Cooper about all that, and I wasn't sure it was necessary. Besides, I had my doubts Myers had been a vampire. He went down too easily and there was the blood from his victims left to dry on the floor of that nasty room.

"Don't do this, Em. It's not your fault. We do what we have to do. They attacked us."

"Next you're going to tell me vampires give presents to needy children on the holidays. You're not going to tell me that, are you?"

Cooper shook his head, a sad smile on his lips. "No, I'm not."

"That's good," I said. I sighed. *Don't get weird about this, Emma,* I thought. Down there, in that hole, it had been my life or theirs. The fact that they weren't trying to save the world—that the majority were, in fact, trying to destroy it—made my life in the now more important than theirs.

Cooper looked at me. "All is fair in war, Em."

I nodded. "Yeah...and love."

"What?"

"All is fair in love and war. That's the saying."

"Right."

On that note, silence. I closed my eyes and listened to the rhythmic bursts of scratching as Cooper returned to de-scuffing his wheeled symbol of freedom. The sound became less jarring, more hypnotic. I sank into my seat. The foam spilling from it carried me like a hundred soft hands to my sleep.

CHAPTER TWENTY-ONE

I WAS BLIND.

Rather, I could barely see. Vague outlines made little sense to my mind.

My head pounded from a nightmare I had prematurely escaped.

I shivered, aware that I had left the dream world with knowledge I didn't have before. As my surroundings got clearer, it hit me.

"He was a vampire," I said, aloud. "The Heart Attacker was a *vampire*."

Movement next to me. I jumped, before my eyes adjusted to Cooper squinting at me from the other side of the car. He rubbed his eyes and managed a stretch in our confined space. "Did you say something?" he asked, in the state of confusion I had just come out of.

"In college, I did my final psychology paper on the Heart Attack killings. Have you ever heard of them? No? Six girls murdered over the span of 120 years, all in the same age group, all killed in the same ritualistic way—blunt trauma to the chest cavity, hearts removed. Pre-vampire era, they're copycat killings. Post-vampire era, they're something very different." I was alert now. My posture had recovered. My mind had the prize. "If a vampire did it, then who was Benjamin Lamb?"

"I don't know, Angela Lansbury," Cooper said. "Who was he?"

I ignored Cooper. At that moment, he wasn't even there. "Benjamin Lamb confessed to two of the murders—the one in 1919 and the one in nineteen-forty-three. He came forward and offered undisclosed details

372

about both crime scenes. He was subsequently sentenced to death in 1943 at the age of thirty-nine. This put him at 15 years old when he allegedly killed the first girl. Could a child be a murderer? Yes. But forensic reports for all the murders had the blunt object being just about the size of a man's fist. Skin fragments were scraped off of ribcage bones. DNA findings came up inconclusive. Investigators in the Lamb case were baffled, but satisfied with a signed confession. The way I see it, either Benjamin was the fall guy for a vampire, or Benjamin was a vampire."

"Maybe he was just a guy who wanted his 15 minutes?"

I nodded. I hadn't thought of that. Lamb could have somehow stumbled across the crime scene details and decided he wanted to make his life more interesting by confessing to murders he had nothing to do with.

"Was there blood at any of the scenes?" Cooper asked.

I tried to recall. I remembered sitting in front of the microfiche reader at the library. I remembered studying the forensic analysis by the man with the funny name, Dr. Beetle Burrows. I remembered my mind tripping from exhaustion. The black and white crime scene pictures started to appear less flat, more real. I remembered the last victim's boyfriend had found her. He stopped by her apartment to surprise her and had had the grave misfortune of being very surprised himself. His girlfriend was dead on the floor with a hole in her chest. He had gotten too close to the body, and blood nudged the tips of his Cons. The boyfriend had described the blood coming out of the girl's body as a stream. I thought he might've wondered at the time where all that blood came from and if it would ever stop. Not for any lack of scientific knowing but for an all-consuming desperation that must have had a hold of him. In my head, I'd heard the boyfriend plead for that blood stream to stop.

Blood—yes, there had been lots of it, at each of the crime scenes. All accounted for. "Yeah," I said. "There was blood."

"Then it couldn't have been a vampire." Cooper seemed to be getting into it. There was nothing like a murder mystery to get away from all that death. "Unless he's a vegetarian, like Leech, but that wouldn't fit. We're not dealing with someone on any moral high ground."

"I think we've got a vampire with an agenda. An agenda bigger than his own basic needs."

Cooper nodded and made a maybe face. "So why the homework?"

I looked at Cooper. He was alien green in the darkness.

"I had a dream."

~

I'm in lecture hall.

Students amble, finding seats. Professor Winnie appears from out of a side door and sets a large pile of papers and books on top of a leaning podium.

"Settle down. Settle down everyone," he says. "Please take your seats. I have a treat for you today. A treat in exchange for your brilliance." He chuckles and motions for the room to be seated.

I look down at an empty turquoise-colored seat behind me and sit.

The professor continues: "Very good. Very good. We will forgo our previously scheduled pop quiz until next week." *(APPLAUSE!)* "We've been truly blessed with an unexpected visitor today. I can only welcome him with open arms and an open heart. Quiet down, now. Please join me in welcoming our most distinguished guest...the Heart

Attacker!" The professor pushes his glasses up higher on his nose and turns to face the same side door through which he recently entered.

Excitement is in the air. Students are gleeful. The door opens, and a man enters dressed in a dark purple suit. He seems to be gliding as if the floor beneath his feet is rolling. The girl next to me lets out a whimper and mumbles something about her destiny. The man's face is there one second and gone the next. Only fuzzy white strokes, like eraser marks, are left behind above the neck.

Winnie is wearing a permanent grin. His eyes bulge, and his overgrown eyebrows arch to meet his hairline. The professor's not that old, but before I can stop myself, I think of an octogenarian dying mid-orgasm.

Outrage wells up inside me. *How is something like this allowed?* Inviting a serial killer to guest speak puts everyone's lives in danger. I turn around to search for others that might be feeling the same way, but any attempt at eye contact is in vain. All attention is on the front. This odd, criminal man is a far cry from Winnie's usual lecturers with their legal pads and key phrases. *No*, this one has something none of these students are familiar with, and to a classroom full of young adults who think they know it all, it's the Holy Grail.

Winnie unsticks his face and clears his throat. He watches the guest like a puppy in need of attention.

The Heart Attacker moves into the middle aisle and gives a grand, sweeping bow. Scared, eager students watch. For me, it's like viewing a horror movie through my hand. I want to look, but don't want to, but do want to, but don't want to. Though a part of me is curious, sensibility reigns and I gather my things to leave. As I start to stand, fabric rips from off the seat and slides like snakes to bind my arms and legs.

"Not until the bell," Winnie says. But there are no bells in college.

The Heart Attacker is now standing in front of a boy. Even though I've never set eyes on this boy before, I know he's a freshman. Even though the idea of a freshman scoring a place in Professor Winnie's class is beyond belief, the detail's minor in comparison. I know he's a freshman because he's yet to shed his boyish aura. His face is zit-mania, his clothes are what a mother might suggest as "real-world," and his energy is the contained, pre-deflowered kind.

His thoughts are in my head as if they are my own. He likes the tall blonde two seats over from him in the tight pink dress and diamond earrings. He wonders when his alcohol tolerance will improve. He worries God might be punishing him for getting aroused after seeing his sister naked at their beach house. He thinks he might go out and buy the cologne his friend recommended that has actual pheromones in it. Guaranteed to attract the opposite sex or your money back.

The Heart Attacker plunges a fist through the boy's chest. The act looks so easy—like the boy's skin, muscle, and rib cage are made out of cake. What looks like strawberry syrup (*but isn't!*) comes out with the heart. The boy continues to think with this organ as it is pulled past his torn skin. He thinks: I know she could have loved me.

I try to yell. My struggling causes the seat straps to tighten. No one else protests or gets up to leave. The boy's eyes go from real agony to agonized glass. The Heart Attacker holds the heart up close to where his face should be. He speaks in a southern drawl:

"The human heart will clock approximately 3 billion beats over an average lifetime. Not Johnny here, though. Just seven hundred and nineteen million, eight hundred and ninety-eight thousand, six hundred and five, and a half." The Heart Attacker throws the limp organ over his shoulder.

The next student is not as young as the boy. He wears his letterman jacket and his vanity like a suit of armor. He has dark brown hair that leans to the side on top of his head, as if combed by a strong easterly wind.

He comes from an upper crust New York family. As a child, outings in Manhattan were frequent and other metropolises just a jet ride away. His parents think of him as their little scholar, but his grades are only exceptional because he's cheated on every test he's taken since he was eight. In tenth grade, he licked his English teacher's cunt for an A minus. That memory never stayed buried. He'd been turned off fish for life.

The Heart Attacker goes slow with this guy. He doesn't punch, he digs.

"The human heart begins beating 22 days after conception, and it pumps every second of every minute of every day until death." Blood spurts. As the boy dies, he wishes he had tried honesty for once.

I shout, "No!" but it comes out an exalted "Yes!"

The Heart Attacker moves down the rows leaving a trail of gore. Hearts are strewn about the lecture hall like wads of crumpled paper. My arms and legs are sore from struggling. With each defiant move I make, the seat straps tighten with their own defiance. A rogue chair has made me helpless, and I watch as my classmates die at the hands of the serial killer who, safely tucked away in books and newspaper articles, has occupied half my senior year.

I never recognize the faces of the victims, but hearing their thoughts before they die forces me to know them intimately. Blood splotches textbooks and drips from desktops. Dead, heartless students are draped over seat backs and bent knees.

A big-breasted foreign exchange student looks longingly at the bloody hand hovering with curled fingers above her chest. It's not until the hand is a couple inches away from her flesh-filled vintage tee that she begins to scream. She screams for *papa* and *mama* and *Santa Maria*. I hear her frantic thoughts but cannot interpret them.

A pinprick of blood between the girl's breasts turns into a gaping hole. Her heart leaps out of that hole and slaps into the Heart Attacker's hand where it beats twice. The exchange student gasps. Her head falls back, before her arms cease their spasms at her sides.

"The heart mass of a normal adult is nine to12 ounces or about three quarters the size of a clenched fist."

Sweat drenches me. This is a dream, but it seems so real. They always do. Smells, feelings, tastes—I get them all in one screwed-up, nightmare package.

I need to wake up. This place is Valentine's Day at the morgue. From the corner of my eye, a heart rolls across the floor onto the Heart Attacker's shoe. A gory pompom.

I close my eyes. *Wake up, Emma.*

I open them, and he's there. His face stutters in and out. I can't retain his visage in my memory. Professor Winnie clears his throat.

"This is the young lady who wrote the paper on you, master," he says. "A talented student, though she got it all wrong. Yes, very wrong." Winthrop hides his mouth so the dead students to his left can't read his lips. He whispers, "I still gave you an 'A.' How were you to know?" He gestures for us to carry on.

"Who are you?" I ask.

"You don't recognize me?"

"I don't know many murderers."

"I'm so much more than all of this," the Heart Attacker said, gesturing at the carnage. "Your subconscious is taking liberties. In reality, I have a much more specific target."

He continues: "For centuries, the heart has been associated with love, when really the brain has a lot more to do with it. When two people are in love, the brain releases chemicals that act similarly to amphetamines, increasing the heart rate and creating feelings of excitement. That pitter patter is the reason this organ has come to represent love. To me, the heart is life. It pumps blood through the human body. Without it, I would die. To me, love is life. Without it, I would die. It's a queer triangle. You don't follow me? Don't worry, you will."

The Heart Attacker leans in close to me. We're just a breath apart when his face flickers and I spot his hollow eyes and large fangs. He brings his hand up. I flinch. His fingers caress my cheek and fall away as maggots that land on my lap.

"Where did you go, my lovely?"

~

"Wow," Cooper said. "That's a rough dream." He stretched, knocking his hand against the steering wheel. She was a small freedom car.

I wondered about my dream. I had had similar ones before, though I couldn't think of when. I remembered loose hearts and sharp teeth. Were these dreams trying to tell me something important? Or was my mind simply attempting to make sense out of my new whacko reality?

"You should go upstairs and get peroxide on that arm," Cooper said. "And get some sleep. It'll be a busy day of shopping tomorrow."

"Shopping," I said, my smile reaching each ear. "I could do with some of that."

~

My second round of sleep, I dreamed of Sullivan.

He took me to Manchester, England to meet his mother. We got along famously and she told me she would be honored to have me join the family. It was a good dream. One well overdue.

~

The next day, we waited for Scott to bury Mary before leaving. It was the right thing to do.

All the hunters were in attendance, plus Sammy and Bugs. We stood over the small circle of newly packed earth with our heads bowed. Scott had placed an unusual pink stone as a grave marker. The palm tree above us threw long, waving shadows across our bodies.

I couldn't concentrate, despite my best efforts. I glanced at Seven and became focused on the deep crevice between her eyebrows.

Earlier that morning, Schizo and I had competed in an impromptu game of tug-of-war in the bathroom. We both had our game strategies. The dog's was to jerk the towel forcefully and repeatedly while mine was to hold on tight and lean back. Schizo gained ground and tugged the towel right out of my hands. He overcompensated and knocked over the wastepaper basket, littering the floor with its contents.

I grabbed a tissue to pick up the scattered trash and found a pregnancy stick with a pink plus sign showing in the window.

"Positive?" I'd said to the bathroom that very often lent me an ear.

Schizo had looked up at me with the wet towel sticking out of his mouth. My shock went unnoticed as he basked in his victory.

At Mary's funeral, Topps said a prayer. I never knew he had it in him. I was learning there were a lot of things I didn't know about the people who were around me every day. Topps did a good job. He had that polite cowboy way about him.

I tore my eyes off of Seven, so she wouldn't notice me staring. The list of potential pregnancy test users was short. One was standing across from me. The other was in the ground. Not like I had a choice in the matter, but which scenario was better? A pregnant woman decapitated by hermits, and a husband not only losing a wife, but a second child, or a young woman carrying a rapist's baby? *It could be Charlie's*, I thought. If there was a God, Seven was the pregnant one, not Mary, and Charlie was the father.

After the service, we packed the car with essentials for our afternoon outing: guns, blankets, food, and water. The fact that it was daytime only made things slightly less dangerous. Human servant patrols existed, so I heard. Myers had been some sort of pawn in the vampire game, but I'd never know specifics.

Less than eight hours had passed since Cooper shared the huge detail with me regarding The Plan, but I had come to grips with it. If anything, it was good news. We could have our country back, citizens intact. The vampires I had killed were killed in self-defense. When I ended a vampire's life, it would be because I had to.

I noticed Seven struggling with a box of food and rushed over to her.

"Let me get that."

She looked at me suspiciously. "Thanks, I'm fine." I wanted to push it, but didn't. Her look warned me off.

There was the possibility the pregnancy test wasn't hers. If I found out it had been Mary's, I'd keep the information to myself. Scott didn't have to know. However, if it was Seven's, I wasn't sure that staying mum was the right thing to do. She could have health complications at an inopportune moment. Plus, if it was Charlie's baby, certainly he wouldn't want her hunting. And given the state of the world, he had a right to know, didn't he?

I decided to feel things out. My bones were telling me that my first official hunt would be soon, and Seven would likely be going along. I would have to get the truth about the pregnancy before then. It would be my first conversation with Seven, and I was not under the illusion it would go well.

Schizo moaned as I lifted him into the back of the SUV. He probably could have made the jump, but in his excitement, he was taking his sweet time. I had suggested to the others that we bring him, and no one objected. Just because he was a dog didn't mean he wasn't sick of living out of a storage facility. I knew he could use the trip as much as any of us.

I closed up the back, and Schizo tracked my progress around the car with big eyes. There were five of us going, with Scott, the kids, and Charlie staying behind. Cooper had learned his lesson after Cara. Sammy would have been okay, but Bugs liked to wander, which meant he needed to stay behind so she didn't feel left out. As the second youngest, it was his sacrifice to make.

Charlie had volunteered to stay. His ankle was better but not yet back to its normal size. Cooper found some crutches for him in one of the units. We dubbed him "Gimpy," and unfortunately for him, the name was not going to be easy to shake. Especially with Rudy as its powerhouse.

"Bye, Gimpy!" Rudy called out from the front passenger seat. "Have fun holding down the fort. And stay off the painkillers until we get back, for Christ's sake." Rudy smirked.

Seven leaned out the window to kiss Charlie. "Bye, baby. I'll bring you back something."

"A new leg?"

"You got it. Adios, mi amour."

They kissed again. My heart felt sad.

"Let's blow this pop stand," Rudy said. "We got shopping to do."

"You're such a girl, Rudy," Seven said.

"Why, thank you!" Rudy said, in his best dainty voice.

Cooper pulled the car from its parked position and toward the garage door. An urge to yell at him to drive fast and to get as far away from that place as possible overcame me. I'd been tempted before in my old life. You slide into the driver's seat, toss your stuff in the back, close the door, maybe leave the seatbelt unbuckled, and the idea to drive and leave it all behind is almost too enticing to resist. But you never go. It never made sense. Until now.

I turned around to pet Schizo and quell my urge. We waved at Charlie, and he waved back before hobbling to his security post.

Poor Charlie, I thought. *Poor all of us.*

CHAPTER TWENTY-TWO

HEAVEN WAS UP AHEAD.

The shopping mall sat, empty streets around it, empty stores inside awaiting their nocturnal customers.

The billboards were what took some getting used to, especially the one on Sunset. Giant vampire models posed in the latest undead fashions, teeth the size of us. The clothes looked the same, just darker. None were yellow—the color of the one thing they thought could kill them.

They had yet to meet us.

We all looked up as we passed, a noticeable shiver making the rounds. We had just wrapped our minds around vampires existing. Giant vampires, even only on paper, set our minds to implode.

There were no food stores, there were blood stores. Signs advertised bulk cartons and shots to go. Each claimed to be the most pure, 99.1% pure, or more pure than that other guy. Cooper told me the UVF had started manufacturing synthesized blood. The real stuff was becoming rarer, and pure portions were reserved for VIVs. Very Important Vampires. The black market was where the rest of the population (the ones with money, at least) went to get the good stuff.

We drove by a single vegetarian bar. Someone had spray-painted *PUSSIES* across the front window. I felt a pang of indignation for Leech.

Schizo bounced around in the back, affording time and runny nose prints to each window. He barked at several crows that flew low to determine our edibility factor.

Cooper took a side street and parked in between two other cars. He said that parking in the mall garage was too risky, and I agreed. I had had some experience with that.

I collected Schizo from the back and attached his leash. The other hunters got out and surveyed the city they had once known well. We checked our guns and holstered our stakes, with a plan to shop and an aversion to the dropping part.

We walked up the ramp to the mall.

~

Rudy got up close to the vampire, sliding his tongue over its lips. He coughed.

"*Blah*," he said, making a face. "Tastes like plastic."

"That's because it *is* plastic, dork," Seven said, with a scowl that was more her than she probably knew.

Rudy moved away from the mannequin. "I'm just building up foreign relations...what?"

"You know the procedure, guys," Cooper said, as if we were on the battlefield and not the first floor of Bloomingdales. "Take what you need and tell me what you take. Anyone need anything they can't get here?" Seven raised her hand.

"I need to stop by the old pharmacy on the second floor. Feminine products."

"*Gross*," Rudy said.

I looked at Seven, she looked back at me.

"What?" she said. "You, too?"

I wasn't about to give the game away. Not yet.

"Yeah," I said to Cooper. "Me, too." Cooper blushed. *Boys are idiots*, I thought.

"Okay," he said. "We'll hit the pharmacy when we're done here."

Rudy, Topps, and Seven broke away, passing makeup and taking a right after purses. That left Cooper, Schizo, and I.

"So, what do you want?" Cooper asked.

That question was such a tease. "Sheets?"

Cooper turned in a full circle before stopping again at me. He pointed, "That way I think."

We traveled in silence mostly, collecting items as they took our fancy. There was no time to try things on, but that had always been my least favorite part of shopping, anyway. We both grabbed a couple pairs of jeans and a few tops. I discreetly slipped several bras and panties into my pile. Cooper had been hand-delivering me my underwear for over a week. It was time to regain my dignity.

We arrived at bedding. Coffins and real beds intermingled.

"Why both?" I asked.

"I don't know," Cooper said. "Leech mentioned something once about new vampires having trouble letting go of some aspects of their human life...maybe sleeping in a bed is one of them?"

These beds were not just beds. They were grand re-enactments of their former selves: four posts nearly touching the ceiling, hand-carved wood with intricate designs, down mattresses, thick and soft. These were beds of kings and queens. I walked by coffins complete with televisions, bars, and satellite radio. Most could fit two comfortably, and some, three or four. They were the beds of the modern undead.

Schizo reared up on one of the coffins. I shooed him down. For all I knew they had a "you damage, you pay" policy, and I wasn't about to lug one of these things home.

Cooper called me over to check out the sheets. And I thought there were choices before. I flipped through sets for singles, doubles, queens, kings, CA kings, CA kings extra, coffin doubles, coffin queens, coffin kings, coffin CA kings, and coffin CA kings extra. By the end, my shopping urge had dissipated. Choice could be such a kill-joy.

Most of the sheets were silk, and the idea of bringing silk into Seepy Storage made me laugh.

"What is it?" Cooper asked.

"Nothing, nothing." I grabbed two sets of white double silk sheets and checked and double-checked for the word coffin. "Okay. We're good."

We went off to find the others. They weren't far. I could barely see Rudy behind the pile of items he was carrying. He had to angle his head to the side to see what was in front of him, making him look like a dog with its head out the car window.

"Enough stuff, Rudy?" I asked.

"I can't believe it's all free," he said.

"Well, it's not really," Cooper said.

"Oh yeah, the IOU project." Rudy turned to me. "*It's all free*," he mouthed, shaking his head.

Seven and Topps had a modest amount but still more than Cooper and I. Topps had a new cowboy hat, this one black.

"A man's got to have more than two cowboy hats," he said. "Anything less is uncivilized."

"Hey, I don't have any…what does that make me?" Rudy asked.

"*Uncivilized!*" we said in unison.

Cooper stepped behind a makeup counter. He ducked down.

"I think you need some rouge, darling," I said.

He came up holding a ballpoint pen. "Forgot mine." He took a notebook out of his pocket, flipped the cover, and began writing. I looked down at Schizo, remembering the IOU I had written for him. He looked up at me, big doggy eyes. *I could never return you, buddy.*

We took turns telling Cooper about our booty. It was mostly clothing, along with some comfort items to make Seepy Storage a bit more bearable. When the last item was disclosed, Cooper shut and pocketed his notebook and replaced the pen under the counter.

We left Bloomingdales and headed for the pharmacy on the second floor. Stores passed us, some familiar, most not. Several places were boarded up, too foreign to a city of vampires and not yet selling something new. Two of the shops used to sell baby items. I turned to look at Seven. She didn't seem to notice me looking or the windows of cribs and teddy bears

I saw a Starbucks and longed for a Mocha Frappuccino.

"You don't even want what's in there," Topps said. Leave it to the coffee house to stick around. When the world came to an end…officially…there would be only cockroaches and Starbucks. I had no doubt.

The pharmacy was boarded up, like the baby stores. Vampires didn't need vitamins, feminine products, ear plugs, or reading glasses. Dirty two-by-fours crisscrossed the entrance. It was all in stark contrast to the rest of the mall and reminded me of a gravesite.

Rest in peace ye olde life.

We stepped between the boards, dodging haphazard nails. I pictured vampire shoppers gliding into the mall that evening to find one female hunter with a nail through her head. Yum, yum. Hunter-on-a-stick.

Thick strips of plastic hung from ceiling to floor behind the boards.

We pushed by them into the pharmacy.

Inside, like in all pharmacies, were rows and rows of things we needed, we didn't need, we thought we might need, and we would soon be convinced that we could not live without. Some stuff had been packed away already. Boxes waited half filled on the floor, empty shelves looked bored without a job.

Seven headed down the DIAPERS, SOAP, FEMININE PRODUCTS aisle. I followed her, brushing several bottles of shampoo and conditioner off of the shelf and into my bag along the way.

She was staring blankly at an empty shelf when I arrived, a dented box of tampons clutched in her hand.

"What are you looking for?" I asked. *She wants to do another test.*

"Um, nothing. They don't have my brand of tampons. It pisses me off."

Boxes surrounded us. I looked down and saw a few dozen pregnancy tests stuffed into a box at my feet. I took one out and placed it on the shelf in front of Seven.

She stared at it for a few moments, then shoved it in her bag.

"You found the test," she said, not making eye contact.

"Yes, I'm..." What was I? Was I sorry for her? I guess it all depended on how she was taking it, and I couldn't see it being taken any other way but bad—especially if the baby wasn't Charlie's. "...how are you?"

"I don't want to talk about it. Shit happens." Seven went into the box to fish out a couple more tests.

"I know about Sisters of Mercy." There, I said it. It was out there. I couldn't take it back.

Seven stopped moving, as if what I had just said shoved a wrench in the space time continuum. She spoke, keeping still. "Well, aren't you just a bundle of knowledge."

"I overheard you talking to Charlie. I didn't mean to. And I found the test. I didn't mean that, either. What I'm saying is that...well, maybe those weren't just coincidences. Maybe I'm meant to help." It was a long shot and I didn't want to get all moon-glow on her, but I had accomplished what I set out to accomplish: I offered her my help.

Seven moved, finally. She shoved another test into her bag and straightened to look me in the eye.

"Can you make this go away?"

Did she mean the baby? The vampires? Everything? I couldn't make any of those go away. "No, I can't."

"Then you're of no use to me."

"But Charlie needs to know."

Seven's eyes softened at the mere mention of him. Her voice grew noticeably weaker. "Charlie has nothing to do with this because *Charlie* isn't the father."

Topps appeared at the end of the aisle. "Anyone see any vitamins?" he asked.

Seven gave me a warning look. Her voice fell to a whisper. "Don't tell anyone, Em. Promise me."

What's a promise between two enemies, I thought. *A lie?* If she was my enemy, why did I want to help her so badly? I cared about Charlie and he cared for her. Maybe more than that, I figured I had too many enemies. Granted they all had pointy teeth, but at the end of the day, I needed friends and I couldn't be the only one.

"I promise." Seven's iceberg melted just a little.

We left the pharmacy equipped for good health and perfect skin.

Cooper had grabbed bandages, ointments, peroxide, and other such things for the injured hunter in us all. I found some Disney movies for Bugs and a couple movies for the rest of us that had absolutely nothing to do with chainsaws.

~

We stopped at a gas station on the way back. We could very easily have siphoned the gas from all the cars at Seepy Storage and had enough to keep the generator running for a year, but why do that when it was available for the taking? Besides, we needed both vehicles and generator running smoothly.

I went inside and grabbed several packs of cigarettes and lighters. A nudie calendar was tacked up on the wall behind the register. A buxom brunette pressed her boobs together. Two small fangs had been drawn on her lips in red marker.

I could smell death in that place, like I had back at the hermit hole. The scent hung suspended in the air, waiting for the undead to awaken and walk the earth again, so it had something to cling to.

The other hunters smelled it, too, and you didn't have to say "leave" twice. We got back to Seepy Storage alive but tired. There had been no time for relaxing between the hermit incident, Mary's funeral, and our shopping excursion. The unlucky took up guard positions. The lucky unpacked their items and rolled into bed. I, as one of two said unlucky, was stationed upstairs.

~

The hunters called the position "The Eye in the Sky." The only windows in the building wrapped the top floor, giving a clear view of the surrounding forest, the driveway, and the one main road that started on the boulevard and ended in Studio City. Headlights showed themselves as distant lights, blinking as they appeared and disappeared behind treetops. From my limited experience as the eye, few cars slowed going past our facility. The entrance was misleading, clogged with overgrowth and broken bottles that we had started to plant as a deterrent. Vampires loved their cars.

That night, I was armed with my pistol, a set of binoculars, a walkie-talkie, and the strongest cup of coffee known to man. My job was to keep moving. The first floor post had limited visibility through two cameras, one at the front and one at the back. As the eye, I was meant to see it all, with particular attention paid to the sides of the building and the main road.

The hardest part was staying on your feet all night and through the wee hours of the morning. By the time relief came, your world was feeling like Jell-O.

Schizo was meant to keep me company, but he hopped up on one of the cushy chairs in the lounge upon our arrival and really only kept me jealous.

Scott was in his office. The telltale glow of candles was coming from under his door. I contemplated going in to talk to him—even stood at the door for a good minute with my hand in a solid knock position—but walked away. I didn't know what to say and was afraid of what I might find. One leader incapable of leading? Brought to his knees because I had unknowingly set off a gruesome chain of events involving his last living loved one? No, better to leave it.

I was on the opposite side of the building as Scott's office, half watching and half lost in thoughts, when Schizo started to growl.

The walkie-talkie jumped on: "Topps to E-girl. Come in, E-girl."

"What's up, Topps? Out."

"Leech is here to see Scott. He's coming up. Out."

"Got it. Out."

There hadn't been any cars. I pictured a caped Leech, his thick arms outstretched, his lumpy body felling clouds in the night sky. My heart jumped thinking of the others asleep and unaware. *What if he slips off on the fifth floor for a quick bite?* I rushed Schizo into one of the offices, though I was tempted to keep him with me and make introductions. But I was too tired to cause trouble.

The elevator dinged. A moment later, Leech was standing in front of me.

"Emma."

"Leech."

"Delighted to see you, again. My better half says hello."

"Okay. Hello back."

"How's Scott?"

"I'm not sure. We went out. I haven't seen him since yesterday."

"It's a shame. Martha is heart broken. She felt quite a connection with Mary."

I nodded. "So how did you get here?"

"Martha dropped me off."

"Oh. I didn't see a car."

"Headlights are out. I've been after her to get them fixed. We vampires have exceptional night vision. We don't need headlights or taillights, but we keep them. It makes the car whole, you understand?"

I wasn't sure I believed him. Maybe, it was just me? Maybe, I could never trust a vampire?

"I should get in to see Scott. Nice chatting with you." Leech turned to go, but then he paused. "I hope to meet that dog of yours one day.

He's a Doberman mix? I just love Dobermans." Leech smiled, running his tongue over one sharp tooth.

Any chance of trust stopped there. "Stay away from my dog."

Leech bowed. "As you wish."

I followed him to Scott's office, leaving seven feet between us. I thought it was a good distance to keep from a vampire and allowed for reaction time. Scott's door was ajar, and Leech pushed through with an unassuming knock. They greeted each other. I heard slaps on backs. Scott sounded *okay*, which gave me relief.

Schizo was going mad. His nails scraped the inside of the door a few doors down. I could feel the dog's growls reverberate inside me. Scott stuck his head out from his office. Whatever relief I had just gotten was now gone. Our leader looked like hell.

"Emma, take Schizo downstairs, please. I can't think with this racket."

"Sure, okay."

"Thank you."

The door was shut by the time I passed it. I walked by slow and listened hard. Voices droned, sounding like space-age robots. Words came at me and it was like being in a foreign country and not understanding the language. Some words you get and you have just those words at your disposal. Then, either the purple dog is baking bread, or the movie starts at eight. It was all about choosing the most logical translation.

I heard my name and the word "feisty" before determining they had opened on small talk. I would have enough time to get Schizo downstairs, come back, and glean the most important part of the conversation. I would not feel guilty. Ignorance was death and I stood by my "no surprises" policy.

What I hadn't counted on was Schizo's stubbornness. He dragged his feet the whole way. By the time we reached the lounge on the same floor, I was exhausted.

"What is your problem, dog?"

Schizo sprawled. He wasn't leaving without making things very difficult for me, but at least he wasn't making any more noise.

"Fine. Stay," I said, pointing a finger down at him. "Stay."

I returned to the hallway. Scott and the vampire's voices floated out to me in a hum. As I got closer, the hum became blips, and, gently pressed up against the door, the blips became words. I knelt and the coldness of the concrete froze my knees. With my ear to the office door, the hum to blips to words became very worth my while.

Leech was speaking: "...and whatever you do, you need to do it *now*. There are surveillance cameras all around town. It's only a matter of time."

Wooden chair legs slid across hard floor. Unease from the other side settled in my ear. Someone sighed.

"I can't remember the last time we got a break, Leech ol' boy," Scott said. "This place...Mary...everything. They're cutting off our food supply. The last grocery store in a thirty-mile radius will be gone by the end of the week. We've got sixty days max worth of sustenance. After that? The world is catering to the undead, and to tell you the truth, Leech, I..."

A long pause. *Do they know I'm here?* I thought. Scott cleared his throat and continued.

"...I'm not sure we can do it. There are just so many of them. "

Another pause. Scott, again: "I don't want anyone else to die."

The plastic fire ticking inside the office kept eerie time with my breathing.

"I'm sorry. I can't promise you no one else will die. But the human race is counting on you, and, well, that needs to be enough." Papers shuffled. "I've got two men…hungry janitors with security clearance. They've agreed to provide you with the addresses for 50 milliliters—a small price to pay. It's what we've been waiting for, Scott."

A tinkling of fine glassware, a cap unscrewed, ice cubes cracking.

"When and where?"

"Saturday evening, half past midnight…it's a club in Venice called The Vein."

"*Damn it*, Leech. What kind of numbers are we talking? Five hundred? Six hundred? I told you to arrange it someplace quiet."

"They were frightened. Of you. The resistance. You should be proud of that. It was either there, or nowhere. I didn't want to lose them."

From inside the room came a loud knocking sound. It made me jump. I noticed Schizo sitting behind me. I glared at him. *Go*, I mouthed. He cocked his ears and tilted his head.

From beyond the door: "Be reasonable, Scott."

Another sigh. "Tell me what you have."

"Photos of the informants, blueprints of each floor, security details—the works. This is it, Scott. This is when we make our move."

"Okay. You'll stay until tomorrow night to help me brief the others."

"Yes, of course. And my room?"

"It's been prepared. The bait's been set. You should have company by now."

"Great! I'm famished." A chair scraping. "Have faith. I do, and if a vampire can, certainly a human can too."

"Yes," Scott said, a tired smile in the word. "I'll show you to your room."

That was my cue.

I got up quietly and slowly. I took Schizo's collar and led him back toward the lounge. Scott's door opened as we turned the corner.

In the lounge, Schizo caught whiff of Leech's approach and began his fight: vampire or die. Scott plus one appeared.

"Sorry," I said. "He didn't want to go downstairs and I didn't want to be away from my station for too long."

Scott nodded. "How's everything?" He spoke loudly over Schizo's snarls. It was a shouting match.

"All quiet on the western front," I said.

"Good, good. Stay alert, Emma.

"Yes, sir."

Leech stared at Schizo, not in fright, but in rapture. I gathered strength and pulled Schizo behind me.

"*Goodnight*," I said.

Leech went reluctantly. Schizo didn't chase the vampire, reluctantly. The stubbornness of predators. The elevator shaft gulped the two. I sighed with relief and loosened my grip on Schizo's collar. A moment later, my furry friend was back asleep on the cushy chair.

No, there's nothing happening out there.

Seepy Storage was where it was all happening.

Cooper came to relieve me at half past five. I dragged feet and canine to my unit and fell into bed. I had the dreadful thought that I was on the same sleep schedule as the legion of the undead and forced my eyes open for another hour and a half with a really bad book. Then, I slept. One human with nothing in common with vampires.

~

One day they were mopping floors, the next they were mopping floors and doing dangerous favors for half a mouthful of rare blood.

Life changes—just like that.

The two janitor informants stared out at me from shoddy photocopies of passport photos. Names were scrawled underneath, not legible, but it didn't matter. Leech and Scott had said both names a billion times, and they were now paperclipped to our brains: Tyson Manning and Lars Wilcox. Looks-wise, they were stark opposites. Tyson's face was meaty. He had blonde hair, light eyes, and a facial expression of pure surprise. Lars' face was long and slightly curved, like an eclipsed moon. He had black hair and dark, suspicious eyes. The word "surprise" wasn't even in his vocabulary.

It was the day after I had *overheard* Scott and Leech's important conversation. The other hunters and I stood in the conference room, surrounded by papers and Styrofoam coffee cups sucked dry.

Scott and Cooper were extended over an enormous blueprint of Club Vein. They twisted and turned their heads, searching for ways in, out, through, up, and down. Every now and again, they would state something out loud and then ask Leech if what they had said was right, to which the vampire would reply, "Right as rain."

I had never seen a blueprint the likes of this one. Each floor, four in total, had a page. It was a giant, risky place to get lost in.

"Okay, hunters, gather round," Scott said. He was looking better. He had the blossoming of The Plan to get his mind off of things. "The club has two entrances, here and here. We'll be entering through the main doors, here. This other entrance is staff only and the last thing we want to do is raise suspicion early on in the night. There are three exits on the ground floor. Wait. Is that right, Leech?"

"Right as rain."

Scott continued: "Okay, I see. There's the main entrance, the staff entrance, and a fire door. All of these can serve as exits, depending on your situation. The other exits are on the second, third, and fourth floors. All fire doors. They're at the back and lead out onto the fire escape. Leech has told me that the alarm will sound if any of these doors are opened. So don't unless you have to. Ideally, you'll be entering through the front and exiting the same. Cooper?"

"We go in as vampires, we leave as vampires," Cooper said, making eye contact with each of the hunters. "Our informants will be on the second floor...is that right, Leech?"

"Right as rain."

"The second floor...right here," Cooper pointed to a spot on the middle page. "There's a row of twenty booths. They'll be in the first one."

"Why the second floor?" I asked. "I mean, if the only exit we can use is on the first floor, shouldn't we meet them there?"

Cooper nodded at Leech. Leech stepped forward. "The first floor is packed by eleven-thirty, and then the crowd slowly filters upstairs. The second floor will give you guys the privacy...to conduct your business."

My eyes lingered on the vampire in our midst. He noticed and smiled. *Right as rain.*

"We stick with our partners," Cooper said. "Charlie, how's your ankle?"

"It's good. Fine, fine," Charlie said, a bit too eagerly.

"You sure? Otherwise, I'll put you with Topps, and Rudy and Seven can partner up."

"No, not necessary, Coop. I'm fine."

Cooper's eyes stayed on Charlie. *Tough room tonight.*

"Who's meeting the transformers, I mean, *informers?*" Rudy said, with a snicker.

"Emma and I will meet them."

"How's that fair? She's new," Rudy said.

"Um, whose blood are we using?" Seven said. "Shouldn't I get some of the action?"

"Emma is my partner. I'm doing the exchange, so we're doing the exchange. Any other questions?"

And it was decided. I got the hot ticket with the vampire janitors. Who knew it was so in demand? I would have quite happily scalped my ticket to the lowest bidder if it didn't mean undermining Cooper's authority.

The room arrived at a general consensus with a moment of sullen silence. I quietly wondered if it would be better for the rest of the hunters to know that I didn't want to, nor did I ever ask to, meet the janitors. Then I quietly decided that that would only pour salt in the wound.

Cooper ran a hand through his hair. The front part split, making horns. "We line up at the front of the club, go through the main entrance, and head to the second floor. We order drinks at the second-floor bar, here...then Emma and I will go meet the janitors, Rudy and Topps will remain at the bar, and Seven and Charlie will move on to the DJ booth...right here. Leech?"

"Alright. Not much to say...just know that every vampire in that club will have a drink in their hand and so should you. There'll be a drinks menu at the bar—it's okay to ask for it. Fortunately for you, Club Vein does have some veggie drinks, though limited. I know you've all done CT, and some of you have already been out in the field. My advice: just sip it. Sip it and relax. Okey dokey, that's it."

Everyone looked around, and another moment of silence followed to let the news to sink in. In two days, we were out. In two days, we'd be mingling with the undead as undead.

"I want you all to study these blueprints over the next two days," Scott said. "I'll leave them right here on this table, so come in when you want. You should know this club like the back of your hand."

I looked at my hand, noticing lines I hadn't seen before. Maybe that wasn't a good analogy for Scott to use? I would have said *You should know this club like your own thoughts*. I didn't always know where my thoughts came from, but I knew them better than anything else.

"Emma, can I see you?" Scott said, his mouth forming a tight line. "You too, Seven."

He knows. He had found one of Seven's pregnancy tests and was trying to figure out who among us was with child. I wouldn't say anything. Seven would have to confess. *And if she doesn't?* If we both denied it, Scott could assume it was Mary, which would be horrible. I had promised Seven, but I refused to do that to Scott.

Scott met us in the corner of the room, his face considerably redder. "This is a bit of an awkward situation," he said.

Stuttering kicked in. "Scott don't...I...don't think...well, you're right—"

"You want to make sure," Seven interrupted, "we won't be

menstruating, because the blood alerts vampires to the fact that we're *human*." Seven gave me a look. That speedy explanation was for me.

"Yes," Scott said, his face a beet.

"Got it already. Loved every minute of it." Seven smiled big. Scott gave an uncomfortable laugh.

"That's…great, and you, Emma? It's just that the menstrual blood has a different smell to regular blood. Vampires don't menstruate, which is why we have to make sure you two aren't either when you duck."

"Duck?"

"Go undercover."

"Okay. Well, I think I'm due in two weeks. I'm pretty regular…in case that was going to be the next question."

"Yes, it was. Thank you, you two. Make sure to study the plans. Get a good feel for them. You can direct any questions to me or Cooper." He walked back to the table, the blood finally leaving his face and not exploding his head.

So that was what it would have been like to discuss my period with my dad, if he had stuck around long enough? I could scratch that one off the list. Seven looked me up and down.

"So much for a white girl's promise," she whispered.

"Has that been your problem with me all along? I hate to say it, but how unoriginal of you. Listen, we need to talk about your…situation."

"Like I said before, there's nothing to talk about."

Charlie, who had been checking out the blueprints, looked over at us. Seven and I had never had a conversation in front of the others. Even standing near each other could've been considered making a scene.

"I think there is."

"Don't you listen? What you think doesn't matter. Got it?" Seven walked back to the table.

Maybe I was wrong, but I had a bad feeling. What were the chances that vampires could somehow sense pregnancy? Smell a fetus like they smelled menstrual blood? *I guess we'll find out soon enough*, I thought.

Cooper approached me. "What's going on?"

"Nothing."

"Making friends?"

"You could say that."

Cooper held a small box out to me. It was black with a gold trim around the edge.

"Why, Cooper, you shouldn't have. I didn't get you anything." I opened the box. Inside were two pointed teeth nestled in velvet cardboard notches. I was speechless.

"We apply them the night before—to ensure that the glue has enough time to dry and that they settle straight. It'll also get you used to talking with them."

I finally found words. "Oh boy."

CHAPTER TWENTY-THREE

I SNEERED INTO THE MIRROR.

A proper rock-star sneer. Fangs and attitude.

"Thank you, Seepy Storage!" I said, to the same empty bathroom.

It had taken over an hour to get the things on. The glue tasted toxic, and the fumes made me lightheaded and giddy. Ten minutes in, I got onto the really bad jokes, and they spilled from my mouth without fear of consequence. I lost my standing audience of two in the first half hour, despite the mind-scrambling fumes that tempted them to stay.

"Is my face melting?" I had asked Cooper, while he applied my new set of teeth.

"No, you're fine."

After he was done, I left and stumbled by Leech on my way to the bathroom. *They suit you* he had said, and I was too fucked up to think of a witty reply, so I just thanked him and beat myself up over it afterward. What was he still doing here, anyway? Wasn't his wife missing him? I wondered if he was coming with us on Saturday. Nothing had been said about it. I wasn't sure whether it would make me feel more safe or less safe to have Leech joining us. He did want to eat my dog, which was two strikes against him, but he also saved my life, which eliminated one strike and left one still remaining. I never liked baseball.

Leech did have another thing going for him: he had to drink blood to live and he chose animal blood instead of human blood, a choice most would deem morally less void. Regardless, if he touched Schizo,

404

he was one dead vampire.

I leaned in close to the mirror and pulled up my top lip. They were caps, but they certainly looked real. I touched both points with my tongue. I made another face except this time I brought my arms above my head and curled my fingers. I had never seen a vampire do this, but it looked like something a vampire might do.

"Weird, huh?"

I jumped. Charlie stood in the doorway. He wore a Sex Pistols shirt. The boy did like his bands. I brought my arms down and picked up my toothbrush.

"I am...yes."

"I meant the fangs."

"Oh, yeah...those...too."

"Be careful with that," he said, pointing at the toothbrush. "Cooper will have a fit if you loosen them."

Cooper has fits? "I'm just going over them carefully and brushing my tongue—to get rid of the glue taste."

"This'll work better." Charlie went into his pocket and pulled out a small bottle of mouthwash. He handed it to me.

"Thanks. So, does that mean you always carry mouthwash in your pocket?" I asked, smiling.

"It helps with the ladies," Charlie said, winking and pulling up an invisible collar.

I laughed. "God, you sounded like Rudy just then."

"Yeah, well if he doesn't stop calling me "Gimpy," there'll be more where that came from. Rudy's worst nightmare is having someone exactly like him around. Telling the same jokes. It would take away his power."

"You mean his power to annoy?"

"Exactly."

I took the cap off the mouthwash and upended the bottle into my mouth. I gargled and swished it over my new set of fangs.

"I want to talk to you about Seven."

Mouthwash slipped down my throat, causing me to choke and cough it out into the sink. *Very subtle, Emma.* After I composed myself, I spoke. "What about her?"

"She's been acting...strange. Distant, I guess. Seven's not always the most forthcoming person, but...I don't know. I saw you talking to her back in the conference room. I thought you might know something?"

My heart ached. He looked so lost, but it wasn't my business to tell Charlie. Come Saturday, if I decided that Seven was a liability to herself or to others, I would tell Cooper. Pass him the baton. For now, I'd keep my promise.

"I'm not sure you've noticed," I said, busying myself with random toiletries, "but Seven and I are not the best of friends. If she had anything to tell, she'd tell you, not me." I looked back at Charlie for that final solid eye contact that says *I'm being truthful.*

Charlie nodded and shrugged, satisfied with my answer. "Yeah, she's probably just stressed about Saturday. I'm probably just being paranoid."

Probably. Probably. Not.

"Partake in a beer upstairs?"

"I'm just going to crash."

"Okay. Be careful sleeping on those." He meant my new teeth. "I advise sleeping on your back."

"Gotcha. Hey Charlie?"

"Yeah?"

"Everything's going to be alright."

"I know." He smiled, making final solid eye contact with me, before leaving me to myself in the bathroom.

Just me and Em the Vampire. I stared at my reflection in the mirror, then bared my fangs. "Yeah...that's right. You should be scared," I said aloud.

You should be very scared.

~

The Saturday arrived faster than a speeding high-performance hollow point.

The nervous tension that shrouded the hunters the morning after the meeting had dissipated by Friday evening. With preparedness came calm.

Over the next day and a half, the hunters took turns testing each other on the club's floor plans. When the time came, we knew them like our own thoughts. Friday day, I spent a couple of hours with Bugs watching the new movies I got her at the pharmacy and a few hours sparring outside with Rudy. There would have been nothing more satisfying than kicking his ass, but he was good and I didn't get my chance. A brilliant fighter hiding in the body of a coward. In a time of war, it was a shame.

Saturday morning, we were allotted our weapons to clean and check twice. I hadn't fired a gun since the hermit hole. A tight grip on the handle sent a pleasurable tingle up my arm and through my body. Power could be a drug to even the most modest.

The evening arrived. Cooper stopped by my unit with a neat pile of clothes for me, like in the olden days. He was dressed in black from head to toe, and my pending outfit looked like more of the same.

"Got black?" I said.

"It's what they wear and it's good camouflage."

"I guess I wasn't expecting a sun dress." I held up a black leather tube top. "Where'd you get this stuff?"

"I had Seven pick out some things for you at the mall. She's been out with us. She knows what's expected." Cooper dropped a set of knee-high boots next to me.

I held one fair-skinned leg next to them. "All I can say is she better be looking like a hooker, too."

Cooper gave me a warning look. "Save it for the vampires, Emma."

"Sure."

I left Schizo with Sammy and Bugs in the residence floor lounge. Bugs was a cocoon in a fluffy new blanket, courtesy of Cooper. She jubilantly invited Schizo in with her.

"I'm gonna be a vampire hunter like you when I grow up," she said to me.

"Don't be stupid," Sammy said, tearing his eyes from a handheld gaming unit.

I ran a hand over her soft hair. "We're doing this so you won't have to," I said.

She seemed to understand.

~

Down in the garage, darker versions of ourselves were busy with hiding weapons. Sharpened stakes and loaded pistols were shoved, squeezed, and covered. The outfit Seven picked out for me had little room for anything else. I had kept her secret, but the joke was on me.

My vindictive stylist had found herself, on the other hand, a gorgeous, roomy number—a frayed, metallic skirt that fell to her ankles—and a tastefully fitted off-the-shoulder top with military buckles down the sides.

Seven kept looking my way and chuckling. *Bitch.*

With the exception of Rudy, who stared openly, the men around me made decent attempts at respect, but their eyes were drawn to my unintentional show of flesh. I approached Cooper.

"Hey...hi...hello...how are you?" he asked. From cool Boy Scout to stuttering fool.

"Can I get a shot at her before the vampires?" I asked.

Cooper scratched his head. "I, um...didn't realize how bad it was between you two. Sorry."

"Yeah okay. Please say you have other clothes for me."

"That's it. Unless Seven will switch with you, but you've got a good four inches on her. Least she got you a jacket. How are the weapons fitting?"

"How do you think?" Cooper looked worried by my response, so I breathed and answered again. "I got them to fit."

"Okay. I'll have a word with her."

A lot of good that would do me now.

"But, Emma?" Cooper said, on his way to my nemesis. "Even though the outfit's not you...that doesn't mean it doesn't look good." Cooper had passed his safety threshold and now reeled himself back in. "Finish suiting up."

Scott and Leech came down to the garage to finalize things and send us on our way. They asked us questions, which were all answered in the affirmative. We were beyond ready. It turned out that the vampire was not going with us. He had to be back at the office in an hour to keep up appearances. I was glad. Ally or not, one less vampire seemed like one big victory.

We wound through the cars to get to the bikes. Cooper said the bikes were ideal because they were fast, could fit through small spaces, and allowed us to drive as a team but still split off from the others, if the need arose.

We arrived at three purple motorbikes. Cooper handed me my helmet.

Outside, we walked the bikes to the end of the driveway. I tried to get used to moving bound by tight fabric and sheaths. Where there had been space, there were now weapons. You could say I was packing wood. Though Seven had been eager to derail my dignity, she had given some thought to my safety. The jacket that came in my clothes pile was proper hunter dress code, falling past my knees and covering up all things deadly.

At the gate, Cooper swung a leg over the bike and sat. He put a key in the ignition and gave me his hand.

"Get on."

I had never been on a motorcycle before. The bike's shape suggested warp speed. I got on, and Cooper's hands guided mine around his waist. My teeth vibrated when the engine came on. I made the mistake of touching my tongue to one of my fangs and tasted blood. The bike slid forward.

The night drew us in.

Chilly air groped blindly, making guesses as to our species: human or vampire?

~

Life was all around us.

Cars whizzed by with music blaring. *People* fumbled with bags, waited in lines, and sat at bus stops with bored faces.

Once more, I allowed myself to believe it had all been just a joke. I let relief sink in. But then it was torn away, and I felt worse than before.

We passed a used furniture store, and a girl a little older than me ran out onto the sidewalk. She was dressed in white, an angel among demons. Blood covered her body. Her arms and legs flailed and failed around her. I tried to look away but couldn't.

I went for my gun.

Cooper felt my movement, saw the girl go down, and said, *"NO."* There was a commanding desperation in his voice. I took my hand off the gun, not because of Cooper, but because the girl was now past our help.

"I'm okay," I said, certain the words had been shooed away by noise and wind, but Cooper turned his head and released the bike's handlebar briefly to put a hand on mine. There were no more incidents on the way to the club. The one had been more than enough. I wished for everything to go well. If everything went well, no one had to die.

Cooper took a left onto Ocean Avenue, then a right onto Twenty-Eighth. Club Vein approached on our left.

Millions of vampires waited.

At least, that was what my mind registered. In reality, there weren't millions, but there were more vampires than I had ever seen together, even at the hermit hole. Comparatively, these ones were dressed, intact, and paying us little notice. A fight at the front of the line garnered their attention. A seven-foot vampire with huge shoulders and

411

neck muscles that rippled when he blinked stepped forward to deal with the troublemakers. His head was shaved. Brillo pad goatee and eyebrows completed the look. The two fighting vampires saw the bouncer approaching and clasped hands, agreeing to disagree.

I tapped Cooper on the shoulder and pointed discreetly. I didn't want to be the bearer of bad news, but that bouncer's existence needed to be made known. He should have been on the blueprints, being nearly the size of the building itself. Cooper nodded and returned his eyes to the packed parking lot we were entering. He signaled the others to follow and stopped on the grass next to an electric blue pickup truck.

The first floor emergency exit was before us, along with a tangled fire escape rising up to the roof. Cooper shut off the engine and kicked the stand down. He offered me help de-biking.

"No, I got it," I said, adjusting the jacket around my thighs.

Cooper took off his helmet and combed a hand through his hair. The rest of us took off our helmets too, hanging them on our bikes' bars. Rudy winked at me and flicked his tongue back and forth between his new set of teeth.

"Charming," I said.

Cooper observed the parking lot. We were alone, for now.

"Let's go," Cooper said. "You know the drill. Stick with partners. Stay frosty."

Commotion.

Three male vampires with their arms around each other stumbled out from behind the building. They were singing and laughing. The one in the middle looked over at us and gestured the peace sign. *The irony*.

"It's *CRAZY* in there, man."

412

"That's what we like to hear!" Rudy said, raising his voice and shaking his head like he was a WWF wrestler entering the ring. The one who had spoken started laughing, and the other two joined in.

"Have a good night, buddy," they shouted as they passed. We overheard one of them mumble something about finding a nightcap of the female persuasion.

We exchanged looks. It was our first brush with the other side, and it had gone well. I was impressed with Rudy's performance, though all in all he had just been himself. I guess I was impressed that he could even do that.

Seven and Charlie joined hands and walked ahead. Topps and Rudy followed. Cooper looked at me.

"Ready?"

"As I'll ever be."

He held a hand out to me. We had discussed this. Pretending to be a couple would help fend off any offertory pints. I didn't want to be drinking more blood than was necessary and I wasn't sure my stomach would be able to take it, so I agreed. Besides, it wouldn't be so bad pretending to be someone's girlfriend. I was sure it would be the nicest part of the evening.

I took his hand, and we went after the others.

"Relax," Cooper said, in a whisper, "and remember what you learned in FT."

The entrance to the club was straight ahead. As we approached the line of waiting vampires, the other hunters seemed to flip some internal switch: human off, undead on. Rudy lit Topps' cigarette while giving him graphic details about a wild, blood-fueled sexcapade, as though it had just happened. Seven put a hand on Charlie's butt and said something quietly in his ear, a wicked smile on her face. Cooper wasn't doing anything in particular, but he looked *right*. It was the look a veteran stuntman might wear before taking a step off a ten-story building.

The line got closer. It felt like we weren't moving at all and the line was floating toward us.

Stay there...we're cooommmmming!

From the bike, the things queuing had looked less vampire, more human, but as we neared, the human fell away, a bit here with the pointy teeth, a bit there with the lascivious hunger in the eyes.

We reached the end of the line and got in behind two female vampires. The one in front of me was talking. She was noticeably prettier than her friend, taller and skinnier, with blue eyes and hair like a Victorian doll. Nature had given her friend the short end of the stick, and the friend was well aware, nodding eagerly and complimenting the prettier one in order to reap any future benefits. Every once and a while, the friend would look around to check out the guys checking out her pretty companion. Then she would return to the conversation her pretty companion had carried on without her, laughing at all the right parts. Her routine was down pat.

The pretty companion: "...and he was like, 'Christine, don't be stupid,' but I could tell from his eyes that something was up, you know what I mean?"

The friend nodded.

"So I said, 'Mark, she's meant to be dinner, not someone you fall in love with.' Seriously, what is his problem? Do you see humans screwing their Happy Meals?"

The friend rolled her eyes and laughed, loud.

"I think it's the scared, helpless thing he likes. The girl's always crying. What do you call it? The...wounded bird syndrome! That's it. *So* pathetic."

The friend's head nodded.

Cooper tightened his grip around my hand.

"And to think that I got her for him! She's rare. B-negative. Nepalese, Italian American mix. Kind of sweet with a flowery aftertaste. To die for."

"Yummy," said the friend.

"Ah, *yeah.* Fucking expensive. Next time I'll get him a tie." The pretty companion turned on her heel to face me, her perfect white fangs in a snarl. "Listen much? Get your own stories." Before I could respond, she grabbed the friend's hand. "Come on. I think Ben's working tonight."

"Does he have any friends?" I heard the friend ask, before the girls were out of view.

I tried to think of how a vampire might respond to such rudeness from a fellow vampire. Rip out a throat? Expunge an eyeball? Perhaps it was my confusion as to what to do that made me do what I did next. Maybe it was something else—something that had always been there, right under the surface, ready to make an appearance.

I drew Cooper close to me and kissed him.

His lips were warm, and he responded. Our new teeth tangled. I forgot where I was, and if he had too, we were in big trouble.

"Get a room," somebody shouted. It was Rudy.

We moved away from each other, reluctantly. Awkwardly. If any vampires had caught that show, they might have seen something too human in how we did it. I looked around. One vampire was looking back. He was my height, wearing a bowl hat and thick eyeliner. He looked away when I met his stare.

I felt a blush rising up my face. I breathed slowly, trying to work it back down. Cooper's hand was warm. I could feel his pulse against my palm. *Or is it mine?*

Cooper pulled a pack of cigarettes from his jacket. He put two in his mouth, lit both, and offered me one. I took it. He inhaled, then spoke, making the smoke come out in a wispy cloud.

"Anyone seen our friends?" he asked.

"Negative," said Rudy, next to us.

"Nope," said Seven, from behind us.

"They must be inside already. Keep your eyes open."

The line moved pretty fast, but it never got shorter. Cars rolled up, vampires got out, and any entering the club were replaced by more at the other end. Brillo-head bouncer started to look less vicious and more dopey and I was glad that some things were less frightening the closer you got. Just a few back now, I could see inside the club and through the entrance. The guests who had just gone in walked beneath a giant heart that illuminated and pulsed to the beat of the music. Inside the heart, a red liquid surged and bubbled. When the heart compressed, the liquid was rushed through hundreds of tubes that wound along the ceiling, into the club. As the heart decompressed, hundreds of other tubes replenished the plastic organ with more liquid.

We moved in past security. Leech had told us that we needn't worry about them, and he was right. Apparently, they were there for show and to break up the occasional fight.

We skipped the coat room, as we were not planning on staying. Plus, my coat was necessary to hide my arsenal. We walked under the giant heart. It had just emptied and was about to refill. A small puddle remained at the bottom. I wondered if it was real blood and felt sick at the thought of how much it would take to fill up all those tubes.

The network continued, liquid freeways above our heads. Further in, the tubes took off in different directions. A few led to a smaller version of the entryway heart behind the bar.

The first floor was full, just as we were told it would be. Cooper softly tightened his grip on my hand as we dove into the sea of vampires. The best thing I could do was to pretend that they weren't what they were, and that the dark red liquid they were sucking down was a foreign lager—the thick kind that sticks to your lips.

The music in Club Vein was the type that banged against your gut repeatedly and made you feel as if it was only a matter of time before the beat would leave you on the floor, *sans* guts.

Cooper was making a beeline for the bar, when the plan had us getting drinks on the second floor.

"Shouldn't we get drinks upstairs?" I asked. "It'll be less crowded."

"I need one now," Cooper said, over his shoulder. Translation: it would look better if we all had drinks in our hands ASAP.

The others followed, and you wouldn't have known anything had changed. They took cues like pros. We got stalled a few feet from the bar as it was four-vamp deep. We didn't talk while we waited. There were too many ears around us, and the less we did that could give us away as human, the better.

Behind the bar, beautiful, lanky vampires bounced to the beat and poured drinks with sharp smiles. One, a female, shouted, "Shots!" and jumped up on the bar with a large bottle. Around us, revelers pushed forward to get some. Cooper was caught in the wave, and I watched helplessly as he struggled against it and was momentarily swallowed up.

Best to stay where I am. He'd get back to me. The others had moved further along the bar. I could just see the top of Rudy's head at the far end but nothing of the others. I thought about ordering the drinks for Cooper and I, but I was nervous and wasn't sure it was a good idea. I was still a couple customers away from the bar, so there would be time to decide.

I danced and pretended to enjoy myself. A forty-something vampire dressed in a light gray suit moved by me with four pint glasses in his hands. He smiled as he passed.

"Take your jacket off, toots. Stay a while," he said, batting big brown eyes.

"I'm alright, thanks."

He stopped short. "Wow, nice teeth."

As he spoke, one precariously balanced pint flipped to the floor, wacking the vamp's knee and coloring the lower half of his right leg crimson red. What followed was a balancing act good enough to stun Barnum and Bailey, and the vamp was able to save the other pints from the fate of their comrade.

"Aw...that's gonna stain. This is a new suit. Shit." He looked at me, finding composure to flirt. "The stuff's a bitch to get out."

I felt pressure to comment. "Yeah, that's why you wear black."

I was going to die. It wasn't the first time I had thought that recently, and it wasn't a pleasant thought—not one you wanted recurring, at least.

The empty pint glass nudged my foot. There were blood spatters on my boots. A puddle hugged my heel. The vampire straightened. He had gotten full control of the pints in his hands. Apparently, three was a much more manageable number. He stared at me. I searched for Cooper in the crowd. The vampire spoke.

"I know who you are."

"You do?" I swallowed and heard the gulp reverberate off of every wall in that place and swore the DJ had recorded it and sampled it into his set.

"Yes, I do." He nodded. "Tommy put you up to this. The *bastard*." The vampire looked at me sideways, very sure that a big joke of a different kind was being played on him. He continued: "Yep. He got you to come over here looking all sexy to distract me, which in turn would make me spill my drink, which in turn would make me comment on the stain, which in turn would give *you* the chance to comment on the fact that my suit isn't black. That stupid asshole can't get over the fact that I want to put a little color into my closet. It's normal, right?"

"Yes, very...normal."

"I went out last week and bought this pristine gray suit to switch things up a bit...stop me if you know this story already...you don't? *Right*. But tell Tommy he makes his point well. I'll step away from the color. Bastard's always right. So...what's your story? How come you're so beautiful?"

"Because she's *mine*." Cooper had found his way back to me. He took my hand and pulled me behind him.

"Hey, it's all good. I don't want to fight—just want to drink." He held up the now-three, clutched pint glasses. "You tell Tommy 'hi' for me." With that, the vampire left my path as quickly as he had scampered into it.

"Tommy who?" Cooper asked.

"Don't ask."

We exchanged looks, grateful no fight had come from that encounter. Our defenses were very different from theirs. One fight with one vampire and we were discovered. And we had yet to get what we came for.

A space opened up at the bar. Cooper moved into it and took a menu from between two candles. A female bartender with an enormous mouth appeared in front of us.

"What'll it be?"

"Two Brockets," Cooper said, replacing the menu.

"Only got Norvies," she said. "Boss has been slow stocking vegetarian. He's of the more traditional kind."

"Two Norvies, then," Cooper said, with some force. He did not want to get stuck in a debate. The bartender caught the hint and went off to fix our drinks. I wanted to ask Cooper what he ordered but didn't dare. I didn't want to raise suspicion and knew that whatever it was I'd be drinking it. This made it better not to know.

Next to us, a male vampire wearing a smug smile and a glittery cap leaned over the bar to summon a bartender. A guy with dreads who looked of American Indian descent came over to take his order.

"What's your flavor?"

"You are, most definitely. The vampire who didn't suck you dry made a huge mistake."

Sexual harassment of the worst kind, I thought.

"Aces. What do you want?"

"The special, of course. Not much else will pass these lips."

The bartender took a glass only slightly bigger than a shot from the top of a tall stack. He dodged the other bartenders and stopped at the smaller plastic heart. Underneath, several tubes ended in taps. The bartender flipped one of the tap levers, and blood flowed solidly to fill the glass below.

"Twenty-five bucks."

Our bartender had returned with the drinks. The glasses were proper pints, and I found myself wishing I had ordered the special, too. I had a quick panic about the cash. I hadn't seen money since my arrival in California and wasn't sure Cooper had any. I guess I had never really thought about it but just assumed vampire currency was something like bone chips, blood, or hellfire.

The bartender stared at Cooper as he dug in his pocket, her mouth in the same thin dissatisfied line since he shut her down. He handed her two Hamiltons and one Abe, then tossed five Washingtons onto the bar. There was nothing like a good tip to bring the smile back.

"Thanks, babe. You guys have a good night."

We pushed back through the crowd toward the stairs. Rudy and Topps had planted themselves in front of a television that was playing music videos. They took daring gulps from their glasses. Charlie and Seven were lip-locked in a corner behind the guys, their drinks sitting untouched on a brass shelf that ran the length of the club. It was a keen strategy. By occupying their mouths in a very human but also very vampire way, having less time for drinking blood wouldn't be seen as suspicious.

I wondered if they could keep it up all night and still keep watch. I didn't blame Seven for not wanting to put the stuff in her system. She was taking care of two, now.

Cooper and I headed upstairs. The others followed, leaving space in between. Now I knew why they did it that way in the movies. If two were caught, the others wouldn't go down. Also, each team could position themselves at a different vantage point and alert the others of problems. We had prepared signals. I was to observe from the booth while Cooper conducted business. To avoid confusion, we kept it down to just two signals: clapping at a partner meant everything was a-okay, raising a glass my way meant trouble was brewing and it was time to leave.

On the second floor, things were looking up. There was a quarter of the crowd. Some vampires milled by the bar, but most sat in the booths next to the dance floor. A different disc jockey worked the upstairs, and he had yet to get anyone dancing. He was playing a song that was familiar to me from my old life, and the heavy beat was less invasive, more comforting. In my head, I sang.

Cooper released my hand to search the floor for the janitors, and I took the opportunity to unbutton my jacket. I looked down to check that nothing incriminating was poking out. It wasn't. My newfound comfort also had me taking a sip of my drink. My mouth puckered with the saltiness of it. I swallowed and felt my throat being coated. I licked the blood off my lips, not because I liked the taste, but because I couldn't stand it being there half a second longer.

I started to feel naked standing there, and against my better judgment, wished for more vampires around us—to hide us. In the masses, it was easier to blend, but being out there in the open would call for our best performances.

I glanced at the other hunters. Rudy and Topps had reached the bar, with Seven and Charlie by the DJ booth. We were in formation: three points. Any additional points and someone had split from their partner, and that was something you just didn't do. Visually, each couple had to be in a position to see and be seen by the others. We were to be each other's biggest fans.

Cooper spotted the janitors. They were in the first booth, where they said they'd be.

"They're here," he said. "Let's go."

We started across the empty dance floor. The song I knew became the wind in my sails. I felt like we were being checked out, so I put it on, licking my fangs and smiling as if being a vampire was the best fucking thing in the world.

Twenty booths were spread out in front of us, each constructed of thick glass, with backs that stretched to the ceiling. Red velvet cushioned the seats, and framed paintings depicting various forms of torture hung from each sectioned wall.

My heels clicked on the dance floor as I concentrated on walking in them. I spotted movement beneath me and looked down to find that the dance floor, like the booths, was made of glass. The club's interior designer had been into some fang shui and thought it important for clubbers to see what was below them.

A strong current of blood passed under the floor. A concrete bed with upraised slabs caused the blood to rise, spray, and curve like a mighty river in the wild.

There's just so much of it.

I tried to stop my reaction before it hit my face, but it came with such force, as reactions sometimes do, and efforts to stop it were futile. My mouth gaped, dry. My tongue was stuck, which may have been a blessing. Loose, I couldn't say what words would have been flung from the tip of it. Cooper followed my gaze, but his recovery time was quick. He hadn't been a hunter that long, but he was officially a veteran, taking the grotesque with mind-boggling nonchalance. His speedy recovery allowed him time to worry about the slowness of mine.

"*Emma*," he said. His voice did nothing to stir me from my trance.

How many people died for this, I thought.

In truth, it could have been animal blood. Best-case scenario, it wasn't even real; though I knew better. Chances were it wasn't being wasted but was eventually being fed through all those tubes. Possibly, it was an advertising gimmick, but weren't vampires already perpetually thirsty? Wasn't it like drilling a hole in the Guinness factory to tempt the Irish already on bar stools?

The length of time that I was staring at that blood river was short, though it felt like ages. Cooper even stole another glance at the monstrosity. It was as if our brains wanted nothing to do with it, but our eyes opted for just one more peek...and another.

I looked up just as a female vampire slid from the booth in front of us. She was wearing a black mink that wrapped her body from cleavage to calves. Long triangles of pale flesh were visible, and with each movement, the dead animal shrunk back to reveal more flesh. Her hair was dark and fell down her back in a ponytail. Her jaw was square, and as she got closer, her eye color appeared to change from black to violet.

I felt envy watching her. She moved as if she knew all the answers—even the ones without questions. The air seemed to part on her approach. She smiled at us as she passed, and spoke in English broken by Eastern Bloc.

"Don't you want to bathe with it? Mabon is genius."

"Mabon?" I said.

She was past us now. The flesh of her upper back visible. Muscles slinked under the skin. She turned around to stare at me.

"Yes. The owner," she said, with a hint of irritation in her voice.

"The owner."

The woman looked me up and down, the irritation now gone and a side of amusement in its place.

"You must be new," she said. "How cute." She raised a hand, flitted her fingers, and turned to walk to the bar. I looked at Cooper.

"Mabon? Where do I know that name from?"

Cooper was still gawking at the vampire. It was my turn to steal him from a trance. I slapped him lightly on the cheek.

"Earth to Cooper."

"What?"

"Who's Mabon?"

Cooper lifted his drink and took a sip. Not even the smallest flinch. I was impressed.

"*A* Mabon kidnapped Scott's son and was the vampire behind Project Sunset."

"That's right. So you don't think it's the same Mabon? How many Mabons do you think there are in this city?"

"Just one," Cooper said, his face turning grim.

"Of all the blood joints in all the towns in all the world, we walk into Mabon's. Don't you think that's strange?"

"I do," Cooper said. "But we don't have time to figure it out now. Let's just meet the janitors, get the intel, and discuss it later. Okay?"

"Sure." It wasn't. Something was wrong, but for sanity's sake, I found another topic. "That female was old. I could feel it, couldn't you? How far do these things go back, anyway?"

"BC."

"As in they dined with cavemen?" I asked, thinking he was joking.

"As in they dined *on* cavemen."

I waited for the smile. None came.

The men from the photographs slouched over big drinks and looked up at us as we approached their booth.

The one I remembered as Tyson scooted over to make room for us. Cooper started introductions and undead hands shook human ones. Their hands were cold, their grips terrifying.

Cooper sat first, so I got the outside. It was all how we had planned it. Once seated, there was a moment of silence and not of the religious kind. Nerves seemed a factor for both parties, but some sizing-up was going on, too. In each head at that table, decisions were being made as to who could take whom.

They were both vampires, so both were dangerous. Tyson was the meatier of the two. He wore the same surprised expression from his photograph, and I wondered if someone had jumped out at him in his human life, causing that look which would stay with him for all eternity. Despite his solid stature, Tyson didn't scare me. Judging a book by its cover, he was someone who was slow in body and slower in mind. I could trust him not to construct any plans that I hadn't first thought of myself.

Then there was the other janitor, Lars, who was the calculating type. I knew from the first glimpse at his photograph that he was someone I wouldn't trust alive, dead, undead, or otherwise. Meeting him only reinforced that feeling. *Oh well*, I thought. With any luck we

426

would be miles away from the janitors in a half hour or so. *Please let Cooper make this quick.* Lars was the first to speak.

"You bring a woman to meet with us, huh? Everyone knows women can't keep secrets."

"Wow, sexist much?" I said. "One could say the same about vampires." I wasn't sure how good vampires were at keeping secrets. I hadn't had any experience telling them any. But what I said sounded good at the time.

"Come on, guys," Cooper said. "None of us like this, so let's just get it over with. Do you have the information?"

"We do," Lars said. "Do you have the blood?"

"We do," Cooper said.

During the nuptials, I shot a look at the others. Seven started some Spanish dancing around Charlie, clapping at him. Topps clapped at Rudy, and Rudy gave a slight bow. Everything was okay.

"Show me," Cooper said.

"You first," Tyson said. It was the first time he had spoken. He seemed quite proud with what he came up with and looked at Lars for approval.

Lars nodded at him. "Yes, you first," Lars repeated.

The meeting was getting off to a rocky start. Goodbye to five minutes that could have had us outside sooner. My plans to take a backseat were just revised. I leaned in closer to the janitors.

"Listen. We called this meeting. We call the shots. Show us what you have or we'll just assume that you have nothing we want and we'll *leave.*"

I was bluffing, but the fangs (the real ones) bought it. Lars went into his jacket and pulled out a manila folder which he slid across the table. Cooper opened it.

"Everything you want is in there," Lars said, aiming a long finger at the folder. In 48 hours, a charity ball is gonna be thrown at the address in there. Masters will be flying in for the event, along with all the other UVF bigwigs who look down on lowly janitors." Lars grunted. Tyson did too. "One place, one night. You go have your fun. Now, where is our blood?"

Cooper studied the contents of the folder. I looked over his shoulder. Inside were a small street map of Los Angeles, with an address on it circled twofold in black, and three dossiers, photos included. The vampires in the pictures looked like car salesmen or politicians ill on bad Mexican.

"Just three?" Cooper asked.

"Yes."

"And what about security?"

"Ample, but your friend has arranged for some holes. It's all there. Now, if you please?" Lars held out his hand.

I paused from the proceedings to make sure the other hunters were okay. As soon as I looked over, Topps held his glass up to me. Something was wrong.

My eyes averted to Seven and Charlie's position. They were gone. I searched the crowd, which had increased since our arrival.

Oh my God.

I found them halfway between the DJ booth and the emergency exit. Seven was vomiting, supported by Charlie's outstretched arm. She clutched at her stomach. Vampires turned to watch.

"Cooper, Seven's in trouble." Cooper followed my gaze. The janitors looked, too.

"Time to go," Cooper said, rolling the folder into a tight tube and shoving it in his jacket.

"Wait. You owe us blood," Lars said.

Cooper reached into his pants pocket and pulled out a small vial which he dropped into Lars' upturned hand. The janitors observed it with adoring eyes.

"Pleasure, Treasure," Lars said, his face now a grin. "Feel free to contact us, again. And let's hope your adventure doesn't end before it even begins." He nodded at the scene unfolding, kissed the vile, and dropped it in a small pocket awkwardly stitched to the front of his jacket. The two were up and moving toward the stairs and the main entrance, as Cooper and I made our way to someplace more unpleasant.

Topps and Rudy had yet to get to Seven and Charlie. Seven was still a mess. She had stopped vomiting, but she stood bent at the waist and holding on to Charlie for support. We had hit worst-case scenario. It was a lesson learned. Intuition trumps all.

"They've got company," I said to Cooper. The worst kind. The kind that insisted on you for dinner. A tall vampire with shoulder-length red hair had stepped in between them and the exit.

Topps and Rudy arrived on the scene. No weapons were drawn yet. Cooper and I ran across the dance floor dodging undead clubbers getting into their groove. I could feel the weapons against my body. They had gotten the call to come out and play.

We were close enough to hear the confrontation, now.

"The bitch got vomit on my shoe," the red-headed vampire was saying. "You can't control the bitch from drinking too much, you make the bitch stay home."

429

The vampire wasn't wearing a shirt. Death tats covered his chest. "Badass motherfucker" ran up his arm in bold italics. Half of his face was scarred. The skin was rippled and pinched. When we reached them, I moved close to Seven.

She whispered, "Something's wrong with the baby." She met my eyes, her face coiled in pain. "*It hurts.*"

Ten vampires stood between us and the fire exit. The red-headed vampire was our only aggressor at the moment, and not because he had found us out as humans, but because Seven had unintentionally gotten vomit on his shoe. The vampires blocking the door were standing there not to stop us from leaving, but to grab front-row seats to a fight.

"What's wrong with the bitch anyway? Bad blood?"

"Yeah, bad blood. We just want to leave," Charlie said, making a desperate attempt at reason. "We didn't mean to cause any trouble."

"Well, you did, man. You did. And there's something I need you to do to make amends." The vampire was showing off now. He eyed the crowd and raised his voice. "I need you to get down on your knees and lick it off."

Vampires gasped around us. Our aggressor basked in the attention. I knew Charlie would do it. He'd do it to save Seven and get us all out of there. He was just that type of guy. But as things went, he didn't have to.

"Hey, is all this shit necessary?" Cooper asked.

"Yeah, come on!" Topps said.

Near us, a small female vampire with short black hair put her nose in the air. A diamond stud in her right nostril glittered. Others were sniffing the air, too. The small vamp dropped her nose and studied me.

Seven buckled over, releasing what was halfway between a moan and a scream. Blood from in between her legs dripped onto the floor.

"What the—"

The tip of a stake poked through the red-headed vampire's chest before being pulled back out. The vampire fell to his knees. It had been his last night for troublemaking and he had spent it well. Behind him, Rudy wiped the tip of the stake on his pant leg and glanced at the exit door group.

"Who's next?"

We made a circle around Seven and Charlie. With just four of us, there were holes. Charlie had his gun out and was ready to fight, but most of Seven's weight was being carried on his shoulder and his emotions were peaked. We could not depend on him.

"What's wrong with her, Cooper?" Charlie asked.

"I don't know...I can't be sure. Just hold on to her. Seven, we're gonna get you out of here, okay?"

We were spinning now. The world blurred around us. We were on the Tilt-a-Whirl with no way off. The female vampire with the nose stud spoke.

"Vein got us a special treat tonight. But those, I don't like," she said, pointing at the weapons. "They've never given them weapons before."

"Yeah and they look like us!" another shouted.

"It's a challenge!" said another.

"They want us to work for it!"

"I'll need to have a word with management," the female vampire said, smiling. She wore blue metallic lipstick and it smudged her fangs. "But first...let's eat."

They came at us.

Eyes were on Seven. She was the weak, bleeding one. I didn't know if they could tell that her blood was rare. Either way, she was their target.

Some of the hunters, including myself, still had full pint glasses. It was beat into us by Leech and Scott to always have a glass no less then half-full in our hand. It was all part of the blending in. Since it was too late for that, we directed them at the onslaught.

The glasses spun in the air, emptying gory contents. Two hit their marks, shattering and sticking broken pieces into undead faces. We didn't expect to stop the vampires with glassware, but we hoped to at least stall them. On the contrary, it excited them. Drove them more. Maybe the act reeked of fright and desperation—aphrodisiacs to vampires. Ironically, our first move in battle just made our enemies want us more.

Bullets were a different story.

I shot off two into a vampire that looked like the *Hamburglar* with a striped black and white shirt and blood from my thrown glass stretched across his eyes in a thick stripe. One bullet hit his shoulder, the other banged through his chest. *Direct hit.* He didn't like that at all, shouting profanities at me before collapsing.

Vampires tugged at our legs from the floor, opting for lower ground to get to Seven. A few clawed at each other, desperate to be the one to have her.

Cooper went down, then Rudy.

I staked haphazardly and stomped on hands and heads.

I checked Seven. She had her gun out now, but it wasn't like one of ours. It was a toy Super Soaker with a cotton ball attached to the end of a wire and positioned an inch or so from the barrel's end. Charlie flipped open a Zippo and touched flame to cotton. It ignited.

"Scatter!" Seven yelled, her voice full of fury.

Cooper catapulted the vampire that had taken him down into Seven's line of fire. Rudy rolled with his, on the upside saving his own life, on the downside sparing his attacker's life. I dove to the right. I couldn't see Topps but had to trust he could take care of himself.

Whoosh!

A spray of flames licked at our heels. The aroma of chemicals pooled in the air. Vampires were on fire, their faces canvases of pain and shock as the promise of eternal life slipped from their grasp. Some collapsed where they were. Others took off running, toward empty space or vampires not yet caught up in the fight. One vampire engulfed in flames ran onto the dance floor, clearing it like a bad song.

Hunters were aflame, too, namely me. The bottom of my coat had turned raging inferno. I twisted in it, trying to get the thing off, but got stuck. I blew at the flames, a panic move I'd never be proud of. I pulled and grappled with the sleeves, finally tearing the coat off my body. I flung it away from me, mesmerized by the flying trail of smoldering fabric.

I stood up to get back to Seven. She was handling things, tossing what I now recognized as a DIY flamethrower and firing off rounds from a real gun. She stood straighter. Her face was determined. She was defending her inherent right to live. No—her inherent right not to be drained by bloodsucking monsters.

Charred vampires lurched and crawled toward her. Even in near-death, great blood had put a spell on them.

Charlie was still at Seven's side. When we got out of the mess we were in, she would tell him about the second baby she had lost to

Death. Maybe he'd find comfort in the fact that it was never his. Then again, maybe he wouldn't.

I had just taken a few steps when something hit me from behind.

I lost my gun. My face smacked the floor. There was a snap. I think it was my nose, but who could be sure? I felt the pain all over.

Whatever was on my back made holds in my clothes and heaved itself upward. I tried to get away, but it was useless. The thing on my back, which (let's face it) had to be a vampire, had me at hello.

My gun was a few feet away from me, my arms pinned beneath my body. The only chance I had was the pocketsize piece in my belt. The small bullets it shot would feel like a bug bite to a vampire. At any rate, I'd need the one on my back to turn me over in order to shoot it and I wasn't holding my breath. The smell of burning flesh filled my nostrils.

"You never know what's in a package," said a female voice, "until you unwrap it."

"Is that right?" I asked.

"Yes. You see, I wasn't even going to bother with you. Your friend's got the blood, that's a sure thing. But then I thought, 'Who knows? That other one just might surprise you.' So, what do you think? Are you ready to surprise me?"

"Oh, I'm ready," I said, pushing against the vampire's weight. I moved my arm down. An inch or so more and I'd have my hand on the gun.

"Stop wiggling, you little worm. Before I open my package, I need it to tell me why Mabon armed the humans." I got my hand further down. No contact, yet. "Stop moving, worm, and answer the question."

"I don't know. Why don't you ask him yourself?"

"Because I'm asking you."

"Like I said, I don't know."

Neither of us spoke. The charred skin smell was making me nauseous. My face had gone from pain to numbness to pain. I inched my hand down some more. The tips of my fingers brushed metal.

"I guess that settles it. I kill you now."

"*No!* Wait. Just wait." The gun's handle was in my hand. I fumbled for the safety.

"You've got something to tell me?"

"No. I promise you...I don't know anything. I don't know why he gave us weapons." Promises made to vampires didn't count. "*Please.* I want to see you. I need to see the person...that kills me."

"Person? I am no person! Look at me!" She flipped my body over.

It was the female vamp with the nose stud that had caused a stir earlier. She had been badly burned by the fire. Most of her hair and her eyebrows had been singed off. Her face was Cajun-style. The diamond and the whites of her eyes were glowing with the contrast. The blue lipstick had come off almost entirely onto her teeth, making her look as if she had just been feeding from the jugular of a *Smurf.*

My unintentional insult had her in a divvy. I thought I might act the same way if someone called me a vampire.

"Look at me. I am vampire. Have no doubt of that."

She grabbed my hair and forced my head back. Her mouth descended toward my neck.

"You're losing your brains," I said.

"We all go a little mad sometimes."

I raised the gun to her right temple. "No. You're losing your brains."

I pulled the trigger.

The bullet went through her head and came out the other side with brain matter attached. I wasn't sure how vampires lived after something like that, but maybe the point was that they weren't actually *living*.

The vampire's face blanked, as if paying quick reverence to what was supposed to happen. She came out of it, snarled, and attacked.

But I was ready.

I pulled a stake from my belt and plunged it through her chest. The vampire screamed, hitting her sides and shaking her head like a child in a tantrum. She fell on me, and I lamented the fact that they always knew to do that. Blood poured from her chest onto mine. Arms came from nowhere to take her off me. I flinched expecting to see another vampire

It was Cooper. He lifted me to my feet.

"You're hurt." It was a statement, not a question. My face ached.

"I'm okay. I'll live," I said, maybe a bit prematurely.

I grabbed my gun off the floor and another stake from my belt. Vampires were all around us. There was no way we would get out alive.

But wait.

"Why aren't they coming after us?" I asked.

"I don't know." Cooper shook his head.

It was not the chaos I had expected. The music still played. The disc jockey still flipped through a case of CDs. Revelers were back on the dance floor, paying no attention to the steaming corpse in the middle. We got a few curious looks over cocktails, but for the most part, we were being ignored.

Cooper continued: "Maybe they think we're the entertainment, and most of them are too full to bother? I'm not sure."

"What about Seven? Can't they still smell her?"

"There's so much blood around...and the fire. It could be covering up the smell."

We moved quickly toward the others with a shared idea: there were time limits on luck. The hunters were near, hurt but alive. By the looks of it, no one would die from their wounds. The vampire carnage, however, was great.

A large portion of our hunter training had been based on vampires not feeling fear, but I was starting to think that that was false information. Maybe they weren't attacking us because they saw what we could do and they enjoyed their undead lives a bit too much to take the risk.

Seven was standing without any support. It was a good sign, but she looked more like a vampire than the vampires—pale, drained of all life, and covered in blood. Her gun darted from one fallen vampire to another daring them to get up and eat more lead. She was crying. It was the first time I had ever seen someone cry without really crying. Tears slipped down her stoic face, as if they had been stored for so long and an overflow was necessary to make room for the next time she chose not to cry. It was simply a matter of making space. I went to her. She pointed her gun at me.

"Sorry...I...sorry," she said.

"Can you walk?" She nodded. "Then let's leave, okay?"

Seven smiled. "Okay."

The fire door was right there. The one we had planned only to go through in the event of an emergency. The one that had been blocked by that group of onlookers we had just annihilated. It now invited us through.

I'm here. So close. Come on through.

Seven and I opened it, and the alarm sounded as we were told it would. I went first to check the other side, followed by Seven.

Someone yelled from behind us.

It was Charlie. A small vampire *(a child? a midget?)* was wrapped around his neck like a scarf.

"Stay here!" I said to Seven, but it was too late.

She was already heading back through the door. I caught her arm. She pulled it away.

The others were working at the vampire on Charlie's neck, shoving their arms between the two in an attempt to wrench them apart. Rudy grabbed the back of the vampire's head with both hands and pulled.

Charlie's skin came away from his neck. He had been bitten. Even with all the screaming, I could still hear the skin *slap* back. Blood spouted from the wound and sprayed the vampire's face. It was just a child after all—a young boy with blonde curly locks and large dimples.

Rudy shot it through the head. Seven got in close and began to beat the vampire's face with the butt of her pistol. She was raising her arm for one more blow when her legs gave out from under her.

I was under the impression she had tripped. Tangling legs would have been an easy mistake; weird things happen to a body and mind when you're pummeling something to death.

But she hadn't tripped.

A vampire had slid into Seven to take her down. Now he was dragging her by her size sixes toward the dance floor. She was putting up a good fight, but the vampire was well aware of what he had. A path cleared for the vampire and his captive. Nostrils flared, and eyes grew big as they passed.

I squeezed off three. They went wide, one nicking the arm of a skinny, neon-haired raver who looked offended at the very notion.

The others were too preoccupied with Charlie to notice Seven's sudden disappearance. I yelled something at Cooper and ran after her.

Vampires had already closed the path and formed a crazed conga line behind Seven and her captor. The more distance he covered, the more interest was peaked, making the scenario analogous to a baker propping open the door of his bakery and setting up a fan by the stove so the neighborhood could get a whiff of his baking buns. I knew he wasn't flaunting her on purpose. He just wasn't familiar with the club layout like we were.

The vampire let out an animalistic roar and turned to face the crowd. He was black and tall with closely cropped hair and a widow's peak. A well-manicured mustache sat on his upper lip. He hissed and let go of one of Seven's shoes to scratch at the air. Seven rammed her freed foot into the vampire's knee. The vampire didn't flinch.

"Get away! She's mine! I found her so leave us!"

"Can't you share? What's a couple drops?" said a voice in the crowd. Others chimed similar opinions.

"No, she's mine. *Go away!*" The black vampire addressed the horde with one eye on me. He wasn't stupid.

Seven was still kicking. She must have lost her gun somewhere along the way, because her hands were empty. She started to sit up, but the black vampire stomped on her belly, making her lose consciousness. I aimed my gun but couldn't get a clear shot, and I had no idea how many bullets I had left.

The music had stopped at some point. We had finally gotten the patrons' full attention and without even trying. They were now neither satiated on pints, nor frightened, but willing and able, and more were on the way. They poured from the stairwell. Soon, the entire club would be on the second floor.

"*You!*" I shouted, shaking from the strength of my voice.

The path cleared again. Vampires split looks between me and Seven's captor, waiting for one to make a move. But things had gotten worse for the good guys. Seven was now hoisted up, her neck poised for sipping.

"Drop it or she dies," he said.

"You're going to kill her anyway."

"Maybe…maybe not," he said, tilting his head back and then forth. "Are you willing to bet your friend's life on it?"

The first thing that popped into my head was that he had it all wrong: Seven wasn't my friend. She had never been. So why was I risking my life for her? Because. We were two people united in an important cause, and that meant something in my books. Besides, I wouldn't wish death-by-vampire on anyone.

I threw the gun, not bothering with the safety. I hoped it would go off and take out a couple vamps on the way to the wall. It didn't. Gun met wall with a sad breaking noise.

"Happy?"

"Not quite yet. The rest, too."

I tossed my small pistol and undid and dropped my belt of stakes. He'd have to have x-ray vision to see the sheathed stakes down my boot and back. I wasn't planning on giving them up, but from that distance and with the vampire holding Seven in front of him, a sharpened piece of wood would do me no good.

I held up my hands. *No more weapons here, fucker.*

The black vampire looked at me warily before smiling like he had just won the big game. He snarled at the others and took a few steps back. Satisfied, his focus returned to Seven. A single yellow fang sprouted from behind the vampire's trembling upper lip.

Oh God…what is that?

Pussy green liquid squirted out of his mouth and landed on Seven's neck.

"No!" I screamed. "We had a deal."

"I don't make deals," he said, the words slurred around that big tooth.

Seven opened her eyes, then.

I noticed for the first time that her hands were tight around a stake. She brought the stake up and plunged it through the black vampire's right cheek. The tip poked out the other side. His mouth was stuck open. He released Seven onto the floor.

I grabbed for my back stake, when shots rang out. Holes appeared in the black vampire's chest. He jerked midair, pummeled by a cascade of bullets. Cooper and Topps pulled up beside me, guns drawn.

Seven was up off the floor now and moving toward us.

Vampires closed in around her.

I ran ahead, shoving my stake through one, two, three vampires. Four, five, six went down from bullets. But it didn't matter. They kept coming.

The path closed, and we lost sight of Seven. Cooper grabbed my arm.

"Come on!"

441

"No! We can still save her." I pulled away from him and thrust my stake into a fat vampire wearing a tight silver dress. Cooper hooked his arm around my waist.

"She's gone, Emma. We need to go. *Now*."

They were coming up the main stairwell in droves. I couldn't see Seven anymore. Where she had been was a writhing pile of vampires. More circled, waiting for their chance. It was too late.

I let Cooper lead me back to the emergency exit, and we made it through the third time. Rudy was there with Charlie, who was draped over the railing and barely holding on. His neck was covered in blood. It seeped from a flesh wound the size of a doughnut.

Rudy took the stairs down two at a time while Topps and Cooper helped Charlie. I followed them, keeping an eye on the door behind us.

At the bottom, our bikes waited. Rudy straddled his bike and put his helmet on. He started the engine and pointed a finger at Cooper.

"You know the rules, man. He's been bit. We gotta leave him."

I looked at Cooper and then at poor Charlie, weak and dying between the two strong hunters.

"What does he mean? What's he saying, Cooper?"

Topps looked at Cooper. "He's right. We can't bring him with us, Coop."

"No, no, no. You're joking," I said. There was yelling in the distance and not enough of a distance to be comfortable with.

Topps slid out from under Charlie and boarded a bike. Cooper looked at me.

"No, Cooper. You don't have to do this. Please. We can't. We can't do this."

"They're right, Emma. He's not human anymore. He's one of them.

We bring him back and we put everyone's life at risk."

"Let's go, man," Rudy said, revving his engine.

Cooper turned and started to walk Charlie toward the wall of the club.

"No. No, you can't, Cooper," I said. "You can't because…because if he stays, I stay."

A vampire burst through the second-floor emergency door. Topps shot him, and he somersaulted over the railing and landed on his back, dead before impact. As if on cue, a group of five or six came around the corner of the building from the direction of the front entrance. It wasn't the welcome wagon. It was the goodbye wagon. Goodbye forever.

"Leave him!" Rudy said.

"Okay," Cooper said. "Help me get him on the bike. We'll need to strap him to my body. Topps, I need your belt. *Quickly.*" Cooper undid his own belt and got on the bike. Topps got off his bike to help us. Rudy stayed put. The goodbye wagon was closing in.

Rudy fired off a couple shots. One vamp went down.

"You fucking assholes," he said, either to us or them.

We got Charlie on the seat behind Cooper. It wasn't easy. Topps had hurt his arm and Charlie was in the process of dying. But we did it, and we tied him to Cooper with the belts.

Rudy fired off more shots. "Come *on.*"

They were closer, now. I made sure the belts were tight and Charlie was secured in the seat. He moaned, "Seven." I touched a hand to his head.

"Go, Cooper."

I got on the bike with Topps. There was only one way out and that

443

was in the direction of our pursuers. We headed straight for them, freeing up space with bullets. As we passed, a vampire caught my foot. We dragged it a good ten feet or so with me gripping Topps' waist for dear life.

I imagined myself falling off the bike and felt the goodbye wagon's frenzied movements on top of me. I felt cold teeth pierce my neck, my thigh, my arm, wherever the feeding was good. I watched the bikes' lights get smaller with distance. *Did they brake?* I wondered as my own lights faltered, set to go out forever. *Did they brake for me?*

As we turned onto the main road, the vampire let go of my foot. What I had seen in my head never happened, but the lingering question of expendability stayed with me through the night and until the sun rose weary the next morning.

CHAPTER TWENTY-FOUR

PLAN B IS NEVER ENJOYABLE.

In order for Plan B to have happened, Plan A has already happened and in most cases gone horribly wrong.

That was where we were, at any rate. The hunters had become the hunted. Plan B was a house in the hills. Not a bad house, mind you. Actually, it was the nicest place I had ever been in.

Rich people had lived there once. They had slept on 1500-thread-count sheets, cleansed with filtered water from rainforest showerheads, sipped Fillico from crystal martini glasses, ate croissants shipped overnight from their favorite Parisian patisserie, and dined on gourmet meals cooked by a celebrity chef in a kitchen they never stepped foot in.

That was then.

Now, four hunters of the undead and one soon-to-be-undead hunter stood in that kitchen, covered in crusted gore and arguing a moot point.

"Look," Rudy said, pointing at Charlie moaning against the wall. "A fucking pre-vamp. *Oh my*, what's a pre-vamp doing here? That's right. *You* brought it here, Cooper, and you should know better." It was strange hearing Rudy reprimand Cooper. Rudy was the fuck-up. I think the reversal threw Cooper off a bit, too. He stood staring at Rudy with no response. I needed to step in.

"Excuse me," I said. "It's a *he*, and *he's* our *friend*. Or have you forgotten?"

"You shut up—because you don't even know."

445

Topps put his hands up. "I think we all need to calm down. We don't want to disturb the neighbors."

A wave of nausea came over me. My face throbbed with pain. I didn't need this right now. None of us did, but it was what we had. *Welcome to Plan B.* My thoughts rested on Seven beneath that pile of vampires. I shivered.

Rudy carried on: "Right. The neighbors. Why not invite them over to join the one we have here? We can play games like...like *Un-Life* and...and *Name That Plot to Kill Your Masters.*"

Cooper brushed a hand slowly through his hair. I wanted him to say something to Rudy in his own defense—in Charlie's defense. Then I understood why he didn't. He agreed with Rudy. He wished he had left Charlie behind, too. He had only brought him back for me.

I looked at Charlie. His face said PAIN. The kind that kills you and then makes you live for all eternity as a walking corpse. He brought his knees up tightly to his chest. I wanted to do something for him but wasn't sure what. I rushed over to the sink and searched the surrounding drawers. I found a clean cloth, soaked it in cold water, and brought it to Charlie. I put the damp cloth on his forehead without asking. His closed eyes opened to slits, then closed again. The moaning ceased.

The argument continued without me. Cooper said that everything was okay and that Rudy losing control was what was making the situation bad and that we should all just sleep on it. Rudy scoffed at the idea that he could sleep with such a huge liability under our noses, stinking up the air. Topps pretty much stayed out of it, stepping in only when things got offensive.

"What about Leech?" I asked. Leech was of the vampire persuasion and we had let him into our home and our plans. I didn't trust Leech, granted, but they did.

"You see, Emma, you shouldn't get into things when you don't know what you're talking about. Leech is a means to an end. He's proven himself. New-bites are different because they can either go bad or good, and ninety-nine percent of the time they go bad. Real bad. You never met Car. Car was a sweetheart. I can pick on just about anyone…but not Car. She was a good kid, and when she turned, it was straight for the throat."

"But there's a chance," I said. "A chance that he won't be like the rest. And we can keep him somewhere. We can lock him up until the masters are dead and everything goes back to normal. He's our friend. He deserves at least that."

I looked from Rudy to Cooper to Topps. Rudy was being the vocal one, but I had a feeling none of them were comfortable with the situation and that Charlie was teetering on the verge of undeath, courtesy of vampires, and real death, courtesy of us.

"He's not our friend anymore, and if you're willing to take the risk, cupcake, then you can do the babysitting. You can count me out."

"I guess we can just count you out of everything," I said, my anger taking on a whole new level.

Topps went to the window. The blinds were shut. He parted them.

"Ladies and gentlemen, if you want a replay of what happened at the club then keep it up. But I suggest we simmer down and hit the hay. There's always tomorrow for arguing."

"Topps is right," Cooper said. "We're all just tired. We'll be able to talk about this rationally once we've gotten some shuteye."

"I'll give you rational," Rudy said, drawing his stake and rushing toward Charlie and me.

I fumbled for my pistol.

"Hold it," Cooper said, his gun already pointed. "Don't, Rudy." He stopped and turned toward Cooper slowly.

"All of this because you have a crush? *Fuck her already*." Cooper's face faltered before his grip tightened on the weapon.

"We haven't made any final decisions here, man. All I'm asking for is that everyone just take a breather. Please. Put it down."

A visible tiredness came over Rudy. His shoulders sagged. There was no defeat there, only temporary compliance. The night had left its tread marks.

"I'm taking a shower," he said, slapping his stake onto the counter and walking out of the room. The wooden weapon rolled to the edge of the countertop before stopping.

Cooper holstered his gun. We all exchanged stunned looks. Charlie was unmoving. His eyes were closed, but his chest rose and fell, indicating that he was still alive, for now. I didn't think he was lucid enough to understand what had just gone down, and I was happy for that. Charlie had his issues with Rudy, but he still considered him a friend and he would have been sad to bear witness to a friend championing his death. And with Seven being gone. It was almost too much sadness for one person to take. *Maybe, it'll be better for him as a vampire?* I shook my head.

"Bad thoughts?" Cooper asked, standing over me.

"Too many," I said. Cooper nodded, and it made me feel a little better.

"Let's go get Charlie comfortable."

We walked down a hallway and up some stairs. The bedrooms were off a mezzanine which overlooked the foyer. An immense chandelier brightened the space like a million stars. Skylights opposite the bedroom doors offered unrealistic views of the city below.

Cooper and I lugged Charlie up the stairs, our feet sinking into the plush carpeting. A person turning into a vampire proved heavier than your average person. Though, full-scale battles against monsters could be tiring.

Topps went to search the place. The hunters had rid the house of its inhabitants two weeks earlier—a family of three which Cooper had tagged as the original owners. I wasn't sure why he thought that and didn't ask. I pictured three vampires dressed in Polo and swinging tennis rackets. They wore nametags: GREGORY, MIMI, and PORSCHE.

We reached the top of the stairs. Cooper pointed to one of five closed doors.

"I think it's this one. Wait a sec."

We sat Charlie down and Cooper went into the room alone with his gun drawn. He came out a minute later.

"It's good."

The room was breathtaking with high vaulted ceilings, a giant bed draped in a silk, beaded quilt, and a bathroom complete with sauna and two toilets.

"Why this one?" I asked.

"It's the only room without an outdoor balcony, and the bed's got a headboard and footboard."

Topps came through the door. "First floor's clean. I found rope." He tossed two rope bundles at Cooper's feet before leaving to check the rest of the house.

"You're tying him up? Like a prisoner?"

"That's what he is right now. We'll make sure he's comfortable."

But not too comfortable. Cooper was right. It made no sense to let Charlie roam free until we found out what kind of vampire he was going to be. At the moment, he was too weak to do much of anything, but I knew that wouldn't last.

We got Charlie on the bed. His restlessness had returned. He made his hands into sweaty fists and gathered the pretty quilt in them. His neck wound wasn't bleeding anymore, but old blood—a mixture of his and the vampires he had killed at the club—was crusted on his neck, shirt, and pants. I took off his shoes and went to the bureau to look for clothes in his size.

"This must be a spare room," I said, sifting through bed linens and sock bundles with the tags still on. "There's nothing in here."

"I know where some are. Watch him, okay?"

Cooper left his gun on top of the bureau and walked out of the room. I ignored the weapon and went into the bathroom. There were two washcloths with seashells on them, and I wet them both with cold water. When I returned to the room, Charlie had gone back to hugging himself.

I sat on the bed and placed one washcloth on his forehead and used the other to clean his neck. The piece of skin that had been torn away was hanging on by just a thread, so I avoided the area. I wouldn't have known what to do if it fell off. Two puncture holes were visible at the center of the wound. Two perfect circles clotted with blood. It was all still very raw. I could see muscle, along with something else: multiple pink spots no bigger than pinheads. They appeared to be moving.

Growing. I got closer. Each spot looked like a tiny pink spider.

I drew a finger close to touch one, when I noticed Charlie's eyes were open. Eyes that had once been blue were now completely black.

I jumped off the bed.

"What's wrong?" Cooper had come in the room with his arms full of spare clothes, and he dropped them now to grab his gun off the bureau. He looked at me to speak. "What's wrong, Em?"

I glanced back at Charlie. His eyes were closed again.

"Nothing...I...he opened his eyes, I think. They were black. All black." Cooper looked annoyed and greatly relieved at the same time. He returned to pick up the clothes he had dropped.

"What do you expect? He's dying."

"I've never seen someone die before. Well, not like this. I don't know what to expect." I went to sit back down on the bed but thought better of it. "His wound has pink spots in it. Do you think it's infected?"

"I imagine that's skin," Cooper said, depositing on the bed a plain gray sweatshirt and forest green sweatpants with the number 26 on the thigh. "The human part of him is dying. The vampire part's regenerating."

"Oh, I see."

We stripped Charlie of his dirty clothes. I turned around to let Cooper get him out of his pants. Cooper wasn't jumping with joy over the task, but he did it dutifully. After we got Charlie dressed and cleaned the rest of the blood off his neck, I helped Cooper tie him to the bed boards.

"Sure it's not too tight?" I asked, when we were done.

"It's just tight enough," Cooper said.

Topps returned and volunteered to keep an eye on Charlie. He said he was too wired to sleep, and I suspected that that would be the case with me but hoped I was wrong. What followed was a polite tug-of-war with each of us offering to watch Charlie. Topps got the honors in the end, and I was okay with that. I trusted Topps not to take matters into his own hands. Under Topps' watch, Charlie would be safe until morning.

Cooper led me out of the room and down the hall. Beyond another door was another bedroom. Inside, sheer white curtains danced frantically while French patio doors, panes black from night, clicked open and shut. Cooper rushed over to secure them, and the curtains tangoed with the newcomer.

"Sorry about that. Topps must have forgotten to lock them."

I stepped into the room and exhaled. It was the most beautiful room I had ever seen. Three times bigger than my apartment at school, with hardwood floors, a king-size bed under a wall-mounted fountain, and several pieces of finely crafted furniture. A fish tank sat opposite the bed, and I walked over to it. Algae clung to the sides of the tank, and the surface was strewn with belly-up fish. One was alive. A small goldfish. It swam over to me and watched me with bubble eyes.

"Hey there," I said, resisting the urge to tap on the glass. They don't like that.

I could relate to the fish—dwindling numbers, surrounded by dead. I found a small container of food, opened it, and pinched some flakes into the tank, away from the decaying corpses. The lone fish swam to the food, at first catching the falling pieces, then going for the smorgasbord floating on the surface. I replaced the cap on the container and the container next to the tank.

"There's a Jacuzzi in the bathroom," Cooper said. "Or I guess it's more like a bathtub with jets."

"And tell me why this is the Plan B house and not the Plan A as in *freaking always* house?" I turned to Cooper.

He smiled, bearing his temp fangs, and I raised fingers to my own. I had forgotten about them. How could I have? As far as I knew, no one had had the chance to forcibly remove theirs. I heard it took a bit of kick.

"We've got neighbors," Cooper said, directing an eye at the window, "which makes this house only good for short-term."

My fingers tasted odd, and I cringed. *Fish food.*

"Is it your face? Let me take a look."

My injured face throbbed from mere mention. Apparently, I had forgotten about my battle wounds too. Memory loss? I'd welcome it like a prisoner welcomed freedom. My nose started to hurt. I wondered if it was broken. I wondered how many beatings my face could take before I needed to work a paper bag into my beauty regime.

Cooper directed me to sit, and I did. He poked, prodded, and asked me if things hurt. He never made it to medical school, but he did have the aggravating routine down pat. Our faces were close and I remembered kissing him and felt the blood rush to my cheeks and hoped the black and blue would mask what I felt, whatever that was.

"I don't think anything's broken," he said. "It looks like the bridge of your nose and the middle of your forehead shared the blow—evened it out."

"Well, that's good," I said, still in a fluster. "Evening out is good."

Cooper looked so tired up close. "You have a slight contusion on your forehead, but it should be okay to sleep," he said. "Do you feel dizzy or nauseous?"

"No more than usual."

"Good." He pulled his face away from mine. Part of me wanted it back. "Maybe put an ice-cold cloth over your face. It'll bring the swelling down."

You mean my monster face? I thought. It was decided. I was not looking in any mirrors tonight. Emma and mirrors were back on poor terms.

"Sure," I said. Cooper opened the door to leave. "Hey?"

"Yeah?" He turned to me.

"She was dead, right? Seven was dead?"

"Yeah…she was." Cooper's eyes glazed over. I looked down at my blood-stained body. I wanted to tell him about Seven's pregnancy. I almost did, when the door shut, and Cooper was gone.

Another time.

~

The hot water was nice on my sore body.

Steam rose in plumes from the tub.

My mind slowed the race, and I closed my eyes. When I opened them, he was with me. The vampire who frolicked uninvited in my dreams.

His head rose from out of the water. From his eyes, blood streamed. It tinted soap suds and caressed my breasts. A hand with twisted brown nails reached for me. I screamed and awoke, slapping at the cold, empty water.

There was nothing there after all.

~

Sunlight tore at my eyelids.

I felt like road kill. Baked road kill. The kind that has festered in the sun for a good week until a minimum-wage employee carelessly and with dry eyes scrapes your smooshed body off the sizzling asphalt.

Above me, water ran down a slab of slate and disappeared with a gurgle into a narrow, pocketed ledge. Gravity, man. It never ceased to amaze.

I kicked off two layers of down comforters. The night before had picked up a chill, and after my bath, I confiscated the spare comforter from the closet, stuffed into a top shelf along with an unusual amount of decorative pinecones. I had slipped into bed naked, too tired to go sifting through clothes that most likely wouldn't fit me, and not about to wear the ones from the club. They were dead to me.

I sat up and peeled one of the blankets back over my naked body. I hadn't locked the door and there were four other hunters in the house.

Just four, I thought.

Or to be painfully specific, three other hunters and one soon-to-be vampire. I thought about Seven, and my stomach turned. I fought back against my emotions, which so rarely worked, but this time did. I swallowed dismay. It was time to prioritize. The day was for saving Charlie.

First, I would try reason. It would be a continuation of last night's discussion, except hopefully we'd all have gotten some rest, and reason would slap Rudy, Topps, and Cooper upside the face and then caress them where it hurt. Guys were meant to like that kind of stuff. If they didn't hear the call of reason, I'd need another plan. No one was going to hurt Charlie.

I rolled onto my stomach and stretched an arm across the bed. I closed my eyes and imagined Sullivan next to me. I tried to remember what it felt like to not be lonely or scared. I heard Sullivan's breathing. He snored sometimes, and the sound would lull me to sleep. I caught the scent of his cologne, which never fully masked his real smell—the reason I liked it.

Behind me, the door opened. Quiet footsteps followed, before the bureau blew it with a heavy whine. I opened my eyes and turned my head.

"You're awake?" Cooper said, his hands in the sock drawer.

"Yeah," I managed. Sullivan slipped away.

A stripy sock flew to the floor. Cooper wore a gray Tulane sweatshirt with green lettering that matched his eyes. The sweatshirt must have been an XXL because he was swimming in it. I recalled a children's show with a lady who sat in enormous chairs and looked very, very small. A cut on his forehead was pink and in need of some attention. He smiled at me, and the smile got lost on the way to his eyes.

"Sorry…I didn't mean to wake you."

"That's okay. What time is it?"

"Noon."

I groaned. There was so much convincing to be done and I had lost half the day. I started to get up, then remembered my nakedness and slipped back under the covers. Cooper took it as me not feeling well and rushed to the bedside.

"What's wrong? Are you dizzy?"

I did feel like crap, but it was bearable and nothing to concern Cooper with.

"No, I'm okay. *Really.*"

It took one more "really" to convince him. Cooper sat on the side of

456

the bed. The blanket got pulled down and he nearly got a nipple show, but I managed to move with the blanket.

He sat bent at the shoulders and drowning in dyed collegiate cotton. I had the urge to throw my arms around him and tell him that everything would be okay, but I wasn't sure that it would be, or that it was at the moment. And I wasn't sure we were at *that* stage. I wasn't sure whether I wanted us to be. In fact, if I was sure about anything, it was that I was completely unsure about everything. Cooper glanced at me.

"So, you're okay? You're still pretty banged up."

"What, do you want me to write it on a blimp and shoot it across the sky?" I poked him.

"If you could."

"I'm still a little tired, but I'll get over it."

"That's probably my fault. I was worried you might have a concussion, so I checked on you every half hour. I tried to be quiet, but the light in the hallway is kind of bright."

"You did that...all night?"

"Yes. Just to be certain," Cooper said, nodding slightly, unaware that this was the stuff of knights in shining armor.

The urge to hug him grew stronger. He smelled of sweat and pine and something sweeter, mustier. Blood, probably. I tugged the comforter up higher and cinched it with my arms against my sides. A self-made straight jacket. The sun outside fled behind a cloud. The room darkened and I couldn't help but think it was because of what I was about to say.

"Seven was pregnant."

Those three words were released into the atmosphere, and it seemed like hours went by and they still hadn't slid into Cooper's ears. He gave no reaction. Not even a twitch. So I repeated myself and only got *preg* out before Cooper charged like a freight train toward the bureau.

I screamed.

The lovely piece of furniture reared up and twirled on one leg like a ballerina, before toppling and ending its dance dramatically, spitting drawers and clothes across the room and falling with a *wumph!*

Cooper stood now unmoving in the middle of his mess. A sock curled over his shoe as if desperate to be worn. I closed my mouth, realizing it was wide open and nothing was coming out or going in. Stillness took over, and I jumped when the door opened and Rudy poked his head into the room. Concerned eyes went from me to Cooper to the fallen bureau.

"How's it going in here?" he asked. "I heard a raucous."

Cooper spoke and the tone was condescending and void of everything him. "We're *great*, Rudy. How's Charlie? Anyone watching him?"

"*A*-ffirmative, boss. Topps is with him. Hey, check what I found." Rudy's head disappeared, replaced by the biggest bottle of vodka I had ever seen. "And…wait for it…" The giant bottle disappeared replaced by another bottle, this one with glass handles in the shape of wings. It was filled with dark liquor and followed by an impressive dust trail that glittered in the waning sunlight like pixie dust. "Old whiskey. This shit is like ten years old or something."

Rudy took half a step into the room and brought the whiskey bottle closer to his face to study the label. "I don't know. It's all in French or something. That means it's really good though, right?"

"Give us a minute, Rudy." To my relief, Cooper was sounding

more like himself.

"You sure?" Rudy asked, stealing another glance at the bureau.

"Yeah."

Rudy nodded and looked at me. "I was kind of a dick last night. It happens, you know?"

It wasn't really an apology, but I knew it was the closest Rudy could get to one.

"Okay," I said.

It wasn't really an acceptance, but it was the closest I could get to one with such a shitty apology. Rudy smirked.

"Girls should be allowed their opinions sometimes. Just sometimes."

"Assholes, too. Just sometimes."

"Touché." Rudy saluted us. "Meet me in St. Petersburg."

He left and closed the door behind him. The repartee was gone, and silence settled in once more to take its place. Dreaded, dreadful silence.

Cooper stood there frozen in place. I blinked my eyes twice to make sure he was real. He looked like a department store mannequin ready for retirement. Too many sales associates dragging him carelessly across the floor. Too many kids sticking chewed wads of bubblegum to his backside.

I wrapped the comforter around me and hooked the two ends behind me with one hand. I got up from the bed and shuffled over to Cooper, careful not to trip over the bunching material. I stopped a few shoe lengths away from Cooper. He didn't turn around, but I spoke anyway.

"I found out. She made me promise not to tell. I didn't think it was anyone else's business." That was a bit of a lie. "No, that's a lie. I had considered the worst-case scenario, but dismissed it. I guess I hoped everything would go as planned. It was stupid of me." I held my breath. Sometimes your whole world depends on what someone will say next.

"It's not your fault," he said, turning to me finally. "Seven loved Charlie. She would have gone to the club even if I told her she couldn't. She always wanted to protect him." I released my breath.

Cooper observed the mess and shook his head. He lifted his foot, and the needy sock fell from it. "Besides, no one could've called what happened. Not even me. I can't even get my head around it now." *Pause*. "It was Charlie's?"

I shook my head and he seemed to understand. I guess he knew the back story. Cooper walked to the fish tank and pressed his finger against the glass. On the other side, the lone fish swam to it. He slid his finger to the other end. The fish followed most of the way before losing interest and beating fins to a floating friend for breakfast. My friendly fish had gone cannibal.

Cooper picked up the fish food, removed the cover, and lifted the top of the tank. He tapped some out, and the fish swam to it. Maybe satisfied he had put enough in to ease the fish's temptation to eat its dead buddies, Cooper replaced the cap and put the food container down.

"The thing is…" Cooper started. I knew there was still a thing. The air is thick when a guy has something on his mind. "…that I'm in charge when Scott's not around and I should have saved them…Charlie and Seven…I should have saved them. They were my responsibility."

"No," I said, tightening my grip on my comforter gown and

shuffling to him. I reached him before I knew what to do. I was never good at this stuff. I put a hand on his shoulder.

Cooper looked at me as if I were a complete stranger. I nearly made introductions, before he spoke.

"It should've been me," he said, and not with sadness or regret, but with certainty. He was the captain meant to go down with his ship.

My hand left his shoulder and grabbed his arm with a grip that meant business. I turned him toward me.

"Don't you ever say that. We're a team," I said. "We're all responsible for each other, and we're working under difficult circumstances. None of us are killers. We're all just doing the best we can."

Cooper stared at me. His face was suddenly inches from mine. I had to fight to keep my train of thought.

"And *he*..." I said pointing to the closed door and the room that was somewhere across the hall and our friend who was tied up in it "...is still alive. And maybe...maybe he won't turn after all. He just ends up being sick. Or he won't thirst for our blood. And if he does, we just leave him. So he'll be undead for a week or so until we kill the Masters and everything's normal again. Seven's dead, but...but the person she loved with all her heart is still alive. That's something, right?"

I was grasping for anything. For the sake of my sanity, but more importantly for the sake of Cooper's. And somehow during my tiny speech, being undead became *not that bad*.

"Last night, Charlie sweat through four blankets," Cooper said. "That's the human still in him...dying. But his throat is torn and he's not bleeding because he has no blood to bleed. That's the vampire. He's turning already. And as for leaving him..." Cooper said, shaking his head "…we just can't do that. He knows too much."

Comforting Cooper had turned into the Charlie debate. I was still a bit groggy, and naked, save for a stranger's blanket, but I felt confident. Reason would start now.

"Okay, okay. We take him somewhere like to an abandoned building or something. You know…someplace where we can lock him up real good so he can't escape. And then, when all of this is over...because it will be...soon…we can go get him."

I had gotten my hands moving, dangerous when your hands were keeping you clothed, but vital to making a point. It was a habit I had acquired from Josie, my roommate. Overdo it and you're channeling a bird with a broken wing, but just the right amount and your opinion becomes much more attractive to any naysayer. I paused. Cooper had bent over the mess and was now busying himself with stuffing clothes in drawers. I couldn't believe how many socks there were strewn about and none matching.

"Talk to me, Cooper."

"I don't know what you want me to say."

"Tell me you'll let Charlie live."

"I can't do that."

My eyes welled and emotion reared its ugly head. A tear ran down my cheek and I cursed myself ten times over. I knew Charlie was turning. I knew it when we got him onto Cooper's bike. I was surprised at how fast it happened. Undeath was so unforgiving. Just one bite and your friends are having a quick, uncomfortable discussion on whether to take your life. It wasn't fair.

"Emma…" Cooper said, leaving one mess for another. He looked concerned, but I didn't care for his concern.

"Would you do it to me?" I asked, realizing I needed to rephrase the question after I said it. "Stake, I mean...would you stake me?"

"There are clothes in the closet across the hall. They look like your size," Cooper said, going for the door.

"Answer my question." The tears had stopped, but my face felt stiff and stained. A headache was coming on.

"I would stake myself."

He was at the door now. "You didn't answer my question. Would you kill *me?*"

The conversation ended with a shut door. I wondered if what had just happened was a case of no words speaking volumes.

"Well, fuck you too."

~

The house was quiet.

An unfamiliar house is unnerving when it's quiet.

I showered and found some clothes in the hallway closet that weren't a perfect fit but would do. I dressed back in my room and returned to the hallway. I had to get my bearings. The house plan was a bit foggy. Of course, the club blueprint was still in my head. A whole lot of good that did us. We were pummeled. But in the end, with some battered and some dead, we had gotten what we came for.

All of the doors in the hallway were shut, except for the one at the end, which was cracked with light coming through. Sunlight—a hunter's favorite kind. Someone in the room cleared their throat, and that got me moving. I was pretty sure Charlie was behind one of those doors, but I needed time before that visit. Cooper had had a look in his eyes when he was talking about Charlie's condition. I was sure he had left things out.

I shuffled down the hallway, an oriental rug under my feet, mismatched socks on them. One sock had orange, yellow, and black stripes, and the other was light blue with little green sailboats. I got to the door and nudged it open.

Rudy sat alone on a brown leather couch. He was thumbing through a magazine. Books and knickknacks filled white shelves. Another oriental rug, this one much more vibrant than the hallway rug with bright purples and reds, covered the floor. A rotund brass Buddha was tucked in a deep windowsill. Behind it, that amazing view of Los Angeles.

"Yo," Rudy said, offering me a second before returning to his magazine.

"I didn't know you could read," I said.

"Just porn," Rudy said, flashing me the magazine cover. A grown woman in a plaid skirt and suspenders, minus a shirt, pouted collagen lips while multiple hands caressed her breasts and tweaked her nipples.

"Classy," I said.

"No. Just porn."

"Sure, whatever."

I skimmed the books, all safe *New York Times* bestsellers, and walked over to the Buddha. I put my hand on its belly and rubbed up and down. This made a little squeaky noise which tugged Rudy from the world of lesbians, breast implants, and discarded morals.

"What are you doing?" he asked.

"We could use some luck, don't you think?" Rudy shrugged and returned his gaze to the magazine.

"Rub my belly and I'll guarantee you'll get lucky."

"No thanks," I said, feeling the need to bathe again. "Where's

Cooper?"

Rudy sighed. I was cutting in on quality porn time, and I imagine it had been a while since he'd seen a naked woman.

"Out for supplies."

"What kind of supplies?"

"More rope to tie Charlie up before he tries to eat us. You know, Cooper got it in his head now that he wants to wait for Charlie to fully turn. I wonder where he got that idea from. You guys are expecting holy Charlie-where-art-thou, and I think you got another thing coming."

"He's changed his mind?"

"I didn't say that. If anything, it's more for show," Rudy said, sniffing arrogantly. "When Charlie tries to eat us, Cooper saves face. We can pop the vamp, and you won't see him as a bad guy for letting it happen."

I didn't believe it. A showy person, Cooper was not. If he did things, he meant them, for better or for worse. I had a vision of Charlie's sweet face lumping, oozing, and changing as we all stood watching. Rudy read me, and what's worse than an asshole? An asshole that can read you.

"Oh yeah, it's going to be awesome," he said. "We can pop some popcorn, put on some tunes…maybe get a strobe light up in there for some sweet effect." I rolled my eyes which only egged him on. "Oh yeah. You take up here, Em, and I'll see what I can find downstairs. We'll need 3-D glasses…a plastic tarp because usually those fuckers squirt." Rudy dropped the magazine on the floor, so the bare-breasted woman was now staring up at me with cum hither eyes. He stood, knocking his foot against something under the couch. "But do you think a spotlight would work better? It's less distracting than a strobe, and we could really get a grasp on what Charlie's feeling." Rudy swayed.

Whatever he had knocked his foot against was poking out from under the couch. I bent over to pick it up and pulled out the elegant and emptied whiskey bottle. I held it by the neck and swung it like a pendulum in front of his face. His eyes watched it. His body swayed some more.

"Yes, I am drunk, drunk, drunk." He raised a finger at me. "And I think you should join me…where I am." He fell back onto the couch and then looked around as if confused as to how he got there. "Where I'm at…is fun, but…but where you're at…not so much."

He seemed to get drunker under my stare. I put the bottle on the table and picked up the magazine, appropriately and creatively titled *Tits*. I handed it to him and he seemed content to return to his original state. The State of Porn.

I wasn't mad, I was more freaked out. The hunters had had their separate moments of losing it. I had taken part in a few myself. But there comes a time when it's no longer *losing it* and it's very much lost. I wasn't sure how to decipher whether that point has been reached or way surpassed. Would the death of Seven and the turning of Charlie cause a rift not just between the hunters themselves, but the hunters and their sanity? Fun food for thought.

I decided to go see Charlie. I felt that seeing him would help me figure out what I needed to do. *Procrastination be damned*. Rudy was now sitting bolt upright on the sofa with the magazine on his lap and his eyelids drooping.

"I'm going to see Charlie," I said.

Rudy's eyelids fluttered and stopped at half-open. He slowly raised and wagged a disapproving finger.

"They're not having *any* fun in there."

I left Rudy and the "Asian Room" and started down the hallway. I passed my bedroom and headed for two doors on the right. Unusual paintings hung on the walls. Dali knockoffs in which various mundane objects floated above glorious landscapes. I tried the first door. The room was empty, but someone had slept there. The bed was unmade. This room, though not as big as mine, was still impressive. A large plasma television peered out from a chest at the foot of the bed. French doors led out to a small patio and a tiled table with a smiling sun on it and two matching chairs. Outside, tops of houses and trees sloped and ascended. I closed that door and went for the next.

This was the room. The moaning gave it away.

I put a hand on the knob, felt it turn, and wrestled with the urge to peek first. If I had been able to catch a quick glimpse of the horror in that room before entering, I might have decided against going in and instead waited for Cooper to return. Maybe if the door had been ajar or open, things would have turned out differently.

CHAPTER TWENTY-FIVE

I SAW TOPPS FIRST.

His body was folded into the far left corner of the room.

His knees were drawn to his chest, and his muscular, tattooed forearms wrapped the front of his calves.

As a kid, I had called this the accordion position, and when I got out of it, I made a sound like an accordion. As an adult, it became the fetal position. It was unnerving seeing a man as tough as Topps in the fetal position. When he realized the door was opening, his legs sprung out in front of him, his arms to his sides, and I listened for, but couldn't hear, the sound of an accordion. Or a fetus, for that matter.

But the moaning I heard. The door had done a good job at blocking most of the sound. In the room, it was near unbearable.

Topps got to his feet and walked over to me. "Got a gun?"

"No."

"Take mine," he said, slapping the weapon into my hand. "I need a break."

He slid by me and mumbled to keep the shades closed. I had never seen Topps like that. He was always so full of manners. I closed the door behind him, not sure it was such a good idea but wanting to block the noise from the rest of the house. I don't know why. It wasn't like the other hunters didn't know what was going on in that room.

The air was moist and smelled of urine. Sunlight teased from behind tight curtains. The room wasn't dark, but gray, like a black and white photograph in need of more exposing.

I swallowed and realized I hadn't moved yet. My hand was sweaty on the door's knob. I made myself take two steps forward. *Charlie's my friend.* I'd be brave for him.

I took two more steps.

Charlie moaned, and it was guttural. He shook his head from side to side, twisting his body and making tight the ropes that bound him. He didn't notice me. I took three more steps, nearing the foot of the bed. The stench consumed me. His body was drenched, as were the sheets beneath him and the clothes we put on him the night before. Most of the damp marks had a yellow tinge. Charlie was bluish green—the color of that thing in the back of the fridge that you know had once been edible, but was now just grotesque.

Charlie's hair was darker than usual. Strands stuck to his pale, off-color skin, and ends of strands disappeared into his earlobes like brain-eating snakes en route to dinner. I took a couple more steps forward and was by his head. Charlie's eyes were closed. His tongue flicked out to wet his dry, cracked lips, and I saw that he was missing teeth. It was all a part of the dying. Rot was taking a hold.

Charlie's eyelids pulsed. His face grimaced and every muscle tensed against the restraints.

My heart beat my chest. I reached out and pushed the hair off his forehead.

"Oh, Charlie," I whispered, trying not to cry for the second time that day.

Still not opening his eyes, he moaned, and his moan became words: "I feel like I'm suffocating, Em. Like six feet of dirt's on top of me. And I'm cold...so cold...but my body won't stop sweating." Charlie stretched and wiggled his fingers. "Do I still have hands? Feet? I can't feel them, Em."

I gripped his hand. It was full of sweat. He held on tight.

"They're going to kill me. Did Cooper tell you?"

"They're not," I said, surprised at how confident I sounded.

Charlie continued as if I hadn't spoken: "They're going to put a stake right through my heart and...and...I don't think I'm even becoming one of them. I think I'm just sick, Emma. Some sort of flu, right?"

Charlie coughed and a sickly liquid slipped out of his mouth and down his chin. I wondered where in the human body something that color could originate from.

"Oh, no...what is it?" Charlie asked. "Is it the blue stuff again?"

It was more olive gray in color. "No," I said. "It's not."

Charlie's face relaxed. I pulled up my sleeve and used the end of it to wipe his chin, trying not to be ill in the process.

"Oh, thank God, thank God, thank God," he whispered, opening his eyes finally and looking up at the beautiful ceiling. Like before, pupil had taken over. He turned his head to me, his face desperate.

"Help me, Em. Let me go."

"I..." I managed, my mind boiling over with second thoughts. Seeing Charlie like this did something to me, but it did the opposite of what I thought it would do. Yeah, it killed me. Charlie had a good soul. He cared for others more than he cared for himself. He loved music and listened to it as a confidant; singers had stories to tell and sadness to relinquish. With Seven, he had worn his heart on his sleeve even though she was someone who threatened to break it. But now his soul was leaving his body, seeping out of every pore. You didn't have to be trained in monster hunting to know that Charlie was changing and becoming something bad. If I helped in any way to free him, it could be suicide. If I didn't, I wasn't sure I'd ever forgive myself.

"...I don't think that's a good idea, Charlie. I'll talk to the others. Make them see. And really, how far do you think you could get if I untied you? You got this...condition...and the others are just down the hall." I left out Rudy's drunkenness and Cooper's absence. I wanted to give Charlie the impression of three alert hunters pacing the grounds.

"You could get me the keys to one of the bikes? I know I can still ride. You might have to help me get there...I'm not sure how good my legs are right now."

"No, I can't. I don't even know where—"

"But you can find them. They're going to *stake* me. I've been trying to understand. They're my friends...you're my friend. I just don't get it." Charlie twisted his hands in the ropes. Bloodless cuts spread across his wrists. Against my better judgment, I leaned in close to his face. His breath smelled like fungus.

"If I let you go and you turn," I said, "it puts everything we've worked for at risk." Charlie shook his head wildly. Sweat sprayed my face.

"I won't tell. I wouldn't do that. If I'm becoming one of them...I'll be good. I'm good in life, so I'll be good after it too. I could even help you guys...like Leech."

I straightened, shaking my head also. Charlie raised his upper body off the mattress. His nipples protruded through his wet shirt. His black eyes were watery. I hated myself for it, but I backed away. Charlie responded in kind, stretching his body toward me to make up for the distance I had made.

"Seven's dead," he said. "Mary's dead. I'll be dead. With so many dead, you'll be dead too. I know you, Em. It hasn't been much time, but I still know you. Your heart is like mine. It will kill you and you'll die inside. I'm begging. Do it for Seven, for Mary, for me...for you. *Free me*." His eyes went from black to blue. They were Charlie's eyes again. He fell back onto the bed, his muscles retaliating for the sudden strain.

He was right.

I had to do something. I couldn't let them kill Charlie. Too many had died already. Even if it made a mess of things, I would fix it...later. Right now was right now and a friend needed my help.

Cooper, forgive me.

First things first. Charlie needed a change of clothes. Someone in the room had peed themselves, and if it wasn't me, it had to be the guy tied up on the bed. Charlie eyed me. They were still his eyes, which made what I was about to do a whole lot easier.

"You know, in poker you're meant to take risks. Either you'll win big or you'll lose big, but at least you played the game." It seemed that I was channeling my deadbeat father. Charlie looked at me regretfully.

"I'm not sure what you mean."

I shook my head. "Me neither, it's okay." I paused to consider my obstacles: rope knots, undead friend, wet clothes, hunters outside, bike keys somewhere, a flight of stairs, and sunlight. I was sure there were more, but I was being optimistic. "I'm going to get you out of here, Charlie."

My friend brightened. It was freaky. It didn't come naturally to the new Charlie. I wanted to beg him to stop, but I didn't want to rain on his parade. He needed a parade. Desperately.

"Yeah? You mean it?"

I nodded. "I do." *I think. Maybe.*

"Thank you, Emma."

"Don't thank me yet. I'm going to find you a change of clothes." I caught a flash of Charlie's inner gunk on my sleeve. "And one for myself. Stay put."

Charlie watched me as I crossed the floor. His eyes said *hurry up*, but he dared not utter a word or risk his second chance at life.

I opened the bedroom door, half expecting Topps and Rudy to fall into the room, bent over with paper cups against their ears, but the hallway was empty. I quickly closed the door behind me and breathed in the new air.

A production line of ideas stuttered through my head. It would be dark in three hours, and we wouldn't leave until then. Charlie hadn't turned yet, but I wasn't sure what effect sunlight had on new-bites and I had no desire to find out. I needed clothes for Charlie to change into, but before that I'd let the other hunters know what I was up to. The fewer secrets I had to keep, the better. If either of them walked in while I was changing Charlie into fresh clothes, suspicions might arise. I'd establish trust by asking permission to change Charlie. I did run the risk of one of them volunteering to help me, but Rudy was three-sheets-to-the-wind and Topps had badly wanted to escape that room. He had been in there all night with the moaning and the smell and the guilt. I didn't think he'd be rearing to return to it any time soon.

The keys would be another issue. Cooper had one set. Rudy and Topps had also driven the night before. Either they would have the keys on their person, or abandoned where they slept. There were no keys that I could see in Charlie's room. I'd have to check the other bedrooms.

I made my way back to the Asian Room. I felt like I was in one of the surrealist paintings on the wall. I passed one with a white rabbit carrying a knife and standing on an ocean floor. Above the rabbit, an upended mirrored cityscape with points and spires facing downward.

Rudy was in the Asian room snoring quietly on the couch, the empty bottle and emptier magazine clutched to his chest. Topps sat Indian-style on the floor, leaning over a stake in the making. He worked at the wood with his knife, long dangerous strokes that would mean digits lost if done by anyone else. His muscles flexed. A hula girl tattooed on his bicep shook her thing. I pushed Rudy's feet aside and took a seat. Topps looked up, his face deep in the shadow of a wide brim. He seemed to pull cowboy hats out of thin air. He hadn't been wearing one at the club. A hat that big would make blind spots. I smiled nonchalantly.

"Charlie's asleep. I figured I'd get some fresh air while I could. Where'd you get the wood?"

"Cooper killed a table. Got only a few stakes between us. How you doing in that department?"

I had to think about it. I counted kills in my head.

"I think I have two."

I remembered seeing the stakes entangled in my crusty heap of clothes before hopping in the shower. In training, Cooper and Scott taught the hunters to always have a weapon on their person. I looked down and realized Topps' gun had been left in the room with Charlie. Constantly being armed was a hard thing to get used to—even with creatures out there lusting after your blood. Topps half smiled without looking up.

"Where'd you leave it?"

Either my fellow hunters were freakishly intuitive, or I was an open book. I'm not sure which I preferred.

"On the table near the window. Sorry."

Topps didn't respond, but I was learning that that was just Topps. He was a less is more type of guy. He was able to say all that needed to be said in half the words as the average person.

"Cooper back?"

"Not yet."

"When?"

"Should be before dark."

If that were true, I'd have to adjust my plans and leave with Charlie sooner. Getting by Rudy would be a cinch. Topps would be more difficult. Add Cooper into the equation and you had Fort Knox. I turned the conversation casual:

"Cooper leave an IOU for that table?"

"What do you think? Boy's a Scout. When all this is over, Coop'll be in debt for the rest of his life."

"You really believe that?"

"Sure do," Topps said, raising the blade to his lips to blow off clingy wood shavings. "We got ourselves a bleeding heart. Even without all those IOUs floating around the city, the kid's destined to be poor."

I shook my head. "No, I meant about this being all over. Do you think it will be one day?"

Topps stopped carving. He flipped his hat up, and the shadow fled.

"I think it's going to be game over soon, and whoever's standing in the end ready to put two more quarters in...well, that's anyone's guess."

"That's vague," I said.

Topps grinned widely and raised his eyebrows, so he looked like Jack Nicholson.

"Well, that's all I got, ma'am."

I waited for a split second, wondering if what I was about to say would be a strange turn of the conversation, or if it would blend like I needed it to. Topps returned to carving the stake. It was nearly done and happened to be the most perfect stake I had ever seen. Each stroke had been evenly distributed. There were no weak points. Mine always ended up slightly curved. Not even Cooper could tell me what I was doing wrong and he was good at that. One second, straight pole, the next, curved like a banana. Rudy got to patting me on the shoulder and saying, "It happens to the best of us." It was a joke that only got old to me.

Speaking of Rudy, he let out a few garbled, choking snores before settling back into a rhythm. I folded my hands on my lap.

"Charlie is kind of a mess in there," I said, unfolding my hands and hitching my thumb in the direction of his room. "He needs a change of clothes, so I'm going to check out the other rooms and see what I can find." I stood. Topps got a hold of my arm.

"Just let me know when you're going to untie him, okay?" He nodded, and I did too. He released my arm.

My feet took me unsteadily to the door. I ignored the voice in my head that demanded I look back to see if Topps was watching me. I opened the door and closed it behind me.

I retrieved Topps' gun from Charlie's room, asking Charlie on the move if there was anything that he needed. "Where do I begin?" he said. I promised to return soon.

I went to my bedroom and decided to start a getaway pile. I thought the shower was a good location for it. There were full baths in every room, so no one would be using mine. I found my clothes from the night before and peeled two stakes from them. The clothes landed back on the floor with a *crunch*.

I deposited the stakes in the shower and collected my boots from behind the toilet. Considering the state of my club clothes, the boots weren't half bad. I placed them, too, in the shower. I grabbed some hand towels off a rack and added them to the pile.

In the bedroom, I stepped over the fallen bureau. My guess was that it would never be returned to its original position. Not now. I picked up several long, mismatched socks from off the floor. They were clean and would work as bandages. My eyes darted around the room, taking inventory. The fish flitted about the tank, committing to an important task of its own.

"Hey buddy," I called to it, heading for the closet.

Mammoth, glitter-encrusted pinecones attacked me when I opened the closet door. I swore and returned them to a box. At this point in time, getting set upon by useless home décor was just the type of thing to push me over the edge. The closet was packed and full of promise, at least I thought, before the discovery that the clothes in it were just large enough to fit an elfin woman.

I speared my arms through the middle and parted the mass. Two surfboards leaned up against each other in the back of the closet, pinned by multiple floral hat boxes full of miscellaneous items that wouldn't be of any help. Ever. I removed the lid of one box. Torn envelopes, photographs, and cards rose with a *hush*. I detached a postcard stuck to the underside of the lid. On it was a picture of a white sandy beach with water so clear you could see through it for miles. An umbrella was stuck in the sand, dropping shade on an empty towel. It was one of those beaches that couldn't actually exist. A paradise envisioned by some graphic designer being paid good money to create a place that people would spend their entire lives searching for. Scrawled across the bottom in flamingo pink it said "The Bahamas" and "Wish you were here."

"Photoshop. Wish you were here," I muttered. The reverse side didn't have any writing on it. I slipped the card into my back pocket and replaced the lid on the box.

I closed the closet door and moved out into the hallway to the other closet where I had found the clothes I was wearing. I did see men's clothes in there, and I could have started my search for Charlie's change of clothes there instead of the bedroom closet, but I was just being thorough. I needed things and wasn't quite sure what all of them were yet, so I'd look. There was time. The light outside told me it would still be a couple of hours until night fell. We would leave as close to dark as possible and try not to run into Cooper.

I eyed the Asian Room door at the end of the hall. I had closed it when I left, but now it was ajar. I had told Topps that I'd be looking for clothes for Charlie, but I still needed to be quiet. Any ruckus was just an invitation for him to come snooping.

The closet smelled like mothballs. I flipped the light switch, but no light came on and the closet was so deep that I spent most of the time groping. Hangers and random articles of clothing slapped my face and went for my eyes.

A couple of suit jackets and light winter coats hung from the main rack. I took down two of the coats, not worrying about sex or style.

They'd fit and they'd be warm. Deeper in, I found a dark blue polyester shirt stuffed in a white nylon bag with other dated clothing. The shirt was perfect. Disco fabric could handle sweat, and sweat we had in buckets. Charlie would soak it, but the material would dry fast.

I found a pair of jeans. I held them up and tried to picture Charlie wearing them. I thought I'd see the old Charlie, but only saw the new and not improved one. Vampire Charlie had yet to be fully realized, but he was already in my head.

The jeans would have to do. It was a nightmare, not an Armani show.

Besides, where we were going, style didn't exist. It would be just him, and style needs other people witnessing it to matter. I had plans to take Charlie somewhere he couldn't do any harm to himself or others. It would be somewhere he could sit tight until things got resolved. I knew there was the chance he'd need to be kept under lock and key, and so be it. I said I'd help him, but I never promised him freedom. That part was later—when The Plan was successfully completed. After I got Charlie safe and situated, I'd come back and face the music with the other hunters.

I found another white nylon bag and pulled it out into the hallway. Inside, wooly winter clothes cozied up to their mothball protectors.

I had an ironic song in my head about things, specifically falling in love, being very easy, and I hummed it quietly.

Of course, nothing had been easy up to that point, and I wasn't expecting my trip with Charlie to be easy, either. I dared not assume he'd go quietly. Even in his weakened, pre-undead state, he was probably stronger than me. And who knew when the change would happen? On the bike on the way there (wherever there was)? *That would be bad.* Charlie behind me, his arms around my waist, and his mouth right at that spot vampires loved so much. A chill with many legs dashed up my spine.

I stretched a long, woolen scarf out of the bag, like a doctor extricating a tapeworm, and launched it around my neck, looping it around four times for added security. It wasn't the Great Wall of China, but at least the area wouldn't be as tempting with an ugly scarf wrapped around it.

I rested a hand on Topps' gun tucked down my pants. I'd be taking it with me, along with the stakes. I would need to trust Charlie if I was going to go through with this, but trust was easier if you went prepared to be screwed over.

I put everything else back in the closet. The smell of mothballs clung to me, and I silently wished we were fighting giant moths instead of vampires, then silently did a take-back. *Jeez, don't wish for freakier shit.*

I returned to my room and deposited the two coats in the shower. My secret pile was growing. Most of it we'd be wearing, but I'd still need a bag. I rethought my plans and decided to go get Topps to help me change Charlie. As I said earlier, we had some time. I wanted to get Charlie comfortable and out of his dirty clothes, pronto. Topps had made a point of telling me to come fetch him when I was ready, so I'd do that and volunteer to watch Charlie for the remainder of the day. When Topps went away, I'd start my search for the bike keys.

Things in the Asian Room were as I had left them, which gave me short-lived comfort. Topps was on his third stake. The first two were lying on the floor next to him, vampire hunter art at its finest.

I wondered if he had already chosen the one he'd use on Charlie.

480

One of the stakes on the floor had a slightly longer point than the other, which meant it would go in smoother and pierce the heart sooner. That was the one he'd use—he was Charlie's friend, after all.

The light was paling outside. A feeling of doom filled me, causing temporary paralysis. Soon the light would be gone and I'd be out there with a vampire at my back and no destination. Rudy snored, and it sounded like a chuckle.

"I'm ready," I said.

Topps put down the unfinished stake and pocketed the knife. He stood and pointed at my neck.

"What's up with the scarf?" he asked.

I'd forgotten I still had it on. "I'm cold," I said, with maybe too much bite. "Is that alright?"

"Sure. That's alright," Topps said.

He walked to the door, his feet dragging on the floor. He wasn't looking forward to this, either. Passing Rudy, he leaned over him and lightly smacked his cheek. "I'll be back, partner." Topps spoke loudly and Rudy's face contorted. Topps snickered.

We slowly made our way back to Charlie's room. When we arrived at the door, Topps went first. I did wonder what would have happened if it had been me. Would I have ended up sprawled on the floor? I wasn't sure Charlie had thought that far ahead, or even if he could in his condition. He just guessed Topps would be first in the room, and his guess just happened to be correct.

From behind Topps, my mind registered two things that were missing from the room. One obvious thing being Charlie, who wasn't in the bed anymore. The ropes that had bound his hands and feet were torn and frayed and empty. The other less obvious thing was a mirror with a frame of white wooden roses. I didn't think Topps noticed that one. If he had, he noticed too late.

"What the hell?" he said, turning to glare at me, before Charlie appeared from behind the door. His arms were stretched above his head, his hands clutched the missing mirror, glass-side down. His skin shined with sweat, his face was still with petrified determination.

I shouted, "No!"

Topps half turned toward Charlie before the mirror was brought down on his head. He fell with such force that the sound of him hitting the floor was louder than the sound of the mirror smashing and raining down a million broken shards.

Charlie nearly tumbled on top of him from the momentum he had gathered. Glass tinkled around us. Topps' hat had fallen off and was now rolling away on its rim. Topps' bald head seemed to split before our eyes, bringing up a red gush. Charlie wiped at his mouth.

"*No,*" I said again.

Charlie leaned the mirror against the wall. He looked down at Topps and tilted his head.

"He's okay. He's still alive."

"*How do you know?*" I said, my voice a shrieking whisper.

"I can hear his heart beating."

"What the fuck are you doing, Charlie? You are still Charlie, right?"

I was trying to keep my voice down, but it was hard. I guess if anything had woken Rudy from his drunken slumber, it was Topps hitting the floor. It had shaken the entire house.

"Yeah, sure I am—but I can hear things. It's amazing, Emma. I heard you two coming. And Rudy...he's still asleep. I can smell the drink on his breath."

I kneeled down to take a closer look at Topps. A small piece of glass was lodged in his head. I got my nails around it and tugged. Charlie talked behind me:

"I had to do it. Maybe, I panicked? I don't know. You were taking so long. I knew that Topps was the only thing standing in our way."

Charlie picked up the clothes I had brought him from off the floor. He undid his pants, shimmied out of them, and kicked them off. They landed with a squish. He smelled. Charlie was wearing boxers and they stuck to him like leeches. He was all skin and bones. His breathing was raspy. Sweat poured down his body. But sweat was good. It meant he wasn't dead yet. He cinched the waist of his boxers between thumbs and forefingers and looked at me. I looked away.

Charlie was right. Topps was still breathing, and his pulse was strong and steady. Oddly, the cut on his head wasn't as big as it had looked when I was standing. His head would hurt like nobody's business when he came to, but the blow wouldn't be fatal. I got up and went to the bathroom. Charlie asked me what I was doing, but I ignored him. I returned to Topps with a damp cloth and gently brushed the rest of the glass off of his forehead and dabbed at the cut. Charlie struggled into his polyester pullover.

"Why, Charlie? Why'd you do it? I had everything under control," I said. "We were just going to get you changed. Then, Topps was going to leave and I was going to go find the bike keys."

"Keys," Charlie repeated. He walked over to Topps and me, half in his shirt, half out. My guard went up. He looked down at Topps and reached toward his pocket. I deflected his hand.

"I'll do it."

I rested the cloth on Topps' head and went into his right pocket, careful not to violate. I pulled out lint. In the left, something jingled. Out came a Honda keychain and two keys. Charlie clapped.

"Ha! We have liftoff." He smiled and I saw fangs.

And not the fakes. Those had been expunged somewhere along the line, together with his human incisors. These real ones weren't yet fully grown. They were just tips poking out of gums, but they were sharp and could do damage. I closed my hand over the keys. Charlie's face fell.

"Give 'em here." He held his palm out.

"Charlie, do you know what you've done?"

"Yeah, I do," he said. "I just knocked out a guy who was supposed to be my friend but had plans to kill me in a few hours. Don't ask me to feel pity for him because I won't. He's gonna wake up with a bad headache. I wasn't gonna be waking up at all."

"Point taken," I said.

I was doing all of this in the first place because the hunters would've staked Charlie by nightfall. The Plan was a higher priority to them, and I was the only one asking *At what cost?*

I opened my hand and slipped my finger through the key ring. I held it up and shook it gently. The keys knocking together sounded like bells which made me think of *It's a Wonderful Life* and angels getting wings. *More like vampires getting teeth*, I thought.

We both eyed the keys. The little metal objects symbolized where everything would go next. Charlie reached for them, and I pulled them away and stuffed them in my pocket. I glanced at the pieces of frayed rope on the bed.

"I'm going with you," I said. Charlie looked at me like I had twelve heads.

"Why on earth would you want to do that?" he asked.

To eventually restrain you again. "To help you," I said.

"Em, I'm okay now. I mean, I've still got some aches in this body. And I know there's more pain to come. I know that for sure. But right now, I'm fine. I feel kind of...strong." He held up his skinny arms, flexing barely-there biceps.

"Hence the ropes," I said.

Charlie dropped his arms and looked back at the torn ropes as if needing a visual reminder.

"Oh yeah, the ropes. I don't know." Charlie gave me a sly smile. "I just got mad and the ropes broke. I can't explain it." Charlie held out his hand again. "Are you gonna give me the keys?"

In my head, I continued that sentence for him with *or do I have to* and then filled in the blank, and it wasn't pretty.

"Charlie, I said that I'd help you, and I'm going to do that. It's not safe for you to drive right now."

"Have you driven a motorcycle before?"

"Plenty of times." *Never.*

Charlie put his hand down. "Okay. Maybe you're right. Thanks, Em. I owe you one."

"You owe me nothing."

He seemed kind of pleased at the prospect of company, and I was pleased that he was pleased. What I had told him wasn't a complete untruth. I was helping him, just not in the way he might've preferred.

Charlie looked at me and smiled and I smiled uneasily back, feeling like a giant, floating pork chop.

"What's with the scarf, anyway?"

"I'm cold." Directing the attention back to Topps, I said, "Let's get him onto the bed."

I stripped the dirty sheets off the bed, and we lifted Topps, with me carrying his feet and Charlie at his shoulders. He didn't stir. Daylight was leaving, and it would soon be our time, too.

"I've got some things stashed across the hall," I said. "I need you to stay here and mind Topps while I go and get them. Can you do that?"

"Of course."

"Please, Charlie. Please do this one thing for me."

"I'll do it, no problem."

He seemed okay. I was a bit worried about leaving him alone with Topps, but I could still see the old Charlie, and no matter how mad the old Charlie was, he'd never hurt an unarmed man. When he had attacked Topps with the mirror, it was for self-preservation, and Topps wasn't about to gain consciousness in the next five minutes. Even if he did, he'd be in a stupor, and I'd be back before he recovered his strength. I waved bye to Charlie and opened the door.

Rudy greeted me on the other side.

"What are you doing?" he asked.

His eyes were puffy slits, and he reeked of several nights on the town rolled into one twenty-minute binge. I swung the door shut behind me and waved a hand under my nose.

"God, you stink," I said.

Rudy stumbled a bit over the flat carpet lying still beneath his feet.

"Gee, thanks. I love you, too. Where's the Topp-man?"

"He went to get more wood…downstairs." I stayed in the doorway.

Rudy turned ten shades of pale. "I think I'm gonna puke," he said, dry-heaving. With a brave face, I moved forward and put an arm around him.

"Well, don't do it in the hallway." I ushered him to the bedroom with the unmade bed, and then further to the bathroom. "Here you go. And close the door, please. We could do without the sound effects."

I waited for him to close the door, and he did. He didn't shoot any wise words back at me. Apparently, he felt too sick. That was nice. The sound of vomit smacking the floor came a half second later. Not so nice. I rushed out of the room, closing the second door tightly behind me. If there was a time for escape, it was now.

I stood in the hallway, my eyes darting from door to door. I wasn't sure where to go, what to do, or how to do it. My feet were being engulfed by a roomy black hoodie that must've fallen out of the closet during my search. I shoved it on.

The ability to move my feet finally returned. Back in my bathroom, the secret pile in the shower was looking small and disappointing. Escape piles were meant to be so much more impressive. Maybe it was a blessing in disguise, since I hadn't found a bag yet. I started dressing, stake sheaths first, then the hooker boots. I nestled the hand towels in the front pocket of my hoodie and pulled out Topps' gun from my waistband, just to check: *Safety on.*

I abandoned one of the coats and kept the other one for Charlie. The hoodie would be fine for me, but he would need something warmer. Becoming vampire seemed to be a process of extremes: pain and elation, weakness and strength, hot and cold. I wanted Charlie to go prepared for whatever extremes he was about to face.

I gave the bathroom and then the bedroom a quick, final scan. Satisfied that I had what I needed, or at least what I could manage, I said goodbye to the fish and headed for the door.

~

Back in Charlie's room, things had changed, but not like before.

I relaxed when I entered to find Charlie not behind the door with a large fatal object, but next to the bed with a still unconscious Topps. The longer pieces of frayed rope had been tied around Topps' ankles and wrists and then around the bedposts. I didn't think restraining Topps was necessary at the moment, but I stayed quiet about it. There was no time for arguing.

The blinds had been lifted, and the last remaining light of day outside spiked through the trees and into the room.

"You opened the shades?"

"Yeah, it's okay," Charlie said. "See?" Charlie moved close to the window, pulled up his sleeve, and thrust his arm into the light. "All I can feel is pin pricks. It leaves little black dots, like soot or something, but they wipe away. See?" Charlie came out of the light and wiped his arm with his right hand. He then raised his hand and wiggled his fingers at me. The tips were black as night, as if they had just been inked for fingerprinting.

"That's good," I said, trying to match his excitement, but not quite making it. "That means we can leave now."

"That's what I thought," he said, smiling and wiggling his fingers once more, before pushing his sleeve back down. "The light hurts my eyes, kind of, but it's not so bad." I felt like he was about to say *yet* but decided to leave that word out. "And Rudy's getting sick in the bathroom. Things couldn't be better."

"I guess. But he's only got a bottle of whiskey to get out of his system. That stuff takes longer going in than coming out. Here, this is for you." I tossed him the coat. "In case you're cold."

488

"No, not right now," he said, bowing his head to tie the coat around his waist.

I couldn't even fathom how difficult it would be knowing that you're turning into a completely different species and not having anyone there to say what happens between now and then.

"I'm sorry, Charlie. For everything. I'm just...sorry."

CHAPTER TWENTY-SIX

THE COLD AIR CAME OUT OF NOWHERE.

In the time it took to get down the stairs, through the kitchen, and out the front door, the light was almost completely gone, so Charlie didn't have to worry. About that, anyway.

I could feel *them* and not just because I had an almost-one near me.

I could feel others perched behind closed doors, mentally shooing the sun away and wearing jubilant grins in anticipation of the descending darkness.

The bikes were waiting where we had left them in a cluster of palms. They wore torn foliage as camouflage. We could have kept them out in the open. After all, vampires drive too. But unfamiliar vehicles might've attracted nosy neighbors.

I removed the foliage from the first bike, took the keys out of my pocket, and poked the ignition with the first key. No luck, it wouldn't go in. The second key was almost certainly the same cut, but I tried anyway. Nothing. I swallowed my heart and moved on to the next bike, which was a match.

I boarded the bike, feeling doom that intensified when Charlie sat behind me and put his arms around my waist. Even though he didn't say anything, he must have felt the gun tucked down the front of my pants. Granted, we were hunters and the first rule of a hunter was to always be armed. What Charlie didn't know was that the gun was protection from him—for when and if he went bad. I had stakes, too, but guns were my preference. The right gun did the same trick with half the effort, more distance, and less mess on you.

My next issue was that I hadn't a clue on how to start a motorcycle. It always looked difficult on television and in the movies. The rider would stand and drop all of their weight onto the foot pedal. Sometimes it would take two or three times. They were generally big, brooding men, too, with lots of tats and packs of cigarettes rolled into the sleeves of their wife-beaters.

Grasping any recollection of how Cooper started his bike back at Seepy or how Topps had done it outside the club was in vain. I was highly preoccupied both times, which only went to show me that preoccupation would be my stealthy assassin in the end.

"You sure you're alright with driving?" Charlie asked.

Yes, because Charlie driving was out of the question. If things were going to go as planned, I needed full control.

"Yep."

I turned the key in the ignition. The engine started up and purred softly, waiting for my next move. I nearly clapped my hands with glee before catching myself. I curved my hand around the right handle and carefully turned it toward me. The motorcycle flew forward with a loud roar, dirt and pebbles becoming the air that we breathed.

I laughed nervously and relaxed my turn on the grip. The bike stopped. I glanced back at the house, just as the front door opened and Rudy appeared. His arms were waving, and he was yelling, but I couldn't hear a word. What he was saying probably had a lot to do with us stopping, that I was being stupid and crazy, and that I was going to get myself and them killed.

I turned the right grip back toward me again, ready for the punch this time, and the motorcycle responded in kind, shooting us down the driveway. My legs flew outward before I forced them against the bike and found a place for my feet. My deadly friend tightened his grip around my midsection. Night let us in, and Rudy's warnings choked and sputtered in our wake.

~

The helmets hadn't been on the bikes. One of the hunters must've gone outside to collect them at some point.

So there we were, buzzing through a city overrun by vampires, helmet-less and without a destination. Anyone else would have said we were asking for it. I say we were putting our cards on the table and we needed to see everyone else's before making that kind of judgment.

"Where we heading?" Charlie shouted.

South. At least I thought. If I had it right, Hollywood and Sunset were somewhere just south of us. I figured if I got on one of the main boulevards and turned east, I could find some old warehouse or factory with the facilities for locking Charlie up. I didn't know how long it would take after the masters were dead for the population to turn human again. I didn't even think the hunters, including Scott, had that information. A couple days? A week? A month? We'd have to see.

After I found a place to put Charlie, I'd head back to the Plan B house and have a whole lot of fun explaining my actions. The thought of it made me ill. I'd have to bear the wrath of three angry hunters. Oh, there would be yelling, and I didn't blame them. I went behind their backs and put The Plan at risk. I'd yell at me. Hell, I'd probably beat the crap out of me. Here was to hoping they didn't hit girls.

I was yet to answer Charlie's question, so he moved closer to my ear and repeated it ten times louder. My ear hummed afterward, and I wondered if becoming undead gave you stronger vocal cords. I decided to tell him the truth. Or half of it.

"South," I shouted back. "I know the area. We'll find a safe place."

I could feel Charlie's chin bob against my shoulder, before he leaned back. Other cars began to appear as if sprouting instantaneously from air particles. Lights in windows came on. A stretched limo pulled up in front of a restaurant, and a woman with spiked black hair moved away from the specials board to greet the first guests. A classic Pontiac with missing hubcaps stopped next to us at a stoplight. The vampire at the wheel was dressed in a mod suit and looked like a young Paul McCartney. Beside him in the bucket seat was a female vampire with straight bleached hair, short bangs, and a pink feather boa wrapped around her neck. She shook her hands in front of her as if she were holding a set of invisible maracas. Through the open back window, a pair of Keds kicked frantically, before going still. A vampire with flaming red hair and sideburns sat up and wiped his wet mouth on the sleeve of his coat.

Eyes ahead, Emma.

The streets were soon congested with traffic and undead pedestrians. I had heard that nobody walked in L.A., but that had all changed. Vampires walked.

Vampires walked in L.A.

I smiled when a large crow attacked a toothy skateboarder wearing a *Skate or Die* tee shirt. The skateboarder won the fight with some spray yanked from his baggy pants. They were both enveloped in a thick green cloud before the crow flapped away.

We had just passed Mann's Chinese Theatre (and I snuck a peek because I was a tourist after all) when Charlie began to shake. His arms tightened around me. It felt like I had a giant pager set to vibrate strapped to my back. I slowed down to look for a place to stop.

There were none.

Because stopping in that area would've been suicide. Vampires were well aware that curiosity sometimes fed thirst, and if we stopped with Charlie in the state he was in, vampires would gather, and then they'd feed. I wasn't sure whether Charlie as a new-bite would make a tasty snack, but I was certainly edible.

Charlie moaned.

The thick wooly scarf wrapped quadruple around my neck might as well have been a single piece of thread. My neck felt naked and glowing in its nakedness, as if it were calling all vamps in the Hollywood area and the one seated behind me had the pleasure of first bite.

I'd go faster, I decided. Fast was good. You could get away from things and get into them, just like that.

Objects on either side of us blurred. Lights became streams of undulating color. A Jeep Wrangler's horn blared as I cut it off to take a lonely side street. People were being drained of blood against their will, but apparently the rules of the road were still abided by.

I veered left again and prayed my memory wouldn't fail me when the time came to find my way back. Charlie dug fingertips into my stomach, and then his hands slid back onto my hips. The gun in my waistband was knocked by the movement and I tried to remember whether I had the safety on. *I did, didn't I?*

The street we had turned onto was quiet. Dark houses displayed broken windows and slanted porches and stoops with cracked plastic chairs. Recognizing desolation as a good thing, I let up on the gas, pulled up next to a fire hydrant, and turned the engine off. Charlie quit shaking. I felt the need to distance myself, but he still held me. I let go of the bike's handles and rested a hand on my gun.

"You okay, Charlie?"

Quiet.

"Charlie?"

"Where are we?" he asked.

His voice was strained. He released me, and I flung myself off the bike, quickly removing the keys from the ignition. My elbow smacked his forehead in the process.

"Sorry," I muttered.

My foot kicked a dead rat on the ground. I lurched back.

"I don't know. I just figured we should stop. You were shaking."

"I'm fine."

"You didn't seem *fine*." I could feel the gun against my stomach. "Have you turned yet, Charlie?"

"You'll know when I turn, Emma."

"You can tell me later how that's meant to make me feel better."

Charlie flipped a leg over the bike and stood. His face was skeletal. Grooves under his eyes and at his temples were so deep that it looked like the skin over these grooves might sink completely in, forming infinite pits. His face was now more gray than bluish green, and his lips were a dead-sea blue. The only thing left bright on him was his hair, which shone, even in the dark.

The house in front of us wasn't friendly like the one we had come from. A chain link fence surrounded the property. It rose to just below my waist, and the purpose of it evaded me since the height would keep few things in and few things out. The house was one-story and mustard yellow with cranberry trim. Steps led up to a porch. A crushed Bud

Light can sat upright on a plastic egg crate. Two director's chairs were on either side of the crate, both with their seat fabric ripped down the middle. Sacrificing beer calories apparently had not worked. Mismatched shutters and plywood, body parts from surrounding houses, boarded a smashed window. Various tags, meaning something only to the person who painted them and maybe a friend or two, were spray painted across the house's façade.

"Looks cozy," Charlie said.

"You know, you're becoming really sarcastic in your deadness," I said, turning toward him. "Is that some sort of requirement?"

I smiled. Charlie didn't.

"I'm not...I'm not *dead*." Charlie seemed to have trouble saying the word. I was afraid he'd have to get used to it.

"I know. Look, I'm sorry."

"Don't be. I'm gonna move the bike."

"Good idea." I nodded encouragement. I shouldn't have said what I said. I was testy. Things seemed to be getting worse. Just when you think it's not possible.

Charlie kicked up the stand, gripped the handlebars, and rolled the bike toward a few hourglass-shaped bushes. I directed my attention to the house in front of us and the others lining the street. They were all in the same ramshackle condition, as if the same person or vampire had gotten a go at each, giving each one a good pummeling.

"Seems we're in the bad part of town," I mumbled. I lifted the latch on the fence door and pushed. I took two steps forward and two steps back. In front of me was a battlefield, and the rats had lost.

Vermin bodies in rigor mortis were strewn about the half-lawn and crumbling walkway. None were moving, but all had the appearance of motion, posed in a final state of struggle. I let the door clang shut and reached over to latch it.

"What's wrong?" Charlie asked, behind me again. Since Charlie had hit the road to undead, I preferred him in front of me with all arms, legs, and teeth accounted for.

"Everything...but if you're looking for something more specific," I said, "there are at least a hundred dead rats on that lawn."

"Oh." Charlie smiled, and what sharp teeth he had, not yet fully grown but getting there. "Is that it?"

I looked over at the bushes and caught the rear end of the motorbike sticking out. But I was looking for it. If someone happened to come by who wasn't expecting a hidden bike, then I was sure it would be harder to spot. Charlie had broken some branches off to cover the top of the bike and placed a couple palm fronds in front of the tires. In the dark, it would do. Besides, if I couldn't find someplace to put Charlie in the next 30 minutes or so, we were gone.

A small concrete building stood a few houses down on our left. There was a sign out front, and I walked over for a closer look. The sign wasn't advertising coffins or crow spray, but something very human: Pepsi and Camel cigarettes.

"Looks like they haven't gotten to this place," I said. "Might be some food left if the joint's rat-proof."

Charlie observed the barred window. Beyond it, things for people in a rush. People on the run. People like us.

"Bars look tight." He brought his hands up, gripped two bars, and gave a light tug.

A black wooden door was pad-locked by way of a rusty latch. I took hold of the door's handle and got my shoulder up against the door itself. I rocked back and forth and applied pressure, careful not to make too much noise. Silence wasn't just a nice gold color, it saved lives.

The latch held. A shop owner's seemingly shoddy attempt at store security ended up being not so shoddy. I wondered if he'd have left it unsecured knowing that two hunters, who might be the ones to save his ass from spending all eternity as a vampire, would come by weeks later for a little food and shelter.

There was about an inch of space between the bottom of the door and the door frame, which was just enough for me to get a firm grip and pull. I got down on the ground, positioned my feet on either side of the door, slid my fingers between the space, and pulled with what might I had left. Above me, Charlie worked on the latch. After a few minutes of no success, I stopped for a breather.

"Where's that kung fu strength of yours when we need it?" I asked, between pants.

"I don't know," Charlie said, shrugging. "I guess I have to really want it."

"You don't want to get in there?" I asked. "Aren't you hungry?"

Charlie shook his head.

"You must be tired? There could be a nice cot in the back room."

Charlie shook his head. "Nope."

"Have to pee?"

No.

Well, if the vampire doesn't want it. I released my grip on the door and held my head. I felt a migraine coming on. My palms were gritty with dirt from the underside of the door. Some fell into my eye, causing it to water up.

"That's just great," I said, wiping at my eye with a hoodie sleeve.

"What?"

"Dirt. Fucking dirt," I said.

A car started up down the road.

Charlie crouched by my side. My eye was now watering furiously. Tears fell down my right cheek. I wiped them with my shoulder and used my good eye to try and see from which direction the car was coming.

High beams turned on and chopped the darkness that had hung over the cross street. Engine noise grew louder. From our position, we could remain unseen until the car was pretty much on top of us. I moved behind a barrel brimming with packing materials and peered over.

A dark-colored truck with a cap moved slowly down the street, toward us, from the direction we had come.

My eye was better, and I opened it to observe the new danger we faced. I grabbed my gun and released the cartridge.

"One fucking bullet," I said. "Just one bullet." I snickered. *This is the point where I lose it.*

I replaced the cartridge and stuffed the gun back into my waistband. Because I was too stupid to check that the gun had enough bullets, I'd need to wait for an opportune moment. I unsheathed a stake.

The truck stopped in front of the rat house. "Charlie," I whispered.

Behind me, something metal snapped and hit the ground. I turned around to see Charlie holding the store door open.

"I'm ready to go in now."

"Thank God," I said, scurrying over to him.

Behind the first door was another door, but this one was unlocked. Going in, I stepped on the twisted metal that was the latch and almost twisted my ankle. I lifted my foot and took a closer look. The latch appeared to have been gnawed.

"Did you bite it off?" I asked.

"Never mind," Charlie said, and I did my best.

I took the latch off the ground and shut the first door just as the truck outside cut its engine. The high beams were kept on and brought a false sense of daylight to our small section of neighborhood. I closed the second door and braced a hand against it.

CHAPTER TWENTY-SEVEN

RED TINGED THE AIR.

The neon Coke fridge was the only thing running in the store, and it hummed. Just another day of keeping beverages cold. A lone six pack of Pepsi sat inside the fridge.

The front counter and cash register were to our right. Behind the counter, enough cancer sticks to smoke one every minute for two weeks. The store was separated into four aisles, and the four aisles were split down the middle by a larger aisle. Things were surprisingly intact. No vampires had been there, just rats, and the rats had showed some restraint. The cereal aisle crunched underfoot. Cheez Doodle remnants stuck to the bottom of our shoes and gave us orange footprints.

After a brief look, Charlie went back around to the front of the store. I grabbed a Twinkie and joined him. There were voices outside, or maybe just one. Too far yet to tell.

Charlie walked up to the counter and hopped over it. He did this in a single movement, avoiding all objects around him except for one lollipop, which was knocked out of its Styrofoam stand by his boot. With his back facing me, he stretched an arm out to the wall of cigarettes and shoved a hand behind an open carton of Marlboro Reds. The box plummeted to the floor.

"What are you doing?"

Charlie ignored me. He ducked behind the counter. Cigarette boxes and plastic wrappers flew into the air. I heard a match strike. Then

Charlie rose, slowly. A lit cigarette dangled from between his new full red lips. His hair was perfect. His skin glowed.

"Charlie," I said, "I know you don't smoke."

"No, but he does." Charlie pointed at himself. He smiled with real fangs. Giant, godforsaken, real fangs.

Inside my brain, swears ricocheted uncontrollably. The effort it took to not go for a weapon hurt. My hands shook with the want to be filled with something that may prolong my life. On the opposite side of the spectrum, Charlie was the picture of calm. He took a drag of the cigarette and blew thick, perfect smoke rings.

"I'm not going to kill you, if that's what you think." His voice had changed too. It was silky.

"How do you know?"

"You helped me," he said. "I remember that in undeath, as I did in life."

The voices outside had moved. They were nearer now. Maybe just at the sidewalk, but they were coming in, I had no doubt. We would get no reprise. We would know no safety. I drew my gun and aimed it at the door. My mind screamed, "Vampire on your left!" and I swung the gun around to point it at Charlie, who was unfazed.

Footsteps sounded outside the door. I swung my gun back to cover the entrance. Whoever they were, they would have already seen the broken lock. They would suspect someone might still be in the store. I heard the groan of weathered metal. Shadows entered first. My heartbeat quickened.

Charlie removed the cigarette from his mouth. He had smoked it down to the filter and clutched what was left between two fingernails.

"One bullet's not gonna save you," he whispered. "There's at least three of them. You have to run. Look, another door." He pointed and there it was.

A sign on the door said EMPLOYEES ONLY, but if there was a king of all exceptions, this was it.

"What about you?" I mouthed back, thinking sign language would be a useful tool for monster hunters.

Charlie shrugged. Confusion marred his perfect complexion. He was going on the assumption that these were vampires outside. So was I. Maybe he was counting on some sort of undead camaraderie. That now that he was one of them, they wouldn't harm him. I wasn't so sure.

"Come with me."

"Maybe I can stall them?"

Maybe. Maybe. But there was The Plan, and my decision to help Charlie was contingent on me protecting it at all costs. Charlie had finally turned. If there was camaraderie, he might get inspired to spill secrets.

The first door opened. There was now only one thin door between us and them. My face pleaded with Charlie. He looked at the entrance, flicked the cigarette into space, and made his way around the counter.

We reached the back of the store just as the second door opened. It was not flung open. It was not yet a chase.

The employees only sign was old. It was tin and rust-munched. Shelves of motor oil and laundry detergent flanked us. A rubber fish hung next to the door. It was attached to a plastic trophy plaque and curled outward, watching the store with shiny eyes.

I had seen this fish before; late-night infomercials had occupied my sleepless nights for years. But when you're running for your life, it's too much to ask that your mind register everything in a calm orderly fashion.

As soon as we passed the fish, it did what it had been manufactured by the tens of thousands to do. It sang. With tail and head flapping, words came out from the fish's gaping mouth in a slow, robotic melody. The batteries were dying but had just enough juice for one more serenade. I looked toward the front as four figures in black cloaks came through the door, as aware of us now as we were of them.

We closed ourselves in the back room. My hands fumbled with the deadbolt. It took three tries to slip it all the way through. Adrenalin had me between flight and collapse. I turned to survey the area and what it had to offer. Charlie moved to the center of the room. He had another cigarette in his mouth, and he inhaled and exhaled without removing it.

"A whole lot of nothing," he said.

A room. Nothing more, nothing less. There were no stairs going up or down. There was no other door that could dump us safely into an alleyway. I felt gypped, and it seemed Charlie did too. *What kind of place doesn't have a back door?* It was the kind of place Emma Spade, the unluckiest bastard on the face of the earth, needed to get out of fast.

A wheeled clothing rack with two aprons hanging from it was up against the far right wall. A desk hid beneath stacks of paperwork and office supplies. A digital wall clock hanging overhead fibbed the time. A contraption that might have been a floor polisher in the 1950s, but was now just awkward, took pride of place in the middle of the room with Charlie. A dressing room with a stained curtain showed us its junk. A row of dented lockers looked to be the exact size of...

"Charlie," I whispered, pointing to the lockers. "Get in."

"In there?" he said. "Not gonna happen. That's the first place they'll look. I might as well just stand here."

"Charlie, they're coming," I said. "Do it now. You owe me."

Charlie stared with eyes that had gone two shades darker. They weren't Charlie's eyes. Would they ever be again? He walked to the locker furthest from the door. I expected it to be full of debris, or worse than that, rats, but it was empty and he climbed in. The locker fit him snugly. He stuck his tongue out at me and closed the door. The locker made a few settling noises, before going quiet.

The main door shook.

I didn't know how long the bolt would hold. It had looked more solid than the front door lock. I moved into the dressing room and pulled the curtain shut. The fabric crackled in my grip, as if it had not been touched since the Eisenhower era, when someone thought it was beautiful. Banded bundles of the *Los Angeles Times* were piled up to my thighs. Above the fold was a photograph of a frail girl of Indian descent squishing her face up as a doctor administered a shot to her arm. The headline read: "Record Number Feel Better Safe than Sorry. Then, "Thousands of Angelinos Get Flu Shot Over Weekend."

Flu, my ass.

The fish was still singing though it had changed its tune to Elvis' "Jailhouse Rock," and I couldn't think of what fish had to do with Elvis or prison, but there were a lot of mysteries in the world and this was just a small one. The people at the Elvis factory had managed to stamp the King on everything, including my father, so what's a rubber fish?

A cracking metal whining and grunts erupted from outside.

Sweaty palms threatened my grip on the gun. I kicked papers aside and made more room. There was a hole in the curtain. I had to bend down to look through it, which was trickier than standing up straight, but if I lost my footing and stumbled forward into our pursuers, then maybe I deserved to die.

I rested my butt on the newspapers. My lashes brushed against the curtain. Through the hole, I could see that the door and lock were still intact, but a strong, jarring force promised not for long.

I glanced at the last locker on the left, the one storing my Charlie. A stream of smoke seeped out from the vent at the top and floated across the room in plumes, before disappearing. A second later, more smoke came through the vent. Charlie was capable of enjoying a cigarette even in hiding. Damn vampires. I debated on whether to say something—a quiet "*Psst*, idiot in the locker. Put the cigarette out!"—but I knew I wouldn't have time, and I was right.

The door finally came down.

Cloaked figures entered the room. A final waft of smoke dissolved around the cracked ceiling lamp. One after the other entered the tiny office until there were four.

Charlie was right about the lockers. I knew it'd be the first place they'd look, but I'd be ready. The first cloaky to arrive at the last locker on the left would have a gun aimed at the back of his head. If he gave me a reason to shoot my one and only bullet, I would. I had two stakes for the rest. Failing that, I could polish them to death. Desperation is the mother of invention.

From my vantage point, the cloakies were big—real big. *Stand up and they're your height*, I reasoned, but had trouble catching my breath. I tried to meditate, but my mind wouldn't allow it, preferring to be scared.

The hoods were concealing their faces. The cloaky closest to me pointed at the lockers, and the one furthest away approached the first locker. A pale fist slid out of a roomy sleeve and punched through the door of the first locker.

Metal succumbed like mashed potato. The fist aimed at the next locker. *Rrronch!* Two more was Charlie's. I swallowed my fear, which clutched handfuls of throat on the way down.

The cloaky was now at Charlie's locker, fist poised. This was it. I pushed the curtain aside and pointed the gun.

"Hello."

The cloakies turned to face me. The one I had my gun on didn't lower his hand or unclench his fist.

"Do it," I said, "and your brain'll be giving this room some color."

They laughed a spit-ridden laugh. Drool sprayed the air. The fist clenched and unclenched, sounding like a leather heart beating.

"Do it," I said, moving the gun to point it at the cloaky that made the order, "and I kill your leader." Laughter again.

"What are you laughing at? You think this is funny? I'm going to blow all your heads off! HA HA HA!" I moved my gun over them, before stopping once more on the leader.

A noise sounded just outside the door. The fish was no longer singing, and what should have been a quiet storefront was not.

"They're laughing, Emma, because that one is not their leader. He's only a hermit. And they know that you've only got one bullet in that gun by the way you're holding it—so you couldn't possibly blow *all* their heads off."

Retarded vampires were moving up in the world. Or maybe we had just misjudged them. Elusive brains and brawn. But more importantly, I knew that voice. It belonged to the toothy, ticking time bomb, our beloved vegetarian vampire. I wanted to scream. I wanted to say I told you so. If I whispered it, it wouldn't be considered bragging, right?

"Show yourself, Leech, you traitor!"

"Not before you put the gun down. You're outnumbered. By the time you pull that trigger, Charlie will already be dead. We might lose a hermit. But newsflash: they're expendable. After you shoot me, you'll be ripped apart. The death of two more hunters would be quite a blow to The Mighty Plan, don't you think?"

Oh no. The Plan. So much of it, if not all of it, depended on information we had gotten from Leech. Never trust a vampire. The hunters broke that rule and would pay in the end. I aimed again on the undead boxer in front of Charlie's locker.

"I'm not putting my gun down."

"I only want to talk." The hermits laughed.

"Shut up!" Leech said. "Have it your way, Emma. Just holster your gun. Can you do that?"

I glanced at the empty doorway, willing death to the Judas behind it. My knees threatened to buckle. All of our planning was for what? For lies, and lies from a vampire at that, which were the worst kind.

I could shoot the undead boxer at the locker before it killed Charlie, but I'd need a stake ready for the next hermit that moved in. Four would remain, to my two stakes. The hermits were strong. Charlie had acquired some muscle with his undeath too, but I didn't think he was any match for these guys.

"Fine," I said.

I'd chat with Leech and figure out my next move. I lifted up my shirt and shoved the gun down my pants. Its imprint was still on my belly, and I winced as the metal slid home.

Leech entered the room, and it was all I could do not to launch myself at him. The others swiveled from his path. He was wearing a blue Cosby sweater with gray tweed pants. His bald spot glowed in the light, like a halo unaware of the demon beneath it. Leech grinned at me. He raised an arm, and the undead boxer backed away from the locker holding Charlie.

"Come out, Charlie," Leech said.

Smoke was drifting through the vent, once again. The locker door banged open, and Charlie stepped out, a cigarette secured between his lips. He glanced at Leech and then the hermits.

"What's happening?" Charlie asked, as if he hadn't been aware of the goings-on beyond his former confined space.

"Leech is screwing us over."

"Oh. That blows."

Leech laughed. "I liked you before, Charlie, but I have to say I like you so much better as one of us."

"Well, don't get used to it, Leech."

Leech put a hand to his ear. "What's that you say? Oh, right. The Plan. From men to vampires to men. Guess I better tiptoe around this one. Oops." Leech bit his lower lip.

"It's all bullshit, then?"

"What's that?"

"The information you gave us was all lies?"

"Most of it, yes. But don't look so glum. Someone amazing wants to meet you." Leech walked over to the desk. He ran a finger through the dust that coated it and brought the finger to his mouth. He blew. "In the political arena, there's always someone bigger than you. With vampire politics as with human politics, blood lines can be a deciding factor."

"I don't get it. This is about politics?"

Leech shrugged: "My boss saw an opportunity in your little band of hunters. He's very smart, you know. That's what almost two centuries of living can do to a vampire. In humans, the brain shrivels with age. In vampires, it ripens."

I glanced at Charlie who looked bored. My mouth was dry. Words were becoming difficult.

"Opportunity?"

"My boss has always taken a keen interest in your leader Scott, and I'm not sure why. As his friend, I found him dull. A straight arrow. My boss tinkered in his affairs…the parents, the son, the wife. Oh, don't look so surprised. The Mary thing was mainly to get you. I told her, 'Bring Emma to this location and you'll get your son back.' I might have thrown God in there a few times. She was easy to lead with all the drugs Scott was feeding her. I certainly couldn't have just taken you. A hunter goes missing from inside the base and who would get the blame? Huh?"

"I don't know."

"You do, tell me."

"The vampire would get the blame. Rightly so, it seems."

"Maybe, but you didn't trust me right from the start. A little trust can go a long way, Emma. I might not want to kill you so badly if you had only just believed in me."

"Fuck you." I spat.

My mouth was so dry that nothing came out. Charlie chuckled, another whole lit cigarette in his mouth.

"You've made your point. Now it's time for me to make mine.

Mary wasn't up to the job. She failed. In the long run, a good thing for her—her son's appetite is insatiable. But it's high time my boss gets what he wants, and what he wants is you."

"Why...why me?"

"Question and answer time is over."

Leech cleared his throat. His hands formed a steeple on top of his head and slid down to smooth his dwindling hair.

"Where are my manners? I forgot to make introductions. *Hermits*."

Quick wonderings of what was behind those hoods had flitted through my head. But I let it go, afraid my thoughts might spin the universe in an adverse direction. *They're covered up for a reason*, I thought. But in the end, the hermits were unveiled anyway. Sometimes bad things are inevitable and every road leads to suck.

These ones looked like the others I had experienced, with bald lumpy heads, fangs like a Python's, and opaque skin. But something was different, too. From my previous encounters with vampire society's lower class, I recalled the wild eyes, bulging with little direction and dripping with a sticky hunger. These ones had red eyes, and they observed me with cold calculation, as if seeing through me, memorizing me from the inside out.

My gun was happy to return. I believe it was smiling.

I pointed it at each hermit, before settling on Leech. Ears twitched. Leech smiled and rubbed his thick hands together.

"And the wheel goes round and round."

"I'll kill him," I said, speaking gun-in-face, a special kind of language. Sure, I only had one bullet, but one bullet was one bullet was one bullet. With good aim, it would do the trick.

Leech seemed unbothered. "They're a bit on the ugly side, but all the better to scare humans with. They take orders and are stronger than your average vampire. I'm not sure where that comes from. Rage?"

I started to feel like he was trying to sell me a hermit.

I'll take two.

My friend will just love them!

Please tell me you gift wrap.

"Strange, I never thought of the coincidence until now."

"What fucking coincidence?" I looked at Charlie, he looked back. My gun felt like it was fused to the palm of my hand.

"The hermits do scare humans…they do. But scaring *vampires* is their forte."

Movement on my left. Near Charlie. I swung my gun hand around.

A hermit was at Charlie's throat, not with teeth but with an enormous needle. The end pierced Charlie's neck. There was a liquid in it. Clear. Unidentifiable. I've never been a fan of needles. Needle fans came in two categories: addicts and grandmothers. But whatever was in that needle scared the crap out of Charlie, and I needed to do something. Leech *tsked*.

"We've been through this before."

"Remind me."

"You've only got one bullet, Charlie would die, you'd die, and vampires would go on to reign for all eternity."

Shit. Right. The damn gun might as well have not been loaded at all, for all the good it was doing me. The hermit at Charlie's neck glared, its red eyes leaking a yellow liquid. It stuck its tongue out and suggestively slid it back and forth, up and around.

Oh, what the hell.

I fired my gun.

It hit the pervert, opening its chest. The hermit let go of the syringe, but a flying bit, possibly a piece of rib, compressed the plunger and forced the needle about a half inch into Charlie's neck. It stuck there. Charlie whacked at it, unintentionally pushing the needle in a fraction more. He started to scream.

The skin around the needle bubbled and blackened, and the smell of burnt flesh filled the air. The cigarette had long fallen from his lips. Charlie's mouth opened wide. He banged his back against the lockers hard, using pain to ease pain. He grabbed at the needle with frantic hands. It dislodged and fell to the floor, unbroken.

Another hermit moved in. I flung my now-empty gun at it. The thing was fast, but the gun snapped its nose and the *crack* of its own face appeared to surprise it. I got the second I needed.

I dove for the needle.

My slick hands wrapped themselves around the syringe, fumbled, dropped it, picked it up again. The barrel was still nearly full with the burning stuff, which was good for Charlie (he hadn't gotten much in his system) and good for me. I turned on the floor to face the hermits with the needle pointing upward and my thumb on the plunger.

The hermit I hit on the nose hadn't taken long to recover. It landed on me and started to writhe like we were screwing and not trying to kill each other. It raised its hips and lowered them, raised them again and began to lower them.

"You want some of this!" I repositioned the syringe between my legs, and the hermit came down on it. The plunger depressed all the way.

The screaming was near-unbearable.

The hermit stood and tore its cloak away, revealing its naked body.

From its groin to its belly, a blackness ate a path through whatever was there. Skin and sex organ were gone. There was a sound like gas escaping, and gore emptied onto me. A lot of it was ash, but I flung a charred intestine from off my bare midriff.

I dropped the needle.

I thrust my foot into the gut-dropping hermit, which was enough to bring the thing down. It fell into another one coming my way and both tumbled to the floor.

Charlie was above me, clutching the lockers like they were a safe zone. His wound looked in desperate need of an economy-size bottle of disinfectant; his dark eyes had turned glassy. If I expected vampire-on-my-side as my next weapon, I had another thing coming.

I got on my feet and drew my stake.

Leech was nowhere to be seen. The fourth hermit ran at me. I misjudged the distance and thrust the stake forward too soon, allowing it to be taken and snapped in two. I removed my other stake, and the hermit thrust an arm out, knocking the wooden weapon over to the other side of the room. I screamed and kicked the troublesome hermit into the dressing room.

I looked around frantically. The hermit with the gut-dropping dance partner was up off the floor and pissed. Movement from behind told me that the one I had just thrown into the dressing room had had a quick recovery. My weapon supply was extinguished.

There was the floor polisher. *No.* There was an unopened package of inkjet paper on the desk. *What, you gonna paper cut them to death?*

A pencil sharpener was attached to the end of the desk. It was one of those old-fashioned ones with the circular dial for adjusting to the correct pencil size and a handle to make you work for your sharpened pencil. My eyes left the sharpener and scanned the desktop again. *Where there is a sharpener*, I thought, *there are sharpened...*

Bingo.

I lunged for the desk. A bundle was held together by a green elastic. Five or six number 2s, probably made of real lead—a no-no in this day and age. Each tip came to a sweet, sweet point.

I ripped at the bundle and got two pencils in my left hand and three in my right. I stuck my arms behind my back, not wanting to give these vamps any reason to be cautious with me. I was a meek little lamb. *Look at me. I'm a meek little lamb.*

"Come to mama," I said, and they did.

They looked like they were flying the way their cloaks billowed out, but vampires couldn't fly. Everybody had said so. I raised my arms up with pencils gripped and points out.

The hermit I had bowled down with the gutless one hit first. I stabbed two pencils into its chest, and it turned to dust. The bundle in my other hand got the dressing room hermit in the shoulder. Momentum carried us to the locker unit. We hit it and landed on the floor. The unit rocked and fell forward.

I scrambled.

Behind me, the hermit grappled for my leg.

The lockers came down on top of us. Pain surged through my body. I cried out and tried to dislodge myself, but my legs were stuck good. In the dark triangle of space formed by my lower half, locker unit, and hermit, I could see the top of the hermit's bald head too close to my thigh.

I couldn't tell whether it still had a grip on me. I hoped the pain in my legs was from the lockers falling on them, but what if it wasn't?

What if it was something more permanent? More eternal? I looked for an object to grab onto and pull myself free, but nothing more than dirty floor surrounded me. I glanced down at the hermit, still unmoving but likely not dead.

The room, it had emptied. Even the gutless wonder had somehow made it out.

"Charlie," I whispered. "Are you there?" I sensed movement near the doorway. "Charlie?"

"No, not Charlie"

Leech. And he didn't have a scratch on him. The one that should be beaten to a pulp didn't have a scratch on him. He stopped a safe distance from my fingertips and leaned over me. The skin on his face fell forward in folds.

"You've made a mess of things, bitch."

"Where's Charlie?" I asked, through gritted teeth.

Leech raised a boot heel and brought it down on my forehead. The pain was excruciating. I tried to grab his foot, but he was too quick. He leaned closer, like a scientist observing his test subject.

"No more questions."

"Fuck you," I said.

His heel came down again, twice, much faster than my injured body could move.

"Learn to be nice."

I laughed. "I can't wait to kill you."

Again, the heel. "All in good time, you violent little bitch."

I didn't want the heel anymore. In my confusion, I tried to appeal: "Please…how can you…do this?"

Leech laughed. "I'm a vampire. Everything's a go."

He raised his heel and brought it down a fourth time. I saw stars. Then the stars became stakes—shiny, sharp stakes. I reached up to grab one, but they vanished. Leech reeled back, thinking I was making a move for him.

"No, no," he said, swaying a finger at me. He raised his heel.

"Your boss," I said, coughing it out. I was grasping at straws now, but Leech took his foot away to listen. "Your boss...would he be pleased if you killed me? Because my head hurts really bad, and I feel weak...yeah...I think I might be dying." There it was. Fear. Vampires could feel fear like us. I laughed. "Go away, you fuck."

Fear turned to anger and I was sure I should have kept my mouth shut, but it had felt so good. Sometimes zipping the pie hole is impossible. I expected the heel again. A few more kicks and my forehead would collapse, and Leech would have the honor of trailing my brain matter through that shitty little store. His boss might kill him, but I would be dead too, so what did it matter? And not just dead, but dead from the heel of a Judas vampire. Such a sad way to go.

Leech's big hands clenched. His face seemed to inflate, as if emotion were helium. I closed my eyes. Then I opened them. I wanted to see it coming. If those were my last minutes of life, I'd live them. I would maybe even make another attempt at grabbing his foot. What the hell. My reflexes weren't what they used to be, but the effort wasn't going to be the thing that killed me.

Leech moved his orangutan face down closer to my face, his eyes daring me to make a move. If I wasn't still stuck, oh the fun I could have. I thought about going for his eyes, but in the end, I'd still be stuck. Whatever I did that didn't kill him would only make him madder.

His fat lips wrapped around words that weren't what I expected: "Wait here."

It was the last thing I wanted to do and the only thing I could do.

Leech returned shortly with two more hermits. He had been holding out on me. Their cold, bony hands gripped my arms. He swung a syringe above my head. This one had a smaller barrel than the one used on Charlie, but the needle itself was longer. Leech looked pleased, and I couldn't say what made me feel worse—that he was about to plunge that point into my battered head or that he was so happy about it.

The needle came down. All the pain in my body transferred to my head. My eyes crossed as the plunger depressed and the contents of the syringe were emptied into me. Leech and the hermits blurred, as did the office behind them. My world went dark except for a tiny pinpoint of color where undeterminable things still happened. It was as if I had been sucked through the needle and was now peering out from it.

Then, the color was gone.

CHAPTER TWENTY-EIGHT

I DIDN'T REMEMBER MUCH.

I remembered floors and ground. Dirt. Eating dirt.

These were the things I had personal contact with during my semiconscious state. There was pain, too. The vampires were not taking good care of my body, but they needn't have to. The instructions had been simply not to kill me. If things went as planned, a bruised, banged-up human body would be of little consequence.

I was dragged for most of the way and picked up only when time or risk became a factor. Pavement was slower-going. I welcomed soft grass and smooth wooden floors. Steps tempted them, I'm sure, but a few good bangs to the head were too chancy.

Stillness was short lived. In the truck, through hazy vision, I thought I saw Charlie lying next to me, beaten and blood-covered. I gathered the strength to move my hand and place it on his shoe. It gave me comfort, and I hoped it did him, too.

I passed out on a decorative rug on which slaves played instruments under weeping willows and white men carried muskets off to war.

~

Silk, rose-scented sheets covered me.

I brought my hands up to my forehead and found a new sore bump. I sat up and ran my hands over my face and down my neck and the rest of my body, expecting to find something missing. All appendages were accounted for, but my clothes were gone, replaced by a backless black negligee with delicate straps. I shivered and yanked the bed's linens up to my chin.

The bedroom was bigger than the one at the Plan B house. It seemed a future on the run held rooms more substantial than ones before, which would've been very nice if I wasn't, well, on the run. This room was dark with an entitled elegance. Three chandeliers spiraled cascades of crystal from the ceiling. A fire in the fireplace jumped and sparked over new wood. Above it, an empty copper candle holder rested on a marble mantle. Two leather chairs sat in front of the fireplace, each with their own table. A perspiring, half-empty glass of water or booze occupied a coaster on one of the tables.

The bed was stately and firm. Three windows were on the far wall. Two doors, one ajar and with light coming through, led someplace, and I was going to find out where. I let go of the sheets and swung my legs over the side of the bed. My toes hung several inches off the floor. Below my feet was the rug I remembered from my daze.

I walked toward the open door and was nearly there when the second door swung open. An elderly woman entered dressed in a servant's uniform. She was thin and small, with hard features and hair the color of fog. She carried a tray of six square glass jars to the fireplace, and with the balancing skills of a trapeze artist, went up on tiptoe to place the jars one by one into the copper holder.

With all the copper slots full save for one, she headed back toward the door, not sparing me a glance. I couldn't tell if she was a vampire. I had yet to see one as old as her. If you asked me, it was quite the bum deal.

I spoke because I had nothing to lose: "Wait."

The woman did not falter. I tried again.

"Please...I need your help." She opened the door, walked through, and went to close it behind her. "No!" I rushed forward and arrived at the door just as the lock was being turned over from the outside. I grabbed the knob and pulled. The knob came off in my hand.

"I've been meaning to fix that."

I jumped. My hand opened involuntarily, releasing the knob to the floor. I turned toward the voice.

A window was open. A man stood by it, but not a man—a vampire. With this one, you could tell. With this one, I was willing to bet that undeath was more him than human had ever been.

The vampire was a bit taller than me, with long black hair strung loosely in a ponytail. He wore black jeans and a gray vintage shirt that had the word "NO" printed on the front. He grinned at me, showing fangs and dimples, as if we had just shared a joke.

"Who are you?" I asked, backing away and attempting to cover up my scantily clad body. He took a step forward.

A familiar song started from the corner of the room and a record player that hadn't been there before.

"The Rolling Stones," the vampire said, nodding toward the player. "'Sympathy for the Devil.' Do you like their work?"

I shook my head.

"Wow, really? I've seen them twelve times live. Actually, Mick's a good friend of mine. He still plays, you know. Sometimes vampires abandon the talents they had as humans for the more…pressing…desire, but not Mick…no. Undeath has been good to him. Tweaked his ability. Made him *better*."

He continued: "Can't say the same for Keith, though. Shame. It was kind of inevitable, I thought. Mick had to find him and put him out of his misery. I don't condone killing hermits, but for a friend…well, you know how it is."

I passed the fireplace, now. Heat licked at my bare legs. I glanced at the jars. Something was moving inside them. Throbbing in a cloudy liquid.

The vampire came forward, slowly, moving like the female vampire I had spoken to at Club Vein—the one that Cooper hadn't been able to take his eyes off of. Every bend and shift of limbs had a purpose beyond my comprehension.

"What have you done with Charlie?"

"Don't worry about your friend. He's being attended to…as one of us." A southern drawl was coming out, not like Topps' Texan accent but more northern in dialect. He continued: "You look like her. The others didn't. That always confused me."

The vampire stuck his hands in his pockets. He looked down at the floor. "I have to ask you something. It's kind of…difficult. I don't know. I'm not usually a vampire that gets flustered." He looked back up at me, eyes big. "Do you…do you think you still love me?"

My heart thudded in my chest and it seemed to be keeping time with whatever was in those jars.

"I don't know you."

"See, that's where you're wrong. You've known me for a very, very long time."

I felt ill. The air in the room had changed—had become stifling.

"*I don't know you!*"

The vampire didn't seem offended by my forceful denial. He unstuck his hands from his pockets.

"Then I'll introduce myself. You see, there were those who didn't understand. Made me out to be some kind of serial killer, killing at random and stalking young girls in the night. But it wasn't like that. I've always loved you and I couldn't let you go. My name's Mabon, and you are Sarah." He motioned for me to sit. I shook my head.

Mabon shrugged and sat himself. He slouched low in the chair and folded one leg over the other. The fire reflected in his eyes like hell itself was trapped in them.

"One hundred and forty-three years and it still feels like yesterday."

THEN:
MABON

The boy held up the bug for the girl to have a look.

She leaned in and brought a delicate finger up to touch it. The boy's grin widened.

"*Bzzzzzt!*" he shouted, raising his palm and the insect to just a centimeter from the girl's nose. She screamed and ran to the porch, a cascade of auburn ringlets bouncing behind her.

The boy laughed. He blew lightly on the bug and it flew off, up over the slave quarters and over the cotton field, which would very soon be ready for picking.

The girl turned on her heel and crossed her arms tightly under her bosom, making it appear bigger. The boy stopped laughing, but a smile lingered. His heart beat in his chest.

"You're not mad, are you?"

"I have never been treated with such disrespect."

The boy knew that wasn't true. Her father was a drunk. More than once he had seen her black and blue, horrid bruises clouding her beautiful face. She would tell him it was a door and he would tell her

523

right back that he was inclined to take that door off its hinges.

"I'm sorry. Can you see it in yourself to forgive me?"

"I'm not sure that I can."

"What if I sing you a song? It's a real nice one."

The girl tilted her head. "Have you sung it to anyone else before?"

"No. It's only for you."

The girl moved over to the edge of the porch. She sat, her dress spread out around her. She folded her hands on her lap.

"Very well, but do make it quick. I must get home for dinner."

The boy knew she was just playing with him, and he went along. He quite enjoyed it, if he were being honest. He bowed his head and cleared his throat. He got down on one knee because Wash had told him it was the only way to sing to a lady. He didn't mind the dirt. The boy had been working in the field all day and hadn't gotten a chance to change. Besides, he was sure the girl would die of shock if she ever saw him in clean clothes, and he would never want that.

The boy sang the song and didn't miss a word. He could learn songs quickly. This one he had memorized the night before. He'd heard Wash singing it to Lilly, and it was the most beautiful song he'd ever heard.

"Sing this here tune to a lady," Wash had said, "and God will shine his light on you, young sir, and that lady will never look at you the same."

The boy remained on his knee until after he had finished. When it came to the girl, it was his Second Favorite Place to be. He was yet to experience his First Favorite Place, but he knew what it was and that when it happened it would be glorious, so he appropriately reserved the moniker.

The girl smiled. The light from the barn played with her hair, which could make a boy jealous. Her eyes welled with tears. The boy stood.

"I didn't mean to make you sad," he said.

"No," she said, wiping quickly at her eyes. "No, you have it wrong. You make me very, very happy."

She stood, too, running her hands down her dress to straighten it. The girl's tears were already gone. She had never been good at emotion. The boy hoped that one day he'd be able to make her feel freely, without being ashamed of it.

"That song...Wash taught it to you?"

"Yes, I learned it last night. Wash's father used to sing it to his mother, and his mother sang it to Wash when he was just a baby in the crib. Can you imagine Wash as a baby? It makes me laugh. All that wicked humor just waiting to get out."

"You know that's why my daddy doesn't like you."

The boy had always known that her daddy didn't like him, but Wash wasn't the reason. It stemmed back to a long-running feud between her father and his father and the woman they both loved: his mother. He wasn't going to tell the girl that. He wasn't sure she knew and he didn't want to contradict her.

The boy didn't respond, so the girl continued: "It's because you're friends with negroes and you go out and work in the field with them like you're one of them."

"But you like Wash," the boy said.

The girl rolled her eyes. "Of course I like Wash. He might just be the funniest person in all the South." The boy laughed at that. He agreed. "But I don't go to market with him, and I don't go around flaunting him as my friend because it's wrong. People don't take kindly to that. Do you know what the townsfolk call you and your daddy?"

"I don't care."

"They call you the White Negroes."

The boy nodded. He knew all this. They had been through it before; it was their bone of contention. The girl didn't dislike negroes, and she'd speak angrily of the horrid way her father treated their own slaves. But the girl's family was much wealthier than his and believed in maintaining appearances. *People talk* she would say *and if you care about us being together one day, you should listen to what is said about you.'*

The girl's father never agreed to the two of them spending time together, and as long as his parents were married and in love, that truth would never change.

The girl glanced nervously across the fields toward her home. "I have to go. It's getting late."

The screen door opened behind them. His mother appeared. She had a softness about her that would stale during the war.

"Mabon, time for dinner. Oh, hello Sarah. Will you be joining us on this beautiful evening?"

"No, ma'am. I'm sorry, but I must be getting home."

"Is your mother feeling better?"

"Yes, she's fine. She sends her appreciation for the tea. She said she's never had tea quite like it."

"Tell her it's a family recipe and she's welcome to it any time."

"I will, ma'am. Goodbye, Mabon."

"Goodbye, Sarah."

For the past year, Sarah Johnson would give Mabon Blackwell a kiss on the cheek before parting. Her lips were so soft that that kiss would stay with Mabon through the evening and the following day and make the task of picking cotton under a hot sun more bearable. Mabon took a step closer to her, but Sarah turned and bounded away like a frightened deer. He looked back at his mother who smiled knowingly before closing the door and disappearing into their home.

Mabon caught sight of Sarah one last time as she slipped into some moonlight. Her white dress glowed fiercely, as if it were a beacon sending messages to far-off planets. Then, she was gone.

~

The war came like an uninvited guest, and in the end, it was anything but civil.

At fifteen, Mabon avoided the draft. His father was too old to be drafted, but he enlisted anyway, he said to do his part. Lincoln's nomination to the presidency had the majority of Southerners talking nervously about the end of slavery. His parents whispered that they wouldn't quite mind if slavery ended, but they only ever did that whispering amongst themselves. This gave Mabon the impression that his family did worry about appearances, sometimes. Hostility and Southern pride were rampant and it was a bad time to be a negro lover.

The Blackwells had three negroes helping them tend a small plot of land that Jim Blackwell, Mabon's father, inherited before his son was born. Wash, Lilly, and their child Titus were bought from a slave runner just outside of town. Jim Blackwell had said he'd never seen anything like it. A billion negroes chained together, some without even the luxury of shoes. He told his family that life couldn't get much worse than that, so he took three, which was all he could afford at the time, and set off to give them a better life. He paid the negroes for their work, and they could end the day when they wanted. Five years of mutual respect led to a friendship between the two families that neither was quick to abandon.

"That's the Southern way," Jim Blackwell said, from his seat on the porch the night before he would go off to war. He used this phrase often, but only upon hearing of bad behavior from his fellow countrymen. It wasn't used to excuse the behavior, but to shine a light on the irony.

"Indeed it is," Wash agreed, before both men broke into fits of laughter. The rest of the group looked at each other, and Lilly rolled her eyes in amusement. Titus sat with his head down and his legs not dangling, but still, over the side of the porch. He was old enough to know what tomorrow meant.

Wash had insisted on accompanying Jim Blackwell into war. Body servants, as they were called, could be brought along to cook, clean, and perform other menial chores for their masters. They were not allowed to fight, but Wash had plans to protect his friend at all costs. Before this opportunity, Wash would lie awake at night wondering how he could ever really repay Jim for saving his family's life and returning to them what Wash believed to be the most precious thing of all: their dignity.

The two families sang that night, but sadness was in the air and what was meant to be a happy song was happy no more. It had always been one of Mabon's favorites, but that was the last time he would sing it.

The following day, the dirt road rose in small clouds beneath the two men's feet. They were crouched over from the weight of their supplies; the women had inundated them with comforts from home.

Fathers said goodbye to sons, and husbands to wives. Jim Blackwell was a kind man of few words, but he put his hand on Mabon's shoulder and Mabon heard his father's voice in his head as good as if he had spoken out loud. *Take care of your mother, you're the man of the house now. Do not mourn me if I pass, but remember that love is the most important thing of all. I love you, son.* Mabon realized his father had said the last part out loud. He cleared his throat.

"I love you too, sir."

Mabon and the others stayed to watch until the two men dropped out of sight. The heat of the morning promised a scorcher. Lilly was the first one to speak, before they all dispersed to get on with the chores minus four strong hands.

"Man gets the killin' in him," she said, "real hard to get the killin' out."

The time would come when Mabon would understand what she meant.

~

Mabon saw Sarah as often as he could, which was never as much as pleased him.

Like his father, hers had gone to war, along with her three older brothers. Unlike his father, hers was a high-ranking officer, which meant that the Southern cause infiltrated her young life. Her mother started a group to make clothing and banners. The women also practiced drilling and shooting. Sarah's mother insisted she take part in all activities, and the girl was usually adorned with tiny confederate flags.

As the years passed, and the war still went on, times got harder. Mabon, his mother, Lilly, and even Titus, who was now at the age he could help, were sore every day from work. Chores never seemed to end, and nighttime would come too soon, but then again, not soon enough. His mother and Lilly sewed clothes for their husbands by candlelight. Well past midnight, Mabon could hear them talking quietly. Paper was scarce and letters from the battlefield became few and far between. The ones they did receive were written on used stationary with old writing crossed off and new writing squeezed into diminishing space, and the two families would crowd around the messy sheets of paper, attempting to decipher them as if they were written in some long-dead language.

Jim Blackwell and Wash were doing "as fine as they could be," and they urged everyone not to worry, until the day the letter came announcing their deaths or "The death in service to the Union of Mr. Jim Blackwell and his property, Wash Limber." The letter didn't have to be deciphered; it was crisp, readable, and new. Mabon wondered how property died and knew it must be a nobler death than most.

His mother broke down. Between tears, she said that she couldn't understand life anymore. Lilly hugged Titus to her bosom as he struggled to free himself, her face grim.

Mabon recalled at that moment the last thing his father had said to him: *Love is the most important thing of all.*

He ran.

His mother called after him, tears choking her pleas. He took the narrow path at high speed. The wind pushed against him, adding resistance, perhaps knowing something he didn't.

Sarah was ahead on the path, coming toward him—a thousand Confederate flags waving from her bodice.

The two stopped an inch from each other, too close.

"They're dead, Sarah. My father and Wash are dead."

"I know, I heard. I'm so sorry, Mabon."

A kiss.

"I don't know what to do. Nothing seems real."

"I know," she said.

Another kiss.

"Help me."

"I will."

They lay down on the cold grass. Her lips were warm. Her body pressed against his. Mabon was finally in his First Favorite Place. In Sarah's arms.

"Are you sure?" he asked.

She spoke through excited breaths. "Choices…are…difficult—"

"—until you make them easy," Mabon finished, kissing her and forgetting everything.

~

A month went by without seeing her. It was hard to breath with her not around.

Mabon went to call at her house twice, but both times her servant had turned him away, saying she was ill and could not have visitors.

"Is it serious?" Mabon had asked.

"I don't think so, sir," the servant had said. "I'll let her know you stopped by."

Mabon was worried. He didn't think her father had been home, but *there is a chance*, he thought. Sarah had said his drinking had gotten worse being away at war. The times he had come home on leave, he was angry and incoherent. *So help me*, Mabon thought. *So help me if he's laid a finger on her.*

For Mabon, life at home had become unbearable. When his father and Wash had left, the farm transformed into a shell of its former self, like what made it good had been taken out. Now that the two men were dead and never coming back, a sadness had seeped into everything and everyone, through timber and bones.

His mother kept at the chores, and little else was allowed to consume her time. Any attempt at communication was met with silence. Lilly tried to take her to a dance in town one night, and they made it halfway there before Mabon's mother went into fits of rage. When the fits had subsided, his mother sat down in the middle of the road with her legs crossed and her hair flying like a banshee's. So Lilly sat too, and they sat there until Mabon's mother decided three hours later to get up and go home. Lilly had told Mabon that God was watching over them that night and it wasn't yet time for two old ladies to join their husbands.

Mabon understood why his mother was acting the way she was, and it took all the strength he had not to join her down that path. He went into town only when he had to. Seeing the townsfolk churned an anger in Mabon he didn't fully understand. They looked pathetic touting their wartime paraphernalia—supporting a government that sent them off to war to die in rags for little more than pride and speculation. If it hadn't been for all of them, Mabon thought, his father and Wash would be alive. The two families would be still together, still happy.

He knew his father had never wanted to go to war, that he hadn't believed in it. But it was forced upon him. In small-town, nineteenth century America, a man needed his neighbors. They may have been willing to look past friendship with a negro family, but to shirk your God-given responsibility as a Southron was unforgivable.

532

As mad as seeing townsfolk made Mabon, it was nothing compared to when he spotted the golden insignia: three stars in a wreath denoting a high-ranking officer, usually a general. *They should know better*, he thought, his jaw so tight it felt like it might shatter. Men with power had the responsibility to know what was best, and they so rarely did. The war was wrong. Sending people beneath you off to die was wrong.

One day, Mabon passed a general in town. He had gone in to trade an old pair of Wash's shoes for two bushels of salt from William Barnwell, the owner of a salt factory visiting from the city. The shoes were too big for Titus and too small for Mabon. They had found a notice for trade in the local paper and thought that instead of waiting for Titus to grow into his father's feet, they'd get to killing the hog and preserving meat for the winter.

The general was in full uniform, clean and well-pressed. His hair was done in ringlets and his beard neatly trimmed, unlike the overgrown and wild beards of most fighting men Mabon had come across. The general was accompanied by a young officer with a gaunt face and several of the town's ladies dressed in their best. He walked with pride and openly flirted with each woman. Mabon could smell perfume on the man as he walked by.

He gripped Wash's shoes in his hands. They folded in his fists, the dry leather cracking. The general glanced at Mabon casually at first, before returning a concerned gaze.

"Can I help you, son?"

Mabon saw red. "Not yet," he said, passing.

Not yet, Mabon thought again, not knowing why he had spoken those words and why they then echoed in his head. He looked down and released his fists. Wash's shoes were scrunched, and he gently pulled them apart. The leather of the right one had split completely down the side. They were no longer good for trade.

"Strange fellow," the general said, behind him now but not quite out of earshot. The women giggled and politely whispered.

His mother cried when he returned home with the broken shoes. The family would have no meat that winter.

~

Sarah called for Mabon one month, two days, five hours, and sixteen minutes after they made love.

He was in the barn finishing chores and he knew she was there before she was. Sarah had a presence about her that Mabon could recognize before it filled any space near him in physical form.

His heart thudded in his chest. Mabon turned just before Sarah came through the doorway. The light from outside was at her back, and he rushed to her, turning her around to get a look at her face. It was flushed but without a mark.

"I've been so worried," he said. "I went to your house."

"I know."

"Twice."

"I know."

"Are you ill?"

"Not quite."

"Then what? What kept you away from me for so long?"

Mabon's hands clutched the girl, as if they could keep her there in that spot in front of him forever. She pulled free of his grasp, and he didn't object, because what she wanted, he wanted.

"I'm with child." His heart stopped.

"How?" It was the first thing that came to his mind.

534

"What?"

Mabon laughed. A short laugh that hardly meant much: nervous energy filling time.

"Are you sure?" he asked, thinking it a better question.

"Yes. I haven't bled. I've been sick every morning. And Clemmy's been dreaming of fish...oh god, I guess since I got back that night." Clemmy was a household servant who had minded Sarah her whole life and, as most stories of the kind go, took more interest in the girl than her own mother.

"Your parents?"

"Daddy hasn't been back from the battlefield in two months. Mother's very busy with her activities. Showed me a flag she made the other day half the size of Virginia. I would've laughed if I wasn't in the middle of a great mess."

"I see," Mabon said. Sarah's eyes watered. She turned away from him. "No...I *see*, Sarah." She faced him again. He smiled.

"I don't understand."

"This is our chance. It's our time to get away from it all. From the war, from stupid pride, from your father and my mother. She's never forgiven me for the shoes."

"The shoes?"

"Never mind. None of that matters any more. Run away with me, Sarah."

"You're insane."

"Maybe."

"Where will we go?"

"Anywhere but here. Europe? We'll have a family and spend the rest of our lives with each other. The horses. Your family still has horses? Yes. Good. We'll take a horse or two and head north…to Boston. What's wrong?"

"The Yanks will steal our belongings and have their way with me…and maybe with you. I hear some of them have horrible deformities. They're monsters, Mabon."

"Just stories, Sarah. Those are just stories. We'll tell them we're on their side, even if we aren't. We'll be okay as long as we're together."

"My daddy will come find us."

"He's got the war now. He doesn't need you."

Sarah looked hurt. Mabon tried to explain: "I meant he's got another release for his anger. He doesn't need you for that any more. I know he'll miss you."

"As sure as day, he'll come for us," she said, all dread and certainty, and seeing her expression the boy knew it to be true.

"We'll be long gone when he does," Mabon said, allowing the reality of what was happening course through his veins. "Is your mother at home?"

"No, it's just the servants, but why—"

"Go, Sarah. To your house. Gather your things. Only bring what you can carry. Meet me at the stables in one hour. Can you do that?"

"Yes, but—"

"Do you trust me?"

"Of course I do."

"Then believe me when I say that we'll get through this."

Hesitancy passed over her face, but her eyes were clear when she lifted them to Mabon's and kissed his lips gently.

"I do believe. I'll be there."

She smiled nervously and patted soft palms against her hair. Mabon accompanied her to the barn door. The smell of wet hay was floral. Dull colors livened. The night outside felt like none the boy had ever experienced. On his hurried path to the house, Mabon turned back to watch her. He wanted to shout admissions of love to her, but he waited too long and in a flash she was gone. He thought: there will be time.

They had their whole lives ahead of them.

~

Her belly.

He placed a hand on it.

The horses kicked and whinnied in their stalls. Mabon wasn't sure how long he had been at the stables. Time was not sacred to him anymore. It would be the fiend that refused to set him free.

He was speaking. His voice sounded far away, like he was listening to it through a sea conch. He made out a word "No" and then another "No" and realized that that was all he was saying. It was that one word joined together so many times to form another word that never ended.

Sarah stared back at him, her mouth slightly open, a contusion on her cheek, her skin no longer rosy but blue. Mabon's fingers worked furiously at the Confederate flag cinched around her neck, but he couldn't loosen it. He spoke coaxingly:

"Please, please come off. I'll do what you say...anything you want...just come off. *Please.*"

His nails dug into her flesh, and he pulled his hands away frantically, his whole face quivering.

There were voices in the distance, men's voices, not his this time. Dogs snarled and choked against taut leashes. They were coming.

Mabon gathered Sarah off the floor and into his arms. He rocked her gently, plucking hay and dirt from off her dress and out of her hair.

Her eyes were vacant and Mabon's belief in the idea of a soul started here. Was there any truth in it, or was it just something he needed to be true? Mabon didn't care to know.

He spoke to his love softly, tears staining his face.

"Sarah...Sarah, my lovely. I'll find you again. We'll be together because...that's what is meant." He laid a kiss on her forehead and started to sing.

The stable doors shot open. Wind and rain came in with men and dogs, too many to count. Sarah's father led the pack, dark gray hair dripping wet and his eyes wide with crazy. He wore his uniform. The stars on his collar caught the dim light. Mabon winced.

"Damn you, Mabon Blackwell," he screamed, his voice competing with the wind in volume. "You killed my daughter, and I will have justice." He raised a black musket. It was too fine for war. This one had come from his private collection.

Mabon placed Sarah's body carefully on the ground next to her packed suitcase. He stood, his body shaking with rage. He raised his head and screamed. Muscles tensed against skin. Dogs that had been growling now whined and cowered behind their masters. Sarah's father aimed and shot.

Another man in uniform lunged and hit the gun with the back of his hand just as it went off, saving Mabon and the untarnished career of a well-respected general.

Mabon made a move for Sarah's father, his anger all-consuming. "It was *you*, you bastard!" he said, but the words came out a jumbled mess, as if he were speaking in tongues.

Several men separated from the group, rushing Mabon. The boy recognized some of them. Townsfolk. And soldiers, too. They shoved fists and metal muzzles into his body and forced him back onto the floor. A hand gripped the nape of his neck and pressed his face into an unpleasant mixture of mud and manure.

"You like to eat shit, don't you boy," one man said. A few laughed.

"Take him. Bring him to the jail," another man said. "*Go!*"

The men responded, lifting Mabon off the floor and dragging him toward the door. Mabon buckled in pain. A rib or two had been broken. A house servant came from around the corner. She was a plump negro with skin the color of fine chocolate. Mabon recognized her as Clemmy. The woman tore through the horde of white men and stopped several feet from Sarah's body. Her hands went to her mouth.

"Oh, my baby. No, my baby. What did you do? Oh no, Jesus, Satan's come a callin'."

Mabon spoke, but Clemmy wasn't looking at him and noise ate his words. She ran to Sarah's body, scooped it up in her big arms and cradled it, much like Mabon had done.

"It wasn't me!" he called to the woman. "I love her!"

~

The jail was filthy, but Mabon wasn't long for that place.

Two weeks and news of the North's fast approach spread on trembling lips. Families left their homes and belongings to go seek shelter deeper south. Sherman's army was coming, and rampant rumors had only ashes left in its wake.

"Take it," Jimmy said, handing Mabon the shotgun. "Go save your family." Mabon accepted the gun, and Jimmy nodded his approval.

Jimmy Gorgas was the jail keeper, and the two men had found friendship in the unusual place and short amount of time. Jimmy was at least 90 with no teeth and blue bulging eyes. He was a gentle sort, and

Mabon thought his only flaw might be that he was a countryman. Mabon told the jail keeper the morning after he was dragged in that he didn't do what they said he did, that he loved Sarah and she had been pregnant with his child and they were going to be a family, and the old man believed him. Two weeks was spent emptying bottles of whiskey and playing the odd game of cards. Under different circumstances, in another life, it would have been a pleasant time.

Jimmy winked at Mabon with long, thick lashes, and the one thing still young on him, and placed a rag of a hat on his head. He took another shotgun from a broken, dusty rack and went to the other occupied cell. In it was Rufus, a big man with questionable hygiene and a constant need to defecate. Rufus was there for armed robbery, and since his arrival two days earlier, an overwhelming miasma had taken over the jail. It skulked around them, and Mabon and Jimmy would hold their breath until their faces turned red.

"Now, Rufus," Jimmy said. "I know you ain't got no family, but it's either keep you here in this cell and let you get done by a Yank, or open this door so you can fight. You gonna fight, Rufus?" Rufus nodded, pudge shifting on his face. "That's good. Now don't make me regret this."

Jimmy unlocked Rufus' cell with a *clink clank* and shoved the gun into his meaty hands. During his crime, Rufus had gotten as far as the door of the bank when he was tackled and brought down by customers and tellers. People in town that day would swear the ground shook beneath their feet. Mabon wondered how a poor man during wartime could collect so much fat on his body.

Mabon thanked Jimmy before leaping out the door and bursting into the night. He ran through the town center, his bare feet painfully pounding dirt and rocks on the main road. His shoes had been taken from him before he was thrown in the cell. Prisoners didn't need shoes. Murderers didn't deserve them.

Just on the outskirts of town, flames licked emptied houses like starving beasts. The townsfolk who had stayed to fight now writhed on the ground missing arms, legs, heads.

The stories were true. Sherman had released hell unto the South.

Mabon passed the house that Sarah grew up in, a glorious mansion now reduced to smoldering heaps of soot and ash. Besides the hole left in his heart, everything Sarah was now gone.

Either her parents had gotten out of the house alive, or they hadn't. Several bodies were scattered across the property, all men, but none were her brothers or the general. The stables where he found her body were in rubble. The family's horses had maybe run off but were most likely escaped on or stolen by Union troops.

Mabon heaved through tired lungs as he followed the path to his home. Overgrown branches whipped his body. His ribs burned. Two had been broken the night of his capture and, a week later, set badly by a local man who played doctor during the war while the real doctor was away healing soldiers. Many died in his care over a span of five years, but only a bullet in the brain from a Yankee gun ended the man's practice.

Through trees and smoke, Mabon caught a flash of his house, still intact and standing, but it was his mind playing tricks. A second look and everything was dead, everything was burnt to the ground, nothing was left to remember anything by, what he saw, no future could be reaped from.

Mabon walked the grounds. Lit embers burnt his feet. Dark smoke clung to his skin like a burial shroud. He picked up stones and put them back down, not knowing why. He stepped over the body of a dead Union soldier naked from the waist up. There was a bullet through his chest and half of his face was burnt off. Ants queued for leftovers.

Mabon shouldered the shotgun Jimmy had given him and bent down over the dead soldier. With strength he didn't think he had, he lifted the body up to eye level and held it there. The soldier's face lacked skin and muscle, but the teeth were there, fixed in a post-mortem grin.

"Why?" Mabon muttered, shaking the body, his arms straining from the weight.

But the dead don't talk. He screamed and threw the soldier as far as he could, which wasn't far, and it landed with a *thump*, face-up and staring at Mabon with empty, grizzled sockets.

Mabon's chest heaved. He could feel that anger in him. It was a seed planted when his father and Wash had gone off to war, and now, as he stood amongst the black remains of his future, the seed was a thorn bush growing inside him, twisting and turning through his limbs and piercing his heart.

His country had wronged him, stripped him of everything he had ever cared about. God willing, he would take them all out. *I'll kill every last one of them*, Mabon thought, but then he laughed and the laughter revolted even the clogged air around him.

"What are you going to do? You're just a *farm boy*." He laughed again and thought he might never stop, when he saw it.

Movement by the edge of the forest.

An animal, Mabon thought. *One of Sarah's horses.*

He took a step toward the woods, which bordered the cotton field not 40 yards away.

There it was again.

Something stepped out from behind the trees. A figure in tattered clothes. Mabon was too far away to see whether it was a man or a woman or whether they were armed. He let the gun strap slip from off his shoulder, taking the shotgun into both hands.

"Hello there?" he yelled. The figure didn't move. It stood in the safety of shadows.

Mabon started toward it, walking fast and then settling into a run. The bottoms of his feet were raw. Every step was pain, but Mabon knew he'd need to get used to that; life and pain were inseparable.

He was aware that running toward the person might frighten whoever it was, and he imagined the figure raising a gun and firing, heard the sound of the bullet slicing the air, felt his skin, muscle, and bone break under the bullet's pressure, and heard himself scream out with elation.

The figure didn't raise a gun, though, or turn to flee. As Mabon got closer, he saw that it was a negro woman. She was wearing a torn dress and a shawl with a hood—a shawl like the one Lilly used to wear.

Mabon stopped abruptly, nearly tripping over himself. "Lilly? Is it you?"

Unless his eyes were playing tricks on him again, something was terribly wrong with the woman's face. The curves were unnatural, the right eye too big, the mouth too long. The woman turned to run into the forest.

"No, wait!"

Mabon cleared the field, jumping burning bushes and plunging through a break in the trees. He saw the woman ahead of him. She moved fast. The forest seemed to give way to her and remain unyielding for Mabon.

"Wait," Mabon said again.

He was losing her. Fog or smoke swallowed her and began closing in around him. He stopped, not able to see where he was going anymore. He leaned over, resting his hands on his knees and struggling for breath. Once he caught it, he used it to swear.

"What was that?" he said, to the black trees. Silence answered him. *The Yanks even killed the crickets*, Mabon thought with unease. A twig snapped behind him.

A flash of movement and the woman was on him before he could turn to face her. Mabon grunted and started to tell the woman to get off him, when her teeth sank deep into his neck.

He yelled out in shock and whirled around. He tried to shake her off, but she clung fiercely. Mabon staggered. His finger slipped on the shotgun's trigger and he fired two bullets. He aimed the next, but the gun had been emptied.

He backed against a tree, ramming her into it. She moaned but didn't fall off and continued sucking.

Mabon felt dizzy. He heard more shots ring out. His hands tensed open, allowing his own gun to fall from them. Another shot was fired somewhere close by and the woman shrieked. Her mouth released his neck with a *glurp*, and she sprang or fell off his back. He twirled and put his fists up, ready for a fight, but she was gone.

A man was coming toward him. Mabon put his hand to his neck to stop the flow of blood. It slid slickly through his fingers.

The man stood before Mabon, now. He was a weathered stranger with strawberry blond hair and a face to match. He aimed a steady gun at the gathering of shrubs the woman had escaped through.

"What the hell was that?" the man asked. "Never seen anything like it. Never in my life."

The man's eyes darted to and fro before finally landing on Mabon. "That's a terrible wound. My house is just over the hill and it still stands." He pointed off to the right. "My wife can...*try*...to mend it."

Blood spat from Mabon's neck, spraying the ground in front of the stranger's boots.

Mabon inched to his shotgun and leaned carefully to pick it up. He wrapped a shaking hand around it and started to walk away.

"Where are you going, son? That thing's still out there, you know. You won't get far bleeding like that. Don't be foolish, now."

Mabon could have explained where he was going, but it would not have made sense to the man. He was going to go find the beast that attacked him, but not to kill it. Mabon would offer himself to the thing and let it finish what it started.

When the woman attacked him, his basic survival instinct had taken over and he fought her. He didn't doubt that she had made a fatal wound, but he wasn't sure how long it would take to kill him, and the less time he had to spend walking that scorched horrid earth, the better. He would find her, and she would end his life quickly.

And set him free.

Mabon could have been worried that the woman was frightened far away by the gunfire, but he knew it wasn't so. The bitch had enjoyed him too much.

Mabon backtracked toward the farm, also the direction the woman had gone. He moved slowly and stopped twice feeling like he might get sick, but didn't. A couple of times he called out "Hello!" and "I'm here!" but quieted himself for fear the strawberry blond stranger might hear and come to his rescue again.

As each breath was forced in, Mabon began to wonder if he'd see Sarah in an afterlife. The idea that Sarah and his father and Wash might be waiting for him made him move faster. Mabon was sure his mother, Lilly, and Titus had made it to safety. Lilly was good at thinking fast. She was a survivor. That beast in the shawl was not Lilly, Mabon assured himself.

The fog was lifting, and everything that could be burned had been, so the smoke was dissipating too. Mabon made it to the farm and then circled back around toward the clearing where he was bitten. The blood from his wound was already drying, and his hand, which he had placed over the wound, was now stuck. He withheld a scream as he used his free hand to tear the other one off and the bite was reopened.

I should be dead by now, he thought. *Why am I not?*

Mabon wasn't a doctor, and, as far as he knew, there were no doctors in his lineage, but he didn't need an education in medicine to know that the beast had torn open a major artery, which meant certain death. Mabon wasn't sure how much time had passed, but he thought enough.

Though he had just reopened his wound, it already seemed to be healing. Mabon's only comfort was that he felt like he was dying. Every step was an effort. He hurt and ached and sweat covered him even though the air was cool. He had smelled rot not long after he'd been bitten and had mistaken the source for the damp woods around him, but the smell was coming from his own body and it was the reek of expiring flesh.

When he found the beast, not waiting and hungry for him, but dead and so close to where they violently met, he thought he might cry.

It was no matter that he brushed the woman's hood aside with the tips of his dirty toes and found nothing human behind it. It was no matter that his eyes fell upon a demon from the deepest depths of hell with bumpy brown skin and pointed teeth filling a mouth that stretched from ear to ear. What mattered to Mabon most was that death had not taken him, yet, and his chance for a quick escape was now gone.

He damned himself and the creature at his feet and the strawberry blond stranger, and his voice got stronger to damn the country that deceived him. His body began to lurch and spasm, and through the sheer pain of it all, he thought with excitement, *This is it!*

Mabon collapsed onto the beast. Instead of revulsion, he felt comfort. He pulled himself up and rested his head on her chest. A brown nipple poked through her rags. Her face was crooked, as if it was made of wax and Sherman's seething flame had recently been applied to it. Her left eye was normal, but the right was set back in a large, soft lump the size of an orange. She had no hair except for two small tufts, one above the left ear and the other at the top of her head, sitting like a very small cap. Her teeth were sharp, and they fascinated Mabon.

Resting in the arms of the beast, he closed his eyes and waited to die.

~

Mabon dreamt he found the general.

He made the general confess to killing Sarah, before he tore out his throat and drank his blood.

"Long live the South," the old man said, cowering under Mabon's glare.

Mabon smiled, and he was himself, except for he was alive and he didn't mind, and he had teeth like the beast's.

"Long live *me*," Mabon said, falling onto the general.

He awoke naked in blood. None of it was his. Dead soldiers surrounded him, their throats gaping, bloodless wounds. Mabon sat up. He slid his hand along the floor. The dark liquid spread thickly across it. He lifted his hand and watched the stuff stretch long and disconnect from his fingers.

It was the first day of his new life.

NOW:

The needle hit the record, and the room filled with angst.

The vampire I now knew as the one in my dreams danced in front of me. He strutted and popped up his shoulders. His hips swayed. His voice was throaty: sweat and blues.

Let the Midnight Special
Shine her light on me
Let the Midnight Special
Shine her ever-loving light on me

Mabon grinned and slumped back into his seat. "If you ask me, the second best way to listen to music is on vinyl. First being live, of course. I've never bothered with tapes or compact discs. Somewhere, someone has the vinyl version of the song you like." Mabon looked at the fire. He flicked a finger against a fang several times before pulling it away. "Sorry, force of habit. Like humans and nail biting." He flicked again.

"Let me go, Mabon. I'm not who you think I am."

"Umbrella on her shoulder, piece of paper in her hand. Did you know that new vampires are born and live with their fangs out and must force them to recede? You see, I'm the other way around, but today there's not the need to hide. It's evolution on the fast track."

Mabon plucked the glass off the table. He brought it up to his nose. He closed his eyes. I thought about running. About doing something. Anything. But his eyes reopened and he smiled like he knew what I was thinking and he'd love for me to try. I stayed put.

"So, where was I? Oh yes...I went to Europe afterward. Traveled everywhere, gaining knowledge. I found more like myself and lived amongst them, letting that thorn bush grow. When I returned to America, I got a job working for the man. Your government hired me to permanently retire enemies of the state...but I decided to let them live. It was classic. Decades of dangerous, powerful enemies of America walking its streets as vampires." Mabon put the glass down. He hadn't taken a sip. Ice cubes became liquid again. "But they got restless slinking in the shadows, as did I. That's when the final stages of my revenge plot began. I turned this country over to a new breed. My breed."

"Who are they—the vampires you want us to kill?"

The song ended. Another began, sounding much like the previous one. "They are my competition. I never would have imagined, but politics intrigue me. I've stepped into it, so to speak, and have decided to run for office. The surefire way to win is to eliminate the competition. I could do it myself, but the UVF frowns on violence for votes. The perfect way to avoid the radar was to trick a silly group of underground hunters into thinking they could save their lovely country."

"You're pathetic," I said, anger, sadness, and defeat bullying for control inside me. "You're too delusional to realize that you've become everything you hate."

"No, no," Mabon said, getting up off his chair and kneeling in front of me. He spread his arms along the arms of my chair. His breath smelled sweet and wrong. Chocolate-covered death. "That's where you're wrong. I *love* me. And you will, too. Oh, and a word to the wise…go easy on the proclamations. If you weren't my Sarah, you'd be long dead. Accept and be grateful, my lovely."

"Or I'll end up like them?" I asked, eyes toward the mantle. "Stuffed in a jar." Mabon stood smoothly. He walked over to the fireplace and the row of jars. The hearts had stopped pulsing. He leaned in close and tapped on the glass of one jar.

"Bodies trap souls like flycatchers. Sarah's not the only one inside you…there are others. That's where complication lies. There's one who got to you first." He turned to me. "If it's Sarah, you'll choose to love me. Otherwise, I'll have to start all over again from scratch. But hell, I've got time."

"Correct me if I'm wrong—I don't live in your fantasy world—but there are a lot less babies being born, and bodies are going to be getting mighty crowded, don't you think?"

Mabon shrugged as if the thought had never crossed his mind but was irrelevant anyway.

"Excuse me…I have a Save the Hermits charity ball to host. Filthy, fascinating creatures." The record skipped. "I'll leave that on. The music might relax you. The room over there is just a bathroom. No windows. You seemed interested. Ms. Mott will be by to add another log to the fire. If you need anything, ask. She's mute but not deaf."

He turned and danced himself to the door. The knob was still on the floor, and he bent to pick it up. He replaced it and stuffed a hand in his pocket for the key.

"On the farm, I used to be really good at fixing things. Not so much anymore. Sometimes, I miss that." He opened the door and paused. "Think about what I said. Once I'm done with your friends, I'll be back for you."

He closed the door behind him. The lock turned over.

I got up and ran. I didn't pull the knob this time but turned it carefully and waited for the catch. No luck. I leaned over and fingered the keyhole. I got close and put my eye up to it.

On the other side, empty useless hallway.

CHAPTER TWENTY-NINE

I WATCHED THEM COME.

They poured from limos and similar cars of class, black silk gowns and tuxedo tails lifting up in the wind and trailing behind like dark guardian angels.

Faces smiled. No smile was pretty. I recognized some but not from any meeting. I thought perhaps from magazines or television. In my head, in my head, flashed a photograph of a stiff man standing behind a podium in front of an undulating, adulating crowd.

Mabon's music was no longer playing. I had silenced it by tearing the record from the player and splitting the vinyl in two over my knee. The pieces were good and sharp. I imagined killing Mabon Blackwell not softly with his song upon his return. In reality, the plastic would be much too soft to penetrate a chest, but I held on to the pieces nonetheless.

I stood looking out the window. Ms. Mott hadn't been back to stoke the fire, and I couldn't find my clothes, or any clothes for that matter, so I remained cold wearing close to nothing.

I moved away from the window and headed for the bathroom. I had done one search already, but I'd do another and another until I found an opening to escape through. Mabon hadn't been lying. The room I'd been eyeing was a bathroom and it was windowless, though windows would apparently do me no good. The ones in the bedroom were locked and I was on the third floor. Jump and I'd be lucky to break a leg. From observation, armed guards with big fangs and big guns circled the house. Five were positioned out front at any given moment.

I crossed the room and passed the fireplace and the hearts on the mantle, motionless in their jars. I wondered if I had seen them beating or if fright had been getting the best of me. Even with training, fear could be a sneaky bastard.

The bathroom was bare. No items adorned anything. The tub was large like the bed. It was freestanding with a silver bird head faucet and scraggly silver claws gripping glass balls for feet. I squatted and looked underneath.

Clean.

I stood, knees cracking, and moved over to the vanity mirror. I avoided my reflection which clearly was avoiding me. I got my hands around the edges of the mirror and tugged. Nothing budged. Apparently, it wasn't the kind that opened.

There was a closet that was empty except for one fluffy white bath towel, a travel-size bottle of shampoo, and a bar of soap, still wrapped. Either the items were meant for me or the previous occupant of that room. I dared to wonder, just once, how that situation had turned out.

My body was fairly muck-free. Multiple bruises might've benefited from a hot bath or shower, but it wasn't going to happen.

I left the bathroom and moved along the wall, knocking at intervals. An oil painting hung of a woman with brown hair and a curved nose. She sat with a fat white Persian sinking into her lap. Both looked out at me haughtily. I took the painting down, expecting to find something worthy behind it—perhaps a lever that opened a secret door, or a safe holding the house plans and a book called *This Way to Destroying the Vampire Race*.

Nothing was behind the painting except for more wall. I continued my search at the fireplace, forcing myself to investigate the jars.

They were white glass and similar to the ones you'd find in a candy store filled with Swedish Fish or gummy worms. Each was sealed at the top. The liquid inside was probably formaldehyde, which, along with a tight seal, would help keep the hearts fresh. The last victim in the Heart Attack murders had been killed nearly two decades earlier, with the first ones dating back to the 1800s. But they were all in the same condition and only slightly varying in size.

I recalled eighth grade science class with Mr. Wendell. Room 201 was home to animal fetuses galore, and above our heads, they danced a long dance in murky brown liquid. We joked that Mr. Wendell had killed the animals himself as a child, not able to resist his murderous urges, and that one day soon he would move on to students.

I picked up a jar and held it in my hand, still after that elusive secret lever. The heart inside rose from the bottom and bounced against the glass. My stomach stirred, and I quickly replaced the jar. I lifted the other five just enough to see if anything was underneath.

I then checked under the entire holder and found I could barely lift it, and I wondered how frail Ms. Mott had done it. Again, no switch or button.

I leaned over the fireplace. The fire was dying but still exuding warmth. I put the broken record on the mantle, faced my palms toward the blinking embers, and rubbed my hands together. They felt warm and empty and good not to be holding a weapon. It was the opposite of what I was used to feeling. *Weapons, if you please, and a different one in each hand.* Fully-loaded and newly-sharpened. Variety was revered and brought spice to hunting. But like I said, things were changing.

I was changing.

If I stopped to admit it, signs were pointing to my early retirement. Maybe I'd wait a few years for the vampire hunter retirement homes to start cropping up. I was a firm believer that if you needed it, one day some entrepreneurial citizen would make it. Of course, the country was much different now.

I collected my makeshift weapons and moved away from the fireplace, back toward the windows. With both shards in one hand, the other was used to continue knocking along the wall, high and then low. With luck, solidness would soon fall away to a hollow sound or a loose panel. I reached the windows and checked behind the curtains and then moved on to each corner of the rug. My thoughts had me starting my own retirement home for hunters: The Done Killing Home for Vampire Hunters. It would be built on that exquisite postcard beach. Vampires may or may not like beaches, I couldn't be sure. The residents would be young and old. They could relax in one of many hammocks linked between palm trees or join in the activities. There would be the usual: Checkers, Bingo, Parcheesi, and ballroom dancing. There would be the unusual: support groups, massage concentrating on the left and right rotator cuffs, and the occasional fight class for those who miss giving and receiving a good kick to the head.

In a storeroom deep in the basement would be a locked door that each resident would have a key to. If ever again a resident felt the call to exterminate the undead, they would take their key, go down to the basement, open that door, and have their pick of the finest weaponry. Then they'd leave prepared, with Done Killing's blessing.

I dropped the last rug corner. It clapped and stirred air that lifted my nightie. I looked down at the split vinyl in my hands. The record couldn't have broken much better, although Cooper might've disagreed. *Stake Nazi*. Each had a slight curve like a cat's claws. On one was "eedence" in bold simple lettering and on the other just "val." The LP had been in good shape before I smashed it. No scratches or bulges. A collector's wet dream. The vampire would be mad.

I hoisted myself up on the bed and propped up two pillows for back support. My eyes were heavy. There was nothing to do now but wait.

~

I dreamt I was grocery shopping. My carriage was full, and with it came the real prospect of eating until my stomach burst...in a good way.

My eyes shot open, feeling a presence outside my head.

I pressed my back against the bed frame, jabbing the record pieces into the air in front of me.

"Am I still dreaming?"

"No."

Seven stood before me. She looked much like she did at the club except vampires weren't attached to her flesh. There was no blood and only one hint at injury.

"You're a vampire."

"You're observant," she said. "Is that what you plan on killing me with?" She lifted an eyebrow and eyed my record slabs with faux interest.

"No, they were for Mabon," I said, raising my own eyebrow, "but I'm willing to make a concession. Have you come here to kill me?"

"Don't be stupid. I'm here to rescue you."

"You're a vampire."

"Are you going to keep saying that?"

"No, I just...Charlie..."

"I know," Seven said, glancing nervously around the room, her calm demeanor fleeing. "Mabon has hermits on him. Oh, it's so horrible, Emma. So horrible." She looked like she might cry. Her face contorted, but her eyes stayed dry.

"But why?" I said. For the life of me I couldn't think of a reason for Mabon to torture Charlie. Mabon had more information than we did.

"Why not?" Seven said, her cool casualness back. She walked to the bathroom, taking in what she saw along the way. "I haven't been in this room before."

"Don't bother with the bathroom. There's nothing in there."

She looked anyway. She wore boots I didn't recognize and they landed heavy on the tiles.

"Can't we go out the way you came?" I said eyeing the door, which she had closed.

"We can, but it's not ideal. The place is crawling with vampires." She exited the bathroom and stopped in her tracks, a crinkle above her nose. "Vampires besides me." The crinkle evaporated.

I hadn't put my weapons down. My hands hurt around the record pieces. It was the trust issue again; humans in my old life, vampires in my new life. I had tackled my mistrust of Charlie, but Seven was different. We had never gotten along and the hunters, including myself, had left her for dead. At the time, we saw no alternative, but I didn't know what she thought about it. There was the chance she was harboring some intense abandonment issues. Maybe Mabon sent her up to play with me. How else did she get a key to the room?

"I'm sorry…for leaving you at the club. We saw no other choice."

She walked by the hearts, not giving them a glance. "You should be."

"What?"

Seven was at the windows, now. She slid to the side of one, hiding herself from what was outside, and coerced the curtain with her fingertips to let her sneak a peek. Her ponytail flopped over her shoulder and landed between her breasts.

"I said, 'You should be.'"

The room held its breath.

"Kidding. I understand. I'm not really sure why Mabon saved me. To be part of his entourage, I guess. Doesn't he know I hate vampires?" Seven let the curtain drop. "Besides me." She turned away from the window. "Expecting breakfast in bed?"

I shook my head and stood, feeling like a soldier in front of her superior. Seven was the same bitch in death as she was in life, but I was glad to have her back.

"You know about Leech?" I asked.

"Asshole."

"And The Plan?"

She nodded. "Should we kill him?"

"Definitely."

"Let's go help Charlie and the others first."

"Okay."

She slipped off the jacket she was wearing. A long dark number with flared sleeves. "You need this more than I do." A stake appeared like magic. "And this."

I took the items, poking my cold arms through the sleeves and plunging the record pieces into the deep pockets of the jacket. I held the stake. It smelled like new wood from the forest.

"Smells like Christmas," I said, with a slight smile.

"Ho, ho, ho," Seven said, without one, before opening the door and spilling like ink into the darker hallway. She blended. I squinted to see her.

"Are you going to say it again?" her voice asked from the hallway.

"Say what?"

"You're a vampire."

"No."

"Good."

~

Fortunately for us, the partygoers were loud—full-up with talk of politics and blood.

We could hear their approach from far and were able to duck into nearby rooms. The hallway was lined with rock memorabilia, sealed away behind glass like the hearts in the jars. We passed signed guitars, cymbals, and snare skins, and photographs of Mabon with his arms around musicians. It was the same young face in every photo, untouched by age. Several pictures hung of Mabon with Bo Diddley at the start of the singer's career, the middle, and nearing the end. In the last photograph, lines creased Mr. Diddley's surprised face.

It's Mabon Blackwell. Remember me, Bo? I'm your biggest fan.

We took a servant stairwell down. I expected to run into Ms. Mott on the way up with a poker and extra logs for my fire. She would stretch her mouth open in a soundless scream, a stub of a tongue jerking back and forth and veined hands reaching for us. The objects she carried would hang in the air, suspended and waiting confidently for the return of the woman's frail arms around them.

Traveling behind Seven, I noticed how she moved differently. She was now hunter and hunted, and she played both roles well, leading the way surefooted and slinking into shadows that seemed to welcome her brief stay.

I misstepped approaching the bottom landing and floundered for the side railings. I caught myself and hung there for a second. Seven looked back at me and put a finger to her mouth.

"*Shhh.*"

"What, vampires don't trip?" I whispered.

At the bottom of the stairs, Seven turned to me. "This goes to the servants' quarters and then the kitchen. It'll be busy. Hide the stake and act subdued."

"Huh?"

"Just do it."

I flicked open my coat in search of a pocket.

"I'm wearing a nightie. Where should I put it?"

Seven took my stake, and I helped her put hers and mine down the back of her pants. It was the only place they'd fit. We adjusted her shirt over them. Seven took the elastic out of her hair, and it fell like black water to her hips.

"You're not looking very subdued."

"How's this?" I curved my shoulders and made my mouth frown.

"It'll have to do." She grabbed my arm, and we went through the door.

The living quarters were empty. Doors opened into small sparsely decorated rooms. Each room had a twin bed and a red side table with two drawers. The walls were white. There were some personal touches in the rooms that I saw: a nice quilt, a teddy bear, a framed photo. I wondered if most of the servants were human, like Ms. Mott, or vampire. I got my answer through the next door.

~

Servants hurried to and fro. Some had fangs, most did not.

The ones giving orders were always undead.

Each servant wore a black and white uniform starched enough to stand on its own. Expensive vessels of blood were being fetched and carried. Ten or so servants queued at a long, aluminum counter, waiting their turn to ladle blood into white bowls on a tray in front of them. A male vampire with a stick face and wearing a chef's hat carefully placed a Lily bloom afloat in the middle of each bowl and wiped spots off the bowls' rims before shooing the servant away.

In the background, a large stove sat unused. Humans weren't the guests at this party. They were serving and being served.

We were the only non-staff in the kitchen and stuck out like sore thumbs. Nervous eyes fell on us and then shot away. For most, it wasn't their place to ask questions, and they knew this all too well.

A female vampire yelling at a girl with a blonde bob for spatter on her uniform looked our way as we passed, then looked again.

"Change *now*," the vampire said to the girl, before barreling toward us like she was being pushed from behind. "Excuse me."

Seven's hand tightened around my arm. We kept walking.

"I *said*, '*Excuse me.*'"

We stopped, and the vampire sidled in front of us like she was very used to keeping people from where they wanted to be.

"Who are you and what are you doing?"

"Mabon asked me to deliver this to the buffet," Seven said.

"Did he specify which buffet?"

"No."

"There are many. We *do* have over 200 guests in attendance."

561

"He didn't say."

The vampire looked at me. She opened my jacket with a quick toss of her hand.

"It doesn't look like the quality Mr. Blackwell usually requires and it hasn't been stripped or oiled. I doubt you even know how to apply presentation tubing. No. You'll stain the carpet. Bring the slab out back. I'll see to it myself." The vampire half turned. Seven stood her ground. "Well?"

"Mr. Blackwell asked me to bring her to buffet, so that's what I'm going to do. If you have a problem, take it up with him."

The vampire's demeanor changed. Her eyes quivered behind thick lids.

"Fine. Well, there's room on the vestibule buffet. You can take it there. I'll send a servant shortly to help with the hooking. It's not as easy as it looks, you know."

Seven nodded and said no more. She gripped my arm and tugged. It hurt, but it needed to. I was just a "slab" after all. We walked away, feeling the vampire's eyes on us. We were nearly home free when she called after us.

"Her?"

"What?" Seven said, overacting impatience.

"Her—you called it a *her*."

"My mistake. It's been a long night."

"It's only just the beginning, my dear," the vampire said, with a cackle, before bee-lining into the middle of the kitchen to find her next victim.

"Tell me about it," Seven muttered.

At the double doors, servants piled in with cumbersome trays.

Emptied soup bowls and glasses, stained red, teeter-tottered. Not many talked and most ignored us with eyes forward. One vampire servant with dark freckle patches found it fit to elbow me as she passed.

"Move meat," she said.

I flipped her the bird. I was human after all. She huffed, before the door swung shut. Seven leaned into my ear.

"*Subdued.*"

"That was subdued," I said, through clenched jaw. It wasn't a lie. I had wanted to jump the wench and tear out her teeth.

We were in the main hallway, now. The ballroom was further ahead with its door open. The inside was opulent. Light pods hung down from a high ceiling, oil paintings the size of buses covered the walls, and on a stage, tuxedoed vampires swayed, crooned, and caressed stringed instruments. At least twenty round tables were decked in whites and seated to capacity. Guests mingled as nervous servants circled their tables, refilling glasses and removing plates. A silver and black banner stretched across the bottom of the stage. It read, "SAVE THE HERMITS. VAMPIRES, LIKE US."

Both servants and guests walked by us. Seven greeted other vampires with a nod or a hello. They looked at me with mixed disgust and hunger, but no suspicion. They thought they knew my fate.

The foyer was to our right. In it, one servant unloaded martini glasses from a tray and restocked a pyramid, while a second tidied the area. The second one opened a small step ladder, which had been propped against the wall, climbed it, and reached up to wipe bile off the chest of a black woman.

The black woman was nude and hung a few feet off the floor, chained by her wrists to the wall. There were two men next to her, also nude and ethnic. The men were unconscious, maybe dead. The woman moaned. Her eyes were closed, but her head shifted heavily back and forth and bile dripped from her mouth down onto her body. Tubes attached to the victims' wrists, necks, and thighs carried blood to polished, sterling silver vats.

The servant tugged the woman's head up by her hair and smacked her face.

"Stop that," she said. She swore and released her. "Now, I have to fetch more rags."

My legs gave out. Luckily, Seven had me. If anything, it helped our act. The second servant stepped off the ladder, propped it back against the wall, and glanced at us.

"Is that for Section Two?"

"Yes, it is."

"Straight ahead," she said. "Prep's under the table." Seven nodded.

I regained my footing and concentrated on not getting sick. We passed the ballroom. Guests were dancing, the meal nearly over. The band beat out an old tune, and couples danced an old dance.

Another hallway, now. I was starting to feel like we'd been walking for ages.

"Do you know where you're going?"

"Yes."

"How?"

"I got the tour."

Behind a door and down some more stairs, we found Charlie strapped to a wall and looking like the *Toxic Avenger*. A UV light had been directed on him. He was barely alive. His skin bubbled, popped, and oozed in a full spectrum of pain colors. Seven let go of me and jumped between Charlie and the light. I switched it off as steam started to rise off the back of her shirt. She hugged Charlie and spoke softly to him in Spanish. She worked desperately at his bindings. Feeling like an intruder in their horrible moment, I went to help her.

We freed Charlie and hoisted him to his feet. I took my stake from Seven.

"He'll heal?" I asked.

"Yes. They gave him something to suppress his regeneration. Make the torture more efficient. It just slows it down, though. He'll be okay."

It was the second time I was to be Charlie's legs and eyes. Man, did he owe me. Seven gripped her stake, and I gripped mine. Our time for being inconspicuous was over. The time for killing was now.

"Tell me you know where Cooper and the others are," I said. She didn't.

I hoped I wasn't being set up again—that another Leech hadn't snuck into the equation. Seven not knowing where the hunters were meant to carry out the assassinations made me feel safer. But maybe that was the idea? I tried to remember the intel we had collected at the club. The envelope from the janitors, the map inside...

"West wing, I think...the library? Do you know where that is?" I asked.

She started for the door and took us with her.

We passed three vampires along the way. Seven ended their eternal lives, separating from us and thrusting deathblow jabs before they could say *traitor*. She enjoyed. She smiled. She even bent down to catch a spray of blood in her face. These vampires were plump, rosy, and full, and by the time we reached the library in the west wing, Seven was juiced with the whites of her eyes the only thing not red on her.

"Too fun," she said, lacing Charlie's arm back over her shoulders.

"Looks like."

We were outside the door of the library, now. Muffled noises sounded from within. Seven and I exchanged a glance. I turned the door's knob.

Stakes were raised.

CHAPTER THIRTY

BUSINESS WAS ALREADY DONE.

The library floor was covered with the color we had become all too familiar with.

Two vampires, not masters but politicians, lay dead with holes in their chests. Three hunters stood over the bodies, waiting for something to happen.

"Emma?"

"Cooper."

"Seven?"

"Scott."

"Charlie?"

"Well, now that we have names straight," I said.

"Seven…you're a vampire," Rudy said.

"Will people stop saying that?"

"What are you doing here, Em?" Cooper asked.

"It was a setup. All of it. They're just lousy politicians. Mabon Blackwell was using us."

"Mabon Blackwell?" Scott said.

"Naw, I don't believe it," Rudy said. "If we just wait…we were just saying ourselves we didn't know how long it would take for everyone to change back to humans. I'm betting 20 minutes. Everything takes 20 minutes in this city."

"Well, we only have zero minutes," I said. "They're coming for us."

"She's right," Seven said, scratching her face and leaving a clean streak behind.

"Where's Topps? And the children?" I asked. *Oh no, did we kill Topps?*

"They're safe," Scott said. "Tell me how Mabon's involved in this?"

"In every way."

Music blared. It was deafening. Doors we hadn't been keeping an eye on opened to armed vampires. They shouted orders over the music. They wore black tactical clothing like the soldiers that had met me at the airport—when my journey to hell began.

The guards pushed us further into the room, nudging the butts of their pistols into our bodies. Rudy and Cooper attempted to draw their own guns but were set upon by guards three times their two, forcing them to disarm.

We were being herded like cattle into the center of the room. Most of us still had at least one weapon, but using it would mean a future as mince meat and we appreciated our solid form.

The guards had us in a tight circle now, and they moved around us counterclockwise. They shouted insults and dared us to make moves. *Go ahead. That'll make our day. We're waiting.* A few had holstered their guns and were bearing their teeth and hissing. One with a face that looked like invisible hands were stretching it from behind bit into his wrist. He made eye contact with Seven as he sucked from the wound. Vampires or humans, he was game.

"Enough," a voice said.

It was Mabon. Scott heard the voice and let out a growl that turned into a painful moan when he saw who accompanied Mabon.

"I brought a visitor."

By Mabon's side was a young boy with fine brown hair and deceptive dimples. Mabon held the boy between his legs and firmly at the chest with both hands. The boy scratched at the air, reaching for us.

"Michael," Scott called out.

"Say hi to your father, Michael." The boy jumped up and down and gnashed his big teeth. "He's strong, Scott. You wouldn't believe how strong. Got the appetite of a king too. A tad overzealous, but that's normal with ones so young. We had to exterminate most of the first batch. There's only so much food and the little buggers have trouble controlling their appetites. But they've got educational videos for that now. I know some elders who could do with watching one." He laughed.

A servant appeared behind Mabon. He handed the child to her. "Take him." The boy squirmed in her grip.

"*No*," Scott said.

"Yes," Mabon said, with a smirk.

"I'm going to kill you."

"You first."

Mabon nodded his head at a guard. The guard raised a gun and fired. Scott collapsed on the ground with a hole spitting blood from the center of his forehead. Cooper charged the guard, and a rifle butt slapped his cheek, causing the skin to split.

"How could you?" I screamed.

"I don't like threats."

"You killed his wife...kidnapped his child!"

"Small details."

"I could never love someone like you."

"Is that your final decision?"

"Yes."

"No. *Don't*." Cooper's eyes pleaded.

"See you in twenty years," Mabon said.

He gave another nod. I clenched for it. I didn't close my eyes but stared beyond everyone as the barrel was pressed against my brow. If I looked at Cooper, I'd want to live. If I looked at Mabon, I'd want to live. Both for very different reasons. But I didn't want to live. Not really. Life as it was now had too little to offer. Some might say I was giving up. Maybe I was.

"We're all monsters in hell, Mabon. Expect my wrath."

The gun barrel vibrated. I heard a sound.

A *whoosh*.

I guessed it was the bullet spiraling through my head, anxious blood flooding the hole. I cursed that I had to hear these things. *Wouldn't you figure*, I thought.

Then, it got hot.

Real hot.

~

Everything happened in explosions of flash laced with fire.

That's how I remembered it—like a daring photojournalist was capturing our tiny victory, and only the scenes lit by bulb would reach print and our memory.

Flash! Topps coming through the door the guards hadn't kept an eye on. Always the cowboy. A UV light strapped to his front, two tanks of propane strapped to his back, and a long gray hose in his hands. Light was the appetizer, flame the desert.

Flash! Guards' mouths wide with pain. Weapons hanging useless from arms on fire. They're collapsing on each other. Flesh is being liquefied. They never expected this.

Flash! The hunters scramble: Cooper grabs my arm. Rudy jumps a desk, his face in a grimace so he's hardly recognizable. Charlie, now out of shock, is saving his girl. The fanged lovers crash through a window.

Flash! The room is swallowed. Fire loves oxygen.

Flash! Mabon pulls me into the hallway. We are both aflame.

Flash! I'm straddling Mabon with a fiery stake point at his heart. My hair moves around me like it's possessed. Flames and music scream.

"All this because you couldn't get past your fucking problems!" I yelled.

"I love you," Mabon said.

It was the first time anyone ever said that to me. I pushed the stake into Mabon's heart. He gripped the splintering wood as it went through him, maybe to guide it home. Maybe he knew it was his time. Maybe he was meant to die in the forest that day. Maybe that day had been God's day off. Maybe God was kicking himself for letting Mabon-full-of-hate slip past him. Maybe, maybe, maybe.

I rolled off the vampire in a lame attempt to put myself out. They made it sound so easy. Stop, drop, and roll. But the shock of being on fire is enough to make your mind shut down. Sayonara and auf wiedersehen.

I shook out of my jacket. Cooper was above me, removing his. I was so happy to see him. He draped me in his coat, patting out hot spots.

"We need to get out of here," Cooper said.

"I'm with you."

A guard shot through the library door. Flames had become him. Pain and rage were displayed on his melting face. He took a few steps toward us before falling. It was a nice try, for a vampire.

We ran. Smoke chased us. We entered a dark room that smelled of soil and rot and incense. Coffins sat in two rows, ten deep. All were open, none were occupied. They were simple unlike the ones we had seen at the department store. There was no television or bar or surround sound in any of them, just dimpled ivory cloth, pinned from head to foot, and a small flat pillow.

We moved around the coffins quietly, as if afraid to wake the emptiness inside them.

No other furniture was in the room. Through a bay window, we could see the mansion's front yard. Some party guests lingered to watch the fire consume the west wing. Others rushed to their limos in a gorged state, throwing frightened glances back at the blaze as if it were about to leap forward and tap them on the shoulder. *Your turn.*

Cooper raced to the window. He flipped its lock and pulled.

"They're nailed shut." Cooper turned and surveyed the room. He went to a coffin and picked up its head. "We'll break a window. Help me."

"But they're out there."

"And they always will be. Help."

I picked up the other side. It was light. We started to swing it and had gotten a momentum going when Cooper shouted, "Now!"

My heart stopped. The coffin smashed through the center of the window. Glass shattered. At the top, a huge piece of broken glass shaped like an upended mountain swung three times before releasing from the window frame and falling to the ground.

The coffin rested half in, half out of the window. Cooper grabbed the end and slid it sideways along the bottom of the frame to clear the glass away. Then he shoved it completely through.

He got up in the window and held out a hand. I took it and stepped up, avoiding glass with my bare feet. Vampires watched us from afar. I couldn't see any guards. There had been so many in the library that it would have surprised me if we hadn't already taken them all out.

Cooper released my hand and jumped down. He positioned arms meant to catch me. Broken glass was spread out across the ground below, looking like thousands of uncut diamonds. I hunkered and went for it.

Cooper's arms wrapped around me. He put me down a few feet from the window, away from the glass. I needed no encouragement, not even a word or a look, to know that it was time to run. Fast. Now.

A town car leaving the party sounded its horn at us as we crossed the driveway, but it didn't slow. Guests dowsed in shadows and orange light watched us warily, but none followed.

"Through there," Cooper said, pointing with his pistol at an area of palms and brush.

A car was coming straight for us. It had been on the driveway heading toward the house but made a last-minute turn off-road. It sped up and then braked, swerving around so it was coming at us sideways. Pieces of pristine lawn flew into the air.

I jumped back and almost landed on my ass. Cooper stood his ground. The car stopped with the door handle at his groin. The window rolled down.

"You kids need a ride?"

Rudy's smug face poked out of the window. He was black and sooty from the fire. A set of three lines had been drawn on both cheeks. His smile said collected, but his eyes said *loco*.

Topps was in the driver's seat, his hands tight on the wheel. Our vampires were in back. Rudy shoved the door open, and we fell in with Charlie and Seven.

"Hello, bitches," Seven said. The four of us fought to disentangle ourselves.

Charlie looked better. Whatever the torture minions had given him was wearing off, and his wounds were starting to heal.

As Rudy closed the door, Topps slammed the gas pedal. A female vamp in a long black gown and with hair to her shoes had come over to investigate or more. Topps drove the car into her and she toppled onto the hood. He braked and she slid off. She barely hit the ground before jumping to her feet and giving us a good snarl, looking like a mummy with her long hair twisted around her face and body.

"Punch it, T-Bone," Rudy said.

The car sped forward. A front tire caught the vampire and dragged her under. We rose up off our seats twice.

The six of us looked back nervously. The vampire was scraping herself off the ground. Even once we reached safe distance, she continued to shake her fists and bare her teeth, as if believing that the sight of her viciousness alone could send us to our graves.

~

The street from the mansion was busy with guests fleeing to beat the sunrise home.

There was still a good hour of darkness left to go, but perhaps the fire had reminded them that their lives were not eternal, despite so much talk of the sort. Those who had pushed the envelope before where daylight was concerned swore to push it no more and always return to their coffins with time to spare.

Brake lights lit up the night like so many demon eyes, then fell away when the street split into double lanes and traffic dispersed. Three fire engines sped past us with sirens blaring, not encumbered by any cars heading up to the mansion. I caught sight of one of the drivers. He swam in a big yellow hat and hugged the big wheel of the truck with his big mouth open and his big teeth out in big anticipation.

I wondered what kind of vampire got into that line of work. Most had probably been firefighters in their human lives. There was no doubt in my mind that these particular vampires had a death wish, and I shuddered at the thought of a confrontation with one of them. *Like meeting a vampire pole vaulter*, I thought, with exhausted amusement.

The car was quiet. There was so much to say, so what was said was very little. We were on our way to meet Bugs, Sammy, and Schizo, and a small band of humans the group had crossed paths with while I was away. They were like us except not hunters, just survivors, and older overall. They had been briefed on The Plan and had asked what they could do to help. Cooper told me they were markedly relieved when Scott asked them to babysit.

I stared out the window at trees waving dark limbs. My eyes started to shut. Cooper's hand was light on my back. I felt it the second he put it there and secretly hoped it would stay. My lids closed completely and I forced them back open. There was no harm in sleep, but staying awake until we reached our destination seemed like a better idea.

After no car for a mile or so, we passed a stretch limo on the side of the road. Its hazards were on, and a vampire dressed like a driver crouched by the right front tire with a lug wrench. The rear window was down, and through it I could see another vampire of about fifty or sixty, with brown hair, a long straight nose, and a down-turned mouth. We made eye contact, and he looked back at me with vacant eyes.

"Stop the car," I yelled, waking even Topps at the wheel.

"Huh?" Rudy said, turning in the passenger seat to give me an annoyed look.

"Pardon?" Topps said, meeting my eyes in the mirror.

"You have to stop the car."

"We're not stopping, sweet cheeks," Rudy said.

"What's wrong, Em?" Cooper asked.

"The man in the car back there."

"What about him?" Cooper asked.

The three other humans in the car looked at me, awaiting an answer. The vampires showed little interest, contentedly curled up in each other like cats. Seven adjusted her arm around Charlie's neck and decided it was worth the second to insult me.

"She's crazy. Keep going."

"No, this is good. I promise." I smiled. I probably did look crazy. I probably did sound crazy. But I was okay with that.

"Is it Leech?" Rudy asked, coming more awake.

"No. Better."

"Who's better than that?"

"Tell us, Emma," Cooper said.

I hate to admit that I was scared to say his name. But I was. And in my head:

Josie was right. She was right all along.

~

576

The desert was dark but ready to greet the rising sun.

Leaning rock formations and funny trees jutted out from the ground haphazardly, like the scenery on an alien planet.

We got out of the Expedition, kicking up dust as we landed.

I squinted and took the sunglasses from out of my shirt pocket. *Better.* They were a gift from our new friends, who had taken up residence in a deserted mall for most of the time. They had collected many more luxuries than we did, and from the sound of it, enjoyed them with less guilt. They laughed and patted Cooper on the back when Rudy told them about his IOU scheme.

I wiped the sweat off my forehead and went to open the back door. Bugs jumped out at me. She snarled and scrunched up her face. I caught her and swung her around in my arms. She squealed.

"Now what did I say about faking being a vampire?"

"Don't do it," she said, laughing innocently.

"That's right, don't do it." I put her down.

"You're a brat," Sammy said from inside the car.

"Am not."

"Are to."

"Okay, that's enough guys."

Somewhere along the line, the honeymoon had ended and the two had started bickering like brother and sister.

Schizo jumped down next. He looked around excitedly and pranced after Bugs as she ran to the other car with her arms raised and her baby teeth bared.

Sammy got out. It was the first time I had seen him looking well rested. He took in the beautiful surroundings like a teenager.

"So are we here to burn that dictator dude?"

"Go look after Bugs," I said. He went without complaint.

The boy could scowl like a teenager, but he rarely took orders like one. I stuck my head in the SUV to make sure the blackout curtain was drawn tight, before shutting the door.

"Think they'll be okay in there?"

Cooper nodded at me as he came around the front of the car. He smiled. "Stop worrying. We've checked a thousand times."

"I know. You're right."

Topps and Rudy stepped out of the other car. They had chosen the 69 Cadillac convertible. Not practical but it did look good. Rudy was as indecisive as a girl. He said that he might still return to Seepy Storage to switch cars before heading north. We would see.

Bugs attached herself to Topps' right leg and pretended to bite it. Topps played along, waving his arms frantically.

"Oh no, oh no, don't bite me, little lady." Bugs laughed with delight. Schizo observed the situation and whined profusely.

"Sammy, take Bugs and Schizo and go check out that rock over there," Cooper said.

"I can't watch?"

"Not this time."

"Is there going to be another time?"

"No," we all said in unison.

All of us had come to do the deed, so we could each bear witness—at least the adults who understood the seriousness of the situation. We needed daylight, wide-open space, and time to spare. The desert seemed like the perfect location. It was where the sun was the strongest, where it would hurt more and kill quicker. Because what we had needed to be dead and extra pain was a bonus.

Sammy took Schizo's leash and enticed Bugs with a grand search for lizards underneath the rocks.

"Why will it be grand?" Bugs asked Sammy as they made their way toward the rocks.

"It just will. Don't ask so many questions."

We went immediately to the trunk of the Cadillac. My heart thudded in my chest more than it had ever done. The sun was half risen. It peeked over the horizon like it was taking frightful interest in what was about to occur. Rudy put the key in the lock and looked at each of us before turning it.

With a flick of his wrist, the trunk flew open.

You could barely see the bag for the carpet. Both were black. But then the bag moved, or rather, the vampire inside it moved, and we each took a corner and lifted it out of the trunk.

Carrying it was tough-going. He was putting up a good fight, despite being properly bound with crosses and rope like we had been taught. We did kind of expect that, though. Vampires hated the sun and no one meek waged a world war.

A lizard got out of our way, leaving behind a hurried path.

The vampire inside the bag went back and forth between English and the language of his homeland. Threats were followed by begging, and then threats again. The bag slipped between my sweaty fingers. The sun was nearly full out now. It was still early morning, but the heat had already arrived.

"How do you guys think he traveled under the radar for so long?" I asked.

"How did any of them do it?" Cooper said.

"No, I mean…with the way he was. He was never a wallflower.

Everything he did was big and destructive. How did he go from that to hiding?"

"It's not like he was turned into a puppy dog," Rudy said. "He went from being a killer to being a killer."

"I guess," I said. No one could ever know for sure anyway.

We came to a clearing. A few stray rocks and sticks gathered, but that was it. There was nothing to grab onto and no shade to hide in.

"How's this?" I asked.

"As good a place as any," Cooper said.

"I concur," Topps said.

We dropped the package in the middle of the clearing. The bag stilled, and noise ceased from inside.

"Who wants to do the honors?" Rudy asked, not volunteering.

"I will," Cooper said.

The bag had a zip down the middle. It was an honest-to-goodness body bag, another luxury begotten from the new arrivals. They had stolen the bags from a local hospital to bury some friends in—just putting them in the ground as is seemed cruel and uncivilized. Plenty of coffin stores were around, but the modern coffin was much too heavy and cumbersome, making acquiring them too risky. In the end, the bags had worked well and the new arrivals had slept better thinking the bugs were being kept away from their friends' dead flesh, at least for a couple of days.

Cooper leaned over the body bag and took the zip between his thumb and index finger.

"*Wait*," I said. "Let's hold him down."

I gripped what were the vampire's ankles tightly through the bag and put my weight on them. Topps and Rudy kneeled in the sand on either side of the bag and pressed their hands hard against the body inside, securing it to the ground.

"Okay. Now."

Cooper tugged at the zipper.

The sides of the bag pulled away from each other like parting flesh. Josie had been right. She had seen Adolf Hitler at the club that night, and now we had him in a body bag, not yet dead but soon to be, God willing.

Halfway down, the zipper became stuck. Still, Hitler was burning. He writhed in the bag, his face blackening, his skin flaking off and falling away. Cooper struggled with the zipper.

"Just pull it, man," Rudy said.

"It won't go. *It won't go.*"

The zipper was stuck on Hitler's clothing: an expensive-looking tuxedo with maroon suspenders and a silk maroon vest underneath.

He was getting to be too much to control. Ropes snapped. The cross fell off his forehead with nothing left to hold it there.

"Do it, man," Rudy said, his face bright red from heat and exertion. "I can't hold him much longer."

"I *know*," Cooper said.

"Cooper?" I said.

Hitler sat up.

Like he had been spring-loaded. We screamed and jumped back, making safe distance between us and the dictator. He brought his hands to his face. They burned too. Everything did. His fingers curled up and scratched at his skin, causing more flakes to fall away like black snow. He looked at his surroundings and then at us. His lids crumbled and left behind manic, accusatory eyes.

I rushed forward, gripped the end of the bag, and pulled. After the third tug, the bag came free and I tossed it aside and out of Hitler's reach. It wouldn't save him, but it might slow the process down and we were ready for it to be over. Sometimes, you looked at torture through rose-colored glasses. Even with something as evil as what we had in front of us, torture had been tried and found lacking.

Hitler turned and belly-crawled toward us. He spoke in German. It was the same phrase over and over, spit from a mouth almost gone.

"What's he saying?" I asked.

"Do I look German?" Rudy said.

"Who do you think you are," Cooper said. "He's asking us who we think we are."

We looked at each other, not quite sure how to answer the question or if we even wanted to.

"We're cowboys," Topps said, putting on a strong Southern drawl.

"We're humans," I said.

"We're vampires," Cooper said, sparing a glance at the SUV where Charlie and Seven slept.

"We're patriots, motherfucker," Rudy said, lifting his heel and bringing it down on Hitler's head. It popped and collapsed under the weight of the boot. Rudy twisted his foot into the ground. One last grind—just to be sure. When he took his foot away, what was left had no more resemblance to the former dictator. Small bone fragments still burned, but the sun had done its job and done it well, and Hitler was dead.

Who do you think you are?

Over the years, I would wonder if we answered his question.

SOMEWHERE IN AMERICA:

In a dusty bar, in a dusty town, a television is on. The bar is empty; the sun is out, after all. Static turns to blue screen and then to a face that would be recognized by humans and vampires alike. He's an older man with absurdly close features and a smile that tells no lies, but a mouth that tells too many. His cheeks are rosy, signifying he has just come from a feeding—very poor form given the current state of his country. Starvation has run amok through the middle class and the poor. Sun-assisted suicides are all the rage.

He pats the mike, "*Is this thing on?*" and runs a hand through his thinning brown hair. He begins. False start. Begins again:

"It is with great sorrow that I come to you tonight, my fellow nightwalkers. Though our nation is young, we have spent its short life supporting certain ideals—that every nightwalker old and new, rich and impoverished, has the right to quality sustenance. Of course, times are tough. This should be expected in the beginning. Every business when it is born has its kinks. But I say to you tonight with all assuredness, we will get through this. Stay strong. Be proud of what you are. Do not cower in the face of adversity. Farms have reported a 23 percent increase in productivity and we are continuing to explore a European outreach. Tonight, I make a promise to you as your leader, and here it is: food is coming. It's on the way…you need not wait much longer. Thank you and goodnight."

www.ingramcontent.com/pod-product-compliance
Lightning Source LLC
Chambersburg PA
CBHW032253020726
47495CB00001B/92